OF THE MORTAL REALM

By Amelia Atwater-Rhodes

Mancer Trilogy
Of the Abyss • *Of the Divine*
Of the Mortal Realm

Young Adult Novels

Den of Shadows
In the Forests of the Night
Demon in My View
Shattered Mirror
Midnight Predator
Persistence of Memory
Token of Darkness
All Just Glass
Poison Tree
Promises to Keep

The Kiesha'ra
Hawksong
Snakecharm
Falcondance
Wolfcry
Wyvernhail

The Maeve'ra
Bloodwitch
Bloodkin
Bloodtraitor

OF THE MORTAL REALM

Mancer: Book Three

AMELIA ATWATER-RHODES

HARPER

VOYAGER

IMPULSE

An Imprint of HarperCollinsPublishers

Digital Edition AUGUST 2018 ISBN: 978-0-06-256217-3

Print Edition ISBN: 978-0-06-256218-0

Cover design by Guido Caroti

Cover photographs © yousang/Shutterstock (mountains); © Maxiphoto /iStock/Getty Images (sky); © CarrieColePhotography/iStock/Getty Images (tree)

FIRST EDITION

20 21 22   HDC   10 9 8 7 6 5 4 3 2

Of the Mortal Realm is dedicated to Rebecca and Michael, the greatest of the many blessings in my life.

OF THE MORTAL REALM

PART ONE

I sing of realms and times before,
when worlds were one and life was more,
than skin and bone, but soul and pow'r
divine and ice and blood and fire.

I sing of terror that kept us swift,
in the ages before the realms were rift,
of claws and teeth, and fire's domain,
darkness whose frolic is mortal pain
in the lakes of fire
lakes of blood
of flesh and need and hungry lust
and the shadows move on
and we survey
the ruin that's left
by Abyssi play.

And I sing a devotion that swept the soul,
defined a fervor, addictive zeal,
creatures of wing, of lightning and frost,
look upon one and be thou lost
to a love like slavery
love like chains
of gold and silk and honeyed rain
and you'd crawl on coals
and pray for hours
for the strength to please
the Numen powers.

From "The Seduction of Knet"
Traditional Tamari Ballad

CHAPTER 1

CADMIA

The high court of the Abyss was a maze of volcanic crystals whose shining black facets reflected the multicolored glow of the tiny luminescent creatures scuttling over them until their highest tips were lost in the sooty sky above. That sky never brightened beyond a dull, rusty radiance, so the tiny dancing lights were delightful—unless you knew they would sear flesh from bone if touched.

Truth be told, Cadmia still found them lovely. Much of the Abyss was like that: achingly beautiful, hypnotic, deadly to the unwary, but ultimately fascinating. Her study of the Other realms—the infernal Abyss and the divine Numen—had been her driving passion for over a decade, even though such interest was frowned upon back in the mortal realm, and especially in the country from which she hailed.

The thought made her press a protective hand to her abdomen. She wished she had the ability to feel the life there, the way the magic users around her could, but it was too early. If the child's father had been as human as Cadmia herself, she wouldn't even have been sure of the pregnancy yet. But the father wasn't human; he was an Abyssi, a creature native to the infernal realm, and thus the pregnancy left a visible aura of power on her.

Cadmia turned her head to see Alizarin, who was standing on the balls of his feet to try to grab one of the glowing wisps.

If he had been serious about catching one, he would have shifted to his true hunting form, but for now he wore what he called his "play" form. In this shape, Alizarin stood slightly taller than most mortals, and though his body was masculine, he could never be mistaken for human. It wasn't just that his lean, hard-muscled form was furred from the suede-like palms of his hands to the soft pads of his feet, or that the fur in question was a dozen different impossible shades of turquoise and blue. It wasn't the claws that peeked out of the tips of his fingers instead of nails, or even the way his eyes glowed like the blue heart of a flame.

It was something else. Some instinct that crawled

along the spine when you looked at him, which whispered to the deepest, most animal part of your brain, *This is the creature that makes us fear the dark.*

And it was the fact that, even though every instinct screamed that his presence meant claws and teeth in the night, he was still the most beautiful man Cadmia had ever seen.

Mortals back in Kavet would call Alizarin a demon. The denizens of the Abyss called him a prince. Cadmia called him her lover, and the father of her child.

"This way?" she asked as they reached a fork in the path.

For the last several weeks, Cadmia and her companions had lived with a half-Abyssi woman named Azo. Azo had been recovering from a grievous magical injury, and as she regained her strength she had taken long, rambling walks that became Cadmia's guided tours to the surface of the Abyss, and particularly the outskirts of the Abyssi royal court. Cadmia therefore knew most of the area well—up until the boundary of the court itself. As Abyss-spawn, Azo was powerful and influential, but even she was not strong enough to protect a mortal who dared approach the royal Abyssi.

The only time Cadmia had seen the court itself had been when the supposedly divine, glorious, loving Numini had blackmailed and threatened her and the others with whom she now traveled on a dangerous trek to the fifth level court—the heart of the deepest level of the Abyss—to rescue a sorcerer named Terre Verte.

Alizarin confirmed her guess with a nod of his head and a curious swish of his tail, then waited for her to take the lead again. He had taken her at her word when she said she wanted to know if she could find her way back to the court on her own.

She continued forward, trying not to be distracted by the spiny vines that struggled to crawl up the slick glass towers. How did any kind of plant survive here, in a place with no sun and no rain? She mentally saved that question for later. Alizarin enjoyed answering her questions, but they were not alone, and the four others in their group were less indulgent.

Hansa and Umber walked closest to Cadmia, but even they had fallen several paces behind, and Hansa's steps had gained a notable drag of hesitation. It was one thing for the once staunchly conservative Quin to embrace his relationship to Umber here in the infernal realm, where no one cared who slept with whom and power was necessary for survival, but quite another to consider what it would mean when they returned to Kavet.

Cadmia wasn't entirely sure which part of the relationship would be considered more damning in the eyes of Hansa's former friends and cohorts: the fact that Umber was half-Abyssi, or the fact that he and Hansa were both men.

In the end it didn't matter. Sorcery was punishable

by death. While the only true sorcerers among them were Terre Verte and Dioxazine, who shared a murmured conversation as they walked at the back of the group, Hansa and Cadmia were still complicit, and Umber had power of his own from his Abyssi father. One did not walk mortal and alive into the Abyss without the use of illegal magic—much less walk *out*, which was what they hoped to do next.

"Here!" Cadmia said triumphantly, as they turned a corner and beheld the wide, slightly irregular arch to the central court.

Inside the massive, black stone obelisk was a vast antechamber with a bone-white stone floor, with irregular streaks of dusty gray and veins the color of old, curdled blood. The surface was pitted in places, and in others juts of rock rose as if shoved upward by tectonic force. The resultant platforms served as the only furniture in the place, and most were occupied by the royalty of the first level court—the highest of the five levels that defined the Abyss.

The first time they had crossed this floor, the monsters within had terrified Cadmia despite Alizarin's protective presence. There were a score of them, and they made no effort to conceal their stares, which were intrigued and hungry in equal parts. Unlike Alizarin's feline aspect on an otherwise mostly human form, the Abyssi of the first level tended to give a more reptilian or even arachnid impression, with heavy carapaces, bristly fur, and frequent scales and fangs.

At least now Cadmia knew these Abyssi were the weakest of their kind. These forms were the only ones they possessed, and Alizarin could best them all together if they dared attack. The strongest Abyssi occupied the fifth level court, the *low* court, which Cadmia had also crossed once. Compared to that, this was nothing.

The high-court Abyssi bowed to Alizarin before their eyes slid to Terre Verte. Tails lashed and eyes brightened, and she overheard a babble of hissing, chittering discussion she could not understand. Alarm? Anger?

Alizarin said he had first heard of Terre Verte in the Abyssi's version of children's stories. According to the Abyssi, the mortal sorcerer was so powerful that, when he died, the king of the Abyss had offered to make him into one of them instead of having him linger in their realm as a spirit. Terre Verte refused, and was locked into a cell in the lowest level of the Abyss for untold years. The other Abyssi were so furious at the king for wasting their time and power on such an ungrateful man that they sacrificed him in the crystal caves so his blood would seed another generation of Abyssi—including Alizarin, who was born from that death.

Cadmia still had many questions, not the least of which was why the Numini had put forth so much effort to rescue a man the Abyssi had once wanted as one of their own. Frustratingly, Terre Verte had evaded such questions in the days they had known him.

At the opposite side of the court was another arch, this one filled by shockingly crimson doors leading to the central well, a stairway that passed between one level of the Abyss and the next. Cadmia groaned softly as she remembered walking down those interminable stairs into smoke and darkness.

Terre Verte ignored the doors and pressed his palms to the smooth black wall instead. His hands were slender and graceful, his nails carefully trimmed, in keeping with his otherwise immaculate appearance. He always seemed to be posing, as if on stage.

He closed his gray eyes. His brow furrowed in concentration.

Dioxazine—Xaz, as she called herself, and as Cadmia had recently come to call her—caught up to them. "Do you need anything?" she asked Terre Verte, patting the pack she carried, which contained precious and powerful tools. Though Xaz was also a sorcerer, her power came from the divine realm, not the infernal one. As a Numenmancer, she had no control over this plane.

Terre Verte on the other hand was something else. None of them knew for sure, except that he seemed to be comfortable using power from either the Abyss or the Numen—something that should have been impossible.

"I'm fine," Terre Verte replied, his voice distant. "It's . . ." He stopped speaking for a few seconds, and then breathed, *"Here."*

A silver sheen surrounded the otherwise dark doorway that rippled into existence under his hands with a waft of sweet smoke. He stood up, tossing his head as if to clear it, and waved for them to go ahead.

Umber moved forward first, and Hansa followed. Cadmia stepped behind them.

The rift was *cold*, like a dunk in the icy Kavet harbor. Cadmia emerged shivering in near darkness. The rift's silver light fell dimly on a cluttered room.

"Where are we?" Hansa asked.

Dust rose when Cadmia moved her feet. "Somewhere dark. And—*achoo*! Dusty."

Terre Verte emerged from the portal last. As it closed behind him, he lifted a hand and summoned an orb of silver-white foxfire, which illuminated a once-elegant sitting room.

"Is there a door?" Xaz asked.

"Of course." Terre Verte pressed a hand to an apparently blank wall, and an ornate wooden door appeared.

The door's appearance wasn't entirely a shock; Azo's home in the Abyss, which she had shared with an Abyssumancer named Naples, had been a warren of concealed doors. Cadmia had never seen such magic in the mortal realm, but given Kavet's laws and her respected position in the Order of Napthol, there was no reason why any mancer would have shown her such a thing.

"We *are* back in the human plane, right?" Hansa asked, less trusting.

"Yes," Terre Verte answered. "But this was a hidden room, not meant for mundane eyes."

Eyes watering from the dust, Cadmia hurried after Terre Verte and found herself in a hallway decorated with cherry wainscoting beneath blue-gray walls, lit by wall-sconce oil lamps turned down low enough to cast as many shadows as light. Hansa, who came through after her, swore under his breath.

Darting anxious glances up and down the hallway, which was empty except for them—for the moment—Hansa declared, "We have to get out of here."

"Where is *here*?" Cadmia asked, rubbing her itching nose.

"We're in the Quinacridone," Hansa said, his voice choked as he referred to the building that was the heart of Kavet's government, as well as the base of the elite group known as the 126—the guard unit specifically tasked with hunting and eliminating sorcery. "I don't know exactly where," he continued, "which means probably one of the private halls, maybe where the monks live. I recognize the—"

His voice choked off as a figure turned the corner, one Cadmia didn't need Hansa to introduce.

President Winsor Indathrone was fifty-three years old, dark-haired, and shrewd-eyed. At that moment, he was wearing slacks and a shirt without vest or jacket; he was comfortably at home, which meant this hall was probably part of his personal residence. He frowned at them all, then focused his gaze on Hansa.

"Lieutenant Viridian? What is the meaning of this?"

Cadmia wasn't sure how good a liar Hansa was, but if he could come up with *anything*, he had a strong chance at being believed. Shortly before their trip to the Abyss, Hansa had been accused of magical maleficence that led to the deaths of nearly a dozen of his companions. Umber and Hansa had never fully explained *how* the spawn had cleared Hansa's name, but whatever lies or manipulation Umber had used had turned Hansa into a hero in the eyes of most of the city. President Indathrone would trust him.

"We . . ." Hansa started to speak, then froze, clearly panicked.

"Hansa?" Indathrone prompted, voice colder this time.

Cadmia had just opened her mouth to say something when Terre Verte stepped past Hansa and said, "Winsor Indathrone, you are the very image of your mother."

"My . . ." The President frowned. "Who are you?"

Terre Verte extended his hand, which President Indathrone reached for as if the habit was so engrained he could never think to resist it.

"How rude of me not to introduce myself. I am

Terre Verte. And I believe you have overstayed your welcome."

Terre Verte accepted the hand Indathrone had lifted, but didn't shake it. Instead he pulled President Indathrone closer, braced his Eminence's body with his own, and broke the neck of the most powerful man in Kavet with a single, undramatic *crunch*.

"We invited that family to supper," Terre Verte remarked, his tone that of a man commenting on a particularly ugly species of cockroach as he dropped Indathrone. "Not to move in."

Cadmia stared at the body on the floor, her chest tight. He just . . .

How could he . . .

It wasn't even the physical *act* that seemed impossible. Reason said Indathrone was as mortal as the rest of them—had been as mortal—and his corpse confirmed that fact, but . . . *no*. This was President Indathrone. He had been Kavet's moral and political leader for decades. Such a man shouldn't be able to die so swiftly, with so little fuss.

CHAPTER 2

UMBER

Umber's first thought when Indathrone's body hit the ground was, *This is going to make things complicated.*

He looked at Hansa, without any hope that the man would be rational in that moment. The Quin's skin had gone gray-pale. His mouth was open in an unspoken exclamation of horror, and the thoughts Umber could hear on the surface of his mind were barely more than white noise.

Hansa had been raised to near-worship the man who was now dead in front of them. He had been one of the privileged majority whose comfort and protection were carefully coddled and sanctified by the laws Indathrone created and defended. Hansa wasn't half-Abyssi, or a mancer born; he didn't even have Cadmia's background as a child raised by the semi-legal Order of A'hknet. Until he had been caught on the wrong side of the law, Hansa's eyes had been firmly closed to Indathrone's many flaws.

Our fault, Umber heard him think. *We brought Terre Verte here. We're complicit.*

Shit. No. None of them had known Terre Verte would do this. None of them had even had a choice about rescuing him, thanks to the manipulations of the Numini and blackmail from an Abyssumancer named Naples. But Hansa wouldn't believe that.

"Now." Terre Verte turned, and his slate-gray eyes swept their group. "I think I'd like to walk about my city. It has been a long time."

It was Xaz who first found breath to gasp, "You just *killed* Winsor Indathrone."

Umber would have been curious to know how Xaz felt about that death, but he knew better than to try to read a Numenmancer's mind. She, too, had gone pale, so much that her auburn hair looked like an unnatural infernal halo, and the faint freckles on her cheekbones stood out like ink stains. But if she felt anything about Indathrone's death other than shock and fear of the immediate consequences, it didn't show in her brown eyes or her pinched lips.

"This is not the time or place to discuss the particulars of what's been done," Umber said practically. "We need to move. Hansa, what is the best way out of here?"

"Someone is coming," Alizarin warned, his voice a soft purr that tickled Umber's skin like a physical thing.

"Which direction?" Cadmia asked. "Can we run?"

Her horrified thought echoed through her mind: *We need to run, or else Alizarin will kill them all.*

The blue Abyssi was Cadmia's lover, and she was carrying his child. If guards attacked their group, Alizarin would fight back. The Abyssi would tear through Quin guards like a shark through a school of krill.

He had done it before, when Xaz had first accidentally pulled him into the mortal realm to protect herself when the 126 had gone to arrest her. That was the slaughter Hansa had been suspected of orchestrating, mostly because the other Quin believed a Numenmancer should never have been able to summon an Abyssi to her aid.

Xaz hadn't done it intentionally. She hadn't known that the Numini had been conspiring to tie her and Alizarin together as part of their plot to rescue Terre Verte, or that one of the Abyssi would willingly come to her aid because he desperately wanted a tie to the divine realm.

That divine link had made Alizarin a different

creature since then, one with a capacity for compassion and even affection, but that didn't mean he wouldn't kill anyone who threatened them.

Umber would fight, too, if it came to that. He didn't have the Abyssi's capacity for violence, but he could hold his own. Still, he preferred running when there was a choice, so he was glad when Terre Verte sighed, pushed open the nearest doorway and said, "Inside. Alizarin, can you dispose of the body without attracting attention?"

The blue Abyssi tilted his head, then nodded.

Indathrone had been dead less than a minute. His blood would still be hot, which meant the most expedient way to be rid of his body would be to eat it. Umber had no objection to Kavet's "beloved" holy moral and political leader becoming lunch, but he was glad Hansa and Cadmia wouldn't see it.

Alizarin stayed behind as the rest of them followed Terre Verte into a well-appointed sitting room lined with bookshelves. A spread of papers arranged on the coffee table and a merrily burning gas lamp suggested the occupant had just stepped out for a moment—as he had, except that now he would never return.

"Tell me." Hansa's voice was cold and tight, and he bit off each word as if it hurt. "Was that a whim, or was it your plan all along to make murder your first task in the mortal realm?"

Terre Verte met Hansa's furious gaze impassively. "It seemed like a good starting point."

"A *starting point*?" Hansa railed.

Umber put a hand on Hansa's shoulder, trying to calm him. They didn't have a good sense of what Terre Verte was capable of, but they knew enough that it would be foolish to antagonize him. Reason wasn't what stilled Hansa's tongue, though. Judging from the thoughts rising from him, he was too furious to form further words.

"Yes, a *starting* point," Terre Verte snapped. "Based on everything you have all told me, it is clear this country is sick. I told you before that I intend to fix it—"

"No," Cadmia interrupted, "you did *not*. It is my job to listen to people, to the hard truths and half-truths and outright lies they tell. You cannot convince me we *misunderstood* you, when it's clear you deliberately led us to believe you had no knowledge of Kavet. Did you worry we would leave you in the Abyss if we knew your plans?"

"Hardly." Terre Verte brushed gray dust off his arm idly. "As I recall, *you* were the ones trapped in the Abyss until *I* opened the rift to bring you back to the mortal realm."

"And how many years did you spend trapped in that prison in the low court before we freed you?" Umber asked.

"Based on what you've told me?" Terre Verte looked up at them again, and now his steel gray eyes blazed with indignation. "A little over seventy years."

He let that statement sink in. It didn't take more than a heartbeat for Umber to make the intended connection: the revolution had been seventy years ago. The fall of the royal house—and the rise of Dahlia Indathrone, Kavet's first elected president and Winsor Indathrone's mother—had been seventy years ago.

"I am *Terre*," Verte declared, wielding the word as if it had more meaning than they knew, making it clear for the first time that it was a title instead of simply part of his name. "I am prince, heir to the line that has ruled Kavet for fourteen hundred years, with only brief interruption by that . . . Indathrone." He spat the name like a curse. "Follow me or don't, but this country is mine, and I will restore it."

Prince. Kavet's royal family had been overthrown and replaced by their first President, Dahlia Indathrone—Winsor's mother—six or seven decades ago. That fact was almost the extent of what Umber knew about the lineage that had supposedly ruled Kavet for centuries before then. It wasn't exactly illegal to talk about those ill-fated days, but it was certainly taboo, and Kavet's school history classes all began with Dahlia Indathrone's election.

He did know the revolt against the royal house, led by the Followers of the Quinacridone, was supposedly the result of the rampant abuse of malevolent sorcery among the royal and noble elite of Kavet.

"Maybe you should clarify what you mean by 'restore,'" Umber suggested, still gripping Hansa's shoulder. "And how you mean to go about it. According to the yearly census, almost eighty-five percent of the country identifies as Quin, and certainly almost all of the rest are staunchly opposed to magic. If you just kill them all, there won't *be* a Kavet left."

"Before we have this argument, can we get *out of the fucking Quinacridone Compound*?" Xaz interrupted, her voice shrill. "I was almost arrested once recently. It went badly. I'd like to not do it again."

As if on cue, Alizarin reappeared among them in a ripple of blue-black smoke.

Xaz sagged with relief. "Alizarin, you've transported me before. Can you do that now, and bring us somewhere safe without our needing to walk past guards?"

Alizarin's tail swished as he considered, and then he shook his head. "A rift from place to place on this plane is hard to travel. I used your bond to me to hold you, and your power kept you together. I couldn't bring everyone that way."

"Can you hide us, then?"

The Abyssi nodded. "We're a big group, but if we're careful, and we don't pass anyone who can see power, I can make people not notice us."

It was not entirely comforting, but better than nothing, Umber supposed.

"How many guards in the 126 have the sight?"

Cadmia asked Hansa. Occasionally people were born with the ability to see power despite not having a mancer's control over it.

"Seven," Hansa answered without needing to think about it. Then he winced, and said more softly, "Six." Hansa's best friend Jenkins had possessed the sight, but he had been among the guards Alizarin killed. "Only one or two are probably on duty now, though, and they may be out on assignment. There are Quin monks who live here who might have it too, though."

"This was the royal family's private wing," Terre Verte said. "If I'm not mistaken, this was my mother's chamber." He swallowed, and for the first time Umber saw the hint of human emotion on his face—stark grief, quickly concealed. "There was a mistress door not far from here, and an entrance to a servant's stairway on the east end of the hall, opposite the central foyer."

Hansa leaned against Umber and shut his eyes as if picturing the building in his head. "Yes, there's a back stairway. Guards don't usually use it, since we're—they're—not supposed to be on this side of the building. I don't know if the monks do though, and I've never heard of that other door."

Terre Verte smiled, but the expression was sad. "It was a *mistress* door. It was hidden, of course. Perhaps it hasn't been found." Before leading the way to the door, however, he looked around the room and opened the drawers of Indathrone's desk until he located paper and ink.

"What are you—?"

"Writing a note." Terre Verte interrupted Xaz's question without looking up from his task. "It will delay the hysteria and search once this man is discovered missing. For a few days, they will think he went off willingly, to deal with a personal emergency."

Xaz moved closer, peering over his shoulder. "You're wrapping it in a persuasion charm?"

"Yes," Terre Verte answered, somewhat distractedly. "So no one will question the difference in handwriting, or the unusual situation."

Umber could see only the vague outlines of the spell the ex-prince wove as he wrote, which was clearly formed of divine magic—the better choice for persuasion.

"Sighted guards will recognize a spell," Hansa bit out. "It will only make them more suspicious."

"Then I will veil it," Terre Verte sighed back, passing a hand over the completed missive with an air of impatience. "Do you think I am some crude novice?"

Umber's awareness of the spell snuffed out, leaving only the paper behind. He elected not to read the words and test if the magic could overcome even his own understanding of the situation.

Once he was done, Terre Verte turned, pushed

past the rest of them and reached for the door. He paused to ask, "Alizarin, is the hall empty yet?"

The Abyssi nodded. "For now."

As the once-prince unlocked and opened the door, Umber watched him, trying to imagine what might be happening in his head. This had been his home—this, in particular, had been his mother's room—and he had been royalty, some time before the revolution had ousted the royal house a little over seventy years ago. Now he was fleeing like a servant sneaking out in the night with a bag of the family's silver over his back. How it must gall him to be reduced to such a thing.

How unpredictable that might make him.

In the hallway, Terre Verte moved confidently. After examining the cherry wainscoting and smooth plaster for a few moments, he ran his fingers over an irregular mark three feet away from the corner. He pressed gently against it, and Umber heard a click.

The door opened silently.

"It's been maintained," Terre Verte said. "Your President liked his privacy, too, it seems."

He didn't wait for them before leading the way. They followed single-file down the narrow passage to a set of spiral stairs, and then to a heavy wooden door with a heavy metal lock plate.

"It should open behind a copse of bushes at the back of the royal gardens," Terre Verte said, looking at Hansa for confirmation.

"Indathrone's meditation garden," the guard said hollowly.

As they passed through the mostly-abandoned garden and into the city, Umber considered their options. His home was best protected, but that was exactly why he didn't want to bring Terre Verte there—not until they knew what he intended, and how much of a threat it was to them.

"Your apartment?" he suggested to Hansa. "It's closest. We can regroup there and make plans."

Hansa nodded.

Thankfully, they'd had the luck to return to this plane late at night. Mars was the capital city of Kavet, and its streets were never *empty*, but they had no trouble skirting the few people they saw. Unfortunately, the hour meant there was no sun to alleviate the bitter cold, and the clothes they had worn out of the Abyss had not been crafted for the frigid Kavet wind that swirled drifted snow into their faces. Umber's Abyssal blood ran hot enough he normally wouldn't have minded, but a dull ache settled into him from his bond to Hansa.

"Stupid," he heard Xaz mutter. "We were all born in Kavet. None of us thought to grab an extra cloak? Gloves?"

"It bothers you?" Cadmia asked. She was walking close to Alizarin, his arm and tail around her for warmth, but was still shivering. "I thought Numenmancers were immune."

"I can't freeze to death or get frostbite. I can still feel *cold*."

"Cold hands, warm heart," Hansa said, chapping his own hands together. "Ruby used to say that about you, because your hands were always cold, even in summer."

The words were a stone in the pool of their wary companionship. Xaz had been friends with Hansa and his fiancée Ruby, before Xaz was reported as a mancer and Hansa went to arrest her. Ruby's death wasn't Xaz's fault—she, too, had been a victim of the Numini—but that didn't mean discussion about her was comfortable.

No one spoke again for a while. What could they say?

When they turned onto Hansa's street, though, Hansa let out a hiss of alarm and put out a straight arm to block the others.

"Damn, damn, *damn*," he cursed, as they scuttled back. "I'm an idiot."

"What's wrong?" Xaz asked when they were safely out of sight.

"There are two men sitting on the front step of a house up the street," Terre Verte answered. "They appear to be soldiers."

"They're watching my apartment," Hansa said. "With everything that happened, and then the way I disappeared, of *course* they're here."

"Can you talk to them?" Umber asked. "It would

be good to know what people know, or think they know, about the situation."

"I know them both," Hansa admitted. "Neither has the sight." Despite the practical words, his voice dripped reluctance.

"Talk to them," Umber said again. "If it goes badly, it will be easier for us to make a problem go away when it's just two men in the middle of the night."

Hansa frowned, an expression that made him appear younger than his twenty-seven years. "Don't hurt them," he said. "I know how persuasive this group can be if necessary." He looked at Umber, as if to remind him of the way he had changed Hansa from a villain to a hero in the minds of everyone in the city. "If I put my foot in my mouth and make them suspicious, I won't believe *anyone* here who tries to convince me violence is the only way to deal with them." This time he looked sharply at Terre Verte.

"Of course," Umber assured him. "Now *go*."

He gave Hansa a pat on the ass just hard enough to make the guard jump. Briefly distracted from his panic about what his fellow guards would think or do, he drew a deep breath and stepped around the corner.

CHAPTER 3

HANSA

Hansa had never been much of a liar, but as the old saying went, necessity was the mother of all invention. It helped that Bonnard and Poll were men in his company, and therefore inclined to trust him.

He approached the pair confidently, reminding himself that the sight was rare and there wasn't likely to be a third man hiding in the bushes. Once he was close enough to make out their facial expressions, he saw incredulity and dawning joy.

Hansa doubted his appearance deserved the sunny grin on Poll's face as he snapped to attention and stepped forward to say, "Lieutenant Viridian?"

"Soldier Poll, Soldier Bonnard." Hansa hadn't been

their lieutenant directly, but they had all served under the same captain before his death at Alizarin's claws and teeth. "To what do I owe this visit?"

The two soldiers puffed up importantly before Poll explained, "Sir, I can't say how glad we are to see you alive and well. When you disappeared while checking out that messy business down at the docks, we feared the worst." His voice dropped and he added gently, "It might not be my place to say, sir, but I was very sorry to hear about Ruby. She was a good woman."

Hansa swallowed tightly. He didn't want to talk about Ruby, or about what had happened that day. Cadmia had run to get him, to tell him that Ruby was "hurt" and to see if he could help. Ruby hadn't been hurt; she had been dead, and Hansa had been sure it was his fault. He'd had no way of knowing that the Numini had killed her, as a way to manipulate him into doing the exact stupid thing he did.

Hansa had drawn blood, summoned Umber, and used the magic of a third boon to demand he do everything in his power to bring her back—an action that cemented them magically together for the rest of their lives, unless Terre Verte really had the power to break them apart.

As if realizing that Poll had in his exuberance neglected to answer Hansa's question, or taking Hansa's hesitation as a cue to change the subject, Bonnard said, "Captain Montag ordered your apartment searched for signs of what had happened, and then watched for further activity or in case you returned."

Apparently someone had suspected Hansa's activities hadn't been entirely wholesome. He tried to remember what his house had looked like when he left it, and for a moment his stomach knotted. The last thing he had done there had been returning Abyssal power to Umber after borrowing it to rescue a little girl named Pearl.

The soldiers of the 126 wouldn't care about motive, not when magic was involved.

Hansa reminded himself that, if sighted men had spotted the residue of sorcery in his apartment, soldiers would have been waiting to arrest him, not greet him.

"I've been on a discreet mission for President Indathrone," Hansa lied. "It had to look like I had simply disappeared. I need a little more time, though, so I would appreciate it if you didn't mention that you spotted me."

They looked suitably impressed to be taken into his confidence, and both nodded solemnly. "Yes, sir."

Hansa knew Poll. He had never been able to keep his mouth shut. He would think he was being secretive, but he would share the news with "just a few people." The rumors would pave the way in case anyone else spotted Hansa.

"I just need to pick up a few things," Hansa said, "and then I'll be gone again. Keep up the good work."

The final, fake words felt like paste on his tongue as his guilt finally caught up to him. Indathrone wouldn't contradict him because Indathrone was dead. Hansa's own captain, Captain Feldgrau of Company Four, wouldn't contradict him, because he was also dead; if these men were taking orders from Captain Montag of Company One, Feldgrau hadn't been replaced yet. Who else would question the hero of Kavet, the man who supposedly single-handedly took down the Abyssumancer and Abyssi responsible for the deaths of a dozen good men?

Slowly, he went into his home. He imagined he smelled the bitter smoke of herbs some sighted guards used to heighten their perception, though surely the smell would have dissipated by now.

Jenkins had always refused to use those, claiming they made his eyes sting and nose run and so were more a distraction than a help.

Gut-struck by the memory, Hansa leaned against the wall of the kitchen and drew a deep breath around the lump of tears in his throat. In truth, the room had an antiseptic smell; someone must have cleaned out the remains of what food he had left behind, probably after it had molded and become foul in his absence.

Then his gaze fell on a familiar trunk, and his heart fell even further. He didn't need to open it to recognize it from Jenkins' apartment at the Quin Compound. He knew it contained the items Jenkins had willed to Hansa. If Hansa had died first, a similar collection of belongings would eventually have ended up in Jenkins' room.

He didn't open the trunk. He didn't even take the time to change, but filled his pouch with spending money, put on a lined vest and cloak, and crammed as many extra clothes into a pack as he could. He wondered what the soldiers outside had made of his strange garments, which were made of material that looked like silk, but had been crafted like parchment, by scraping and stretching the tough skins of certain Abyssal beasts.

He couldn't stand to be in the apartment any longer. He bid good evening to the two soldiers and walked back toward where he had left the others with as much composure as he could muster. He had a brief moment of panic when he couldn't see them, and thought they had left, then realized he had gone outside the edge of Alizarin's concealing illusions. When he focused on magic instead of what his eyes could see, he was able to identify the telltale edge of Alizarin's power, and the others within it. As Alizarin had said, he couldn't hide them from someone with the ability to see Abyssal magic.

Once he reached the group, the illusion dropped completely. Hansa leaned against Umber, tucked his head down against the spawn's shoulder and drew a deep breath to keep from shaking. Umber didn't complain when Hansa's hands snaked under his shirt to find his bare back, even though they had to be cold as ice, but wrapped an arm around his waist to hold him close.

Umber's skin had a faint musk like clove smoke. Touching him felt like putting the final piece into a masterful stained glass window, perfect completion.

The compulsion to seek the spawn's skin and the deep contentment of finding it were heightened by the bond between them. It was more than sexual attraction, which Hansa had felt well before he had demanded the third boon; it was like the need for water or food, something vital he would die without.

"We can't stay there," Hansa said. "They searched my house and have been watching it. Even if we can sneak past them, Alizarin can't hide us forever, and as soon as the others know I'm back, they'll come looking for explanations. Someone with the sight is sure to show up."

"Do we have another plan?" Terre Verte asked, his voice crisp and unsympathetic.

Murderer, Hansa thought, lifting his eyes to the supposed once-prince. *Verte*, he thought, mentally correcting what he had been calling the man in his own head. Hansa had thought the double name was a style from some far-off country, but Verte's earlier rant had made it clear that "Terre" was a title.

He isn't my prince.

"I was a suspected mancer," Xaz said practically. "They will have gutted my apartment and burned everything I owned by now." Hansa squelched the unhelpful guilt he felt at Xaz's utterly flat remark.

"What about the Fens?" Cadmia asked. Despite having snuggled against Alizarin for warmth, she was shivering steadily and had a bluish cast to her lips.

Hansa raised his brows at the suggestion, and Umber let out a sharp half laugh and said, "Sister, your knowledge surprises me."

"The Fens?" Xaz asked.

"It's a semi-abandoned series of buildings not far from the main docks, but not quite in the village," Umber said, bright blue eyes dancing with amusement. "Very popular among men and women seeking illicit deals and assignations."

"Guards get called down to try to clear it out every now and then," Hansa added, "but everyone knows we're just going through the motions. The regulars have some kind of early-warning system set up, and the place is a rabbit warren of exits. There's never been any sign of sorcery, so the One-Twenty-Six doesn't bother with it except when someone makes an official complaint and we're required to make some noise."

"People squat there, don't they?" Cadmia snapped. "Sometimes people who come for counsel mention it."

Just as Hansa had been a loyal guard in his former life, Cadmia had been a well-respected Sister in the Order of the Napthol, which provided medical services and spiritual counsel to Kavet. Cadmia specialized in advising the general scum of Kavet—

drunkards, thieves, and other petty and more serious criminals.

In short, the kinds of people who would know the Fens well.

"It's a good idea," Hansa admitted after thinking it over. "It's a place out of the snow where no one looks too closely at anyone, and where guards generally don't bother to come—much less anyone with the sight." Cadmia's stomach rumbled audibly and she rubbed at it, then dropped her hand lower as if to cup the tiny speck of life sheltered there. Hansa added, "Hopefully we can also trade for something to eat."

"Then it's decided," Umber said, with the alacrity he tended to demonstrate whenever he was reminded of Cadmia's pregnancy. Hansa couldn't help but wonder if his solicitousness was caused just by Cadmia's condition, or whether it was specifically because her child would be Abyss-spawn like Umber himself.

They left the city proper, then skirted the edge of the Kavet docks district and the surrounding village. Most trading vessels preferred warmer southern ports at this time of year, but there were still enough ships tied up and therefore enough sailors in port to make this area wilder than the city proper. The mingled clamor of tavern bards, carousing, and bawdies hawking their wares felt surreal. Normally, when

Hansa walked down here in the tan and black livery of the 126, these raucous noises fell into silence.

Now, with the help of the Abyssi, he was invisible.

The noise died away behind them as they approached a string of ramshackle buildings—the remains of old warehouses that had seen better days. Most had been partly gutted by fire many years ago, or had roofs staved in by untended ice and snow, and had never been repaired.

"This?" Verte asked. He had been so quiet that Hansa, walking in the front of their group with Umber, had almost forgotten him. Now he was looking at the structures with his usual disdain. "Why are these warehouses in this condition?"

Hansa shrugged. "There are superstitions around them of bad luck," he admitted, "but mostly, no one's had the money and motivation to buy them and either break them down or rebuild them."

Verte scoffed, but before he could make another disparaging remark about "his" Kavet, Umber cut him off.

"Alizarin, can you hide everyone else for a few minutes, but let Hansa and me be seen?" he asked. "We'll secure a room, then the rest of you can follow in a few minutes."

The Abyssi nodded.

"This way," Umber said to Hansa. "Tuck your head down so your cloak hood hides your face. We don't want anyone recognizing you."

"That won't look suspicious?" Hansa asked, though he obeyed even as he inquired. He had learned that hesitating when Umber suggested he do something never improved matters.

Umber laughed, and cinched an arm around Hansa's waist to pull him tightly against his side. "In this place? Absolutely not."

Inside, there were signs that some repairs had been done, probably by regular occupants, but enough doors and walls had been left with gaping holes to make it impossible for anyone in this area to get cornered.

Hansa expected Umber to let him go before they reached areas with people in them, but the spawn kept him close. Only as they pushed aside a hanging blanket and entered a room where several groups were set up playing dice and card games did he realize that Umber wasn't holding on to him for comfort, but camouflage.

As several men and a few women looked up at them, Hansa's face heated. Even if these strangers didn't recognize him specifically, his cloak wouldn't hide the fact that he was obviously a man, pressed close enough against another man that they had to be lovers. In any other area of Kavet, they would have been derided and told to break it up or face arrest for public display of perversion.

Not long ago, *Hansa* might have been the one doing the deriding.

In the Abyss, where sex was considered as vital as air and shame was a divine and thus unwelcome complication, it had been easy to accept his relationship with Umber. To *revel* in it, once he had overcome his anxiety. After so many years fighting to be who he was supposed to be, pursuing his relationship with Ruby because it was what everyone expected, and dreading having anyone notice what was wrong with him, honest passion with the handsome, experienced half-Abyssi had been a revelation.

Now that they were back in Kavet, his skin crawled with the need to hide.

The man acting as dealer looked them over and asked, "What kind of room are you looking for?"

"A private one," Umber answered, "with a lock. I have cash."

Without waiting for a response, Umber tossed a coin to the dealer, who caught it, glanced at it, and pocketed it. Hansa thought it was a silver bit, though he hadn't seen it well enough to be sure; it wasn't a princely sum, but it could have bought them a room and meal at a proper inn if they hadn't wanted to avoid more-reputable areas.

"Pardon me," the dealer said to the players at his table. "Put your cards down. Cheat and you know I'll cut your fingers off." He made this threat with a sunny smile that somehow reinforced its sincerity.

He didn't have anything as solid and immovable as an innkeeper's key board. Instead, he opened a battered satchel, rummaged through it with consideration, and tossed Umber a heavy brass key.

"Room four," he said. "You know the way."

It wasn't a question, clearly. Umber nodded. How much time he had spent in this place—and with whom?

In the last weeks in the Abyss, Hansa had been able to pretend the real world, this world, didn't exist. He had been able to ignore the fact that he barely knew this man who had become his lover.

Now, as Umber led him up a staircase and down a dark hallway that Hansa was half convinced might collapse under him, Hansa couldn't help feeling that all the messy details of the mortal realm were going to catch up to him soon.

He was so lost in his own thoughts that a scoff from behind him made him jump half out of his skin as Umber unlocked the door.

Umber chuckled. "Didn't see them?" he teased, as Hansa realized it was Verte who had made the disapproving sound. He, Alizarin, Xaz, and Cadmia were right behind them, hidden in Alizarin's power until that moment.

Hansa didn't deign to answer as he stepped forward and examined the room. He had passed through the Fens enough on required raids that he knew there were places here that would be worse than staying in the snow—areas where damp and neglect had left rot and ruin, where a misstep could easily break a man's ankle, and where refuse attracted flies and crawling vermin.

This room was cold, and dark enough that Verte once more lifted a hand to summon foxfire. The silvery light made every surface appear frosted as it revealed a simple but clean chamber with a scarred but serviceable table, two mismatched chairs, and a wide mattress in the corner. There was a faint smell of damp, but that was the worst of it.

"This is much nicer than I expected," Hansa admitted. He had seen more unpleasant rooms at tavern inns.

"It will be even nicer if the fireplace works," Cadmia added, as she spotted a fireplace with a haphazard pile of logs next to it.

"It should," Umber answered as he moved to arrange the logs on the hearth grate. He didn't bother with kindling; instead he drew the ever-present knife from his belt and nicked a fingertip. The moment his blood touched the wood, flames rose to lick at it like kittens at cream.

"*Nice?*" Verte echoed, looking around incredulously as Umber whispered the fire into merry life and blessed heat filled the room.

Apparently the room wasn't *palatial* enough for the prince. Yes, it certainly had its flaws. For starters, there was a large gap in the far floor, which had been half covered with a fishing net Hansa couldn't imagine was particularly helpful except to make the hole invisible in the dark. There was no way to let in sun or moonlight, because the only window had been boarded over. Still, what had Verte expected?

"It's clean," Cadmia elaborated, "and it has a working fireplace."

"There are only a handful of rooms like this," Umber said, "and House, the man who runs this area, guards them fiercely. If you trash one of his rooms, he'll add your blood to the mess before he makes you clean it up with your tongue."

Once the feeling had returned to his extremities, Hansa felt a bone-deep weariness take him. He glanced at the mattress, and couldn't help briefly considering what might have been done on it. After all, this was a place he knew mostly as a spot for the types of trysts Kavet's culture and laws declared perverse and criminal.

As was often the case, Umber responded to Hansa's engrained Quin disdain with an amused question: *Are you imagining things you think people have done here, or things you would like to do here? I can't tell.*

As usual, Umber had a point. Hansa had spent twenty-six years as one of Kavet's elite. Now, even after he had accepted how ignorant he had been and how much his own status had changed, he was still daily faced with examples of his own habitual arrogance and assumptions.

Hansa and Umber had had a few conversations on that subject previously, and he wasn't in the mood for another one right then. He had just opened his mouth to make a snarky retort instead—hoping he could come up with one by the time he started speaking—when Verte announced, "I think I'd prefer to find my own lodgings."

The once-prince's gaze swept the room, as if challenging them to argue with him.

"You . . . what?" Hansa asked. "You can't possibly plan to go back out there tonight."

"A few more minutes in the snow won't hurt me," Verte said. "I refuse to stay in this slum."

"You don't know the city— anymore," Hansa argued, amending the last when he saw the spark of challenge in Verte's gaze. "You don't know the laws. You'll attract attention."

The prince's impassive expression suggested he expected as much, and was waiting for Hansa to explain why that was a bad thing.

"If they capture you, they will kill you. Do you understand that?"

Why was he even trying to talk sense into this man? So what if the Quin captured him? Unlike most of the mancers the 126 had captured and executed, Verte was actually *guilty* of a crime worthy of arrest, and Hansa didn't doubt he was able and willing to commit more.

Xaz spoke calmly. "He'll have a guide." Her lips quirked on the last word, as if she hoped to be far more than an advisor. "If he wants one, that is."

"A guide would be deeply appreciated." Verte smiled and held a hand out to Xaz. "If you don't mind a few more minutes in the snow, lovely lady, I'm sure we can find better accommodations."

Xaz accepted Verte's hand. "I'm intrigued to see what you can come up with to try to impress me."

In the years Hansa had known Xaz, she had always been reserved and demure, and uninterested in any of the men Ruby had thrown her way. Apparently Ruby's choices had lacked a special something—such as powerful sorcery, and the ability and willingness to murder a man with his bare hands.

We can't just let them walk out of here, Hansa thought, unsure if he intended it for Umber or not.

Did you expect them to stay with us? Umber replied. *I'll feel safer with them gone.*

If not for the commands of her divine masters driving them together to the depths of the Abyss, Xaz would never have been with them, so it shouldn't have been a shock that she was willing and perhaps anxious to leave—but it still was.

Spotting the blue Abyssi crouched by Cadmia, as if hoping not to be noticed, Hansa said, "But, Alizarin—"

Xaz shrugged, and spoke directly to the Abyssi. "I have no power over you, just as you have no power over me. That was why you wanted to bond to a Numenmancer in the first place, wasn't it?"

Alizarin's half nod, half shrug of response seeme strangely uncertain, though Hansa had been unc the same impression, that Alizarin had chosen Xaz because he wanted a tie to the mortal realm without being subject to an Abyssumancer's commands.

"Then we're both free to go about our lives."

"As for myself, I haven't forgotten I am in your debt," Verte said, glancing briefly away from Xaz to Hansa and Umber. "Once I have regained sufficient strength, I will seek you out and we can discuss severing your unwanted bond to each other."

Unwanted, Hansa thought. It was, or had been, but that single word was too simple. He had changed since demanding the third boon, too much to simply go *back* now.

There was Umber to consider, too, though. He didn't have Hansa's hang-ups about family and peer expectations, and a societally-indoctrinated dream of a respectable career and a wife and classic little children, but he had a *life*. Hansa had forced this bond on him, and though Umber had been remarkably sanguine about the whole thing—better than Hansa deserved, considering it was his pigheaded selfishness that had dragged Umber into this entire mess—he clearly wanted to shake off his unasked-for Quin appendage so he could go back to whatever he did when he wasn't taking care of Hansa.

"Thank you," Hansa managed to choke out to Verte. "But are you sure you—"

Firmly, Verte interrupted, "For now, I will bid you farewell."

CHAPTER 4

UMBER

Hansa turned an incredulous look his way, and Umber realized he had made a vast error in judgment. He had been focused on survival—always his first priority—and Hansa's and Cadmia's safety. He didn't trust Terre Verte or Dioxazine, but hadn't had a way to suggest separating that didn't insult them, which he couldn't afford to do.

Now Umber saw the way Hansa's jaw set and his brown eyes hardened, and realized he had forgotten one crucial detail: Hansa wasn't the kind of man who sat back and took care of himself while the world burned.

"You think we should just let them go?" Hansa challenged.

When it came to sex or sorcery, Hansa tended to do a lot of blushing and stammering. The Followers of the Quinacridone believed in abstinence outside of marriage, that same-sex relations were deviant, and that any contemplation of the Abyss or the Numen was the first step toward an inevitable decline toward madness and destruction. Since Quin made up the vast majority of the democratic Kavet, the laws reflected these views. Therefore, Hansa's education on certain subjects had been so lacking that Umber sometimes struggled to comprehend just how naïve he still was.

On the other hand, a Quin man in Kavet didn't have to spend a lot of time ducking his head and hustling just to survive. Umber had spent his life focused on surviving tomorrow; Hansa had spent his focused on protecting the country in which he lived. That made their perceptions fundamentally different.

Umber had seen a sorcerer break a powerful man's neck, and had decided that sorcerer was a danger to him personally and therefore best avoided. Hansa had seen a murder—an assassination, even—that he perceived as a prelude to more violence. He wanted justice. He wanted to fix it, whatever that meant.

"Verte started by killing Indathrone," Hansa said,

emphasizing the once-prince's name in a way that made it clear he had consciously dropped the title. "What do you think he will do next?"

"He clearly thinks he has a right to this country," Cadmia said, with a grimace. "Terre. Prince. I know the Quin deliberately eradicated all records of the royal house, but I feel like such a fool that I didn't know."

"It's obvious he intentionally misled us," Hansa speculated. "Every time we spoke of Kavet, or asked where he was from—"

"And what if you had known?" Umber asked. He hadn't realized Verte had been royalty, but it had been clear from the start that he was a man used to privilege, power, and prestige. "Leaving him in the Abyss wasn't an option, just like keeping him with us now wasn't an option. Trying to force him to stay would not have ended well."

Her voice uncharacteristically quiet and strained, Cadmia said, "Xaz was hoping Terre Verte could help her break her bond to Alizarin. What will happen if he does?"

Umber winced, wishing he had assurances he could give her. "Abyssi and Numini cannot stay in this realm without some kind of mortal bond," Umber said. "The immediate result would be Alizarin falling back into the Abyss."

"And the less immediate result?" Cadmia pressed.

Alizarin, knowing the answer already, curled

himself against Cadmia and tucked his face against her hair.

"Magic can change who we are," Umber answered, glancing at Hansa, thinking of their long conversations about how their bond may have affected him, and how once it was broken he might look back on the last few weeks with a completely different view. A fleshbond was only supposed to affect physical attraction, but who could say anything for sure? "Alizarin has traits I would say are impossible for an Abyssi, which must be enabled by his connection to the Numen through Dioxazine. If he loses that connection . . . it may be for the best that he won't be able to stay on this plane, since it's likely he will turn around and eat us all without a second thought."

Alizarin lifted his striking turquoise eyes, and Umber could see sorrow and fear clearly etched on his face. He knew.

"People keep telling me Abyssi can't plan, either," Cadmia pointed out, "but we've seen them do it. Maybe some Abyssi, like Alizarin, are just different."

"No one said Abyssi were stupid," Alizarin interrupted, his voice holding a touch of growl that Umber thought came from sorrow, not anger. Actually, Umber thought, many people have said that, though he also knew it was false. "Abyssi do not plan unless they need to, because planning is boring. But Abyssi can hunt. Stalk. Play a game. Some make mancers. But the world is full of food and fun, so planning isn't needed most of the time. Because food and fun are all that matters. And not being eaten."

The last words were muffled, spoken as he once again nuzzled at Cadmia's hair, acknowledging the irony. Obviously, to this Abyssi, many more things mattered.

Umber wasn't often speechless, but what else could he say? He had no power to hold Alizarin in this realm, or to protect his connection to the divine one.

Alizarin swished his tail once more, then shook himself, smoothing his fur in a gesture of anxiety Umber saw too often from him. "We do need those," Alizarin said, changing the subject from the abstract threat to their more immediate needs. "We came here for food and rest. Is there food?"

"I can barter for mortal food downstairs," Umber said. "Can you hunt without attracting notice?"

"I can."

"Umber, how much time have you spent in the Fens?" Hansa asked. Umber smiled despite the circumstances. He had wondered when that question was coming.

"It was a favorite haunt when I was younger," he admitted. "I've moved up in the world since, but I still know my way around well enough."

He started toward the door. Cadmia called after him. "Can you tell us about yourself?" she asked. When he turned to look at her, she met his gaze directly, despite the hint of new color that rose on her cheeks. "When you get back, I mean. I'm curious about you, and about the spawn in general, but even Alizarin doesn't know much about your kind."

Again her hand drifted toward her abdomen, an unconsciously protective gesture.

Umber nodded. He would have to decide how much to tell her. He had spent most of his life actively cultivating the belief that his kind didn't exist, not deliberately sharing details, but there were some things Cadmia should know.

He had time to think as he sought the ever-present yet ever-changing flea market, which was half inside and half outside, wedged in a sheltered alley between three buildings. Individual merchants lit their booths with oil lamps or hooded candles just enough so the wares were visible, but the faces of merchants and customers were left dark.

Umber found a woman selling simple food, and bought a loaf of dense barley bread, goat cheese, and smoked fish. The woman looked particularly down on her luck, and normally Umber would have deliberately overpaid for the purchases, but he wanted to avoid drawing attention. From another merchant, he purchased warm woolen blankets, which were slightly worn but clean and serviceable.

He was on his way out of the market when the glint of candlelight on steel caught his attention. The merchant had his wares arranged on a blanket, which could be rolled up and hauled away over his shoulder at a moment's notice.

One more purchase, and Umber returned to the others. Alizarin was still gone, hunting, but perhaps that was for the best. This story might be better to tell without an Abyssi nearby.

Once he and Hansa and Cadmia had gathered for their simple meal, Umber contemplated how to begin. As he thought, he watched Cadmia pick at her food despondently, uninterested but grudgingly forcing it down because it was better than nothing. Umber thought she should be able to tolerate human food soon, as her body became used to being back on the mortal plane, but in the meantime, he hoped Alizarin could bring something back from his hunt.

"My story isn't as sweet nor my father as solicitous nor my mother as loving as you and Rin," Umber began at last.

He still found it hard to credit the relationship between Cadmia and Alizarin, but that was only because he had never heard of an Abyssi being able to care for anyone but itself. Abyssi and Abyssumancers were drawn to each other, but that was a physical draw, closer to the fleshbond Umber shared with Hansa than the emotional connection Cadmia and Alizarin shared—and besides, Cadmia wasn't a mancer. She had chosen her relationship with the

Abyssi, as she had chosen her pregnancy, entering into each situation with her eyes open.

"My mother was a member of the One-Twenty-Six," Umber continued. "A lieutenant, actually, named Bonnie Holland."

Cadmia had known that already, but Hansa visibly started, then blanched, his imagination filling in the blanks accurately enough. He already knew part of the story, because it was told as a cautionary tale to newer guards. Bonnie hadn't done anything wrong, and what had happened to her could have happened to any man—except for the pregnancy, of course— but President Indathrone had used it as an excuse to stop accepting women into the 126, and to start forcibly retiring those who remained.

"Holland went as part of a team to investigate a report of suspicious activity—strange noises, missing livestock, the usual indications of an Abyssumancer who isn't being careful enough."

Abyssi inherited memories from their sires. To a lesser extent, so did spawn. Umber's mother had never told him the tale of his conception, but he remembered it with the brilliant horror of a fever dream.

Walking up the step, careful not to slip on the ice from a recent storm, beneath a gray and hazy sky. Knocking. Nervous, despite the half-dozen others she was with. They were all well trained with the weapons they wore, but they also knew the damage an Abyssumancer could inflict.

"They were ill-prepared to deal with an Abyssumancer whose carelessness had to do with the fact that he had spent the last week building power to open a rift. I imagine he assumed that, with an Abyssi at his command, he wouldn't need to fear Quin reprisals."

Bonnie was the only one who had the sight and so could see the black void that opened behind the Abyssumancer's left shoulder. She shoved one of her team back—a young man who had only recently been promoted to full soldier, out on his first assignment—and ordered him to run to the compound to warn the others and get more support.

He hesitated for a heartbeat. He knew it would be over before he returned, that she was trying to save his life. A human being could not fight a monster from the Other realms.

Bonnie lunged at the Abyssumancer. The rift would close when he died. The action threw the mancer off-balance and disrupted his ceremony, but not before the beast stepped into the mortal realm.

It was on the others before Bonnie could take her next breath. A wash of blood later, it turned to her where she was still grappling with the mancer. Its claws dragged deep gauges in her skin as it pulled her away from the Abyssumancer.

"Wait!"

When the Abyssumancer called to the invisible beast, Bonnie thought for one foolish instant that he intended to save her. She was wrong.

"Don't kill her yet. I need her to tell me who reported me. As soon as I'm finished here."

"The mancer stopped his Abyssi from killing her so he could interrogate her. But first he had to complete the ritual to bind the Abyssi to this realm."

If the Abyssi had wanted, it could have helped the mancer create a stable link between them, as Alizarin had helped Dioxazine. Umber's sire, however, had had no interest in being a mancer's slave, so he resisted the link, making the ritual a painstaking and time-consuming process.

"There are a limited number of ways that an Abyssi kept from feeding will entertain itself. Eventually the Abyssumancer lost control, and the Abyssi killed him and was pulled back to its native plane, but not before it had raped . . . my mother."

As Umber fought against memories that weren't his own, Hansa reached over and put a hand on his. The contact, the opposite of the viciousness in his mind, made him jump.

He pulled away from Hansa to avoid getting distracted, and caught a scrap of thought from the guard:

Stupid, Hansa chastised himself. *Why would you touch someone as he's describing his mother's rape?*

It was an irritating misread of the situation, though this wasn't a good time to correct Hansa's misconceptions.

The fleshbond between them affected the purely human Hansa most, but Umber felt the pull of it as well. He wouldn't wither, starve, and succumb to madness without the touch of Hansa's skin, as Hansa would without Umber, but Hansa's presence was like the wafting scent of rich chocolate in the air. His touch stirred hunger no matter how sated Umber had previously been.

Given a choice between describing this story and tumbling into bed with Hansa, Umber's preference should have been obvious—but it wasn't, not to Hansa, because he had been raised to think of sex as a dirty indulgence best met in secret with one's lawfully-linked partner. It would never occur to him that passion with a willing and tender lover was *exactly* what Umber wanted after dragging his mind through these memories.

Instead, he forced himself to continue the story. "After the attack, Holland was given leave from the guard with a generous pension."

After Hansa had been the only survivor of a similar attack, he had used Bonnie's deal as the basis for his own demands. Hansa could live quite well in Kavet for the rest of his life even if he chose never to return to work.

Hansa should have died that day, when Xaz had summoned Alizarin. Umber should have left well enough alone when he saw the bloodied guard struggling to lift himself from the cold street. But he couldn't. He had meddled. He had pushed enough Abyssal power into Hansa to stop the bleeding and heal the wounds. He had made plenty of excuses at the time, and even more since—oh it was tempting to blame the Numini who had manipulated them all— but the heart of the matter was that he had seen a downed Quin guard in the same uniform his mother had worn, and despite knowing the action would cause a bond between them that would give Hansa a dangerous amount of power over him, Umber had been too stupid to walk away.

"Bonnie became a recluse by her own choice before she realized she was pregnant. She kept the child. Bore it. Nursed it." Abyss-spawn nursed on blood, but his Quin mother hadn't hesitated. "About the time I was learning to walk and talk, she dumped me at the doorstep of an Order of A'hknet witch, walked off and never came back."

Cadmia and Hansa both looked at him with horror as he narrated that portion of the story, but even when he had been a child, Umber had understood. After all, he had his mother's memory of his conception. He wondered sometimes if she would have cared for him without any magical coercion, but she never had the opportunity to make that decision, so as the Abyssal taint faded from her so did her dedication to her unwanted spawn.

"At the time she intended to leave Kavet on the first ship that would take her. I don't know if she made it, or if she died like rumors say she did."

He stopped with his personal history then. He had known Cadmia when they were both children in the Order of A'nknet, though there was no reason she would remember him. She had been the daughter of the famous Scarlet Paynes, a much-admired dancer and the highest paid courtesan in Kavet; Umber had been the scrawny kid no one claimed, who lived off scraps left behind by the sailors and merchants until he finally came into his power as an adolescent.

He continued with more important, general facts.

"Eventually human-born Abyss-spawn do learn to eat the same things as humans, but the first few months they nurse—blood, not milk, which at least means Alizarin can feed the child as well as you can." Cadmia twitched involuntarily when he said "blood," but like his own mother, she would do what she had to. She didn't question it. Was that just her practical nature, Umber wondered, or the unborn child's magic manipulating her? Unlike Bonnie, Cadmia had willingly chosen to conceive her child. That changed everything, didn't it?

"My first solid food was strawberries," Umber recalled aloud. "In summertime they grew in my mother's backyard." That one was a pleasant memory.

"After that . . . well, the spawn are among the more powerful creatures in Kavet," he said, without false modesty or arrogance. "We are human enough to hide the Abyssal taint from Quin soldiers with the sight, but Abyssi enough that we are substantially sturdier than other humans. We can feed on any of the coins of the Abyss, or eat human food. And in my experience, we are often more *human*—more able to control our Abyssi side and the impulses associated with it—than Abyssumancers.

"Which brings us to the dangers your child will face." He gazed down at the scraps of bread left on his plate, because he didn't want to meet either Hansa's or Cadmia's gaze.

"The two largest dangers to the spawn are bonding, and Abyssumancers. A full bond usually takes some form of intent, but partial bonds can be formed through accidents. Simple favors. Any unequal transaction." Like saving the life of a Quin guard. "The Abyssal power seeks a mortal connection. A mortal granted one boon has the ability to demand another, and another, and each one ties spawn and bond-partner tighter, until harm to one is harm to the other." Since humans were significantly more fragile than spawn, such a bond could be a significant weakness.

"As for mancers . . . well. Like I said, spawn can feed

many ways, which means they are a valuable power source." Abyssi created Abyssumancers to heighten their own strength. They used their mancers like lamp oil, burning through them, which meant mancers constantly craved power. They could raise that power through fire, through blood, through sex or through pain—the four coins of the Abyss—but the kind of sacrifices that met their needs also drew the attention of Quin guards. Spawn could raise power in those same ways, but also produced it as a natural body process, just as pure humans generated body heat.

Cadmia set her jaw as if preparing for a fight. Hansa attempted to look casual as he avoided looking at Umber.

Hansa had stumbled into trouble with an Abyssumancer named Naples in the Abyss. The strange laws of the Abyss had kept Umber safe from the mancer, but hadn't afforded the same protection to his human bond. Half-starved due to circumstance and as blind to the thought of right or wrong as most Abyssumancers eventually became, Naples had identified Hansa as an easy target the moment he had walked in the door.

As for the other danger, Hansa *was* exactly the kind of bond most spawn tried to avoid.

Well, not *exactly* the type. A fleshbond with a handsome individual of one's preferred gender was hardly a catastrophe. Speaking—or thinking of—it had been a while . . .

"I know that look," Hansa said, startling Umber from his thoughts.

"What?"

"That's the 'thinking of sex on the table' look," the Quin elaborated. "If you're trying to change the subject, you can just say you don't want to talk about it anymore."

"Are you objecting to sex on the table?"

"Not in concept, but--"

Cadmia waved a hand to cut him off. "Can *I* object to sex on the table? This room is good enough for sleeping, but not large enough for privacy." She cleared her throat, and met Umber's gaze squarely as she added, "Thank you for sharing what you have. I know I'll have questions in the future, but I don't want to force you to tell more than you're comfortable with, especially all at once."

Umber nodded. "I'll answer what I can." Before Hansa could decide again to feel guilty for mentioning sex, he silently half teased, half assured the guard, *Don't worry, I know plenty of secluded spots we can use tonight.*

"What's our next step, anyway?" Hansa asked, a little too loudly. "We sleep here tonight, and then what? We've set a crazy sorcerer prince loose in the city."

Hansa's description seemed to give them a good deal more agency and responsibility than Umber recalled their having in the matter, but that was a bridge for another day.

"Tomorrow we need to teach you both how to veil your power," Umber said. "With effort, you should be able to hide yourselves from sighted guards, and hopefully Abyssumancers." He slid the last package he had picked up in the market across the table to Hansa. "Happy birthday."

"It's not my birthday," Hansa said, skeptically, as he opened the felt-wrapped satchel to reveal a belt-knife in a simple leather sheath. He drew it with a look of horror, the words clear on his face even if Umber hadn't been able to read his mind: *Why does it always have to involve blood?*

"It's sturdy, not fine steel but good enough for now, and simple enough no one will remark on it if you wear it openly," Umber said. Hansa knew enough about Abyssal power by now that he didn't need further explanation, but Umber continued for Cadmia's benefit. "There are four coins of power in the Abyssal realm: blood, fire, flesh, and pain. Blood is the easiest to use and manipulate. Neither of you has a natural tie to the Abyss, but as long as you're bound to it, you should be able to use it at least a little." He met Hansa's gaze as he said, "Anything else you want to accomplish starts with this. You have power. You need to know how to use it."

CHAPTER 5

CADMIA

Cadmia had a thousand more questions about the spawn, but followed Umber's lead and let him change the subject. She didn't know yet how she felt about his assertion that she needed to learn how to use Abyssal magic—while she had plenty of academic knowledge, she had less experience with it practically than even Hansa—but if it was necessary, she would cope.

But Alizarin was right. The first thing they all needed was rest.

Hansa and Umber insisted that Cadmia should have the room's one bed, and after several minutes of pointless arguing she capitulated. She didn't like being treated like spun glass just because she was pregnant, but it would be stupid for them all to refuse the bed on principle.

The two men snuggled together on the floor near the fire, a blanket under them and Hansa's cloak spread across them both, while Cadmia lay sleeplessly on the bed. The mattress wasn't new, and had never been excellent quality, but it was clean and her nose suggested the hay stuffing was relatively fresh.

Given what she knew of the Fens, she had expected the familiar reek of misery and indulgence: drug-smoke, sex sweat, vomit, and human waste, as one often found in the pockets of this world kept for those who had been driven from society.

There are places here like the ones you imagine, Umber said, responding to her thoughts in the occasionally-irritating way the spawn had. *There are people here who make their livelihoods on the addictions and weaknesses of others, and they make sure they always have a steady supply of misery. There are more people who come here because they have no other choices. They take care of their spaces, little as they are. Even here, we're among the lucky. House's rooms don't come cheap.*

Cadmia had the sudden image of dealing with a child or adolescent who could actually *read her mind.* Oh dear.

Umber chuckled, then smoothed a hand over Hansa's shoulder when the guard shifted and murmured something too soft for Cadmia to hear.

Cadmia sat back up, giving up on pretending to

sleep. There was a cold spot at her back that Alizarin was supposed to occupy. She would sleep once he returned from hunting.

Umber patted Hansa's shoulder again, then sat up as well. He eased away from Hansa, stood and stretched. Shirtless for sleep, he cut a handsome figure —lean body, dark hair that had grown unfashionably long since it was last trimmed, and those brilliantly blue eyes.

"I've decided I will go back to the Cobalt Hall as you suggested," Cadmia said, keeping her voice soft to keep from disturbing Hansa, "but not for the reasons you think. I'm not going to hide."

For reasons no one understood, mancers were unable to cross the threshold of the Cobalt Hall, which would keep her and her child safe from *that* threat— but not from the continual, eroding wear that came from living a lie and hiding who and what you were from the world.

Umber nodded, holding his tongue as he awaited her next words.

"If I return to my customary tasks at the Hall, I'll be in a position to hear rumors from both the Quinacridone Compound and the sorts who live at the edges of society. If Terre Verte starts stirring unrest, I'll know."

"And in the meantime you'll be warm, well fed and as safe as any of us," Umber said approvingly. "I on't experience the kind of debilitating discomfort mancers do when they approach the Hall, but the only time I slept there I had disturbingly vivid dreams. I don't know if that was a result of what I am, or the situation I was in at the time, but I'll warn you anyway. I'm also not sure if Alizarin will be able to follow you there, or if the power that holds mancers at bay will also keep him out."

"*No! What did I—*" Hansa shouted, and reached out in his sleep. Umber moved swiftly, and caught the other man's grasping hand.

Before Hansa had settled again, Alizarin appeared in a waft of spicy smoke that coated Cadmia's tongue with the smells of the Abyss, and consequently made her stomach rumble with hunger. At Umber's urging, she had eaten a bit of the fish and cheese, but she hadn't been able to tolerate more than a bite of bread, and what food she had taken was now sitting oddly in her stomach.

She tried not to look disappointed when she realized Alizarin hadn't brought anything back for her.

"How was the hunting?" she asked.

"I have to range far to find large prey that won't be missed," Alizarin replied apologetically. "I saw the big wings in the sky."

"The Osei?" Umber sounded incredulous. "You hunted *them*?"

Everyone in Kavet knew about the Osei, though here in the city no one thought much about them. The dragon-like creatures claimed territory off th southern and eastern shores of the country, but never flew above it and rarely interacted with the population except through trade.

Alizarin lashed his tail in a way Cadmia knew indicated discomfort. Had he been afraid of the massive beasts? Cadmia hadn't realized there was anything on the mortal plane that could intimidate an Abyssi, but she also hadn't seen any creatures near the massive bulk of the Osei in Alizarin's native realm.

"Of course not," Alizarin said, fluffing his impossibly-soft fur. "I just looked at them. I've heard stories, and wanted to know if they are true." He shrugged, as if his curiosity was inconsequential. "I could not tell. You're hungry?"

"Yes," Cadmia admitted. She bit her tongue to ask if looking at the Osei had distracted him from bringing meat back for her.

"Here." He tucked his tail tightly around her waist and pulled her against his chest. Under the fur, his body was that of a well-muscled man, and her own body always gave an appreciative shiver when she pressed against it.

Alizarin drew a claw down the underside of his forearm, which, like his palms, was covered only with fine, suede-like fur. The blood that welled to the surface was thick, inky violet with an iridescent blue shine. Cadmia started to pull back, but Alizarin's tail tightened.

"It will feed you better than dirt," he said in his

practical way. To the Abyssi, all food that didn't still run with hot blood was inedible dirt.

"But you—"

He put a finger on her mouth. The tip of one claw rested on her upper lip, but she trusted him not to hurt her. "I can hunt here, but I cannot bring prey back through town without being noticed and I cannot carry it through a rift. This is the best way." He licked her cheek affectionately.

She should have been disgusted. She expected to need to brace herself and force her mouth to that wound, but it was easy to lean forward and set her lips to his arm. The blood tasted like fire and smoke, and satisfied in a way human food—*dirt*—never could. She closed her eyes and Alizarin wrapped her in his arms while she fed.

In another world, another life, the concept would have horrified her. Drinking *blood* would have been beyond any acceptable notion, and even if she could have stomached that, the idea of feeding off her lover would have undone her.

Except that he *was* her lover. And she was carrying his child. And the Abyss was a very practical place. Turning his offer down over Numen concepts of *should* was silly.

She snuggled closer. She wasn't sure when she stopped drinking, and her arms weren't just holding on to him but caressing him.

She heard the door open, and Umber's word·

floated through her head—*We'll give you some privacy, and seek some ourselves.*

Priorities of the Abyss-tainted, Cadmia thought with wry amusement. There had been absolutely no judgment in Umber's tone, no irritation that—despite their close quarters and dire situation—she and Alizarin would choose now to be intimate.

The first time she and Alizarin had made love, weeks ago in the Abyss, Umber had pulled her aside the next day to make sure she was all right. His concern, combined with things she had learned from their half-Abyssi host Azo, had made it clear that what most Abyssi considered sex was brutal and bloody.

Cadmia understood that Alizarin's connection to the divine realm through Xaz was what had supposedly given him the capacity for deeper emotions and complex reasoning, but that didn't seem enough. Humans had that aptitude, too, but Cadmia had known plenty of men and women who didn't show it.

"Who taught you to be gentle?" she wondered aloud, as Alizarin's palms skimmed down her body with the softest of caresses. Claws capable of rending stone tickled her skin so lightly they raised no weal, drew no blood, and hands strong enough to snap bones eased her gently to the mattress.

"A Numini," Rin answered. "Veronese. He came to the Abyss." He paused and tilted his head as he considered, causing his long black hair to slide silkily across her chest. She might have forgotten the subject entirely right then, but he said as if realizing for the first time, "He must have been the one who tried to rescue Terre Verte, the one who failed. He didn't tell me that, but it makes sense."

"Mm." She didn't want to talk about Terre Verte right then. "He was your lover?" She had always imagined the Numini as sexless creatures, but perhaps that was a Quin conceit.

Alizarin nodded, then continued with a dreamy voice. "He used to tell me stories. And he gave me a feather." He tucked himself against her body and tickled her stomach with his tail as he spoke. "It was pink and yellow and white and black. But I lost it. I hid it somewhere, but . . ." He shrugged. "I don't remember where. I was different then."

She had never heard Alizarin speak with such awe in his voice. She wished she could meet this Numini, Veronese. Surely he had been different than the rest, if he had befriended an Abyssi.

"Is he what made you want a tie to the Numen?"

Had Alizarin hoped that, through his link to Dioxazine, he could see Veronese again?

Alizarin nodded, then snuggled his face against her chest, hiding the glow of his cobalt eyes an instant after she glimpsed pain in them. "Modigliani destroyed him," he murmured in a tight voice. "I was prince of the third level then, and might have won if I fought for the fourth, but Modigliani was already lord of the low court. I couldn't protect Veronese there."

She felt warm wetness on her breasts, and realized it must be tears.

She hadn't known an Abyssi could cry.

"I'm sorry," she whispered, stroking his hair.

She felt the tickle of his eyelashes against her skin as he blinked rapidly, and then the barest brush of his teeth, a gentle nibble that shot sparks down her body and made her catch her breath. In response, she ran her fingers though the thick fur on his upper arms and shoulders, urging him up so she could kiss him.

When they made love, it was solace and passion, release and connection. Perhaps Alizarin had learned from the divine how to be a considerate and gentle lover, but it was with an Abyssal immediacy that they put aside their fears, hurts, and concerns for a little while and found comfort and pleasure in each other.

CHAPTER 6

HANSA

The details of the nightmare had slipped from Hansa's mind before he and Umber had left the room, but he still felt shaken by it. Had he been back in the Abyss? Back at the fifth level court? In reality, he had only glimpsed the Abyssi of the low court before Umber had covered his eyes, shielding him from a sight capable of driving a mortal mad. In the dream—

Perhaps turn your thoughts away from that, Umber suggested quietly as they ghosted through the halls of the Fens. He gave Hansa a half hug with the guiding arm around his waist. *You saw more than was healthy down there.*

Is it safe to talk out loud? Hansa asked. He was getting used to this form of silent communication, but still didn't prefer it.

"As long as we keep our voices low and mind what topics we discuss," Umber murmured. With a side-long glance, he asked, "Did you bring me out here to *talk*?"

"I thought you brought me."

"We brought each other," Umber suggested.

"It seemed like Cadmia and Alizarin could use some privacy."

"I assumed you would want some, too, for the things I'm hoping to do to you," Umber teased, paus-ing to spin Hansa toward himself so they were eye to eye. Before the bond, Hansa hadn't been able to see the glow in those indigo depths. Now it was hard to imagine that the average man on the street couldn't see the flickering Abyss all around him.

"You're suddenly so serious," Umber said when the silence between them stretched too long. "What's wrong?" He caught himself, and amended, "Specifi-cally, right now."

"How can you stand to live this way?"

Umber tensed, his expression going steely. "Which . . . way?"

That cool, deep voice used to frighten Hansa. Now he recognized it as Umber's defensive tone, the one he put on when Hansa had just said something arrogant and judgmental, tainted by Quin prejudice and fear.

Hansa shook his head, realizing he had offended the other man and struggling to clarify his meaning. "Not *this* way," he said, gesturing to the dilapidated building around him. "I mean . . . all of it." That wasn't any clearer. "You've told us the spawn are among the most powerful creatures in Kavet. When I was arrested, you waved your hand or something and I went from being a condemned traitor to the hero of Kavet. Winsor Indathrone shook my hand and—" He choked off, remembering that Indathrone was dead, and it was at least partially his fault. "Kavet is *broken*, and you live in it, which means you're forced to hide everything, from what you are to who you like to bed. How can you stand to live like that and do *nothing*?"

Umber drew a long, slow breath. His fingers drummed on Hansa's back, an idle caress, as he thought.

"I don't have the kind of power you're thinking of. To get your charges dropped, I had to push several carefully-cultivated contacts and burn most of the influence I had in the Quin Compound. I can't sway a country."

"I'm sorry," Hansa sighed. "I didn't realize. You acted like it was easy." *And I didn't care, at the time, if it caused you trouble,* he thought.

Umber had granted the first boon willingly when he saved Hansa's life, and it had put him in a position where he couldn't refuse when Hansa demanded a second. That was the way a spawn's power worked.

Hansa hadn't known anything about him except that he was half-demon and he had the power to save Hansa's life.

"Of course I pretended it was easy," Umber scoffed. "I was trying to scare you off. I wasn't about to admit I had limits." With a raised brow, he added, "Clearly, it didn't work."

"Sorry," Hansa said again.

"I'm not *entirely* disappointed with how things turned out." His arm snugged around Hansa's waist meaningfully.

Hansa was starting to get used to the way his body tightened in response to remarks like that, and Umber's direct gaze. He *wasn't* prepared for the way his heart gave a quick little lurch, too.

He wanted to pass it off with a quip. Something suggestive and witty. Something that would acknowledge that, while he wouldn't have chosen a sojourn into the bowels of the Abyss, he had no complaints about the quality of his time in Umber's bed—or wherever else they ended up.

Umber's lips quirked again. "Take your time, Quin," he teased, well aware that sexual banter had most decidedly *not* been among Hansa's skill sets when they first met. "You'll come up with something eventually. Mind if I distract you in the meantime?"

"Please."

Umber's fingers trailed down Hansa's cheek and over his jaw, a tickling rasp that made him shiver.

"Your beard didn't grow when we were in the Abyss," he remarked.

Hansa scrubbed a hand over his own face. He was looking forward to some quality time with a mirror and a blade to remove the shadow that had grown in the few hours since they returned to this realm. Then, curious, he smoothed a palm over Umber's jaw.

"Give me a month and I'll still fail to grow proper stubble," Umber said.

"Funny, for someone whose parent had fur."

"Not mine," Umber replied. "Some Abyssi have scales. Let's go a little farther down this hall. I know a quiet spot where we can examine the issue in detail."

By the time they returned to the room, the fire had dropped to a few burning coals—which was a good thing, since the faint light they cast was enough to show that Cadmia and Alizarin were both stark naked, fast asleep, and tangled around each other. Despite their changed situation, Hansa still felt awkward seeing a Sister of Napthol that way. Umber, far more comfortable with casual nudity than Hansa, threw a blanket over the two of them before he and Hansa settled into place in front of the fire.

Languorous and content, Hansa drifted into sleep with his head on Umber's shoulder, listening to the spawn's oh-so-slow heartbeat.

He woke to the sound of the door closing. Blinking, confused, he realized that Umber was no longer with him, but had apparently just come in from the hall. Cadmia was also up, and thankfully dressed once again. Alizarin was nowhere to be seen.

"You tossed and turned most of the night," Umber said, before Hansa could clear his throat to ask. "I wanted to let you sleep."

"Where's Alizarin?"

"Hunting," Cadmia answered. "He left just a few minutes ago."

As Umber arranged new logs on top of the barely-glowing coals in the fireplace, Hansa glanced through the bag, which was full of simple, portable foodstuffs. "Are we preparing for a siege?"

"We need to teach you and Cadmia how to veil your power today," Umber said. "I didn't want to have to go out again, and the work will make you both hungry."

"Oh. Right," Hansa said, grimacing. Abyssal sorcery always seemed to involve his getting cut up and bleeding.

"Where do we begin?" Cadmia asked.

"Do you still have the knife Alizarin gave you?" Umber asked.

Cadmia patted the weapon sheathed at her belt. Hansa wasn't sure "knife" was the right word for something crafted out of black Abyssi bone, with a blade as long as his forearm. The Abyssumancer Naples had helped Alizarin create the weapon so the

Abyssi could form a bond with Dioxazine. Alizarin had given it to Cadmia before they left the Abyss.

"Hansa?"

"I have it." Hansa unenthusiastically pulled the knife Umber had given him the night before.

"Good. Now come here."

Umber sat on the floor not far from the fireplace and drew his own knife from somewhere. Hansa knew for a fact that, even when the spawn stripped naked, the sheath that held that knife wasn't visible. It was a neat trick.

"Abyssal sorcery is about power and will, not much else," Umber explained. "You raise power, and you direct it with your mind." As if it were the simplest thing in the world, he pulled the knife across his fingertips and casually flicked the drops of blood at the fireplace. The fire sprang merrily up, licking along the fresh wood as if Umber had nurtured it with fresh pine kindling. "In your case, you're directing your power *inward*. Normally it reaches out, seeking. Hansa, you'll find this task harder, because the bond instinctively reaches for me and for flesh, while Cadmia's child is still used to receiving its sustenance from its mother. You need to stop that grasping, since it's the aura that a guard with the sight—or a passing mancer—picks up on." He looked at both of them, then said simply, "Try it."

"Excuse me?" Hansa smiled at Cadmia's shocked tone. For once, he wasn't the only person in the room uncomfortable taking a wickedly-sharp blade to his own flesh.

"In my experience," Hansa said through half-gritted teeth, "every question I ask tends to make it worse. Umber, what's the trick to getting the wounds to heal so I don't bleed to death if I cut too deep?"

"There's no trick. Abyssal power is very practical. It doesn't waste." The spawn held up his unmarked hand.

So their lessons began.

Set his teeth. Pull the knife. Once he was sure it would heal and he wouldn't cause himself permanent damage, Hansa found the easiest way was to grip the blade in his palm so he didn't need to look at what he was doing.

That was the easy part.

The next part was visualizing what he wanted to happen, commanding the power that continually reached toward Umber like a flower leaning toward the light to curl up tight inside him, and then holding it there while the magic fought like a caged raccoon.

By lunchtime, he was glad to throw down his knife and eat ravenously. Cadmia ate more food than she had the night before, but also gladly accepted when Alizarin returned and offered blood. Hansa was considering dragging Umber off somewhere private to help recover some of his own power when Alizarin suddenly tensed and growled, his tail lashing as he looked around the room as if to catch a glimpse of something elusive.

Cadmia pulled back from him. She wiped the back of her hand across her mouth and asked, "Alizarin? What's wrong?"

Most of the time, Alizarin wore what he called his "play" form: the masculine body with blue fur and an expressive tail. That form wasn't a lie, precisely, but it wasn't true. When the Abyssi fought, the tangible part of him faded into a smoky darkness made of heat and claws. Even now that Hansa knew he was an ally, looking into that living shadow still made every mortal instinct scream, *Run!*

Right then, Hansa could see that true form peeking out. Alizarin perched on the balls of his feet, tensed as if listening. His lashing tail left afterimages, and a plum-colored aura of heat spread from him, as if darkness could leave a residue on the eyes like a brilliant light could.

"Something watching us," he said in a voice that rumbled like thunder. "I can't quite see it."

They kept their blades in their hands as they waited, watching the Abyssi snuff the air. What they were doing here was grounds for arrest and execution. If someone had seen them and then ran to report them, the only question would be: Run, or fight?

"It fled," Alizarin rumbled. His voice was a lilting growl, a match to his half-solid form. "This way."

"Should Cadmia stay behind?" Hansa asked, as they all tried to go through the door at once to follow Alizarin. Surely a pregnant woman shouldn't—

"No," she snapped, in a tone that warned him his concern had been offensive once again. He made a mental note to stop suggesting ways to protect her, no matter how hard he had to bite his tongue to ignore all his training.

They followed Alizarin down the hallway in the opposite direction as they had gone the night before. As the Abyssi squeezed through a half-blocked archway, Umber stepped forward to go first; when they emerged on the other side, he put one arm around Hansa, and then one around Cadmia.

"What are you—?"

"Shh." He cut off Cadmia's hissed complaint and refused to let her go.

They entered a large room half-full of broken crates and other odds and ends. The bitter tang of crystal smoke, a dangerous and addictive drug that was controllable in Kavet mostly because it couldn't be produced natively, coated Hansa's tongue and made his eyes sting. He also couldn't fail to recognize the sounds of passion rising from the debris, which clearly concealed at least several pairs, or perhaps a larger group. He didn't want to know which.

They skirted the outside of the large room and slipped through a gap in the wall to enter a narrow corridor lit only by occasional streams of sunlight flickering through gaps in the ceiling. For a moment, looking at the rows of numbered doors, Hansa thought he was looking at a massive inn. Then he realized this must be an old storage warehouse. The room behind them had been a main cargo area, but these were smaller units, which might have been rented out to trading vessels or merchants. There were two floors, with the upper one accessible by stairs and a narrow catwalk.

Unfortunately, Alizarin led them up.

The condition of the floor made the floor of their room seem well made. Pieces were missing from this one, and snaking rot was clearly visible. Hansa was watching his step so carefully he barely noticed when Umber let go of him and drew his knife instead.

Umber's voice in Hansa's head whispered, *Stay sharp. There's nothing I can do to make us fit in here, and the kind of people who stay in the warehouse protect their privacy with blades.*

Alizarin paused outside a doorway. The door had long since broken away, replaced with a hanging rag of a blanket. Whatever colors it had once been had long ago faded to smeary browns and grays.

Alizarin nodded significantly toward the curtain.

At the thought of pushing aside that piece of fabric, Hansa's flesh crawled. It was a rotten thing. All he could imagine looking at it was black mold and graveyard fungus. Surely if he touched it, the pestilence would seep into him, his skin would slough off, and he would die in leprous agony.

"In there," Alizarin said, sounding puzzled at their hesitation.

Hansa looked at Umber and Cadmia, who seemed equally reluctant to proceed.

"Is there another way in?" Cadmia asked.

Hansa swallowed and took a step back, wary of breathing in whatever spores might billow out from the pestilent rags.

Alizarin tilted his head. He looked at the curtain. "This way," he said.

Umber rubbed his hands on his arms. Pale-faced, he said, "It's spelled. It isn't really—" He broke off, as if the next words were too foul to say aloud. He drew a deep, hitching breath.

His words were enough for Hansa to realize what was happening.

In another time, it would have been his second lieutenant Jenkins with him, using his sight to identify power. Jenkins, who had also been Hansa's best friend since childhood, would have been the one to say, "There's some kind of spell here, probably trying to keep us out." Now it was Umber, whose half-Abyssi blood must have made him slightly more resistant than the mere humans.

Once it had been pointed out, Hansa was able to recognize the kind of power blocking their way: necromancer.

The 126 caught Abyssumancers most often, usually men and women in their early twenties who didn't have the restraint to keep their Abyssal impulses under control and avoid coming to their neighbors' attentions. Numenmancers like Xaz were the next most often found, as their desperate meddling with the divine realm could create a frost that ate through stone and metal, blighted crops and damaged livestock.

Necromancers were rarely caught because they could do things like *this*—create an aura around themselves that made you absolutely certain death was waiting for you, so most people avoided them and never noticed their work.

Umber had identified the spell, but it was Hansa who stepped up to enter the room first. His hand ached for his sword, which was surely sitting in its case in his apartment, as he eased the curtain aside. Even knowing it was a spell, it took all his will to push past the bone-deep revulsion that coiled his guts and drove bile up his throat as he put a hand on the cloth.

He had walked through Abyssumancer lairs where the viscera of small animals—and sometimes larger ones—smeared and popped under his feet. He had entered Numenmancer refuges where the air singed his lungs with cold and icicles threatened to drive into his flesh. He had seen necromancers curled up asleep on beds made from the bones of the dead.

He had no idea what to expect here. He braced himself against what he might find.

CHAPTER 7

LYDIE

Lydie squeezed the heel of a brown hand against her temple, trying to push away the throbbing pulse of blood that felt like it would split her skull. She leaned forward, clutching to her chest a tattered doll whose buckwheat-hull stuffing concealed shards of bleached-white bone, dry earth, and a generous pinch of pyre ash.

Almost time to get rid of your doll, Mama, she thought.

Mama didn't answer. She had been gone a long time.

When Lydie was younger, she had been able to carry the doll everywhere without exciting comment, but she was fourteen now. It would be noticed. She needed to replace it with something less conspicuous. She had been telling herself that for months, but kept putting it off. She didn't have much. How could she part with the last gift her mother gave her?

She pressed her face against the doll's homespun wool body and again tried to visualize high stone walls encircling her. Within her imagined tomb, it was cool and quiet. Nothing could reach her.

The wall of power shattered as intruders pushed through the curtained doorway to her room, shredding her laboriously-crafted illusions and protective spells like spider webs.

The man in the front of the group was broad shouldered, with fair skin losing its summer tan to winter, brown eyes, and slightly darker brown hair, which looked like it had been cut short and then allowed to grow several weeks past when it needed a trim. After he crossed the threshold, his eyes locked with Lydie's, and he held out a hand in a sharp, clear gesture for those behind him to halt.

He was armed only with a shoddy-looking knife, and he wasn't wearing a uniform, but Lydie didn't need those cues to recognize a soldier.

She gripped the doll tighter, scrambling to focus her power, as two others entered behind the soldier, one a slightly-plump woman with strawberry-blond hair and brownish-green eyes, and the other a tall, lean man with fair skin, black hair, and startlingly blue eyes. Neither of them looked like fighters, but they also clearly weren't from the Fens.

Lydie projected an image of rot and decay as she said, "There's nothing here for you. No coin, no crystal, no food that isn't spoiled. Not even a clean blanket. And you don't want me."

The spell should have worked, would have worked against the drug-seekers, slavers, would-be pimps and common thieves who were the most common threats she faced here.

The guard swallowed thickly, but didn't flinch.

Instead he said, "We're not here to take what's yours or to hurt you. Put down the doll and we'll talk."

She felt the spirits swirl around her, their whispers rising to howls as she raised as much power as she could without complex ritual. She would have to try the aversion spell again.

The woman eased forward, a hand on the lead soldier's arm to urge him to back off. Her voice was gentle as she said, "We just want to know why you were spying on us."

"Spying? I haven't spied on—" *The shades.* Something had disturbed the shades, and caused them to batter restlessly against her walls until she had commanded one of them to go see what was going on. "—you. You're the ones who've disturbed them."

Simple guards, even those trained and tasked with ...ting mancers, would not have upset the dead.

"Necromancer." Lydie flinched as the man in back said the word, though it didn't sound like an accusation. It sounded, inconceivably, as if he were on the verge of laughter. "*Now* we find a necromancer."

"No." Lydie gasped, reflexively. "I'm not—I'm just—" She drew a breath and declared, "So what if I am? *You're* consorting with a demon."

That was the news the shades had brought her, had *screamed* at her, until she had needed to go into a trance despite not having the tools she needed in order to hear the whole story. Her headache now was a result of their distress.

"That's quite a curious thing for you to know," the lean man in back purred.

"Its presence disturbs the dead," Lydie admitted. One of them looked like a guard, but if so, he was a renegade one. Maybe if she told them the truth they would go away. "They've been battering at my shields all night. I finally ordered one to tell me who and where you were, so I could *avoid* you. That's all. I didn't expect him to bring you right to me."

The three others shifted their gaze simultaneously toward an empty space in the room, as if listening to something. Lydie followed their gazes, knowing what that movement had to mean. "Hello?" she said. "I can't see you . . . or hear you . . . but I know you're there." *Abyssi.* The shades had claimed there was one nearby.

"It is probably for the best," the black-haired r said, "that you cannot see him."

"You're an Abyssumancer?" Lydie asked him, trying not to shudder. She had always done her best to avoid *all* other mancers, but especially those who worked with the infernal realm.

This time, the man laughed out loud. "No mancers here but you."

Lydie flinched from the word, an accusation that was usually tied with arrest and a death sentence. "Don't call me that."

"Umber," the woman said, voice chastising. She moved forward, pointedly distancing herself from the two men. They both let her take charge, though the soldier remained tensed and the dark-haired one called Umber maintained a haughty smile. "I think we should talk," the woman said. "Perhaps in our room? It's more private than this, and I believe we have breakfast waiting for us. You look like you could use a meal."

Lydie tensed, trying not to show how much the offer tempted her. This had been a lean week, and the yammering of the shades, the trance she had utilized to speak to them, and the spell she had attempted to use to chase away the soldier had all drained her reserves.

The soldier's frame wilted. He sheathed his knife awkwardly, as if he had just realized it was out and didn't want to draw further attention to the weapon. "We won't hurt you," he said, with what sounded like attempted gentleness. "I'm sure you understand why we were worried when we thought someone was spying on us. We expected something else when we came in here, just like you expected something else when we barged in. Can we start again?"

Hansa Viridian. The name came to her, most likely from the shade she had spoken to earlier.

"Hansa Viridian," she repeated aloud. "That's you?"

This time, Hansa was the one to flinch. She wondered what kind of judgment he feared from her. Now that she knew his name, she knew who he was. *Everyone* knew his name. Was he worried she would despise him for betraying the 126 and meddling with the Abyss? Or that she would fear and hate him for the role he had played who-knew-how-many times as he arrested and executed people like *her*?

She hadn't decided yet, but she supposed it was worth talking to him more.

Hansa nodded, not speaking.

"I'll go with you," Lydie said. She smiled at the woman, attempting to look more confident than she felt. It was always better if people thought you were stronger than you were. "If you're really offering breakfast."

Hansa glanced back at Umber, deferring to him, or maybe waiting for him to object. The woman glanced toward the empty space Lydie assumed contained the Abyssi, then focused on Lydie. She hustled the men ahead, and walked protectively close to Lydie. Lydie expected that she might try to chat, but she didn't, which made it possible for Lydie to focus her attention on the hissing voices of the dead. She caught the woman's name from them, and other bits of information she hoped would make sense later.

Umber led them in a roundabout way back toward the House, a collection of rooms run by a man who went by no other name, and which Lydie usually avoided. She couldn't pay House's prices, but apparently this group could.

They could also afford real *food*, which they offered without hesitation and which Lydie scarfed down as if the offer might be rescinded at any moment. For all she knew it would. The last time she had accepted a proffered meal, the kindly-seeming man had put a hand on her thigh the moment she started to eat, and extricating herself had taken more power than was usually wise to wield in public.

Umber opened a sack full of apples, cornbread cakes, thick slices of ham, and a jar of real maple cream. Lydie couldn't remember the last time she had tasted maple cream; she slathered it unashamedly on the cornbread cakes, only idly noting that Hansa took one tiny bite before shuddering. The energy around him shifted in a way Lydie knew meant one of the dead had just crossed his thoughts.

Ruby, her mind whispered. Someone dear to him.

He pushed the jar of maple cream toward Lydie, and ate his own cakes dry.

They let her eat mostly in silence, waiting until had put away a whole apple, two cakes, and a good-sized piece of ham before the woman asked, "What's your name?"

Her name wasn't attached to anything incriminating—or much of anything. "Arylide." *Honey, you hate that name.* Grudgingly, she added, "People call me Lydie. I know you, too. Cadmia Paynes. You're a Sister of the Napthol, or you're supposed to be. I still don't know who *he* is." She looked at Umber. Cadmia had said his name, but the spirits had little to say about him.

"I'm surprised you recognized her, or Hansa," Umber remarked. "Did you live in the city before you came here?"

Lydie let out an incredulous snort and shook her head. "I don't go up there," she said. "A girl with brown skin down here in the docks district is just another sailor's get, but in the higher city I get noticed. Besides, I can't go to the Cobalt Hall for healing or counsel, and I don't want to be near Indathrone's—"

When Hansa had tasted the maple cream, there had been a faint ripple in his aura; she might not have noticed it if she weren't paying such close attention. When she said the name of Kavet's President, the shift of power was tectonic, a rumble as if the ground might split beneath her. A piece of apple fell from her numb fingertips as she gasped with breathless horror, "You *killed* Winsor Indathrone?"

"No!" Hansa nearly shouted, distress painting his face.

"I can feel his death on you, on *all* of you," Ly

snapped. "His shade isn't walking with you, but his essence is smeared across your skins. That could only happen if you were there when he died."

"We were there." Umber spoke calmly, less distressed than his cohorts. "But we were only witnesses. None of us knew what the man with us intended until it was too late."

"Terre Verte." Again, the name came to Lydie. She normally tried to avoid speaking this way around others, but there were too many words and names and deaths flying in the air around her. Trying to control it was overwhelming.

"How do you know about him?" Hansa asked.

Lydie crossed her arms and paused, trying to make out comprehensible details in the overlapping, barely-coherent ranting of the dead.

"Alizarin—the Abyssi with us—said he could sense the shade you sent because it was tainted by the Abyss," Cadmia said aloud. "Is that shade the one talking to you now?"

Lydie nodded slowly, her eyes sliding from Cadmia to Hansa as she did so. The shade she had spoken to in trance had wanted to share several pointed words with his once-friend.

"Who is it?" Hansa's voice was hoarse.

Lydie sighed. "He said if I told you, you would probably cry like a little girl. I find that offensive, by the way."

"Jenkins." The guess brought an answering flash

of power, both in Hansa's aura as he recalled one of the dead whom he had cared for deeply, and as the shade standing next to Lydie was named. "He's *here?* He's—Is he—"

Lydie clenched her jaw, biting back a sharp retort, and let Hansa get to the conclusion on his own. He broke off as he realized what he had almost said: Is he all right?

Of course Jenkins wasn't all right. He was *dead.*

"Can I talk to him?" Hansa asked again.

She should have predicted this. "I went with you because Jenkins tells me you're a good man." Her eyes flickered to Cadmia and she added honestly, "And because you offered food. Maybe, *maybe,* with the proper tools I could find a way for you two to talk to each other, but that would call for powerful magic of the type that tends to bring guards and blades. It isn't something I would try out here in the Fens."

She would have liked to talk to Jenkins for longer herself. Maybe, if she had been able to maintain the trance, he would have gotten around to telling her about Terre Verte and Indathrone and the Abyssi, instead of just assuring her that *Hansa Viridian is a good man. You can trust him. He can help you, and you can help him. Please help him.*

The dead couldn't lie to her, but they could be wrong.

Sometimes, they could be so very wrong.

CHAPTER 8

UMBER

Umber reached out to Hansa, trying to offer comfort, but the other man was so focused on the necromancer and the possibility of speaking to his dead friend he shook off the touch without a glance.

"Could you relay what I say?" Hansa asked desperately. "Or tell me—"

"It doesn't work like that," the young necromancer snapped, eyes a bit too wide and near black with anxiety. They darted to the door, as if she were considering making a run for it.

If she did, should they let her? She knew they were here. Was their presence disturbing enough to ⸺er that she would report them? Umber knew from personal experience that sorcery was the only thing that would make the vicious man who had run this slice of the Fens for two decades cooperate with authorities.

Lydie would have to run, too, in that case, but she would risk it if she decided they were a more immediate threat to her. A teenage girl living alone in the Fens had to have wits, grit, and a keen sense of self-preservation.

Tentatively, he reached toward her mind. He wouldn't have tried to read the thoughts of an Abyssumancer or Numenmancer, since their connection to the other realms made doing so dangerous if not impossible, but a necromancer was only—

The burst of white noise that filled his head the instant he opened his mind to hers shot a spear of ice into his temples. He clamped his teeth shut to keep from cursing. Lydie, thankfully, was too focused on Hansa to notice the attempted intrusion.

"How *does* it work?" Hansa continued his interrogation, probably without realizing that's how it sounded. "Could you—"

Hansa. Umber spoke in the guard's mind, knowing that irritated him and would therefore distract him from his desperate quest to talk to his late friend. *You're frightening her.*

As expected, invoking Hansa's better nature worked where any plea to his common sense might have failed. He took a good look at Lydie, then san down in one of the rickety chairs, which groaned beneath him.

His despondency must have touched something in the young necromancer. She explained in halting terms, "Normally, shades are like leaves in the wind. I can hear them rustle, and feel them scratch against me. Sometimes I see an afterimage, or hear a faint whispering in my head. When a shade has something so important to tell me that they use all their strength to scream it at me, I might . . . it's hard to explain. It's more like suddenly *remembering* something, suddenly knowing it, than it is like hearing it. Like when they told me the name Terre Verte." She shook her head and bit her lip. "I know he's powerful and I know he talks to the dead, too, but I don't think he's a necromancer." She refocused on Hansa. "If I need to speak to a shade more directly, I can go into a trance, but in that state I wouldn't be able to talk to you. I can't sit here and act like an interpreter, back and forth."

"I see. Well, thank you." Hansa nodded woodenly. "If you do talk to him, would you let him know—"

He broke off, and Umber could hear the rioting thoughts ricocheting through his mind: *Tell him what? Tell him I'm sorry he's dead? I'm sorry his sister is dead? I'm sorry it's all kind of my fault, and I'm now friends with the Abyssi who killed him and we helped the Numini who killed her? Tell him I'm sorry I went to the depths of the Abyss to try to save him, then left without him or any of the rest of the men who served under us? Tell* him I'm sorry we did save a man who then murdered the President we both served and may now be plotting Abyss-only-knows against the country?

"Tell him I'm sorry," Hansa said, "and I'm doing my best."

Lydie nodded tightly. Umber wondered if she had any intention of relaying the message.

He looked at the rest of their group. Alizarin and Cadmia had stepped out of the way as well as they could in the crowded room while Hansa pleaded with the necromancer. Now, as if realizing that moment was over, Cadmia asked, "Did you say Terre Verte speaks to the dead?"

"We were told he's a Gressumancer," Umber reminded her.

"Really?" Lydie's deep brown eyes brightened with curiosity. "I thought they were a myth."

In general, mancers worked with one of four planes: the Abyss or infernal realm, the Numen or divine realm, the realm of death, or the realm of life. Those powers were antithetical to each other, yet rumors persisted of Gressumancers, sorcerers who had mastery over all four.

"We know he has power over both the Numen and the Abyss," Umber said, looking at Alizarin for confirmation. Alizarin had heard fantastical stories about Terre Verte, the man locked in the deepest dungeon of the Abyss, for longer than Alizarin had been alive. He was the Abyssi version of fairy tales, really. "That combination is far more surprising than his also being able to speak to the dead."

"Do the shades just know he *can* do this," Cadmia pressed, "or has he *been* doing it?"

Lydie glared at her, as if to remind her that idly conversing with the dead was not easy.

"I know it's hard for you to clearly understand them," Cadmia said, "but this is important. He is a dangerously powerful man, and we need to know what he's planning. If he's actively talking to the dead, something you say takes preparation and ritual, he's doing it for a reason. We need to know that reason."

For that conversation, Umber would far prefer a direct "face-to-face," rather than accepting the necromancer as an interpreter after the fact. Perhaps Hansa would get what he wanted after all.

"If we brought you somewhere private and secure," Umber suggested, "and helped you acquire the tools you need, would you be willing to help Hansa have a conversation with Jenkins?"

Umber didn't need to hear Lydie's thoughts to see them reflected on her face. Living in the Fens, any man who offered to take her somewhere private was most likely someone she should run from, fast.

Lydie looked thoughtfully around the room. Her eyes snagged on the bag of food, like she was weighing the risk against the possibility of more than one solid meal. Her gaze settled last on Cadmia, who looked back with the thoughtful, accepting expression she probably used with the ruffians who came to her for counsel.

"I could do that," Lydie said. Her green eyes fixed on Umber's like a cat's. "But it would be hard, and I'm putting myself at risk to do it. I know of your kind. I know you'll make me a fair deal in exchange."

I know your kind. She had already told them she received insights from the dead, but the statement still startled him.

"Yes, I will." Ever since seeing her, he had wanted to help her, but his power made it dangerous for him to offer charity. Unbalanced favors tended to create a tie that could lead to a bond. This would balance the scales nicely and assuage her pride and his power.

"I need to get some things from my room," she said, "and make preparations. I might not be back until late. You'll still be here?"

"We'll be leaving in the morning, just before dawn," Umber answered.

Walking to the Fens from the Quin Compound under Alizarin's spell had been risky, since any sighted guard could have spotted them; Umber didn't intend to repeat that gamble if he could avoid it. Waiting until dawn would give Cadmia and Hansa a chance to rest and regain the strength they needed to hopefully hold the veils over their power for long enough to make it through the city.

Besides, they would all look less suspicious in the early hours of the day instead of the middle of the night. The docks woke early to put out fishing boats, and any sighted guards who spotted them in the city proper wouldn't be surprised to see a group of respectable citizens out for an early-morning walk, perhaps to pick up just-baked pastries.

Lydie nodded—then, with an expression that suggested she was being daring, she swiped one more cornbread cake before waving a curt farewell.

"Do you want someone to walk you back to your room?" Hansa offered, ever the gentleman.

Lydie gave him a haughty look that was older than her years. "I don't want to have to protect you."

Then she was gone.

Cadmia laughed at Hansa's dumbfounded expression. Umber pointed out, "A necromancer might not be as frightening to us as an Abyssumancer, but she still has power. I suspect she can walk alone through this place like a ghost, without ever drawing a single eye." He started clearing the remnants of food away. "Any thoughts on our young friend?"

"Looking at her breaks my heart," Cadmia admitted. "I keep telling myself to be rational, that she is a mancer and a stranger and I should be more suspicious, but she's a *child*."

"A hungry, homeless child," Hansa added, "who can't go to the Cobalt Hall for aid. Do you really think she can help us get more information on Terre Verte, or did you just want an excuse to help her?"

Umber shrugged. "Somewhere in the middle."

"I could go to the temple."

The slightly surprised-sounding suggestion came from Alizarin, who was thoughtfully twitching his tail back and forth around his waist.

"The temple?" Cadmia asked. "Why?"

"You said you want to know what Terre Verte is doing," Alizarin said. "Abyssi have always gossiped about Terre Verte. They must have noticed he's escaped by now, and might be talking about him. The Numini might be talking about him, too, since they wanted him. If I go and listen I might learn something."

"That's a very good idea." Hansa sounded as startled as the Abyssi had, and probably for the same reason—they were all still caught off guard whenever Alizarin demonstrated his capacity for complex planning.

Except Cadmia. She had seen Alizarin's potential first. She asked, "Is that safe for you?"

Alizarin shrugged. "As safe as being here is for you. I can go now, while we wait for Lydie."

Alizarin didn't turn to Umber or Hansa to say, *Take care of her.* Abyssi didn't do that for each other, and in many ways, Alizarin treated Cadmia as a fellow Abyssi.

Once Alizarin was gone, they all returned to their practice. As expected, Cadmia was better at creating and holding the veils over her power than Hansa, both because her power cooperated more and because she was less squeamish. Umber had never truly appreciated how practical the once-Sister of the Napthol was.

The amount of power they used as they worked was staggering. Once Cadmia and Hansa had perfected the techniques, holding the veils in place would be easier than this repetitive raising and tamping of magic. It was easier to brace and carry a heavy weight than it was to repeatedly lift and lower one. Umber siphoned power into Hansa as he worked, grateful that they would be able to replace it as soon as they found a little privacy. That was one of the greatest advantages of a fleshbond; sex was the oldest and most effective ritual in the world for raising Abyssal power.

The knock came on the door earlier than Umber expected, a little before sundown. Maybe Lydie was hoping to share dinner with them. Why hadn't it occurred to him to invite her?

Limbs heavy from too much blood-work, he opened the door cautiously, peering around it.

The figure on the other side shoved it open the rest of the way with enough force Umber stumbled back, surprised. He opened his mouth to protest—

And words failed him.

Pale brown hair, like some shades of blond turned if they never saw sun. Soft blue eyes, a match to skin as fair and sun-innocent as his hair. Tall, broad shouldered, strong body under warm, practical clothing. Every line and plane and shade of that body was familiar, and seeing it here, now . . .

The newcomer's eyes widened when he saw Umber, and his expression brightened. He smiled widely. "I hoped it was you."

Without further talk, he stepped up to Umber and wrapped one arm around his waist, caressed his cheek, and tilted his face up to kiss him.

Too sudden. Too unexpected. And Hansa was watching. Hansa wouldn't understand.

Umber tensed and managed to put his hands up between himself and the other man's firm chest, but he couldn't make his body further obey him so he could pull back or push away.

The kiss started soft, but didn't stay that way long, and the gentle hand on Umber's chin became a tugging clutch at his hair. The man's mouth tasted of blood, smoke, fine wine, and honey, flavors that would probably have disturbed Hansa but called to Umber with whispers of rough play and sex that could never be characterized as "making love."

A choked sound from Hansa broke through Umber's deer-like trance. It was followed by the sound of a throat clearing, and Cadmia's sharp query, "Umber?"

He flinched at the sound of his own name. The man holding him pulled back and asked, "That what you're going by these days?" Though he had broken the kiss, he kept his arm around Umber's waist.

Umber nodded, one silent move, almost a tic. "And you?"

"Cupric. And these must be Hansa and Cadmia?"

"And you know us how?" Cadmia asked coolly.

"Terre Verte asked for a volunteer to go speak to you," Cupric said. "I barely dared hope my—*Umber* would be the spawn in the group, but given their scarcity it seemed possible."

"Terre Verte?" Umber echoed, the closest to an intelligent response he could manage.

"Oh, don't look that way, my dear," Cupric teased. "The Terre credits you all with freeing him. He means you no harm. He hoped you would take this as a good will gesture, but I see you're taking it with your normal cynicism instead."

"He could have found a different messenger," Umber said. Finally, he found the self-control to draw out of Cupric's arms.

"He could have, but I wanted to see you. I volunteered."

Reluctantly, Umber looked at Hansa, and saw the exact hurt and horror on his face that Umber had feared. Cupric either didn't notice or else ignored the expression. He offered his hand to Hansa as if they were meeting at some kind of afternoon social.

"Hansa Viridian, it's an honor to meet you."

Hansa shook himself and pushed to his feet, but only to step back around the table, farther away.

Cupric frowned at Umber.

"Come now, surely your bond knows you're not some kind of innocent Numen-spawn." As if it might possibly help the issue, he added, "Oh, of course, you're flesh-bound. I'm sorry. Don't worry, Umber is an exception. Men aren't my usual—"

"Why are you *here*?" Umber demanded, before Cupric's "comforting" words could drive Hansa from the room. Yes, the fleshbond could make Hansa more vulnerable to pressure from men like Cupric, but that wasn't what had put the panicked look in his eyes.

Cupric looked around, taking in each stony face, then sighed. The friendly teasing was replaced by an expression that was all focused business. "I met Terre Verte and Dioxazine in the mancers' temple in the early hours of the morning."

"Good for you," Umber snapped, when Cupric paused as if waiting for applause. "*And?*"

"*And,*" Cupric replied, bristling, as if he had only then noticed their hostility, "we ended up having quite a long chat. That man has some crazy ideas— not that you're apparently interested."

"Did Terre Verte send you just to say he means us no harm, or is there more to the message?" Cadmia prompted, not rising to Cupric's bait.

"He's hosting a soiree of a sort," Cupric said, the amused lilt back in his voice. "A social-political gath- ering, as he puts it. I'm here to officially invite you to join him."

The words were so far away from anything Um- ber might have expected from this man, who he hadn't seen in as much as a decade, that he couldn't find words to reply.

Luckily, Cadmia once again responded. "Can you clarify what that means? Join him how?"

Cupric finally looked at her fully. His brow quirked, a familiar expression that could still make Umber's body tighten. "Terre Verte wants to organize a meeting of any and all individuals of power—small magic users as well as mancers. It will be held in two weeks at Amaranth Farms, which is also where he's staying for the foreseeable future."

"*How?*" Cadmia asked. "How does he even expect to contact them?"

"I know he's gone to the mancers' temples to talk to the Abyssumancers and Numenmancers, and that he's sending messages with shades to try to reach the necromancers. I don't know how he plans to reach the others, but . . ." For the first time, Cupric's nonchalance appeared posed instead of sincere. "I suspect that, what that man wants, he gets."

"And what's the point?" Cadmia asked. "Assuming he can get them there and they won't just fight with each other, why is he doing this?"

Cupric gave a dismissive half shrug. "Who knows?"

"Someone will report it." Hansa's voice was hoarse as he raised that objection, but at least he had returned to the conversation—albeit from the opposite side of the room. "He can't contact that many complete strangers and not have the word get out. What does he plan to do then?"

"Again, I didn't ask." Apparently deciding his errand was complete, Cupric turned back to Umber with a slow smile. "As long as we're here, let's take a walk downstairs, shall we?"

Umber's throat tightened, stifling his response, before Cadmia interjected. "We were in the middle of something."

"We won't be long."

"Yes, we would be," Umber said. "And I'm needed here. And you've delivered your message. So it's time for you to leave." Each phrase came out stilted from a mouth that felt sandpaper dry. The effort it took not to reach for him, to follow him, to walk out that door with him and find some secluded spot like he had suggested, was dizzying.

"Excuse me?" For the first time, Cupric seemed just as shocked.

"You heard him." Cadmia stepped up like a soldier, her tone frosty. "Go. Tell Terre Verte you delivered your message."

"I—"

"*Out!*" Umber managed to snarl. "Now!"

For a wonder, Cupric went. The dismayed expression on his face might even have been genuine.

That just left Hansa.

Even if he hadn't been able to hear the rioting, self-recriminating thoughts slamming around in the guard's overwhelmed, exhausted mind, Umber still would have recognized the way Hansa was desperately trying to compose his expression.

"I'm sorry," Hansa said. "I overreacted. What he said is true. I know you have other lovers." He flinched, and corrected himself. "Real lovers. Ones you chose. I don't have any right to . . ." He seemed to lose his train of thought there, as if he couldn't put the rest into words.

"Cupric is . . ." Umber hesitated, also at a loss. "Never mind. Cupric doesn't matter. By the time he can go back to Amaranth to report to Terre Verte, we'll have moved on."

CHAPTER 9

CUPRIC

He *threw me out.*

No matter where else Cupric's thoughts traveled as he left the Fens, they kept returning to that one point.

Umber *threw me out!*

He would have stayed to argue the point if Terre Verte hadn't emphasized that he didn't want to anger Alizarin, Cadmia, and Hansa.

The Terre had included Umber in the list, but he didn't know Umber the way Cupric did. Maybe it was the Abyssi in him, but Umber liked to fight. When pain and blood were just another form of power, a good argument was a fine form of foreplay.

It wasn't a quick trip from the Fens, through the heart of Mars, and then farther north to one of the first large, landed homes outside the city, but Cupric still hadn't entirely calmed when he reached the manor house late that evening. He paused outside the front door, trying to compose himself before entering. It wouldn't do to walk into the prince's presence still bristling with fury.

But Umber had thrown him out! To avoid offending *Hansa Viridian*, of all people, the Quinacridone's pride and joy. Oh, and the Sister of Napthol staring over his shoulder like an offended cat.

The door opened in front of Cupric, and a preoccupied-looking Dioxazine nearly ran into him.

"You're back already," she remarked, dancing out of the way before they collided.

The Numenmancer crackled with power. Of course, she had spent last night in bed with Terre Verte. Cupric would whore himself out for that kind of glow, too.

When he had first met Xaz, he had been prepared to dislike her on principle—she was a Numenmancer after all, and the Numini tended to be a rigid, moralistic lot who disapproved of his kind and all they stood for. But any person willing to say screw you to the Numini, bond with something as powerful as Xaz's toy Abyssi Alizarin, go to bed with a man whose power blazed ke the noonday sun, and wake up like a cat who got aws into cream was all right in Cupric's book.

"The Terre made it clear he wanted me to report back," Cupric said. He didn't intend to disclose the more embarrassing points of the discussion, which he was still struggling to come to terms with.

"True. We simply expected you to stay with them longer. I'm sorry if you felt hurried."

"Hansa took exception to my presence," he admitted with a shrug.

Xaz gave a sympathetic smile.

"The Terre should be in," Xaz said. "We have a new animamancer who thinks she can cast a fence around the property that will alert us if anyone unwelcome crosses it."

"An animamancer?" Cupric repeated, intrigued. He had never met one of the healers before.

"She and another Abyssumancer came to talk to Terre Verte today," Xaz said. "Separately, of course. They're both staying on."

Of course they are.

Cupric thought back to his own first meeting with Terre Verte—had it really only been that morning? He had been in the mancers' temple. Cupric had listened to the man's words, then suggested fatalistically that, if he really wanted to overthrow the Quin, Terre Verte somehow needed to get all the magic users in Kavet to work together. He had said it sarcastically. He had said it *knowing* it was stupidly impossible.

Yet here they were, less than twelve hours lat

Cupric wasn't sure how Terre Verte had known the owner of this land and building was a necromancer. He had knocked on the door and, after a long conversation, the necromancer had turned over the main house for the Terre's use.

Cupric opened the door to that house now, then stopped, taking in the sight before him.

The bite of Kavet's early winter wind was replaced by the warmth and gentle teal glow made by orbs of foxfire—floating balls of pure power, which cast off light and in this case even heat. Silver magic frosting the windowpanes was the most likely reason the light hadn't been visible from outside. The carpets were still the same, simple woolen weaves that had been there that morning, but under the glimmer of the foxfire and the silver mist of the windows, even they seemed elegant.

The parlor was empty, which meant Terre Verte was probably in the master bedroom.

Cupric had just lifted his hand to knock when he heard the prince's clear voice call, "Come in, Cupric."

That was starting to annoy him—the Terre's casual knowledge of seemingly everything, from who was standing outside his door to what was going on in the city. Nevertheless, Cupric bowed his head slightly as he entered. It was enough to avoid giving offense, and as far as he intended to go.

Thus far, the Terre hadn't objected aloud, though e first time they had been introduced—when Xaz had made it clear who the Terre was, and Cupric's refusal to scrape and grovel had been most obvious—he had been able to see the annoyance in the prince's expression.

Now those aristocratic features were perfectly composed.

"I take it the visit didn't go as well as you hoped," the Terre said.

"No, but I delivered your message. They don't trust you, and Umber doesn't trust *anyone*, so I don't know what you hoped to accomplish."

"Umber is justifiably wary around mancers," Terre Verte replied. "If I can convince my sister to attend, I hope she can help assure the other spawn of their safety. Until then, it's just common courtesy to keep in touch with Alizarin and the others."

The fact that Terre Verte had an Abyss-spawn half sister was one of many alarming and unusual facts the man had shared in their first long conversation about how they might be able to find allies in Kavet.

"If they go to ground, will you be able to find them?" Cupric asked. The last time Umber had chosen to disappear, he had vanished from Cupric's life like smoke.

"I may not be able to find *him*, but we can find Alizarin easily," Terre Verte said dismissively. "And while I would regret not having Hansa's and Umber's support, if they desire their privacy, they can have it 'He paused, and seemed to consider before specul ing, "Though I don't imagine they will stay hidden very long, unless they miraculously come to terms with the effects of the bond."

Little comments like that were why Cupric was staying on this man's side. According to everything he knew, there was no power in Kavet capable of breaking the bond created by one of the spawn granting a third boon—and he *would* know, since he had researched it extensively. After all, he had been closely involved with Umber. He needed to know the risks.

Every source he had ever found had made it clear the third boon made a permanent, magical connection. It could take many forms; no one knew how to control the outcome, which could range from a fleshbond, like the one Hansa and Umber had, to an all-encompassing physical, mental and emotional addiction that left the human partner a sniveling wreck, incapable of functioning outside the presence of his half-Abyssi bond-partner. The witch who had described the different types of bonds to Cupric had mentioned offhand that a strong enough Abyssumancer might be spared the worst effects, or might even end up the master in such an arrangement; but Cupric didn't plan to risk it, not when the consequences lasted forever.

Supposedly. Unless you were friends with Terre Verte, who seemed confident that, with a little work, he could learn how to break that bond.

"I have another assignment for you," Terre Verte

said. Cupric drew a deep breath to keep himself from responding sharply to the tone of authority. Yesterday, it had been quite possible that he was the most powerful mancer in Kavet. He had been cautious, but never *afraid*. Then the Terre had strolled into his life.

"There are two documents I would like to read. One is the Citizen's Initiative One-Twenty-Six. The other one would be older, from before One-Twenty-Six was enacted, and I imagine would be kept wherever the Quin keep their more valuable—and *private*— records. It would be among the first documents written regarding the practice of sorcery in the city after Dahlia Indathrone came to power."

Dahlia Indathrone had been Kavet's first President, which, if Cupric understood the history right, meant she was the one who had taken charge when the royal family—Terre Verte included—had been deposed. The *fact* of that revolution less than a century ago was covered in every schoolroom in Kavet, but in accordance with Quin beliefs about the dangers of too much knowledge, the details were absent. As a schoolchild Cupric had known how many times Dahlia had been reelected, the name of the man who had briefly been President after her shocking and unexpected death, the exact year in which her son Winsor had been officially elected for the first time, and how he had passed a resolution declaring biennial elections unnecessary. Supposedly the people could call for a Presidential election at any time by gathering some number of signatures, but sparing that, Winsor stayed in power.

Even now, Cupric remembered all those details, but he had never been taught *why* or *how.*

"There are copies of One-Twenty-Six available in any library in Kavet," Cupric confirmed. That weighty law was the one that had declared all sorcery punishable by death and created the guard unit by the same name to enforce it. "The second request . . . anything about sorcery would be in the private archives of the Quin monks or the Order of Napthol. I don't have access to those."

"Hmm." The Terre gave the matter a little thought, but not as much as Cupric would like before he said simply, "Find a way to get it."

"Find a way to get something the Quin don't want me to have when I don't even know exactly what I'm looking for?" Cupric repeated. "I'll bring you a copy of One-Twenty-Six, but as for the rest, I can't help you."

He wasn't sure how much of the last sentence he said out loud, because somewhere in the middle of it, Terre Verte gave him that *look.* The one that said, "I could kill you, here and now, and I would lose no sleep over it, and no one would miss you."

That was the problem of choosing to side with the most powerful son of a bitch around: Terre Verte could probably make good on that silent threat.

It had been a long time since Cupric had been frightened of one man.

He hoped the Followers of the Quinacridone felt the same.

"I'll try, but I make no promises," he said grudgingly.

Terre Verte nodded. "Dismissed."

Fuck you, Cupric thought back. But he didn't have the gall to say it aloud.

Cupric knew one Quin who would be allowed into restricted archives if anyone would be. Unfortunately, Hansa hadn't been too pleased to see him before and probably wouldn't be anxious to help him now.

On the other hand, people said Hansa Viridian was a "good man." That usually meant someone was a sentimental, protective sap. Hansa would probably look at the document before giving it to Cupric and therefore Terre Verte, but something the Quinacridone wanted to hide wasn't necessarily something the lover of an Abyss-spawn would find threatening. As long as he didn't think doing so would endanger his own friends, Hansa might agree to help just because he was that nice.

First though, Cupric had to find and talk to Hansa when Umber wasn't about to make things uncomfortable. It was hard to be around the Abyss-spawn without remembering him sprawled across the bed, and Hansa obviously didn't appreciate reminders that his lover had a past.

The Quin could get over it. There were Good Deeds to be done, after all.

CHAPTER 10

CADMIA

As dawn approached, they prepared for the day ahead. While Alizarin scouted the mancer temple, Hansa and Umber exchanged moping, uncomfortable glances, and they all waited for Lydie to arrive, Cadmia meditated—and planned. She sat in front of the fire with her knees crossed and her eyes closed, blocked the sounds of her companions and the rest of the Fens from her awareness, and silently put pieces together in her mind.

Like Hansa, Cadmia feared what violence Verte intended, but before they could respond they needed know his plans. Cupric had implied the once-nce wanted to overthrow the Quin government and take back Kavet. It seemed a plausible motivation, but what would gathering the mancers together accomplish?

Rose might know. Cadmia had been born in the Order of A'hknet, but had craved a higher education and more "respectable" life and had gone to the Order of Napthol. Rose Atrament had joined the Order of Napthol as a child and had been admired as a scholar there before she walked away from it to join the Order of A'hknet. Their paths had crossed many times since, as Rose refused to be dissuaded from her study of magic no matter how often the Quin arrested her. She could be a valuable resource, if Cadmia could convince her to talk to them.

And one I won't need to counsel for relationship problems, Cadmia thought, as a moment of worry about Hansa and Umber wormed into her attempt to form a solid plan. When Umber had first kissed the stranger at the door, Hansa had looked startled and awkward, but had made an attempt to keep his always-so-readable expression unflustered and even welcoming. *I can be mature about this*, that expression had said.

It was only when the kiss hadn't *stopped,* when it had become something that sang of sweat-slicked nights and sated days, that Hansa's self-control had slipped.

It's not my problem.

Unless they made it her problem.

Back to the matter at hand. She noticed a thread of her power peeking loose from the careful cocoon she had spun it into that morning and tucked it back away, then turned her mind back to Verte, Rose, and mancers until she heard Lydie ask, "Where are we going?"

Cadmia jumped, startled that the necromancer had made it into the room without her noticing, and opened her eyes in time to see Hansa do the same. Umber was in the middle of packing up the last of their supplies, and turned toward Lydie slowly enough Cadmia had a feeling he was pointedly trying to pretend he *hadn't* been surprised.

"My home," Umber answered. "It's in South Bay."

"South Bay—and you've been sleeping *here*?" Lydie asked incredulously.

"How did you get in without our hearing the door open?" Hansa asked Lydie, at the same time Umber answered, "We had other guests previously, who I didn't want to invite to my private residence."

Lydie shrugged understanding and dismissal at Umber's answer, and rolled her eyes at Hansa.

The young necromancer looked better today, less ghastly—or so Cadmia thought. Even when making a conscious effort, Cadmia found it hard to focus directly on Lydie. Her eyes wanted to shut out the girl. Lydie's seemingly-soundless passage into the room meant her ears wanted to as well. Cadmia didn't remember having the same difficulty the night before, so decided this must be one of the ways Lydie had prepared herself to come with them.

Safety means being ignored, to her, Cadmia thought, reminded suddenly of Pearl, the orphan child she had helped raise in the Cobalt Hall. Pearl was Lydie's opposite: bold and outgoing, an eternal optimist who would make friends with anyone who let her and therefore knew and was known by every guard in the 126. Her mismatched blue and green eyes were shadowed sometimes by her own personal fear of abandonment—her own mother had left her on the steps of the Cobalt Hall, walked away, and never returned—but as vast as that anxiety was, it couldn't compare to the everyday terror Lydie must feel.

"How old are you?" Cadmia asked. She wanted to ask, *How have you survived in Kavet?* The girl might be as old as fourteen or fifteen, if she was a late bloomer; she also might be as young as eleven or twelve.

"Why do you care?" Lydie shifted the sack on her shoulder and said, "Let's go. I don't like walking around like this."

Umber looked at them each in turn. He must have been satisfied by what he saw, because he nodded, and said, "Keep your heads down until we get out of the Fens. Once we're to the dockside market, don't hurry, don't dawdle, and for Abyss' sake *don't* look around to see if we're being watched or followed." The reminders were clearly for Cadmia and Hansa, not for Lydie, who shifted impatiently as she listened. Cadmia felt anxiety curl and flex in her stomach like a restless lizard. "Remember you have every right to walk these streets, but also remember now isn't the time to test the self-control holding the veils over your power. If someone recognizes you, be polite, but end the conversation as quickly as you can without drawing notice."

"If you tell me where I'm going, I can meet you there," Lydie grumbled. "I don't need to walk through Kavet with a pair of celebrities."

"You won't be able to get inside without me," Umber answered, "and you'll look out of place idling on the street."

"I wish Alizarin was here to do his magic trick again," Hansa sighed.

"I'd make you both do the walk anyway," Umber said. "Cadmia says she plans to go back to the Cobalt Hall as soon as possible, and you'll want to leave the house at some point, too. You need to know you can do this."

Lydie let out an exasperated sigh. "I'll meet you at the fish market when you're done talking about your—"

"We're going," Hansa said gruffly. "Lead the way, Umber."

"You're new to all this, aren't you?" Lydie murmured as they stepped out of the Fens. She had ghosted up beside Cadmia's left elbow, and her sudden, soft voice startled Cadmia from her hyper-focused, anxious daze. "You and him." She nodded toward Hansa, then flicked her eyes briefly to Umber. "*He* knows his way around here and looks comfortable in it, but you two look like you're expecting a lynching. Which, by the way, is the best way to *get* a lynching."

"I should know better," Cadmia sighed. She rolled her shoulders and twisted her head side to side, trying to dismiss the tension that had turned the muscles in her neck to stone. "I grew up in the Order of A'hknet. Scarlet's daughter." She glanced at the necromancer, wondering if she had any words to say on the subject of Cadmia's mother, who had died five years previously.

If Lydie recognized the name or felt any presence of Scarlet's shade, it didn't show.

Thankfully, getting from the Fens to South Bay didn't involve passing through either the docks market or the upper city, where Cadmia and Hansa almost certainly would have been recognized. Even so, they took smaller back alleys Cadmia would normally have avoided. Alone, even as a Sister of Napthol she would have invited robbery; together, they weren't a good target for a single alley-thief, and this area was too close to the upper city to be home to any larger gangs. Cadmia tried to keep her head up, as if she were taking a quick and familiar route, and not skulking.

Umber had stepped away from Hansa once they

left the Fens, and they once again walked with a careful distance between them, avoiding any visible sign of their bond.

That empty space felt painful even to Cadmia.

Soon enough they left behind the narrow, winding alleys in favor of a wide thoroughfare and a footbridge over the rocky river outlet that marked the southern edge of the city of Mars and the beginning of the outskirts. The streets here were broad, and cultivated beds in raised planters were replaced by naturally green spaces—not large ones, granted, but even a few paces between one home and the next made a difference. Instead of the low-slung buildings that made best use of the often-marshy land under the A'hknet village near the docks and the Fens, this area's rocky footing provided ample support for two-and three-story buildings with elaborate steeple roofs, fanciful balconies and porches, and tall windows that sparkled in the dawning light.

"You're teasing us," Lydie choked out as they turned from the cobbled main street onto one of the well-maintained paths that ran parallel to the shore. "You have a lover who lives here, or . . ." She trailed off as Umber turned without comment toward one of the homes.

Here even Cadmia hesitated, trying—and failing—to come up with a plausible explanation for how a child orphaned as a toddler, who had clearly spent time homeless and hungry, had ended up living in a private residence on the banks of the South Shore. This particular home wasn't the fanciest in the area, true, and it was situated on the least desirable piece of waterfront, which overlooked the harbor and the lower city instead of the open ocean, but it still sat, alone, on almost a quarter acre of land, within two miles of the city center or the docks.

"You don't want to know," Umber said, as if one of them had spoken aloud.

"But . . ." Hansa sputtered, looking at the house and ignoring Umber's attempt to divert his question before it left his lips. "How . . ."

Lydie, less discreet, asked bluntly, "Did you kill someone for it?"

"No, I didn't kill anyone," Umber sighed. "I'll grant I didn't gain it in an entirely lawful manner, but I didn't hurt anyone. Not much, anyway, and it wasn't anyone who—look, that's a story for another day. It has two bedrooms and a dormer that I've usually used as a study, but which should suit you, Lydie. It's private, has a couch that should be plenty large enough to use as a bed, and the door locks."

As a child, the only truly private space Cadmia had called her own was a nook under the stairs off the kitchen, which was low-ceilinged but had enough space for her bed and a small trunk. It didn't have a real door, but her mother had repurposed an elaborate embroidered shawl one of her lovers had gifted her to make a curtain, and everyone in the household knew that it was Caddy's space, never to be violated.

When she had joined the Order of Napthol, the room they had offered her had seemed cool and impersonal at first, cut off from the rest of her community by stone walls and a heavy wooden door, but it had been palatial nevertheless.

As far as Cadmia could tell, Umber never used a key. He put his hand on the front door latch and Cadmia heard the *click* of a lock disengaging before Umber pulled the door open, triggering a burst of blessedly warm air that made Cadmia close her eyes with a sigh.

"Is someone here already?" Lydie asked, as they stepped into a front parlor with painted walls and floors of gleaming hardwood instead of stone. She looked around, and frowned at the empty fireplace in the scarcely-decorated room.

"There are spells set into some of the brickwork to generate heat," Umber explained as he hung his cloak on a rack next to the door. "They keep the place above freezing."

The furniture was all fine quality, but oddly scarce, and though the built-in shelves boasted occasional books or knickknacks, they too seemed more empty than full. The only other piece in the room was a cherrywood entry table holding a handful of casually discarded items, including a wrapped package Cadmia remembered his buying not long before their adventure in the Abyss. It contained a red silk scarf. Whatever he had intended it for hadn't happened.

"The house is warded," Umber said, "so casual visitors won't come by, and most mancers or other magic users won't be able to get in if they do come calling. There's a washroom there." He gestured vaguely as he walked toward the back of the house. "Upstairs, the master bedroom is the one on the right, there's a guest room on the left—Caddy, that will be yours—and Lydie, you'll see stairs there up to the study. I'm going to put these things in the kitchen," he concluded, hefting the bag of food supplies he had bought in the Fens in explanation.

Cadmia trailed after him, wondering at the juxtaposition of luxury and emptiness and whether they represented the man himself.

The kitchen spanned the rear of the house, blending into a rotunda that served as dining and living room both. The windows here were unshuttered and looked out over the river and across to the Mars harbor, which at this distance seemed full of toy boats. A deep window-sill bench occupied one wall, next to a low bookcase haphazardly stuffed with a combination of bound books and loose notes held down with chips of polished stone.

Unfortunately, it was hard to enjoy the beautiful view due to the ghastly stench that rose up as they entered. Cadmia's stomach, always a bit sensiti these days, twisted and heaved, and she hastened in the direction Umber had identified as the washroom. As she puked in what turned out to be a rather nicely equipped bathroom—Umber must have a cistern on the roof, since he seemed to have running water—Hansa came in and matter-of-factly gathered up her strawberry-blond hair to lift it out of the way.

"Apparently Umber was in the middle of making dinner when I summoned him," Hansa remarked. "He and Lydie are going to clean it up. She says the smell doesn't bother—sorry." He broke off because just the reference to that scent brought on a fresh bout of retching. He tucked her hair behind her, stood long enough to run the tap, and put a bracingly cold cloth on the back of her neck.

She pulled the cloth off to wipe her mouth instead. "Thanks," she murmured, trying not to look at the sludge in the bowl. She thought she was done for now, but didn't dare stand yet. Not until the shakiness passed.

Hansa shrugged. "I don't know if you knew him well enough to remember, but Jenkins had that stupid long hair. They don't tell you in the brochures, but when you first join the One-Twenty-Six, you spend a lot of time puking your guts out before you get used to the things you see. Having the sight made it worse for him."

As he spoke, he found the chain to run the water and clear the basin.

"You're really planning to go back to the Cobalt Hall?" he asked, subdued, as she rinsed out her mouth.

"You're really *not* going back?" she countered. "I can get information from small magic users and others who live at the edge of Kavet's society. That's valuable, but not enough on its own. We need to know what the Quin have heard, what they believe, and what they plan to do about it."

Hansa froze at the words, like a rabbit caught under a hedge.

"What were you planning to do?" Cadmia prompted. Despite her earlier, pointed words, she kept this question neutral, the way she might have asked it in a counseling session. "You said earlier you wanted to do something about Terre Verte."

"Something about *him*, yes, but not . . ." He trailed off with an overwhelmed sigh. "I'll see what Jenkins says. Maybe, between his information and what Alizarin can learn at the mancer temple, we'll have a better idea of our next steps."

She nodded, and something in her expression made him flinch defensively. "The work you do at the Cobalt Hall *helps* people. If I go back, not only will I be around some of the most powerful sighted individuals in the country, I'll be expected to track down people like Xaz, and Lydie, and Umber—and you. I can't go back, then refuse to perform the basic function of my job." He let that sink in, then added,

"As for Terre Verte, I don't think he's a problem that's going to be solved with soldiers."

Cadmia shivered. It was as though Hansa's words had brought the chill of the divine into the room. When traveling with Umber and Alizarin, it was easy to feel almost safe. They were powerful, and knew what they were doing.

Hansa's words reminded her of a simple fact: In Kavet, people "like her," and like Lydie and Umber and Hansa, were caught all the time. Caught, arrested, branded, and executed. Despite the illusion of Umber's rich and magically warded home, the mortal plane was no safer for them than the Abyss had been.

CHAPTER 11

HANSA

It took hours to make Umber's home livable again. As he helped discard rotten produce and open windows to chase away the stench, Hansa had to keep swallowing down guilty apologies. He had spoken one of them aloud—two, actually, since Umber had only grunted in response to the first—and then Umber had snapped at him to stop sniveling.

"You should be able to salvage this pan," Lydie said, wrinkling her nose as she scoured a cast-iron pan that had been abandoned with half-cooked chopped potatoes in it for the last several weeks. "It will need to be seasoned again, but the rust isn't deep."

Yes, cast-iron pans were expensive—Hansa had

mostly copper himself—but Umber's relieved sigh still seemed disproportionate to the possible loss. He mulled it over, then risked a cautious question.

"Did you design this kitchen, or was it like this when you moved in?"

Umber's tense shoulders as he lovingly dried glass-ware and put it away warned he might not respond, but at last he said, "It was mostly like this, but it was one reason I chose the house."

"I didn't know you liked to cook." He didn't know a lot of things.

"I'm half-Abyssi," Umber said, flashing a grin that was a shadow of his usual one. "I have a deep appreciation for food."

Lydie scoffed, looking up from her pan. "I still can't tell if you two love or hate each other. Why don't you just *talk to* him instead of making quips? This is obviously your favorite room in the house. It obviously upsets you that it was trashed, but you're trying to be tough because . . . well, I don't really know why. Because that's what you do, I'd guess. Is it such a vile weakness to admit you love to cook, you love this room, and you're upset to see it in such poor condition?"

"We have bigger problems than some moldy potatoes," Umber huffed. "Thank you both, though, for helping clean up."

Hansa dropped his gaze, as if that would stop Umber from hearing his thoughts. Umber didn't want him to apologize, and he didn't know what else to do. He was the one who had dragged the spawn abruptly out of his home and into the Abyss for weeks, and therefore he was the one responsible for the kitchen's condition.

"I'm going to check on Cadmia," he finally said. After the initial bout of puking, she had insisted on helping, but had taken several breaks on the back porch for fresh air.

She wasn't alone in the frequent need for fresh air. It wasn't just the toxic scent of the weeks-rotten potatoes; there was spoiled meat in the long-warm icebox, a generous pile of imported citrus fruits from Tamar and Silmat that had turned to greenish slime, and a half-empty bottle of hard-curdled cream.

"She's fine," Umber replied. "Alizarin returned a few minutes ago. I thought I would give them some privacy." He looked around the room, which was bright with mid-morning sunshine and now only had a faint, dissipating odor of rot, with an expression of resigned contentment. More in control of his affect now that his kitchen was restored, Umber remarked, "Well, I apologize for that rather atrocious welcome to my home."

"I've seen worse," Hansa replied, still off-balance from the vulnerability he had seen in the other man. He was sure Lydie had identified it right, but he didn't think Umber would accept any attempt at sympathy from him.

Umber and Lydie both looked at him with horrified skepticism. Lydie asked, "What kind of friends do you *have?*" Then, abruptly, she must have remembered who she was talking to. He saw the shutters go down in her eyes and her body tensed as she realized the "worse" he had seen had been in the course of his career in the 126. She answered her own question. "Not friends. Of course. I forgot." As she turned away to give the pan one last scrub, she hissed something to herself that Hansa thought included the phrase, "*idiot for coming here.*"

Cadmia and Alizarin entered then, her arm around the Abyssi's waist and his tail around hers. It must have been an interesting image for Lydie, who couldn't see the Abyssi.

Cadmia's color was better, and there was a mischievous light in her eyes as she said, "Alizarin has some bad news for you, Hansa."

He didn't need more bad news. "What's wrong now?"

"I spoke to Antioch," Alizarin said. Hansa's stomach dropped at the unfortunately familiar name. Antioch was an Abyssi who had tried to claim him as a mancer. Alizarin had saved Hansa by challenging the other Abyssi's claim, but the fight had seemed like a close call. "He says you are involved with too much ow that makes him nervous. He doesn't want you more."

Hansa blinked, and finally processed Cadmia's

amusement regarding Alizarin's news. "Oh . . . too bad," he murmured.

"Antioch is old and cautious," Alizarin said. "He is afraid of who you may have angered in the low court, and of who you might anger if you stand either with or against Terre Verte."

"Well, there goes my lifelong dream of being an Abyssumancer." Antioch hadn't even crossed Hansa's mind since they left the Abyss. He certainly wasn't disappointed to learn Antioch wasn't going to make another effort to claim him, but didn't like the idea that they were all in so much trouble that even a fourth-level Abyssi didn't want to get involved.

Alizarin tilted his head as if puzzled. "If that is what you want, it would be easy for another Abyssi to take you. Your body accepts Abyssal power well, and Antioch did all the preparation."

Umber cleared his throat. "Hansa was joking," he clarified. "So, the other Abyssi know Terre Verte is free?"

"Sennelier and Vanadium have Abyssumancers allied with him," Alizarin reported. "Sennelier would prefer not to be involved, but doesn't curtail his mancer's actions. Vanadium is curious about Terre Verte's plans. Nyanza has forbidden her Abyssumancer from coming near, and has enough control to keep him away."

"Vanadium—queen of the second level, righ Cadmia recalled aloud.

Alizarin nodded.

"Did you say Sennelier?" Umber sounded startled.

"You know him?" Hansa asked. "Or, remember him?" Umber had explained that spawn inherited memories from their parents, a trait that had been useful in the Abyss, but Hansa still didn't fully understand how that worked.

"We've never met personally," Umber said. "I suppose I knew he had a mancer, though, since that was why he was close enough to the mortal realm to get caught in another Abyssumancer's summoning, but strong enough to resist it." He grimaced. "He's my . . . I don't think the word *father* is appropriate in this case."

"Abyssi use the word *sire*," Alizarin provided. He continued with his report. "I could not find many Numini, and the ones I saw would not speak to me."

"Can someone tell me what is going on?" Lydie interrupted. "I'm missing half the conversation."

"I apologize," Umber said. "We can explain, if you wish, but given the trouble we may be in, it occurs to me that you might actually want to know *less* about our plans."

"I like the old cliché, forewarned is forearmed," Lydie replied. "Besides, I've said I'll do the spell so Hansa can talk to his friend. I'll hear what they say."

"You may not want to once you've heard the whole story," Hansa admitted. "And you said you need tools for that spell. Is that something one of us can get while the others tell you our tale?"

Lydie paused to consider. "Mined salt if you can find it, but I usually use earth and flour instead, since most of what you find in the market is sea salt." Her voice gained strength and confidence as she discussed her . . . Art? Was that the word for it? "I'll need something to help me focus the Abyssal power as well. I don't know as much about that kind of magic, but there must be some kind of tool that usually—"

The necromancer was still speaking slowly, thinking aloud, when Cadmia drew the knife Alizarin had given her. "Would this help?" she asked, turning it to offer the knife handle-first.

Lydie stared at it. "Is that . . . What *is* that?"

"Abyssi bone," Cadmia answered. "I wasn't sure you would be able to see it."

"It's . . . dark, like it's in shadow, but visible. Is it carved?" Lydie reached toward the knife, hesitated until Cadmia nodded, then took it gingerly. "No, not carved, I don't think. It's . . ." She examined the slightly-irregular, wickedly-sharp blade with what looked like a combination of wonder and horror.

"It was crafted by an exceptionally powerful Abyssumancer," Umber explained. "I don't know what methods he used. He's dead now, if that matters, though the Abyssi who provided that bone isn't."

"I can tell," Lydie said. She put the knife down on the table, and briefly glanced in Alizarin's direction as if she could at least partly see him. "He needs to leave while I do the spell, incidentally. I won't summon a shade while the creature who murdered him is in the room."

Murder. Hansa didn't like the word, but couldn't contest it.

"I want to restock the kitchen, so I'll look for mined salt and flour," Umber offered. "You two can tell Lydie as much of our story as she needs to know."

After Umber left, Hansa looked at Cadmia. When it came to sorcery, he tended to defer to Umber, and their entire story had to do with sorcery. Cadmia was the next best expert.

She sighed. "The short version is, Terre Verte was imprisoned in a cell at the lowest level of the Abyss, and the Numini wanted him back. They manipulated us, along with a Numenmancer who was with us, so we would rescue him. All we know about Terre Verte is that he used to be prince of Kavet before the revolution, that the Abyssi admire him so much they wanted to make him one of them, and that the Numini tried at least once before now to get him back . . . and, of course, that one of the first things he did when he returned to the mortal realm was murder Winsor Indathrone. We've been told he is trying to gather mancers and other magic users for some kind of meeting, but we don't know his motivations." She looked up at Hansa. "Is there anything you think we should add?"

He blinked, considering her summary, which had

skipped large chunks of the story that he would have included if the telling had been left to him. On the other hand, his version probably would have been less coherent, and would have focused on the human aspect—those who had lived or died—while forgetting key points Cadmia had succinctly shared. Lydie didn't like or trust him; she didn't care about his spat in jail, his conflict with his now-dead fiancée, or any of that.

Though there was one more part Lydie needed to understand.

"The Abyssi with us is named Alizarin." Hansa looked at the blue Abyssi, who was waiting quietly for them to finish their explanation. His eyes, the same shade of blue as Umber's, met Hansa's. "He found a way to bond to a Numenmancer. Someone reported her. When we went to arrest her, she summoned him for the first time. I don't think she even realized he was an Abyssi. That's how Jenkins died."

It felt odd, telling the story while looking at Alizarin's drooping ears and slowly swishing tail. The Abyssi's usually vivid aquamarine and turquoise fur paled a shade with what Hansa could only interpret as shame.

"You didn't know, then," Hansa said to him. "You were protecting your mancer."

Lydie shifted, crossing her arms and looking away. Hansa expected her to respond to the story, but instead she cleared her throat and said, "After Umber gets back with supplies, it will take me a few hours to prepare a space for the ritual. I need to eat before that." She glanced back at Hansa and added awkwardly, "You should probably eat and rest, too. You look drawn, as if you've been burning too much power."

"You're right," he sighed. He didn't think he would be able to sleep despite his fatigue, but he was still queasy from the cleanup and didn't want to stay in the kitchen while Lydie and Umber stayed downstairs to cook, either.

Determinedly, he climbed the staircase, and found the bedroom Umber had indicated was the master. While it wasn't as stark as the rest of the house, it was still simple, though the bed showed Umber's taste for comfort in its elegant, strong lines and piles of soft sheets and blankets. In fact, every item in the room was well made, but there were no fabulous decorations or elaborate luxuries—other than a handful of bricks near the bed's headboard, which cast a wonderful radiant heat.

He left his boots by the door, climbed under a quilted down blanket, and closed his eyes. The moment he did, a wave of fatigue struck him. He felt a faint burn in every muscle, as if he had run across the country. The flesh-hunger for Umber came to the forefront, singing its demands in the form of a tingling across his skin, and he didn't think he would be able to sleep until the spawn came back . . . But before he could fully consider that thought, he was dreaming.

He had forgotten something. He wasn't sure what it was, or why it mattered, just that he had forgotten it. And it was lost now, lost forever, and he didn't know how to get it back . . .

Drifting through darkness. Wrapped, trapped, contained by the shadows. A world of fire and blood. He set his lips to the flame so he could drink deeply.

"You need your strength, my love."

Cupric, gazing at Umber with that sudden expression of joy. "I had hoped it was you."

And then it was Naples, the Abyssumancer, standing on the balcony, copper eyes hot.

"No, he isn't the jealous type," Hansa said.

"Good. Then he won't mind."

Pushed down, and it wasn't just the bond and lust and the Abyssumancer's power that held him, but shackles. Cold metal bit into his wrists.

Trapped.

Wrapped in black silk and shadows, blood at his lips—

He woke screaming, wordlessly this time. Another body was against his and arms clutched his torso, and he thrashed away from them in a panic.

"Hansa? What's wrong?"

After another heart-pounding moment, Hansa's mind cleared enough for him to recognize Umber's voice. The other man must have spooned against him while he slept, but was now standing on the opposite side of the bed with his hands held up in a gesture of harmlessness.

"Nightmare," Hansa gasped out, easing himself back to sit on the bed. He couldn't remember dreaming in the Abyss, or even very much before that. The nightmares had only started when he had needed to return to real life. Return to *life* at all. "I think a few of those are the least I can expect, given all that has happened. They'll pass."

"You might consider talking to Cadmia about everything on your mind," Umber suggested. He crept onto the bed slowly, giving Hansa time to pull away again. When Hansa leaned toward him instead, the spawn took that as an invitation to wrap him in his arms again. "She does listen to men's troubles for a living. She might be able to give you some perspective I can't."

"Maybe." Normally, going to a Sister of the Napthol would have been the best solution, but Hansa knew Cadmia so well now that it would feel odd speaking to her as he would have to any Napthol counselor.

He started to turn so he could put his head against Umber's chest, but then the joyful expression on Cupric's face flashed through his memory. What right did Hansa have to occupy this space, which another man was clearly meant to hold?

"Cupric and I aren't lovers," Umber blurted out. "Never have been."

"He seems to think differently."

"We fucked," Umber said, bluntly. "A lot. I was . . ." He stopped, swallowed tightly. "Fifteen? Fourteen maybe. I had never met anyone who knew what I was. I haven't seen him in years. I would have been fine never seeing him again."

He started to slide his hand down from Hansa's arm and around his waist, but this time it wasn't thoughts of Cupric that distracted Hansa, but Naples' smoldering embrace and the cold kiss of chains. The nightmare had been so much worse than the reality, where Umber and Azo had interrupted Naples' attempted seduction—one which had included magical manipulation against which Hansa had been vulnerable, but no physical force or restraint.

Umber, catching the image in Hansa's mind, cursed and pulled back. When he stood, cold air rushed into the space he had previously occupied. "I'm not good at comfort, Hansa, not the kind you need. Distraction, lust, blood, power, that's the best I have to offer. That and the hope that whatever Terre Verte is up to, we can nevertheless get him to break this bond so you can have what you really want."

What you really want. What *did* Hansa really want these days? He had lost so much of what he had expected to have in his life—his career in the 126, a wife, children someday—but lately, lying in Umber's arms felt right.

It felt like more than lust.

Fuck.

A sharp rap on the door saved him from needing to answer.

"Hansa? Umber?" Cadmia called through the door. "Lydie is ready whenever you are."

Hansa let out a breath of relief at the welcome interruption, but couldn't help remembering Lydie's criticism about how he and Umber both avoided talking about anything important. They had been able to talk before, during the weeks in the Abyss, as they waited for Verte to gain enough strength to open the rift.

Hansa missed those lazy conversations, which had been a mix of serious and playful. Like peaceful, uninterrupted sleep, they had disappeared with their return to Kavet. And all he could wonder was if they would ever come back.

CHAPTER 12

LYDIE

Not *your best idea, girl*, a voice whispered through Lydie's head.

She didn't respond to the ghostly warning. She agreed with it, but what *choice* did she have?

As far as she could tell, her possible paths had swiftly narrowed to three options: join Terre Verte and his mancers, join Cadmia Paynes and her rag-tag band, or attempt to stay uninvolved. Despite her youth, Lydie wasn't naïve enough to believe Terre Verte would tolerate neutrality long. If she wanted any information, she needed to seek it, and if she wanted allies in the trouble she could see on the horizon, she needed to claim them now. Most of the shades who clamored at her mind insisted that Terre Verte was trouble, and Hansa and Cadmia were less likely to be vindictive if things went bad and Lydie decided to run.

That logic had brought her here, preparing to tie her spirit to the Abyss so a Quin guard could talk to the dead. If it failed, or went bad some other way, she hoped she would be able to get away before anyone could stop her.

It didn't help her nerves that she had set up in the mostly-empty front hall of Umber's house. The half-Abyssi assured her that his spells would keep anyone from coming unexpectedly to the door, but it still made her feel exposed, especially as she picked up the Abyssi-bone knife. It trembled in her hands.

If the bone had come from a dead creature, she would have felt that creature's shade, no matter how far away it was. She might not have been able to reach it, especially if it were deep in the Abyss or past the golden walls of the Numen, but she could sense and probably call to it.

This creature wasn't dead, but nevertheless the bone was stained with all the deaths its owner had caused or witnessed. Abyssi were born from death.

Setting her teeth, Lydie touched the flat edge of the blade to the back of her forearm. Abyssumancers had ways to keep from bleeding once a ritual was done, but she didn't trust that magic to help her, so she had chosen a spot where she could make a tiny cut without damaging herself too badly. As soon as her hands stopped shaking.

She had hoped the blade was sharp enough not to hurt. She had heard people say that in the past— "too sharp to hurt." This knife wasn't. Or maybe that was a myth. Or maybe it was the Abyssal power that made it sting like nettles as she dragged it across her skin just enough to draw a fine line of blood to the surface. As she watched, a black ooze of power crept up her arm, sending tendrils out toward her core. Every instinct said to fight them, to raise her mental walls and try to protect herself, but instead she beckoned them in.

She touched her fingertips to the rising blood, then smeared it through the jar of mined salt Umber had provided, staining the already-pinkish grains with flecks of eerie scarlet.

She hoped she had her logic right. Short of killing him, she couldn't force Hansa to see the realm of the dead directly; her only hope was to use his Abyssal power to heighten his awareness of the Abyssal taint on Jenkins' shade, and let the men share awareness that way. Unfortunately, to do that, she needed to tie *herself* to the Abyss temporarily.

There weren't guidebooks to this kind of sorcery. To *any* kind of sorcery.

She had not confided to the others that this whole thing might fail to work. Or worse. There was a slim chance she could do something unfortunate, like drain the life from Hansa when she tried to tie her power to his, or drive him mad, or—

Don't think about that. Was that her thought, or the voice of one of the innumerable shades? Sometimes it was hard to tell.

She walked a circle in the parlor, dropping grains of salt along the way to create a symbolic wall, which she turned into a higher, harder barrier in her mind. She didn't need such elaborate ritual to speak to the dead—she could have closed her eyes and let herself fall into their level with a single exhaled breath— but without a wall she would be swarmed by shades, some who knew they were dead and some who did not, some who flickered like candle flames as they fought the pull of the Abyss or the Numen and some who lamented that they could not find their way to the next realm. Some who were sane, and some who had been driven mad by their passage out of life.

She sat comfortably cross-legged in the center of her circle and called, *"Jenkins Upsdell."* The use of a second, family name marked him as someone who had been a member of the upper echelon of Kavet society. The tradition to identify by a family name instead of a community name, like *of A'hknet* or *of Napthol*, had only come to Kavet in the last few centuries as their nation firmed its ties to the distant, aristocracy-obsessed Silmat.

A leaf-rustle reply let her know Jenkins had arrived. Once she dropped into the plane of the dead, she would be able to see and hear him more easily, but she didn't want to do that until she was ready.

She turned. Her heart pounded as she opened a gap in her salt-and-magic wall with a wave of her hand and a firm image in her mind. She swallowed back her dread. This was where it could all go wrong, but if she focused on the horrible things that might happen next, her power would be just as likely to obey that thought as it did the circled wall.

"Jenkins Upsdell, enter my circle. Hansa Viridian, enter my circle. All others stay out."

She shut her eyes to avoid being distracted by the sight of Hansa, and instead focused on the feel of him—specifically, on the way the slithering black power exploring her blood responded to him, and to a similar taint on Jenkins' shade. The Abyssal magic felt hot and foul, like a fever-infection. It was unnatural to her; her body recognized it as alien, and wanted to get rid of it.

She wouldn't be able to maintain the connection long.

Holding the threads of Abyssal power tightly, she let out a breath. As the air sighed out of her lungs, she dropped from the world of mortal flesh and into the realm of the dead, dragging Hansa with her like a reluctant dog. He couldn't help fighting her—he was alive, and so his flesh and spirit protested crossing this veil—but inside this circle, she was stronger than he was.

Hansa's choked gasp let her know the exact moment the two men were able to see each other.

"You keep some interesting company these days," Jenkins asserted as a greeting. "My best friend, an Abyss-tainted pervert. *That* takes some getting used to."

Lydie flinched at the casually used epithet despite the shade's light tone. She understood that he wanted to get the topic out in the open as fast as possible, but couldn't he have found a less coarse way to do so?

"Jenkins—"

"Well, not all of it," Jenkins continued thoughtfully, cutting Hansa off when he tried to choke out a greeting. "I always suspected you were . . . oh the Tamari have a great word for it, what was it? *Aft*, I think. Someone who's into both men and women is 'fore and aft.' I think they have a word for someone who doesn't like either, too, but—"

Lydie's circle shuddered around her, bucking against the strange magics within it. Lydie opened her eyes and pressed her hands to the ground to brace herself and keep her walls from tumbling down on them all.

When Jenkins paused, watching Lydie with concern, Hansa drew a shuddering breath and asked in a tone he couldn't quite keep level, "You came back from the dead to tell me Tamari words for sexual deviance?" Hansa was staring at Jenkins with his lips pressed together tightly, a slight quirk in them as if he almost wanted to laugh at his dead friend's chatter, but couldn't bear to do so. Jenkins' energy was wild and confused, and Lydie knew the rambling was born of his fear to address his friend more frankly.

The shade's form was semi-solid, and a red-black aura rippled around him. He looked at Lydie a moment more, then sighed, "I'm not *back*, Hansa. I'm just here. While you've been doing . . . whatever you've been doing the last few weeks . . . I've been taking a hard look at Kavet, and at my life. I—"

His voice choked off and he shuddered as Lydie's grip on the Abyssal power slipped again; the force slapped against her walls, cracking them. Hansa's life-force burned like a star, and it took a physical effort for Lydie to resist its song and the instinct to draw it into herself to fuel this work.

Both men responded to her control's momentary wavering. Hansa grimaced, and Lydie saw him tense. Jenkins' form became paler and more transparent.

"We don't have much time, so I'm going to skip the small talk and apologies and all of that," Jenkins decided aloud. His sudden focus tamed his energy and helped Lydie pull the spell tighter. "I know you, and I trust you, no matter who or what you're in bed with. I *don't* trust Terre Verte. He's promising the mancers who flock to him a better life, free of persecution and fear, and I don't see how he can hope to accomplish that without bloodshed." Jenkins looked at Lydie, and his gaze met hers sadly as he said, "The has already been bloodshed. No one knows that better than Hansa and I do. I'm sorry, so sorry . . ."

Guilt. Damn it, Lydie hated guilt. For the dead, guilt was a predator; it devoured their essence, and made them impossible for even her to hold. As Jenkins turned toward her, considering his role in the arrest and execution of so many sorcerers who had probably just been trying to survive, he started to flicker and fade.

"Jenkins?" Hansa asked in alarm, reaching for his friend.

Lydie pressed her hands harder against the floor and imagined the ground below. She anchored herself and the shade to it, holding him fast. Her body trembled at the effort. She wanted to tell the men to hurry this along and say whatever else they desperately needed to say, but didn't trust herself to open her mouth without devouring the defenseless mortal trapped in her magical walls.

As Hansa's hand passed through Jenkins' insubstantial arm, Jenkins gathered himself. His form flowed back together like mist. "When I—" This time, the force that tried to pull the shade apart was remembered fear and pain. "I hear the Abyssi sometimes. Because—" He had to stop again, unable to refer so explicitly to his own death. "They talk about Terre Verte, but not just about his power. They also talk about the things they did to him in the decades he's been trapped among them. I don't see how anyone could have survived that without going mad. He talks to the dead and the living about wanting to protect Kavet and heal it, but I don't think we can trust him to be logical or predictable. Someone needs to watch him, and be ready to control him."

Hansa started to shake his head, but Jenkins declared, "I know you. I know you're going to want to stay here and see what happens before you step in, but you can't. You need to get involved preemptively, and you need to *fix* things."

Hansa's attempted protest creaked from his tight throat, incoherent.

Jenkins spoke over him once again. "That's the same look you gave me when I first suggested you apply for a position with the Quinacridone guard. I won that argument. It's the same look you gave me when I suggested you should ask Ruby out. I won that argument. It's the same look—"

"You've made your point," Hansa choked out. "But you might look how all those things turned out before you keep giving advice."

Jenkins shrugged dismissively. "How *is* Ruby? Was she the one who called off the engagement, or were you? I know you're too honest to cheat on—"

Jenkins might have said more, but neither of them heard it. Hansa's sudden guilt and horror, combined with a frigid wind that could only have been the echo of a shade that had already passed into the Numen, stormed Lydie's awareness and sliced through her, severing her link to the Abyssal power and shattering her carefully-crafted walls. Any attempt Jenkins might have made to further communicate drowned in the cascade of other shades who mobbed her, screaming their woes, and the ringing of Numen ice.

Lydie curled her body, pulling her knees to her chest and wrapping her arms around them. She rocked, trying desperately to ignore Hansa's blazing life, the wailing of the dead, and the rhythmic pounding of wings that eclipsed even her own heartbeat. She slapped vaguely in Hansa's direction and he backed away.

There were mortal voices talking to her, too, but she couldn't understand them.

"Salt water," she managed to say aloud. Her voice seemed the barest whisper in the din. "Ocean water. Please. And my doll."

Someone pushed the doll into her hands, someone whose form shone darkly, mortal power wrapped tightly in a protective shell like the carapace of a lobster. Lydie clutched the doll to her chest, triggering the spells stored inside it. The chaos and noise faded a little, enough that she could start to think, try to reform her walls—and curse herself for an idiot for trying this.

A few more minutes passed, and then the same person returned, this time with a bucket of cold ocean water still frigid from the sea beyond. To

Lydie's power, it felt like an empty void—exactly what she wanted. She plunged her hands into it and felt the shock through her body as all the power she had raised rushed into the sea.

As the voices of the dead and the shining auras around her faded, Lydie looked up gratefully at Cadmia, who was standing a few feet away and watching warily.

"Are you all right?" Cadmia asked.

Lydie half nodded, each tiny move of her head requiring a fantastic effort. As she pulled her hands out of the bucket of ocean water, the muscles in her arms twitched and trembled.

"Can you help me get to my room?" Lydie asked. "I need to lie down." She would be helpless for a while as she recovered both physically and magically; she wouldn't even have the energy to ward the door before she slept. She could only hope she had chosen the right allies.

CHAPTER 13

CADMIA

Lydie leaned heavily on Cadmia's arm as they walked up the stairs together. The young woman's body felt frail and bony, and she was shivering hard enough that Cadmia struggled to keep her balance.

"If-f you don't mind my asking," Lydie asked as they climbed the tightly winding stairs, "what are you?"

The question caught Cadmia off guard. "What am I?"

Lydie flinched. "Sorry. Mama says I'm too curious."

Cadmia noticed the present tense, and made a mental note to ask the girl about her mother later.

"I understand. I've been told the same thing about myself," she said, as they reached the upstairs landing. As a case in point, Cadmia was grateful to have an excuse to peek at Umber's study, which she had resisted looking at earlier in deference to both Umber's and Lydie's privacy. The couch Umber had mentioned was indeed deep and long, upholstered in plush damask, where gray-blue and chestnut birds cavorted against a bronze sky. As Lydie dropped onto it, it sank invitingly around her small body. "But I'm not sure how to answer. I'm human. I'm not a mancer, or spawn, or even naturally have the sight."

"You have power," Lydie said, "but it isn't the same as Hansa's or Umber's."

Cadmia cleared her throat, feeling unaccountably awkward. To cover the moment, she picked up a sable-colored throw blanket whose perfect softness reminded her of Alizarin's fur, and tucked it around Lydie's shoulders.

"I'm pregnant," she said at last, deciding it was best to be simple and forthright. "Alizarin is the father. That's the power you sense."

Lydie nodded thoughtfully, clutching the blanket around her shoulders. "I always thought the spawn were myths. Cautionary tales for Abyssumancers and Numenmancers. I should have known better." She yawned widely.

"Do you need anything else?" Cadmia asked. Lydie shook her head, and Cadmia ventured, "Is there someone you want us to contact for you, to let them know you're safe? Your mother maybe?"

Lydie shook her head sleepily. "She died when I was six." She yawned. "I was a sunset baby. That's what everyone called it. It's hard enough for a Silmari woman to be respected as a sailor—that's what my mother did for almost thirty years—so she didn't have me until after everyone thought she was too old to have more children. She blamed that for my oddness when I was little, that she and my father settled here and had me when she was past bearing ages."

"Oddness?"

"I saw things, heard things no one else saw or heard. I would spend hours staring at nothing, unresponsive, or suddenly start screaming." She shrugged. "After my mother's fever, I saw her at her funeral, and she saw me, and she realized what I was. She helped me control my power."

"And your father?" Lydie looked ready to drop from exhaustion, but she also seemed to want to talk.

"My father became very devout. He moved us to the city and wanted to give me to the Order of the Napthol as an apprentice. I ran away. That was two years ago, when I was twelve, around the same time Mama moved on."

Cadmia bit her lip and resisted the urge to say something sympathetic or comforting, because Lydie's no-nonsense tone asked for none of it. Instead, Cadmia considered Umber's story about his mother, about all the individuals who had been investigated, branded, and executed because of whispers of mancer leanings.

"It's kind of nice," Lydie said in a small voice, "being able to have conversations like this. It's been a long time since I've actually really *talked* to anyone who isn't dead."

Just hormones, Cadmia told herself, but the words brought tears to her eyes, and she couldn't resist the urge to pull the necromancer into a hug. Lydie tensed at first, and Cadmia had started to pull back, started to apologize for the unwanted contact, before Lydie's arms wrapped around her. The young woman's body relaxed by inches and her breathing slowed.

Only seconds later, she realized Lydie's form had slumped into a deep, exhausted sleep.

We'll fix it, Cadmia thought, fiercely. *My child will not grow up in a world like this.*

She eased Lydie down onto the couch and tucked her in with the throw blanket and a second, down-filled coverlet before slipping quietly out of the room and back downstairs, where she found Hansa and Umber sitting together on the window-seat, Hansa leaning against Umber's chest. Two glasses of wine sat nearby at hand, one half-empty and the other apparently untouched.

"How is our necromancer?" Umber asked, the usual lilt in his voice notably depressed.

"Exhausted," Cadmia said. "The spell clearly wore her out, but she didn't seem hurt. She says she just needs rest. What happened?"

When the spell collapsed, both Hansa and Lydie had ended up on the floor. Cadmia had trusted Umber to see to Hansa, and had gone to Lydie herself.

"Jenkins didn't know about Ruby," Hansa said hollowly. "He didn't know she's dead. How could he know so much, but not know *that*?"

Umber snugged Hansa closer to himself and leaned a cheek down against his hair with a sigh, as if they had already discussed this point and he wished he could find a better answer for his lover's distress. He explained, "Jenkins shared his thoughts about Verte's meeting, and the promises he's making to mancers in the city. He believes Verte means to fight, and that he might be mad from his long captivity in the Abyss. Beyond that . . ." He looked at Hansa with an expression too soft to be simple lust. "They didn't get to talk long."

"Jenkins is right, though," Hansa said hoarsely. He looked worn and ragged. "*You* were right," he added, focusing on Cadmia. "I can't wait here to see what Verte does, or what the Quin do. If he is gathering mancers for a war, the best defense Kavet has is the One-Twenty-Six. They need to be prepared."

"And if he *isn't* planning to fight?" Cadmia asked. She agreed that Hansa should go, but not if he only intended to use the guards to fight Verte. As far as

Cadmia was concerned, the 126 was just as much a threat to this household.

"Then he's gathering sorcerers in one place, leaving them vulnerable to attack," Hansa replied instantly. "Verte has said sorcery was different in his day. That means he probably doesn't know the methods we use to fight it, either. If I go back to the compound, maybe I can avoid a slaughter if the One-Twenty-Six hear about Verte's plans and decide to march on Amaranth."

Umber nodded, agreeing, then added, "Tomorrow. You're exhausted."

"I've only been up a few hours," Hansa protested.

"Lydie's spell must have used your power to fuel the connection to the Abyss," Umber said. "If you try to go to the Quin Compound in this condition you'll never make it there, much less keep the veil over your power long enough to accomplish anything."

They returned to their room. That left Cadmia as the only one still standing—more than awake, she was buzzing with anxious energy. She wanted to act, to move, to *accomplish* something.

She paused to remove the knife sheath from her waist and, though it hurt her heart to do so, tuck it under her pillow in the guest room. Unfortunately, the Abyss-bone tool could never be mistaken for a simple work knife, and Umber hadn't taught her whatever spell he used to keep his own weapons hidden. Alizarin would sense its power and find it when he returned. He would keep it safe for her.

She used one of Umber's kitchen knives instead to draw blood and veil her power. It was harder to do with the simple steel blade than it had been with the more powerful knife, but she wanted to make sure she could replace the veils with mundane tools if she needed to do so before she returned.

Once she felt safely hidden, she turned her feet toward the city, intending to be Cadmia Paynes—Sister of Napthol, counselor to the ones who scrabbled, fell, fought, and lost as they sought to survive in this world—for the first time in several weeks.

After weeks in the Abyss, Kavet's central market at midday felt oppressively crowded, yet strangely vacant. She hadn't had the ability to sense magic long, but had already become accustomed to feeling the feral, Abyssal energy of the creatures around her. To see such a press of bodies with her eyes yet feel no power gave her vertigo.

She focused her eyes on the crowd, keeping her expression calm and welcoming while she slowed her breathing and reminded herself, *This is what the mortal realm is like. This is home.*

At this hour, the sprawling cobblestone plaza between the Quin Compound and the Cobalt Hall was full of merchants. In a centuries-old tradition, they sold their wares from brightly-colored carpets, wheelbarrows, and small wagons, and called out to passers-by in jovial voices that proclaimed their goods and services. This time of year, they came early to clear snow from the cobbles and stake their claims in the most advantageous spots, creating a wagon-wheel pattern around the plaza's central fountain.

Guards patrolled the plaza regularly, ensuring the walkways remained wide and clear enough for commercial traffic to make its way through them— and, of course, looking for sorcery, as were the two soldiers of the 126 stationed at the front door of the Quinacridone Compound. Cadmia hitched her disguising spell tighter around herself, aware that this was where she was most likely to find someone with the sight.

She started to pick her way across the plaza, keeping a generic, welcoming smile on her face to respond to anyone who made eye contact, and rehearsing the excuses she had prepared for anyone who asked her where she had been. She briefly acknowledged several familiar faces before she spotted the child launching herself across the plaza like a shooting star.

Ribboned hair only half-up and streaming behind her, Pearl dashed between and occasionally over merchants' wares until Cadmia caught her up in a laughing hug.

"Where have you *been*?" Pearl demanded breathlessly. "I—" Her words broke off abruptly, and she froze in Cadmia's arms. Her eyes widened.

The first time Cadmia had met Umber had

been just after Pearl had been kidnapped by a Numenmancer. When Cadmia had wanted to alert the guards, Umber had cautioned her against it—specifically, he had said they didn't want *sighted* guards looking for Pearl, implying she had some power of her own.

Cadmia still couldn't see any magic on Pearl, but it was obvious that even with the disguising spell in place, Pearl could see something on Cadmia. Perhaps physical contact had allowed her to see past Cadmia's veils.

Why did the Numenmancer kidnap her? That question had seemed unimportant in the scope of everything else that happened, but now it reoccurred to Cadmia.

"Are you all right?" Pearl asked, with a discretion that seemed unnatural in a seven-year-old child.

"I'm fine," Cadmia answered, hoping Pearl wouldn't ask questions in the middle of the marketplace.

There were a few people who would be sympathetic to her recent shift in views, but far more would report any suspicions to the 126.

"Let's get inside," Cadmia said. "I need to get into my own clothes and let everyone know I'm back."

"And tell them where you've been," Pearl said. "What are you going to tell them?"

She didn't ask again, *Where have you been?* She ~~knew~~ Cadmia was going to lie.

"While I was at the docks, I ran into an old friend in crisis," Cadmia answered. "I traveled with her to a family funeral. I sent a letter to give my whereabouts, but it must have been waylaid in the storm." The first flurries had been starting to fly when Cadmia had stepped into the Abyss.

Pearl rolled her eyes, apparently seven-years-old going on thirteen. "Sienna says kids say too much when asked a question," she said in a conspiratorial whisper. "That's how she knows when they're lying."

Cadmia smiled, and hugged Pearl to her side. "I'll do a better job when Sienna asks." She was actually quite good at lying. She had given Pearl the whole manufactured story at once because the child already knew it wasn't true.

Like Lydie, whatever power Pearl had was probably why she already knew so much about being sneaky. Sadly, at seven years old, she already had to hide to survive.

CHAPTER 14

UMBER

Hansa had lost enough power to the necromancer's spell that Umber would have been worried, if they didn't have such a convenient and pleasant way to generate more. They went back to bed at mid-morning, where the sex was lazy and tender, in deference to Hansa's exhausted body and fragile emotions. Afterwards, Hansa fell asleep with his head tucked down against Umber's chest.

Once he was confident he wouldn't wake his Quin bond, Umber slipped away long enough to check the wards around the house, tend to some worn patches the protective spells, and reacquaint himself with horses. There was a local A'hknet woman who dropped by regularly to feed and exercise them in exchange for a nominal salary, access to the animals when she wanted or needed to ride, and the right to sleep in the hay barn when she needed to get away from home for a few hours, so they were in good condition despite his long absence. The only sign in the stables of the time that had passed was an invoice and a note from the woman telling him she had bought the last sack of feed on credit because the money he had left was gone—and when did he plan to pay her salary again?

He refilled the coffer where he left funds for supplies and the groom's payment and brushed down the horses and gave them apple-core treats. But though he longed for a ride, he knew now wasn't the time.

Instead, shaking his head in recognition of his own folly, he climbed the stairs back to the second floor and the master suite where Hansa was still sprawled naked on his stomach on top of the blankets. It was a nearly irresistible image, and Umber had never been much about resisting temptation, but Hansa *needed* this sleep. Since they had come back from the Abyss, Hansa's nights had been infected with nightmares, keeping true rest far away. Combined with his magical exertions, his body had been battered by overuse.

Gently so as not to disturb him, Umber climbed back into bed and wrapped an arm around Hansa waist. The other man's body should have been and relaxed in sleep, but his muscles were tense and his heart was beating quickly. His eyelids flickered as Umber spooned against his back, and Umber caught a brief image that was most certainly *not* a nightmare.

He stopped to consider, letting Hansa's mind brush against his own. The dream was Abyssal, hot and sensual but dark. The sensations of fire and fur and claws were at the edge of everything, and the center of the dream was lust and blood. The secondhand experience was enough to make Umber press himself closer to his lover, but he tried to think how it would seem to *Hansa*. He might enjoy the dream as it was going on, but upon waking maybe it would seem like a nightmare.

Hansa was bonded to the Abyss, but he didn't understand all that implied. What *Umber* wanted to do was roll Hansa back onto his stomach and make love to him, letting the dream and reality slip together, but Hansa had responded to his recent dreams with panicked awakenings, and even with the fleshbond, Umber's attentions would be unwelcome while he was trapped in that fear.

If these were the dreams finding their way into Hansa's mind and disturbing him so deeply, though, there needed to be a conversation. Hansa might not be ready to accept these fantasies, but if he kept fighting them the way he had so far, they would rip him apart.

Later, though.

For that moment, Umber let his own eyes half close. One hand drifting down Hansa's chest, he submerged himself in Hansa's fantasies.

One way or another, when Hansa woke, Umber would be there for him.

Then, abruptly, the dream shifted. Instead of being wrapped in shadows, he was being held by pale arms. He was staring into copper eyes. *Naples.* Umber wanted to reach out and fight, but in Hansa's dreamscape the Abyssumancer was all-powerful.

What have I done? he thought with horror. He had deliberately let Hansa go off alone with this monster, thinking that it would be better for him to learn the dangers of Abyssumancers and of the fleshbond in a situation where Umber could step in and stop it before too much harm was done. It had taken only the barest push of power—and a classic Abyssumancer's disdain for others' preferences—for Naples to seduce Hansa. He hadn't needed to use physical force, because the newly-formed fleshbond had been starving for Abyssal power. But lack of force did not equal consent.

In the dream, the magical coercion and the helplessness Hansa must have felt at the time manifested as shackles holding his wrists in place above his head. There was a flash of blade, and then the Abyssumancer was leaning over him, licking blood from a fresh wound on his chest.

That had never happened. Not with Naples. Not to Hansa.

No. No. *No, no, NO.*

Umber ripped himself from the dream, throwing himself back from Hansa so violently that he tumbled from the bed and struck the ground. He should wake Hansa—

He fell when he tried to stand. His limbs were shaking too badly to support him. Still on the scuffed wooden floor, he drew his knees to his chest and dropped his head onto them, drawing deep breath after deep breath and trying desperately to get himself under control. Hansa couldn't see him this way.

He needed to be able to stand up, to wake Hansa, to comfort him.

Comfort him *how?*

Umber finally managed to stand. And like a coward, he fled the room. There was one thing he could do. After all he had inflicted upon this poor man, it was the only thing he *should* do. He left a brief note, then rode as hard as he could while still reaching his destination with himself and his horse intact.

Outside the city, cobbled paths gave way to dirt roads, which wound into the first of the farming communities. This close to the city, the farms were still relatively small, a few acres at a time.

He thundered across the bridge into Amaranth at midday and was not surprised when three people immediately appeared to intercept him. They seemed

more surprised to see *him*, especially the auburn-haired woman at the front. The others dropped back as she stepped forward.

"You're looking well, Xaz," Umber commented. He didn't have time for pleasantries, but neither did he want to appear as desperate as he felt.

Unlike Hansa or Cadmia, whose Abyssal power also came from an external source, Umber could usually faintly see the shimmer of divine magic when it was present. Until now, though, he had never been able to see Xaz's under the brighter halo of the Abyssal taint she had gained from Alizarin. But as she stood before him on the bridge, both auras blazed bright with pride and confidence.

"You're looking . . . alone," she said, sounding surprised. "Where's Hansa? He's all right, I hope?"

Umber shrugged. "As all right as we all are. I was hoping to speak to Terre Verte on just that subject."

When Hansa had demanded a third boon and cemented the bond between them, Umber had resigned himself to his fate, such as it was. Everything Umber had ever learned about other spawn from illicit texts, covert conversations with scholars—sanctioned and not—and even full-blood Abyssi had told him a bond like the one he had with Hansa could be broken only by death. Even that was chancy; when Naples died, Umber hadn't known for sure whether Azo, the spawn to whom he had a heartbond, would survive,

and if she did, whether the false emotions caused by the bond would remain or dissipate.

At the time, Umber had simply been grateful the consequences weren't worse.

"Verte is in the middle of a fairly complex ritual," Xaz said, "but I am sure he will be happy to speak to you once he's done. Let me show you where you can keep your horse. Can I get you anything to eat?"

Xaz had never been this solicitous. Umber knew some of the personality change could be explained by her increased comfort; she was surrounded by other mancers here instead of individuals who would turn her over to arrest and death if they knew what she was, and she seemed to have a leadership role. Even so, the shift was unsettling.

He dismounted to walk with her to the stables, though his skin crawled to put the other two guards—almost certainly mancers, though their powers were more tightly suppressed than Xaz's and therefore harder to identify at a brief glance—behind him.

"What are you *really* doing here?" Xaz asked once they were alone. "Even if you want the bond with Hansa gone, it's not a threat to you right now, and I know your feelings about mancers." She paused, and then amended her words. "In general. You seem willing to ally with some of them, when it works for you. We were all surprised that you let Arylide stay with you."

"She's a kid," Umber replied, dismounting and beginning the process of tending to the horse, who was sweating and breathing heavily. "And just a necromancer. She isn't a threat. I should cool Olive down before I stable her," he added. He didn't want to spend more time here than necessary, but he had pushed the horse hard.

"I'll get the stable hand to tend to your horse. He's an animamancer. She'll have the best care of her life," Xaz replied, waving to a young man who had been lingering politely out of earshot. "Do Hansa and Cadmia know you're here?"

"You're chatty today," he observed.

She scowled. "I told Verte I would be nice to you. Don't be a bastard and make it difficult for me, all right?" He actually smiled at that; there was the Xaz he knew.

She led the way to the main farmhouse, revealing a parlor more in the style of a manor in the Abyss than a cabin in Kavet. "You can wait for the Terre in here," Xaz said, ushering him before her. "You'll even have company. I believe you and Cupric are . . . familiar?"

She said the last word very flatly, as if it was a struggle to keep the judgment out of her voice. He wondered vaguely if she disapproved of the fact that Cupric was a man, or that he was an Abyssumancer, or if the distaste was more personal. He didn't care enough to ask.

"Who have you brought me, Xaz?"

Cupric's voice was exactly the same as it always had been. It made Umber's heart tighten and skip a beat before the other man even looked up. Then those sky-blue eyes met his, capturing his attention so firmly that Umber didn't even hear Xaz say farewell before she left.

"Umber!" Cupric said brightly. He was lounging on a sofa with his legs crossed and propped up on its arm. He rotated, setting his feet to the floor and clearing space for Umber to join him. "Did you come to visit me?"

"I came to visit the Terre," Umber said, leaning back against the doorway. Back at his own home, they had all chosen to drop Terre Verte's title from their speech, but here it seemed better to be polite and humor the once-prince's pride. Especially because he was here to ask the man a favor.

"He's trying to scry into the Cobalt Hall," Cupric said. "He's curious about what magic protects it. I always assumed it was Numen in nature but he says he doesn't recognize it at all. This is his second attempt and he just started, so we probably have a while to wait."

"Maybe I'll take Xaz up on that meal, then," Umber said, preparing to go.

"Hansa's not with you, is he?" Cupric asked. Umber shook his head. Those long legs uncrossed and Cupric sat forward, lifting one hand in invitation. "Come here."

"I really should—"

"*Should,*" Cupric interrupted, laughing. "You sound like some kind of Numenmancer. Come *here*, Umber." More softly, he added the name he had known Umber by so many years ago. "Attish. Whatever you're answering to these days. Get over here so I can do things to you your Quin bond would run screaming from."

CHAPTER 15

HANSA

Hansa stretched, waking without screaming for the first time in—he didn't know how long. He knew the nightmares had come and gone, but he had sunk into a deeper, dreamless sleep after them. The brief respite felt glorious, even if he hadn't slept long enough to feel truly refreshed. He considered rolling over and going back to sleep, but he was hungry.

Bleary-eyed, he put on pants and made his way down the stairs only to discover that he seemed to be alone. Lydie's and Cadmia's doors had both been closed, so they might be in their own rooms, but where was Umber? Hansa wasn't surprised that Umber had gotten up while he was sleeping, since it appeared to be early afternoon, but he hadn't thought he would go far without telling anyone his plans.

Returning to the bedroom, Hansa belatedly spotted the note on top of the dresser. He skimmed it, expecting it to say Umber had gone to the market, or something mundane like that.

Hansa, I've gone to speak with Terre Verte. Stay in the house. You'll be safe here. I will return as soon as I have news. —Umber

A wave of hot-and-cold fury washed over him, and he heard his voice exclaim, *"Who the fuck do you think you are?"*

The door across the hall had just opened, and Lydie froze in it, eyes widening at his hostility. She looked like she might bolt, but Hansa couldn't find the words to explain. Instead, he pushed the note toward her and turned back toward the room to find a shirt.

"'Stay in the house,'" he spat as he finished dressing. "He is out of his Abyss-cross mind is what he is."

"He's going to Terre Verte?" Lydie asked. "I thought—"

"He's gone to talk to him about breaking the bond," Hansa growled, as he collapsed next to his boots in order to pull them on.

"Didn't you *want* the bond broken?" Lydie asked.

The answer to that question, Hansa could admit to himself, was incredibly complicated. His inner conflict, however, wasn't why Umber's latest move infuriated him.

"Terre Verte is collecting *mancers*," he bit out. "Abyssumancers are dangerous to him. To both of us. I don't know what is going through his head that makes him think going there is a good idea but I'll be branded before I'll let him do this alone."

Hansa had thought he knew all there was to know about Abyssumancers from his time in the 126, but Umber had taught him how naïve he had been. As a guard in the 126, he had been nothing but a threat to an Abyssumancer, which meant they had tried to avoid him or, failing that, just kill him. A half-Abyssi spawn could be so much more— most especially a pure, easy source of power—which meant an Abyssumancer had strong motive to seek one out and find a way to trap and control him.

Why would Umber have risked it? Why *now* of all times? Hansa knew this bond hadn't been Umber's choice, but he hadn't thought the spawn was miserable enough to do something like this.

"I can make it to Amaranth Farms in about an hour on horseback."

He didn't wait to hear Lydie's further thoughts on the situation. She would be able to tell Cadmia where he went, so he didn't even bother to leave another note. Fueled by fear and fury, for once he didn't hesitate to use the knife Umber had given him to draw blood as he crossed the front hall. He pulled his veils into place, hiding his power, then sought the stables. Umber's favorite horse was missing, but Hansa had ridden the sorrel mare left behind before, and knew she was a good mount.

He *tried* to be subtle. He stabled the mare at a public inn about a mile before Amaranth and approached the farm on foot, arriving around dusk. A stream, just a little too wide to hop over, marked the southern boundary. The bridge was occupied by a woman dressed in what might have passed for a farmhand's clothes, if they hadn't looked quite so crisp and new.

Her posture as she leaned on the rail and watched the water below appeared casual, but he wasn't surprised when she stepped back to block his way as he approached, tossing curly hair out of her face.

"Can I help you?" she asked. Hansa couldn't see power on her, but that meant little given his limited ability—either she didn't have Abyssal power, or she was hiding it the same way he was.

"I'm on my way to visit a friend," he said, trying to sound casual as he continued to walk forward, wondering whether she would try to stop him and what he planned to do in response.

She *did* move in front of him, then hesitated, letting out a startled, "Oh!" Brown eyes assessed him frankly, traveling down and then back up his body. "Hansa. I didn't recognize you right away. Not a bad job on the power veil, all things considered. It's a little patchy here, though." She started to reach forward, and he jerked back. In order to see Abyssal power, she needed to have some herself. That meant she was probably an Abyssumancer.

"Do you know where I can find Umber?" he asked. Given she apparently knew who and what he was, there was no point in trying to conceal his intention.

She frowned, thoughtful, apparently not offended by his instinctive recoil. "He was here earlier. Xaz took him to see Terre Verte."

Given Hansa could still feel the bond as a coil of power in his viscera and a persistent itch across his flesh—one he always felt when Umber was more than arm's length away—Verte clearly hadn't made good on his promise yet. That didn't mean he couldn't do so at any moment.

Before Hansa could ask if she could bring him to Verte and Umber, the Abyssumancer leaned back against the railing again and dropped the veils over her power the way a lover might drop a piece of clothing. This time, as she sized him up more slowly and deliberately than before, he felt her gaze as a hot caress that pushed his own disguising spell aside.

Even with her standing several feet away, the "touch" made him squirm and say, "I'm not interested in women."

It was more polite than saying, *I will shove you off this bridge if you don't stop that.* It was also strangely odd to say. Despite his relationship with Umber, he thought this might be the first time he had admitted the full truth aloud.

"And Cupric doesn't usually like men," the Abyssumancer said with a shrug. "It's always possible to make an exception for the right kind of power. Personally, I'm—"

"Keppel, leave him alone." And there was one of the last people Hansa had ever expected to be so grateful to see. Hansa's stomach did a strange twist as he looked at Cupric and felt relief and dislike war inside him. "I felt you cross the wards and thought I should come out to greet you. And rescue you, if necessary."

Keppel crossed her arms with a "hrumph." "I know the rules," she said. "I was just talking, wasn't I?" she asked Hansa. At his expression, she laughed. "Flirting, I'll admit to," she added, "but we both know it would take me a few drops of blood and about three seconds to rip that disguising spell off you and have you like a cheap doxie under this bridge, no matter what your normal *interests*. Given you and your friends in the One-Twenty-Six ran me out of my last house a few months back, I figure you owe me." At Cupric's warning look, she shrugged. "But Terre Verte says we need to be *polite*."

"I'm looking for Umber," Hansa said to Cupric, a bit desperately. There was no point in responding to Keppel, since he believed every word she said. The fleshbond made him especially susceptible to Abyssumancer coercion, and unlike Umber, he didn't have a lifetime of practice defending himself.

For a fraction of a second, Cupric's jovial expression darkened. It returned to normal before Hansa could fully register the new emotion on his face, but the fracture in his composure was enough to make Hansa start walking.

Given Terre Verte's clear preference for the best, and his disregard of anyone else's opinion, Hansa guessed he would have claimed the main house, so he turned his steps that direction. There was a curl of smoke rising from the chimney.

"He's meeting with the Terre," Cupric said, shadowing Hansa. Keppel's laughter followed them.

The words made Hansa's heart skip a beat, but he tried to hide that. He continued walking.

What would happen, he wondered idly, if the bond to Umber snapped while Hansa was here? Someone like Keppel might be less interested in him as an easy source of power, but the mancers here had plenty of reason to hate him. Without his tie to Umber, would Verte's "rules" still defend him?

"It would probably be best if we didn't interrupt," Cupric added, lengthening his stride to keep up.

"I don't care what's 'best,'" Hansa replied with a cold smile.

The main house wasn't set far from the road. Hansa had almost reached it when Cupric grabbed his arm and pulled him around. "Okay, I lied to you!"

"Where is he, then?" Hansa asked, his stomach

plummeting as he pictured all the trouble Umber could have run into.

"He's all right, he just . . ." Cupric hesitated, and ran a hand through his dark blond hair. "He's asleep."

"Why would he . . ."

Oh.

Oh.

"I felt you crossing the wards," Cupric said. "I thought I should intercept you before you walked in."

It was possible that this man wasn't a *complete* bastard, but it was still very, very difficult in that moment for Hansa not to fling himself forward and try to strangle him. Even more so when he said, "Look. I know this is a stupid time to ask, and you didn't like me very much in the first place . . . but I have a favor I need to ask of you."

Hansa was sure his expression said everything that needed to be said. Cupric had saved him from Keppel, yes, though it sounded like Verte's rules would have kept her off him anyway, but Hansa didn't owe him favors.

Cupric drew a slow breath. "There's a document Terre Verte wants. Now, you've met the prince, so I'm sure you understand why I don't want to be the one to tell him I can't do something he has ordered me to do."

Having seen Verte break a man's neck without hesitation, Hansa could understand fearing how he might react to disappointment. "I don't know Verte's plans," Hansa said, "and I'm not sure I want to help him with them."

"If he wants it so badly, he'll find a way to get it eventually. At least if you help, you will have a chance to look at it first." Cupric shifted his weight. "I don't disagree with you that he is unpredictable and potentially dangerous. I'm on his side because the Quin are, in my book, just as dangerous. But I'm in this for myself and people I care about—people like Umber. So if you find the thing and think it's too dangerous to give it to Terre Verte, that's a decision I'm comfortable leaving in your hands."

Hansa sighed, trying to listen to Cupric's arguments rationally, despite his savage dislike of the man. "What is this document, and why do you need my help to retrieve it?"

"The Terre wasn't very specific—he said it was from just after the fall of the royal house, has to do with regulating sorcery, and won't be public."

"And you can't get into restricted areas," Hansa said, recognizing the problem.

Cupric nodded.

Supposedly, Winsor Indathrone's personal library contained copies of materials the Quinacridone considered inappropriate for public consumption. Hansa could probably get to it.

"I'll . . . try," Hansa agreed, reluctantly. "If you'll do something for me."

"What?" Cupric asked, eyes narrowing with suspicion.

"Delay Umber's meeting with Terre Verte." Hansa didn't know what Verte would say; the last time they had spoken with him about the bond, he had said he would need to study it extensively before he had a chance of breaking it without harming them both. Hansa just knew he didn't want that bond to snap when he wasn't there. When he hadn't had a chance to talk to Umber again.

Cupric quirked one brow. "I can do that." The expression and tone were familiar; Hansa had seen and heard Umber make both. One of them must have picked the tendency up from the other. "And, thank you, Hansa. I doubt the Terre would be willing to see Umber today, anyway—he has been doing some very difficult, tiring work—but I will delay Umber if necessary."

Hansa decided not to think too hard about how that "delay" might be accomplished.

"If I can find what you're looking for at all, I should be back before dawn," Hansa said.

That was assuming he could restore the mask over his power that Keppel had damaged, and keep it up long enough to get to the Quinacridone, make excuses to the guards there, look for the document, and get back here.

He wouldn't be in any better shape if he waited, though. Not unless he had Umber with him.

clear thought pulsing in his mind: *damned coward, Hansa Viridian.*

horse probably been less than a hundred yards Umber. He could have pushed open that spoken to him, to at least let him know he ready yet for this bond to be broken. Maybe would have laughed at him; maybe Umber have explained why it needed to be done now. Maybe the explanation would have involved his lover.

Either way, Hansa had grabbed onto Cupric's "family like a drowning man grabbing onto a sinking anchor because it was easier than thrashing at the surface waiting for sharks. True, Cupric had made some persuasive arguments; knowing information Terre Verte wanted before he managed to get it could only help them. But that was not why Hansa had agreed, and unfortunately, even Hansa knew it.

"I'll keep him safe while y MORTAL RE
"I'm stronger than any of the
here, so I can make sure they sta Cupric
inclined to break Verte's rules." uman

Hansa nodded silently, not w the
knowing he might as well do this no

He had just turned to leave when C bu
his wrist to pull him back, then clo
wasn't lingering or even invasive, but it w
for, either. Hansa jumped back, rubbing
with his wrist.

"What was—?"

"To tide you over," Cupric said, at which p
Hansa realized that in the brief contact, Cupric
pushed power into him. *Familiar* power. Umber's.

"How . . ."

"I had two boons of Umber once," Cupric explained. "It was years ago, but the connection lingers enough that I can draw on it. You need the
power to make it to the city and back safely, and
to keep from unraveling from the effects of being
without your bond-master. That will hold you a
while."

Hansa started to open his mouth to ask another
question, maybe about the boons or about Umber or
about how Cupric had just done that . . .

Then he shut his mouth, because there wasn't
thing he wanted to know.

He returned to the inn stables and mounted

CHAPTER 16

UMBER

Umber opened his eyes, trying to remember where he was, and why.

He was on a bed. That much was obvious. He was naked. Also obvious. Every muscle in his body ached deeply, in a way that meant both physical use and a *lot* of burned power.

Oh. Of course. Cupric.

Umber rolled from his back onto his side, a prerequisite to sitting up. It had been a long time since his body had taken that level of abuse, and even if it felt good at the time, he wouldn't be up to dancing for a while. How long had he slept?

The thought gave him enough adrenaline to let him

shove himself to his feet. *How long had he slept?* When Umber had been younger, Cupric's particular variety of sex had been enough to put him under for a week, if the Abyssumancer wasn't careful. Umber hadn't meant to leave Hansa for more than a few hours, much less the possible *days* he could have been here.

Outside, night had fallen, leaving the room full of shadows and Umber struggling to orient himself. The rope-frame bed he was on took up most of the room. A clothing chest doubled as an end table and held an oil lamp, which Umber lit with a thought and a burst of power as soon as he found it. Blankets shoved from the bed occupied the only remaining floor space.

The door opened to frame Cupric within it, his fair body lithe and perfect in the shadows. He had always been comfortable in the nude; he would dress only if he had to. Umber knew Cupric had a knife on him, probably held by a sheath on his thigh or upper arm, but it was concealed by the same spell Umber often used.

"You've grown up, Attish," Cupric observed with a wolfish smile. He crossed the room, kicking blankets out of his way as necessary. "I think I like it." He smoothed his hands around Umber's waist, the grip firm. "I also like that you're still not taller than I am."

One abrupt shove, and Umber was on his back on the bed again. He caught himself on an elbow, trying to leverage himself out of the way before Cupric could join him—unsuccessfully. He was still shaky and exhausted. He wasn't up to evasive maneuvers.

"I can't be doing this," he managed to say before Cupric pinned him with one hand on his shoulder and the other twined in his hair, holding him to the bed. "Hansa won't be—"

"Hansa will be fine for a while," Cupric said. "I gave him some of the power I pulled off you the first time."

"You saw him? *When*? Was he *here*? Is he still here?"

"Hush," Cupric whispered, leaning down to brush his lips over Umber's. "He came looking for you while you were sleeping. I didn't think either of you wanted him to see you in this condition, so I sent him off to run an errand for me."

After that, Cupric obviously lost interest in talking. He dropped his head to lick and nibble his way down Umber's skin from throat to chest to stomach. The love-bites were gentle, though Umber knew they would be repeated later more forcefully.

While he *could* still speak, he struggled to do so. "I'm—supposed to—" A harder bite, accompanied by a shock of pure power, broke off the sentence for a second. "Need to talk to Terre Verte. Why I'm here."

"Later," Cupric replied. "Hansa made me promise to keep you distracted until he came back."

"He . . ." Umber found himself staring into Cupric's sparkling sky-blue eyes, searching for the lie, because what he was implying was impossible. Hansa was conflicted enough over the bond he might have been convinced to do something else, but he wouldn't have handed Umber off to another man.

He *wouldn't*.

Cupric smiled. "Hansa's not as bad as I thought. He is a bit fragile—a bit *Quin*—but he learns fast. I can see what you see in him." He returned to what he had been doing, pausing only long enough to add, "Fleshbond. As tasty as you are on your own, I bet you two *together* would be—"

He hadn't finished the sentence before Umber found the energy to sit up, flinging Cupric off him, off the bed, and down to the floor, all in one movement.

"You are not going to lay one *hand* on Hansa, do you hear me?"

On his back on the floor, Cupric started to laugh. "You know I wouldn't damage him. He's your bond. I've *felt* that link before, or what it becomes after only two boons, and it isn't pretty."

"I know your definition of 'damage,'" Umber pointed out, for the second time managing to find his feet. Now if only he could find his pants. "Stay away from Hansa." He had to step over Cupric to move toward the door; he was surprised Cupric didn't stop him, but tried not to let it show. "If you hurt him, or you take advantage of him—"

"You'll . . . what, exactly?" Cupric purred, still on the floor. "Disappear for a decade to punish me? Change your name so I can't summon you by blood?

Tell me, during those years when the second boon still twined us, would you have come to my defense if I had been captured by the Quin? Or would you have sat back and let them brand and execute me, even if it killed you, too?"

Umber crossed his arms, fighting the sudden chill that passed through him. "I don't know," he admitted. He found his pants under one of the wayward pillows and tugged them on. "Now excuse me, I need to speak to the Terre."

The bedroom was directly off the kitchen, indicating that this was probably one of the smaller tenant houses. Umber couldn't remember getting there from Verte's parlor.

He had to speak to Verte, and then get back to his home—to Hansa, Cadmia, and Alizarin. If Verte couldn't break the bond right away, Umber needed to make sure Hansa was all right. If the Terre *could*, well, then it would all depend on how Hansa reacted.

He paused at the front door, blinking against the afternoon sunlight. It was impossible to judge if this was the same day he had arrived, or the next.

Cupric caught up to him and wrapped his arms around Umber's waist. "Terre Verte is busy," he said. "He won't be inclined to do you favors if you interrupt him."

"Then I'll come back tomorrow."

Umber tried to pull out of Cupric's arms, but they only tightened around him. "Umber, I don't know what it is about Hansa that has put you into this panic to get rid of the bond. Not that I'm objecting—it all works out fine for me—but maybe you should settle down. Hansa will be fine for one night without you. And if the Terre can't help you and you end up keeping the bond, Hansa is going to need to learn the limits of his independence anyway."

"He doesn't need to learn independence by my abandoning him for another man."

Cupric circled Umber, never letting his hands leave Umber's waist as he moved in front of him until Umber's back was to the doorway and Cupric was between him and the rest of the world.

"Are you in love with him?" Umber started to object to the question, but Cupric cut him off. "I'm serious. Obviously it's natural to feel *some* affection. You're bonded to him, after all. But we're talking about *Hansa Viridian*. Even before you made him Indathrone's darling, he was a Quin guard. You're the one who warned me countless times about the consequences of the third bond, so listen to your own warnings:

"You're not talking about 'abandoning' him for 'another man.' He's your bond. Not your husband. And if you keep coddling him, he's never going to learn the difference. He'll continue to be hurt every time he's faced with a reminder that you aren't in love with him."

Umber shook his head. Cupric was probably right,

but damn it, Umber *did* care for Hansa. Maybe that was the bond or maybe it wasn't, but the emotion was still there and he couldn't just rest easy and ignore it.

"Hansa's bright," Cupric said. "You'll confuse him if you keep sending him mixed signals, but as long as you're consistent, he will be all right. He settled down about me and my relationship with you fast enough."

Too fast for Umber's tastes, maybe.

That was a painfully selfish thought.

"And what *is* my relationship to you?" Umber snapped. "What in the Abyss am I to you, or you to me? I haven't seen you in ten years, and for good reason."

Cupric gave a half smile. "Well. We'll see what we are. But I know what we used to be." He leaned forward, pulling Umber closer. "I used to be your everything."

CHAPTER 17

HANSA

Hansa took a few minutes to leave Umber's horse in the public stable at the edge of the city and to tidy both his clothing and the veils on his power, then crossed the city and the central plaza with determined strides, as if there were nothing suspicious about his approaching the Quinacridone Compound in the middle of a winter night. The brisk pace kept him warm, as did his pounding heart and the effort it took to hold his veil in place when it felt like every frigid burst of wind tore at it.

As he reached the Quinacridone Compound, the building that had been his aspiration and then like a second home, the two guards at front snapped to attention and one called, "State your—Hansa! Welcome back, sir." Neither guard on the door asked where he had been, which meant Poll had done his job spreading rumors. One did fall into step behind him as he crossed the threshold, and started updating him in a swift murmur. "Glad to have you back. Company Four is still short several men, including the captainship. You're first in line for the position, but with you on leave . . ." He trailed off with everything but a conspiratorial wink, as if he "knew" Hansa's leave was a cover for the covert work he had been doing for Indathrone. "*Are* you back now?"

That question, heavy in so many ways, made Hansa hesitate. He had to clear his throat to say, "Yes, I'm back. And I will accept the captainship if the offer is still in place. First, though, I have urgent business with President Indathrone."

"I—I'm sorry, sir," the guard replied. "He is still away on his own business. Or perhaps it is related. Do you know anything about—"

Hansa gave him a look learned from Umber, and the other guard murmured, "Of course. It's need-to-know, I understand. But he *is* still unavailable."

Verte's spelled note must still be working, then. Hansa had kept his initial words vague and planned appropriate follow-ups for multiple situations, depending on whether or not the President's disappearance had triggered alarm. "If he hasn't returned yet, he should have left me instructions," Hansa explained. "If General Norseth is available, he can escort me while I look."

The general wouldn't be available, not at this hour of night. Hansa had deliberately put the low-ranked soldier in a position of needing to decide whether he wanted to wake the general and call him in, delaying Hansa's supposedly urgent mission for the President in the meantime.

The soldier cleared his throat. "That isn't necessary, sir. I will inform Captain Montag that you are back, though, and that you plan to take charge of Company Four. He was put in charge temporarily until the ranks were filled, so you will want to talk to him about what new recruits he has assigned and what other men he had in mind."

"Good idea."

The other guard left him alone, and Hansa finally opened the door into the familiar hallway. He closed it behind himself, then slumped against it as a wave of dizziness hit him. He was exhausted physically, mentally, and magically, and didn't entirely trust that his veils were as tight as they should be; he could only hope the hour would help him avoid the sighted guards left in the unit.

As he caught his breath, he realized something: he didn't feel guilty.

He had expected to feel guilty, or at least awkward, returning as the enemy and a spy to a place that had held his loyalty, but he didn't. The lies had come easily to him, spoken to a soldier from another company whose name Hansa didn't even know.

Thankfully, Indathrone valued his solitude and had no guards outside his private rooms, including his personal library. Hansa stepped inside, rubbing his hands over the goose bumps that rose on his arms as he did so. He was no necromancer, and thankful for that. Was Indathrone's spirit still here?

The manuscript Cupric wanted was something older than Citizen's Initiative One-Twenty-Six, important enough that Terre Verte would need it, and confidential. There were leather-bound volumes around the room, varying in subject from agriculture to the distant land of Silmat. There was also one case. The door included a panel of heavy, ancient glass with a wire core. The sturdy wooden frame was locked.

That looked promising. If Indathrone had been carrying the key with him, it was long gone, but maybe somewhere else around here . . . No, he didn't have time to search.

He took the knife Umber had given him from its sheath, wondering if he could jimmy the lock in any way that would be remotely subtle if someone looked at it.

An idea came to him, unpleasant but the most likely recourse. Instead of using the knife to try to force the lock, he drew blood from the fingertips of his right hand, recalling Umber's instruction: *Draw power. Then it's just a matter of directing your will.*

Hansa tried to avoid the thought, *this is never going to work*, as he touched the blood to the outside of the lock, and instead thought as clearly as he could, *Open!*

For a moment, he could sense the iron in the lock, and then the *snick* the bolt made as it turned made him jump. He pulled the glass door open. As he retrieved the two manuscripts within, he noted the cuts on his fingers had already healed, the blood done with its work.

The smaller of the two books, set on top, was bound in soft leather, with its title inlaid in silver. It was no more than twenty or thirty pages, and the title emblazed on the cover was, *Citizen's Initiative One-Twenty-Six, recorded by Dahlia Indathrone this day, 2.29, year Twenty-One of the New Reckoning.*

Hansa was familiar with New Reckoning, which was used after Kavet had discarded its ancient calendar but before they had switched over to the Realms calendar used by most of the world. The New Reckoning calendar was counted from the day Kavet had elected its first President, Dahlia Indathrone, which meant One-Twenty-Six had been passed twenty-one years after that time.

Hansa leaned closer, fascinated by the revered manuscript, even though within its pages were the laws that would swiftly sentence him to death. This had to be the original document, written by Dahlia Indathrone herself.

He double-and triple-checked to make sure there

was no blood left on his hands before he lifted it carefully to look at the larger manuscript beneath. This
one was more simply bound, and its title was inked
into place on its first heavy page in a hand that looked
like it had shaken slightly: *Recorded by Henna of the
Naphthol, Madder of the Naphthol, Ginger Cremnitz of
the Quinacridone, and Dahlia Indathrone President of the
Council. Approved by majority vote, 1547:413, day 8.14,
year 1247.*

That calendar had to be Kavet's ancient reckoning, which meant this tome had been recorded before One-Twenty-Six had passed. Judging by how
it was locked away, it was either like the original
manuscript of One-Twenty-Six—very precious—or
else very dangerous. In short, probably exactly what
Terre Verte was looking for.

Hansa turned the first page with a trembling hand.

*In order to protect the populace of Kavet from the ris-
ing threat, the sorcerers of the Napthol Order have helped
draft this initiative, which after much debate within the
council is in final form separated into one-hundred and
twenty-six provisos.*

Sorcerers of the Napthol Order?

And two of them had been behind writing this.

He didn't have the time to read it here. Instead, he
tucked the bulky manuscript inside his vest, where
it would be hidden well enough to pass a casual in-
spection. He planned to read every word before he
handed it over to Verte. Knowledge was power.

Power *is also power*, he thought cynically, as he stumbled, dizzy, on the last stair back to the main hall. The guard who had spoken to him earlier caught his arm to steady him. "Are you all right?"

Hansa nodded, remembering the story that had brought him here. "I've been living rough the last few weeks. Must have worn myself out." As a precaution, he added, "His Eminence seems to be out. I'll return first thing tomorrow."

Such bullshit, but Hansa knew *he* would have fallen for it, weeks ago before this all began. The other guard nodded, but then Hansa weaved again and the guard said, "Perhaps you should stay here tonight, sir? Or see one of the Sisters of Napthol? You don't look well, if you'll pardon my saying it."

Sister of Napthol. Yes, that would be good. He would never make it back to Umber's home in this condition, but Cadmia had said she would return to the Cobalt Hall. She could help him.

"I've been working with Cadmia Paynes," Hansa said. "Would you—"

"I'll see she's summoned," the guard said, hooking an arm matter-of-factly around Hansa's waist to help him stagger across the plaza. Once at the Cobalt Hall, Hansa thought the guard said something, but by then his awareness of the mortal world had started to blur and dangerous dreams had taken over.

Around him were all the sounds of the Abyss: the hiss of claws over stone, the crackle of fire, and the noises of the hunt. He was wrapped in fur, kept warm by flame and his lover's arms. Claws scraped gently down his back and he sighed.

"You shouldn't struggle that way," the Abyssi murmured. "You'll damage yourself."

"I'm impatient," he said.

He stared at the walls of his room . . . his prison. The walls undulated and rippled like the wind-swept surface of a lake, but in colors that would never have been found in the nature of that world. Beautiful colors, for which he had no name.

They burned and screamed if touched.

"I want to hunt." He reached out, but didn't quite press his hand to the trembling wall.

The Abyssi sighed and pulled his pet away from the minor rift. "You can barely walk," the Abyssi said. "You won't survive outside."

He sat down, his limbs awkward and ungainly. His skin was nearly white, with barely a breath of fur. His teeth and nails were short, and he had no tail, no horns, no scales or spines. A few hours before, he had put those facts together and cried when he realized what they all meant. He had been born in the crystal caves, like the cannibalistic baby Abyssi, but he wasn't one of them.

The Abyssi pulled its pet closer, until the human rubbed his cheek against silky black fur, then ran his hands through it as arms and tails wrapped around him to hold him close. He couldn't purr, either; he would have, if he could.

The Abyssi tasted like fire and smoke. It used a claw to

make a short cut on the underside of its jaw, where the fur was thin, and the human stretched up, rising onto his toes, in order to meet his lips to the small wound and drink. The blood met a constant, aching need.

The same need, nearly, that was hinted at by the slide of black fur along his body, pulling a moan from his throat so that, once he had stopped drinking, he rubbed his cheek along the Abyssi's chest.

CHAPTER 18

CADMIA

"Thank you for agreeing to see me," Cadmia said, as Rose settled into a chair nearby and helped herself to one of the lemon cakes that had been set out for this meeting. Cadmia had nibbled on one politely earlier, but hoped to have something more substantial for dinner once this was done.

Rose Atrament had been born the second daughter of the premier Kavetan merchant family. Had she wanted, she would have had at least one merchant ship from the family fleet as part of her dowry. Instead she had decided to join the Order of Napthol. She had studied everything she could about the other realms and the creatures and sorcerers who associated with it, then decided that path was also too restrictive for her. For a while she had remained unaffiliated; she used the money she had left before her parents cut off her allowance to buy an accessory shop, which continued to make her a comfortable income despite frequent raids by the 126 to make sure she didn't have any sorcery paraphernalia.

These days, she was affiliated with the Order of A'hknet. Everyone knew sorcery still fascinated her, but she didn't practice it herself and was careful to avoid any overtly illegal actions, so her family ties and her background with the Order of Napthol had been able to protect her from lengthy prison sentences.

All that meant she could make a powerful ally—if Cadmia could convince her to risk it.

The middle-aged woman's expression remained impassive, the only hint of her thoughts a slight deepening of the faint wrinkles in the tawny brown skin next to her mouth.

"I know how you helped Hansa," Cadmia continued, when Rose sipped at her tea but said nothing. When Hansa was wrongly imprisoned, Rose was the one who had taught him about the spawn and told him how to summon Umber to demand a second boon.

"I did nothing," Rose answered calmly. "I shared some idle speculation about a species most people believe to be mythical. If he did anything with that information, it has nothing to do with me." Cadmia knew that Rose had *seen* Hansa summon Umber, had seen his first meeting with the spawn, and had explained how the boons and bonds worked. Black brows drawing together, Rose added, "*You*, on the other hand, gave the testimony that put him in that cell in the first place."

Cadmia needed to take a risk, or else Rose surely never would. "I made a mistake," she admitted.

"You believe he's innocent now?" Rose queried, sounding almost bored.

"I believe," Cadmia said carefully, "that guilty and innocent do not mean the things I thought they meant." She drew a deep breath, trying to decide the best way to broach the subject she needed to discuss. If anyone would know about sorcery in pre-Quin Kavet, it was Rose. She also had contacts all through the city, most likely including some who would have told her about Verte's meeting.

Before Cadmia could speak, a rapid knock on the door interrupted, followed by a young man's voice calling, "Sister Paynes, I am very sorry to interrupt, but you are needed urgently." Cadmia opened the door to find a novice, face flushed with anxiety or exertion, and eyes like saucers. He explained in a whisper that probably wasn't soft enough to keep his words from Rose's ears, "One of the One-Twenty-Six just carried Hansa Viridian to our door. He said he needed to see you, but now he's unconscious. I had him put him in the hospital wing, and summoned a doctor. Do you think it's sorcery, though? He's the one that foiled that big mancer plot back at the start of winter, isn't—"

"*Hush*, Rev," Cadmia chastised. "Remember your lessons on confidentiality. This is important information, but not something that should be shared in front of others." Hansa. Unconscious. And *here*. If Rev suspected sorcery, or if the other soldiers from the 126 did, they would send someone with the sight to check him. That didn't leave Cadmia much time. "Rose, I'm sorry but I—"

Rose interrupted, saying, "My specialty when I was an initiate here was the identification and treatment of malevolent sorcery, and I continue to practice healing arts—legal ones—for members of the Order of A'hknet. May I accompany you?"

"Yes, please," Rev answered, before Cadmia glared at him again.

It wasn't appropriate for Rose to come—she wasn't a Sister of Napthol any more—but her words and the urgency of the situation made a good enough excuse. Cadmia nodded and said, "That would be appreciated."

They walked together to the hospital wing of the Cobalt Hall, where Cadmia dismissed the doctor who had just arrived to check Hansa. Once the door was closed, Rose asked bluntly, "Is there any purpose in my examining him, or do you know his ailment already?"

Cadmia didn't know exactly what was wrong. She tentatively shifted her awareness the way Umber had shown her, but wasn't sure if Hansa's aura of power really was significantly weaker than usual, or if she was doing something wrong. The Cobalt Hall might even be suppressing her abilities; she hadn't tested them since she arrived.

She looked at Rose, who was looking at Hansa with curiosity, but no alarm.

"I don't know," Cadmia said. "Do you think you could tell?"

"Perhaps." Rose stepped forward, then leaned down as if to listen to Hansa's heartbeat.

Cadmia was curious to know what Rose could do, but more importantly, she had wanted the other woman to look away long enough for Cadmia to pull a hat pin out of the fold of her cloak and jab it into the pad of her own thumb. She formed an image of her Abyssi lover in her mind and whispered, "Alizarin, I could use your help." She had already discovered that Alizarin couldn't come into the Cobalt Hall any more than mancers could, but it was all she could think to do. She couldn't get Hansa back to Umber's house on her own.

Rose looked up, considered Cadmia in silence, and said, "First, you should know he seems to have stolen something." She tugged a battered manuscript out of

Hansa's clothes. "It isn't as shiny as most of the things children of A'hknet bring home, but I don't know any other reason he would have concealed it. As for the more pressing matter, I am not a sorcerer, and I do not have the sight, so I cannot read power directly. I can however recognize the symptoms of power exhaustion. Either someone has been feeding on him, in which case the One-Twenty-Six can try to trace the attack to its source, or he himself has been using too much magic, in which case the One-Twenty-Six will arrest him and execute him. I can delay their inquisitors a few minutes on my way out, and leave up to you whether you want to try to move Hansa before they arrive." She stood with a stretch, and added on her way to the door, "I am curious to see what you decide."

And I am equally curious about you, Cadmia thought, giving a polite nod to the older woman and saying, "I hope we can continue our conversation soon." If Cadmia failed to turn Hansa over to the 126—and of course she had no intention of doing so—it would prove to Rose that Cadmia was complicit in his magic, and not setting up a meeting to try to trick Rose into admitting to illegal actions. All things considered, Hansa could have picked a worse time to pass out.

He also could have picked a *better* one.

Cadmia hoped Alizarin would come, but couldn't be sure. In the meantime, she hid the manuscript beneath a pile of papers in the corner; whatever it was, if Hansa had taken it from the Quin Compound, she couldn't risk soldiers coming to examine him possibly noticing and recognizing it.

That done, she studied Hansa herself. She found his knife, which wasn't as powerful a tool as her own but was far better than her pin, and nicked her fingertips again. Pressing the bloodied digits to Hansa's brow, she focused on trying to mask his power as well as her own.

She thought she had made some progress when two guards in the 126's black and tan uniform pushed open the door and hurried inside. Cadmia stood imperiously, inwardly praying that either these men didn't have the sight or she had successfully hidden his power, and stepped between them and Hansa.

"This is a sickroom," she proclaimed. "Why are you here?"

"He has been on special assignment for President Indathrone," one of the guards explained, a disclosure that earned him a look from his partner much like the ones Cadmia had given Rev. "We have good reason to suspect sorcery as the cause of his condition."

Cadmia nodded, but only in acknowledgement, not permission. "And you two have the sight, so you can examine him?"

The two men exchanged a look.

Cadmia breathed a discreet sigh of relief, then pressed her advantage. "He is already within the walls of the Cobalt Hall. We will examine him, and if we find evidences of malevolence we will of course report it to you. In the meantime—"

A rasping voice behind her said, "Bonnard. Poll. Thank you for your concern. I think I pushed myself too hard the last few nights trying to get back and report as soon as possible, and caught a bit of flu." Cadmia turned toward Hansa's voice and saw him sitting up at the edge of the bed. His clammy skin and the feverish sparkle in his gaze did make it seem like he might be struggling against a flu.

"Do you want us to stay on guard on the door?" one of the soldiers asked.

Hansa shook his head, then grabbed at the edge of the bed as if that move had made his head spin. "Mancers can't come into the Cobalt Hall, remember? I will be safe here while I recover. Please let the others know I intend to return to work as soon as I can." They both hesitated, until Hansa added with a voice that cracked slightly, "Dismissed." Hansa stayed firmly upright until the door had closed behind the two doors, then collapsed back against the bed.

"Rose said you had signs of power exhaustion," Cadmia explained swiftly, worried Hansa might not stay conscious long enough to ask or answer too many questions. "Is there any chance you can walk? I called Alizarin, but he can't come in here to help."

"We just need to make it outside?" Hansa asked.

"Yes," Cadmia answered. "Hopefully after that Rin can hide us."

Wanting to avoid the crowded mess and questions about her lack of appetite, Cadmia had deliberately scheduled her meeting with Rose to conflict with the evening meal, so they passed few Brothers or Sisters of Napthol in the hall and we able to evade too many questions. Even so, Cadmia was sure rumors would begin—Rev would make sure of that— and she would need to come up with more lies to explain why this soldier had come here, and then left again so quickly in such a state.

Hansa swooned into Alizarin's arms the moment they crossed the threshold to meet the Abyssi in the alley behind the Hall. Cadmia looked frantically up and down to make sure no one was watching them, but the Abyssi must have successfully shielded them from sight, since the only passers-by she saw gave them no notice.

Rin meanwhile tilted his head, in the way he did when he was looking at something the rest of them couldn't see. "What are you doing?"

"Doing?" Hansa asked groggily. "I'm not doing anything."

"You're leaking power."

"I'm not . . . I don't think I'm doing anything," Hansa said, leaning against Alizarin. "I'm not *trying* to."

"Is this the longest you've been away from Umber since the bond?" Cadmia suggested.

Alizarin pulled Hansa close enough that Hansa let out a squeak of surprise, then nuzzled his neck and bit him just hard enough to draw blood. Hansa yelped. Rin licked the blood away, looking contemplative.

Cadmia knew the Abyssi could taste the individual gradations of power the way a connoisseur could taste a wine, and then discuss the subtle flavors of oak or tannin. The process was obviously uncomfortable for Hansa, but he bore it, understanding.

"Mancer," Alizarin pronounced. "And Abyssi. And Umber. All pulling power from you."

The first was problematic and unsettling; the second was downright frightening, since Alizarin was the only full Abyssi they knew; and the third had its own reason to be upsetting.

"*Umber?*" Hansa asked. "What does that mean?"

"It means he needs the power," Alizarin said.

"That would seem to mean he's in trouble," Cadmia said.

"Then we'll go get him," Hansa said. "He was with—" He pushed away from Alizarin, then wobbled and would have fallen if the Abyssi hadn't scooped him up like a child.

"You're in no condition to travel," Cadmia pointed out.

"I'll be—wait, where's the manuscript?"

Cadmia patted the bound pages tucked beneath her cloak. "What is it?"

"Something Verte wants," Hansa answered. His color was a bit better than it had been, and Cadmia realized Alizarin must be siphoning power into him.

How much was it taking just to keep him conscious and coherent? "I didn't read much of it, but it's from before One-Twenty-Six, and before they started with the New Reckoning, so it must have been written just after the overthrow of the monarchy. And it's . . . weird. It refers to the Napthol Order as sorcerers."

"We can examine it closely at home," Cadmia said, though she couldn't resist flipping through it as they walked.

In order to protect the populace of Kavet from the rising threat, the sorcerers of the Napthol Order have helped draft this initiative, which after much debate within the council is in final form separated into one-hundred and twenty-six provisos.

What rising threat? Mancers, maybe? Verte hadn't known what a mancer was until they told him, but maybe it was a modern term. Clearly he and others in his line had used mancer-type magic.

She read bits and pieces aloud as she walked, trusting Alizarin to keep their path clear.

"This part is asking all sorcerers of legal age to be voluntarily branded . . . here, dropping the legal age to fifteen, with parents' consent . . . the permanent sealing of the *temple* in the Cobalt Hall?" She looked up with surprise before continuing. "Cessation of all training by the Order of Napthol, and a request of similar cessation by independent parishioners . . . this is insane. It goes on and on." She kept flipping. "Oh, this is cute: incentives for premarital chastity. Hmm, and here, fines for public swearing, including the use of terms referring to the Abyss or the Numen. Taxes on any butcher or farmer selling bone, blood, fur, or leather for use in sorcery. Nothing in here makes sorcery *illegal*. It just discourages it. Strongly."

Curious, she flipped to the last page, which she also read aloud:

"Oh. Provision One-Twenty-Six: *Giving this council authority to initiate and authorize future measures as necessary with a simple majority approval of the voting body.*"

"Citizen's Initiative One-Twenty-Six passed about two decades later—fifty years ago," Hansa said slowly. "Maybe not enough people fell into line with this 'polite' request, so the majority decided to use this provision as a basis for stronger laws."

CHAPTER 19

LYDIE

Lydie chewed slowly, thoughtfully, enjoying the feel of the dense fruit bread in her mouth—such a luxury—and the quiet in her mind.

She had awoken to find herself alone in Umber's home, as far as she could tell. If the Abyssi was around, he hadn't made Lydie aware of his presence, so it was just her and a handful of ghosts. She had tranced to have a longer, more coherent conversation with Jenkins, which had given them both a lot to think about. She had also attempted to reach the previous owner of the house, which she should have been able to do if he were murdered anywhere nearby, but his spirit was beyond her reach. If Umber had done away with him, he had done so peacefully, or far from here.

That was good. She wanted to like Umber. Under the thick skin that anyone of a magical persuasion needed to develop to survive in Kavet, she suspected he was soft-hearted.

Then she had reset her walls even higher, because ever since that ritual, it had felt like something was *scratching* at her.

Reaching for a canister of mint and citrus tisanes, she noticed the bandage on her left arm and frowned at it. She had hoped she would heal instantly after the knife wound, the way all the others in the household did when they drew blood for magic, but her necromantic power remained stubbornly uncooperative.

She had just set the kettle to heat when the front door opened with too much force, accompanied by shouting voices.

"Don't be foolish," Cadmia snapped. "You can barely walk even *with* Alizarin's help. You are in no shape to go back to Amaranth Farms."

"If Umber is in trouble—"

"Alizarin, can you knock him out so we can stop having this argument?"

Lydie rushed to greet the others in the barren front hall. Cadmia was flushed from the cold, a brisk walk, or anger—or perhaps all three. Hansa, who was leaning on a figure Lydie couldn't make out as more than a vague haze in the air, was gray-faced.

He must have burned himself out trying to do too much. Of course he had. Unlike a mancer, he hadn't spent most of his life learning the limits of his power. He was too ignorant to realize overuse of his magic could kill him.

Hansa looked at Lydie, as if she might be more reasonable than Cadmia. "I'm not just being stubborn. I'm not a mancer. I'm bonded to Umber," he said. "If Umber isn't here, coming here and *resting* isn't going to help me—stop that!" he snapped at the Abyssi, in response to some provocation Lydie couldn't see.

"Did you find Umber at Amaranth Farms?" Lydie asked. Umber clearly hadn't broken the bond yet.

"No. Yes. It's complicated," Hansa said. "Cupric asked me to get something for him from the Quin Compound, something Verte wants."

"A laundry list of provisions passed shortly after the election of Dahlia Indathrone, it looks like," Cadmia summarized. "We already knew sorcery must have been legal or at least less vilified during Verte's time. This gives us some insight into how the change happened. That may be all Verte wants—to understand how his world turned into ours." She paused, considering. "I don't see any reason it would be dangerous for him to have. I know why you want to run off immediately, Hansa, but if we take a little time to read through the rest of this and confirm it's something we're comfortable handing over, we can use delivering it as an excuse to visit Amaranth

Farms and look for Umber. It will also suggest to Verte that we're on his side somewhat, which might put us in a better position to understand what he might do next."

"What makes you think Umber is in trouble now?" Lydie asked. "He went to Amaranth willingly, and it's only been a few hours . . . hasn't it?" When she was a child, she used to lose hours or even days at a time when her power overwhelmed her, but that hadn't happened in years. As far as she knew. She hadn't been around enough people to be sure.

"Alizarin says Hansa is having power pulled from him by an Abyssi, an Abyssumancer, and Umber," Cadmia explained. There was a tone almost like a teacher's that she fell into whenever she answered questions. "We haven't had time to consider the first two yet because Hansa is busy panicking over the third one."

Lydie understood, and shared, Hansa's alarm. There was no reason for Umber to leach power from Hansa unless something was very wrong. Could the spell to sever the bond have gone awry somehow? An Abyssumancer might have been involved in a ritual like that; could he or she have accidentally or intentionally linked to Hansa? In that case, the Abyssi might be the Abyssumancer's patron.

She didn't bother to pose any questions to Hansa or Cadmia, who would have no better basis for speculation of that kind than Lydie herself.

"I can go to Amaranth Farms," she offered. It would give her a chance to see Terre Verte's operation while also protecting her safe, comfortable spot here at Umber's home. In the hard reality of her world, the fact that she also genuinely wanted Umber to be safe was secondary.

Cadmia looked at her with protective skepticism—that expression that was usually paired with words like, "But you're so young."

"Of the three of us," Lydie said, arguing before Cadmia could, "I'm the only one who has a hare's chance of successfully using my power to defend myself if I need to—and I'm the one least likely to need to, since I am not a walking buffet for an Abyssumancer. Besides, I know how to stay unnoticed when I need to. That makes me the logical choice."

Cadmia nodded, though reluctantly. Hansa frowned, too dazed and distracted to follow her points. He seemed to be wilting before her eyes. Alizarin curled close to him, lending power, as Cadmia hurried to read and take brief, sloppy notes before pushing the manuscript toward Lydie and urging her to go.

It was a few miles from Umber's home to Amaranth Farms. Lydie caught a ride for a couple miles on a pig cart going that direction, but it still took her longer than it would have taken Hansa on horseback—where had he left the poor beast, anyway?—so she arrived late enough that any good Kavetans would already be asleep.

As she approached the bridge, she stretched out her power, gently examining the gauzy spell-wall that surrounded this property. It didn't seem harmful and wasn't solid enough to keep anyone out, but she suspected passing through it would trigger some kind of alert. She was contemplating if she could make a hole to pass through without alerting the locals when she felt the rustling of a shade, followed by the brush of another necromancer's power.

Two guards appeared momentarily: one man whose necromantic power wrapped him like a coat, and one woman Lydie couldn't easily identify. Both looked a little rumpled, as if they had been sleeping—or *not* sleeping, if the man's crookedly-buttoned coat and the woman's wild hair were anything to judge by.

"Arylide, welcome to Amaranth Farms," the necromancer said before Lydie could speak. Given what he was, she was unsurprised he knew her name, but the familiar greeting from a stranger felt abrasive all the same. "Terre Verte mentioned you. Are you thinking of joining our family?"

If Lydie had been considering it, the strangely feral gleam in the other woman's gaze would have convinced her otherwise. "I'm looking for Umber," she said, since it seemed clear she wouldn't be able to sneak about and look for the half-Abyssi man on her own.

The response seemed to amuse the woman, who

replied brightly, "I would *love* to show you where he is. Stay on the bridge," she added to the necromancer. "I'll be back in a few minutes."

Without a further word, she started at a brisk pace toward one of the smaller buildings.

"Why are you so anxious to help me?" Lydia asked as she followed the Abyssumancer's bouncing steps.

"You're allied with Hansa and the rest, which means we're all under strict orders to be polite," she replied. "Also, Cupric deserves to be interrupted. Greedy bastard."

She pounded on the door of one of the smaller farmhand houses and flourished her hand toward it. "Good luck. I need to get back to my . . . duties now," she said with a suggestive lift of an eyebrow, "so you'll excuse me."

Lydia wasn't sorry to see her go, whether back to her guarding or her liaison with the other necromancer. She did, however, hesitate to knock on the front door as she considered what might be going on inside. Cupric seemed to be more or less an ally, and the Abyssumancer's words implied he was enjoying himself. Amaranth did not want to walk in to find him and Umber happily and consensually having sex.

She also didn't want Hansa to die of power exhaustion while Umber was happily and consensually having sex—and, almost more important, she had no way of knowing if anything going on in that house was happy or consensual. Cupric was an Abyssumancer, one whose name Lydie had known through whispered warnings even before recent events.

Without taking the time for more than a cursory protective circle, she closed her eyes and let herself fall into the power level where the dead resided, hoping she could ask a shade to take a peek for her.

Moments later, she realized a personal circle wasn't necessary; part of securing Amaranth must have included expelling any shades who could pester the local necromancers, or be used as spies by outsiders like Lydie.

Returning her awareness to the plane of the living, she raised a hand and struck the door with her knuckles once, twice, three times. The sharp *rap, rap, rap*! sounded much more confident than she felt.

Much to her relief, a man's voice answered almost instantly, "Come in."

Lydie pushed open the door.

A man with close-cut dirty-blond hair, blue eyes, and a broad-shouldered physique was standing at the wood stove, stirring a pot emitting the spicy smell of mulled wine. He glanced at Lydie as she entered, looked her over with a quick up-down that seemed to dismiss her out of hand, then spooned up a taste of the wine and contemplated it a moment before adding more honey.

"I'm Arylide," she said, hoping that would suffice for an introduction with this Abyssumancer as it had with the other guards. Hansa had said Cupric sent him for the manuscript, so she held it up. "I think this is supposed to go to you."

Cupric managed not to snatch the heavy bound pages from her hands, but relief shone in his eyes. "Good," he breathed. "Was there any trouble?"

Lydie hesitated. She didn't know this man, and wasn't sure of his motives.

"Hansa's all right, isn't he?" Cupric asked, concern escalating when she didn't immediately answer. "I promised Umber he would be. He seemed to have a good grasp on his disguising spell, and I pushed enough power into him to last a couple days. Did something happen?"

Lydie found herself suppressing a sigh of—what? Disappointment, almost. Had she worked herself up to fight a wicked Abyssumancer? She of all people should have known that being a mancer didn't neces-sarially make a man a villain.

I'm as prejudiced as the rest of Kavet.

On the other hand, the only way for a mancer in Kavet to live was by deceit. Cupric looked six or eight years older than Umber, which meant he was almost twice Lydie's age. He wouldn't have made it this long unless he was an excellent liar.

CHAPTER 20

UMBER

The next time Umber opened his eyes, the darkness pressing against the window indicated it was late at night. He stared at it a long time, not sure he had the motivation to roll over and try to get up—especially if Cupric was just going to show up and throw him back on the bed again.

Slowly, as his senses started working again, he became aware of voices in the next room. Hopefully that meant Cupric was distracted, either by another would-be conquest or the actual work he was supposed to do here for Verte.

Deeply sore and so tired the air felt like molasses, Umber stood and dressed with exacting care. It was impossible to rush when he was this drained; it was hard enough to do each task. He wanted a bath, or to at least dunk in the river, but he would settle for getting away from Amaranth Farms first. Though he still hadn't spoken to Verte. But he had to check on Hansa.

Hansa made me promise to keep you distracted . . .

Once he assured himself the Quin was all right, he might have to smack him silly. What had he been *thinking,* coming here in the first place, then running off to do whatever "errand" Cupric had given him?

Umber contemplated the window, and whether he could sneak out without going past Cupric again. It took almost all his energy just to lift the thing a few inches; the wood was warped, and in his current state, he didn't have the strength necessary to force it.

Fine. He would go through the kitchen. Cupric had to know he was too burned out for *anything* more at this point.

Umber hesitated in front of the door a long time before easing it open, straining his ears to hear the conversation in the next room. Cupric and . . . Was that *Lydie?*

Umber leaned an ear on the door, and was able to pick up Cupric's next words. "It sounds like you need a real sorcerer to help you work this out—one who works with the Abyss, that is," he corrected swiftly, as if he hadn't intended to slight Lydie, though Umber was certain the casual insult had been deliberate.

"We have an Abyssi," Lydie pointed out.

"Abyssi are good at *reading* power, but not manipulating it. Could you bring Hansa here? If—"

Umber pushed the door open. Cupric was good at sounding sincere and charming; Umber couldn't blame Lydie for falling for the act and answering Cupric's questions. But he would swear himself over to the Numini sooner than he would let Cupric touch Hansa.

Or Lydie, he thought, as his gaze swept the room. Cupric had one hand on the counter and was leaning toward Lydie, the picture of helpful concern. Rationally, he knew Lydie was too savvy to be in any real danger from the Abyssumancer, but seeing Cupric there, hanging over the girl, who was no older than Umber had been when Cupric first targeted him—

He missed Cupric's next words because he was busy wishing he had an Abyssi's ability to reduce a living body to a crimson stain on the wall with the speed of thought. He settled for storming across the room, grabbing Cupric's shoulder, and flinging him away from the teenage necromancer. Adrenaline and fury replaced the exhaustion he had felt an instant before; the pure anger felt even better than the sex had.

Cupric let out a curse as he slammed into the corner of the table and fell to his knees. Lydie, recoiling from the unexpected violence, let out a wordless protest.

"What in the three worlds do you think you are doing?" Cupric snarled, pushing himself up.

Umber moved toward him, all too aware that if

Cupric fought back they were all fucked. Before Umber had taken a single step, Cupric had a knife in his hand.

"Umber?" Lydie queried, two syllables that said so much: *What's going on? Are you okay? What do you need me to do?*

"Get out of here," he told her. "This isn't your fight."

She tossed her head, took one step closer to the door, and reached into her cloak pocket—searching for a tool, he suspected. *Not* planning to run.

Cupric looked from Umber to Lydic, his eyes narrowed.

Anyone else might have missed the brief moment when Cupric clearly considered killing the necromancer, then decided it would cause him too much trouble. Worried about Verte? Probably; he certainly wasn't worried about Umber.

The instant ended, and Cupric shook off his tension with a shaky laugh. "You scared the breath out of me, storming in here like that," Cupric said with a smile that looked absolutely real—and absolutely wasn't. "What's wrong?"

Umber choked on his answer. Lydie was still looking at him for guidance.

It wasn't worth arguing. Umber couldn't kill Cupric, couldn't even make him hurt, which was what he *really* wanted.

"We're going now," he said. Lydie nodded, but didn't move until Umber led the way.

Cupric let them go. In his mind's eye, Umber could see the Abyssumancer's smile slipping from humor to wry amusement to dry irritation once no one was looking.

"Were you looking for me?" he asked Lydie.

She nodded. "Are you all right?"

"Just tired." Now that the adrenaline of the moment was fading, all his aches and fatigue had returned. He had turned toward the stables where Dioxazine had left his horse before he realized there *was* one thing he could do.

"I just need to make one stop," he told Lydie, before crossing in swift strides toward where he believed Verte was staying. She trailed behind; after seeing her with Cupric, Umber appreciated having her at his back.

He knew he looked terrible, and this wasn't a good hour to ask favors, but he needed to anyway. He was relieved to find the once-prince in his sitting room alone instead of in bed with the Numenmancer.

"Are you all right?" Verte inquired, as Umber knocked politely on the open archway's frame.

Umber nodded, not about to discuss his own condition with Verte or in front of Lydie. He said, "I can't stay long. I need to get back to Hansa. But I have a favor I need to ask you."

"About the bond, I imagine?" Terre Verte asked.

"Not right now." No, he had other threats to address first. "It's about one of your followers."

Verte's brows tensed, the beginning of a frown. "Is

there a problem? I've given them all strict instructions to be helpful if they can, and not to bother any of you. Even your recently-adopted necromancer," he added, with a smile to Lydie that almost looked paternal.

Probably as fake as Cupric's, Umber thought.

"I need you to keep Cupric away from Hansa."

Verte looked surprised by the words. How could this man who wanted to take back Kavet, who could walk between the infernal and mortal planes, and who had been offered a position as a prince of the Abyss, be so ignorant of the *nature* of the Abyss?

"Has he given you two trouble?"

Trouble. That was one way to explain it.

Umber couldn't go into the detail he needed, so he focused on what he thought Verte would understand and believe. "Hansa was raised in a very restrictive culture. He isn't comfortable with casual sex, but because of the nature of his bond to me, an Abyssumancer's attentions would be very difficult for him to refuse. Cupric doesn't understand. He can be . . . pushy."

At that, Terre Verte looked amused, no doubt convinced that Umber was a jealous lover trying to keep either Hansa from Cupric, or Cupric from Hansa. No matter what he thought, he said, "I'll speak to him about it. I want you to feel comfortable."

"Please."

"If you do want Cupric to leave Hansa alone," Verte said, with the tone of someone working up to a bribe or blackmail, "then I am going to need to ask something of you. I believe Hansa was helping Cupric retrieve a document for me—"

"Cupric has it now," Lydie interrupted, somewhat too sharply. She, too, had clearly distrusted the prince's tone. "So that matter's done with. You'll keep your side of the deal?"

Verte didn't try to conceal his irritation at Lydie's brisk, protective assertion, the way Cupric had, which in some ways made Umber feel more at ease.

"I will," Verte said. "As long as you're here, will you tell me if your group plans to come to the meeting?"

"I would be curious to know what it is going to be *about*, before I decide to show myself there," Umber hedged.

Verte smiled. "It will be about many things, but the primary goal is simply to have it *happen*," he said. "From what you have told me about these times, and what I have observed, getting multiple mancers, spawn, and small-and large-magic users in one place and cooperating would be a miracle in its own right. The rest of the agenda is secondary."

Umber believed that—as much as he believed in chaste Abyssumancers.

"I'll consider it," he said, with a smile just as fake as any of Cupric's. "Thank you for agreeing to speak to Cupric for me." Saying those grateful words caused a familiar, dangerous tug at his power, like a fishhook snagging in the edge of his skin and pulling in Verte's direction. There had been no exchange of blood, but

Verte was enough of a sorcerer, he could utilize the link to call Umber in the future if he wanted. It would be naïve to hope Verte wouldn't know that.

Verte's lips parted and the gray of his eyes briefly brightened to blue; Umber braced himself as the sorcerer across the room noticed and examined the faint bond now between them.

Deliberately, Verte said, "Your bond-partner put himself at great risk to help me acquire something I needed. You and I are even."

The pressure around Umber's chest lessened as Verte waved away any possible debt—and therefore tentative bond—between them. Umber wasn't sure whether to feel glad or frightened at Verte's swift management of the situation, and the way he added thoughtfully, "Though that was informative. Before I break your bond with Hansa, I think we should negotiate carefully, and decide what you can do for me in exchange. For now, I'm sure Hansa is expecting you. I will see you soon."

Were those words intended to be threatening, or comforting? Or were they just the way a prince spoke, with a casual assumption that his will would prevail, and everyone else would accept his actions and judgment? Either way, they were clearly a dismissal, which Umber and Lydie heeded.

"You came to Amaranth to give Cupric something?" Umber said once they were outside, trying to understand what had happened while he was distracted.

"Mostly, I came to find you," Lydie answered. "Hansa is losing power at an alarming rate. The Abyssi is with him right now, siphoning power into him to keep him stable, but he says somehow Hansa is losing power to an Abyssumancer, an Abyssi, and to you. It made us worry you might be in trouble."

Trouble was one way to describe Cupric. Could the bond have enabled him to pull power not only from Umber, but from Hansa, too? It seemed the most likely explanation, and if correct, the problem was already half solved now that Umber was away from Cupric. He and Hansa could generate more power once he reached home.

"Do you mind riding double?" he asked belatedly, as they reached the stables. "You're light enough, Olive shouldn't mind carrying us both back to my home."

Lydie's responded wasn't immediate, as if she needed to consider if she wanted him so close to her for so long, but after a few moments she nodded. "You look like you'll need me to keep you awake."

He couldn't argue with that.

The ride back was uneventful. He said good night to Lydie once they were inside, then found Hansa and Alizarin curled together on the couch downstairs, Hansa's cheek against the Abyssi's turquoise-blue fur. Hansa had his pants on but was bare-chested, and even though Umber knew nothing sexual had happened between them—or ever *would* happen between them, most likely—he couldn't help a brief fantasy, which wasn't diminished by the images Umber found in Hansa's mind when he touched his shoulder.

Alizarin looked up sharply, blue eyes burning in warning, then recognized him and relaxed.

"He dreams of the low court," Alizarin said, "and of Abyssi there."

"Real or imagined?" Umber asked. They had passed through the low court on their way to rescue Verte, and even though Hansa had only seen the beasts of the deepest level of the Abyss for a moment before he put on a blindfold, that glimpse was enough to be dangerous to a mortal mind.

"Real, maybe," Alizarin said. "I have not met Modigliani, but he was often around the old king, and I remember him when I taste Hansa's dream." It took Umber a moment to remember that, like himself, Abyssi had memories inherited from their progenitors. Alizarin had been born of crystals seeded by the last king of the Abyss.

"Do you remember Verte that way?" Inherited memories often lay dormant unless something provoked their recall. Alizarin had shared all the information he knew with them when they had first found the late prince, but he might have remembered more since.

"A little," Alizarin answered. "The old king, Grumbacher, had him many days before the other

Abyssi revolted. Grumbacher killed many Abyssi to try to work the spell to make Verte alive again."

"Do you know why Verte refused when the king offered to make him Abyssi?"

Alizarin shook his head; Hansa shifted sleepily as long black strands of hair moved across his shoulders. "I remember the taste of Verte's flesh, and of his power. If Verte explained why he said no, the king did not pay attention, or did not understand."

Umber's memories from his mother were fragmentary, but when they came to him, they were full of detail and color and thought and consideration. Abyssi memories tended to be more like a watercolor painting, focusing on sense and either pleasure or pain instead of words and specificity.

"Do you know why Hansa might be dreaming of the lord of the Abyss?"

"Images from you, if you remember Modigliani?" Alizarin suggested.

Umber frowned, scratching at his own memory. "I don't think Sennelier ever met him. Does that make sense?"

Alizarin pondered for a moment., "Sennelier returned to the second level court around the time I joined the third. He is cautious for an Abyssi, and prefers the higher levels. He might never have met the Abyssi of the low court."

That still left the blazing question of Hansa's

dreams, which Umber suspected couldn't be answered unless Umber took a closer look at them.

"I'll take Hansa now," he told Alizarin, before
reaching forward to lift the still-sleeping man. To
a passer-by, the image might have looked comical,
since Hansa was larger than Umber, slightly taller
and broader in the shoulders. If Umber were at his
full strength, he could have lifted him easily despite
the difference; as it was, it took a bit of stumbling and
help from Alizarin to get him upstairs, where Alizarin padded into Cadmia's room and Umber continued
to his and Hansa's room.

I'm sorry, he thought, as he lay Hansa down on the
bed, then curled behind him. He had hoped to get to
Amaranth and free Hansa of all this.

If Hansa wanted to continue a physical relationship once the bond was broken, Umber wouldn't object, but damn it, the man should have a *choice*. Hansa
was the one who demanded the second and third
boon and created this bond between them, but he
hadn't known what he was doing. He hadn't known
the danger. He still didn't understand what he had
tied himself to.

CHAPTER 21

HANSA

When the shackles were finally removed, he had to bite back a whimper at the pain that bit through his shoulders as they were allowed to move for the first time in days.

"You don't need to be there, Hansa."

The voice half roused him, shaking him out of the dark dreams without fully waking him. Familiar arms wrapped around him, turned him, until he rested his head against Umber's shoulder and found softer, hotter dreams.

He slept restlessly a bit longer, then woke to Umber nibbling his way down Hansa's stomach.

"I thought that would wake you up," Umber said.

"It's a good way to wake up," Hansa agreed blearily, before blinking with confusion. "You're back."

"I am. I'm sorry I left so long." Umber moved back up to meet Hansa's lips, gently, holding himself just above Hansa's body as if afraid of breaking him.

"I'm sorry," Hansa said, for what felt like the five-hundredth time in—how long had it been? The sunlight streaming through the window seemed the same angle as it had been the *last* time he had been in this bed, as if the last day or so—Umber's note, Hansa's trip to Amaranth Farms, going to the Quin Compound—had all been a dream. "You had to come back for me, didn't you?"

Umber shook his head. "You're an enjoyable sight to come home to," he said, with a grin that didn't loosen the tense knot in Hansa's belly as he remembered where Umber had been, and who with. It wasn't fair that Umber had Hansa for a leash, dragging him away from his lover.

"If you want to—"

He broke off with a yelp as Umber bit him on the rise of muscle on his chest, hard enough he knew it would bruise.

"Cupric," Umber said, the word sharp, "Is. Not. My. Lover. Never was. Get that through your head."

"Well, I'm sorry!" Hansa shouted, shoving Umber back to make space for the argument they were apparently about to have. "Apparently your leaving me sleeping and going to Amaranth to tumble into bed with him gave me the wrong impression. Maybe he's just a really good lay—Abyss knows he has more experience than I do. But if that's the case then—*ow!*" That last as Umber shut him up by biting him again. "Then tell me! Tell me what I've misunderstood."

Umber sat up, anger hot in his blue eyes, but an expression of sadness on his face. It was enough to make Hansa draw a breath, and say more softly, "Just tell me what's going on. Please."

Umber started to stand up, and Hansa couldn't stop himself from reaching for him and pulling him back down to the bed. For once, sex was one of the furthest things from his mind; he refused to let Umber walk away until they had figured this out.

Umber didn't fight him, but put his head down on the bed and closed his eyes to draw a deep breath. Hansa wished he had Umber's ability to read minds, and could pull from Umber's head whatever was bothering him.

He started at another angle. "How did you and Cupric meet?"

Umber's eyes half opened, just enough for him to glare. "I don't remember, and why do you care?"

Because Hansa was trying to imagine the riot of conflicted emotions that could come to the surface in this situation. For the first time in a decade, Umber had been confronted with the man who had been his first—whatever they had been. Maybe not lovers, but according to Cupric, Umber hadn't wanted to leave. Maybe that was normal. Maybe, to a kid who was only fourteen or fifteen, it had felt like love; recognizing it as something different now didn't mean old wounds instantly disappeared.

"If you really want to console my poor, trampled heart, can we have sex now?" Umber asked, the tone too tight to be properly teasing.

"Are you going to bite me again?"

Umber gave one of his half smirk, half smile expressions. It was a little forced, but the effort was there. "You might find that you like it."

The quip was enough to bring Hansa's Abyssi dreams to mind, which made him blush, which made Umber laugh. Suspicious, Hansa asked, "Can you see my dreams?"

Again, that mostly-smile. Umber nodded. "Mmm-hmm."

"Can I ever see yours?" He could use a little variation from his recent selection of nocturnal terrors.

Umber froze. It was just an instant before he shrugged and suggested, "If you're enjoying the Abyssi dreams, I can give you new things to dream about," but Hansa saw it and recognition left a cold lump in his stomach.

More firmly, Hansa asked, "Can I ever see your dreams?"

Umber sighed, as if bored with the academic discussion. "I've heard people say the bond can allow that, yes. But right *now*, sleep is not the highest thing on my—"

"*Have* I ever seen your dreams?"

Again, there was the briefest moment where Umber's impatient but sultry expression cracked. "Hansa—"

"*Have I?*" Too many pieces were beginning to settle into place, and forming a picture Hansa absolutely needed to fully see and understand. He squashed the guilt he felt at the panic he could see in Umber's gaze in that unguarded instant, his guilt at pushing a question upon someone he knew couldn't lie. Not outright. Umber could evade and he could manipulate words and he could twist the truth, but like Abyssi and Numini, spawn couldn't lie flat-out.

"Drop it, Hansa," Umber said, all pretense gone now.

Hansa dropped that question because he didn't need Umber to answer it; his refusal said enough. Instead, he went back to an earlier thought. "How did you meet Cupric?"

"I told you, I don't remember," Umber snapped. He rolled over, set his feet to the floor, and started toward the door.

Hansa followed. The dreams made sense now—as did the fact that he never dreamed of the Abyssumancer except when Umber was with him. In Hansa's mind, "Abyssumancer" had translated to the only mancer he had ever been intimate with, but the base of the dreams—the situation and emotions—weren't his.

If those dreams had been Umber's—and they had started as soon as he had seen Cupric again . . .

"Dear Numen, Umber," Hansa swore, slapping a hand to the door to hold it shut before the other man could disappear through it. "Why didn't you *tell* me? I—"

"There's nothing to *tell*," Umber shouted.

"Nothing to . . ." Hansa trailed off, horrified. "I *left* you with him! I thought maybe you loved him, maybe you were just looking for variation, I thought a thousand different things but I *left* you with the man—with the *monster* who chained you down, tortured you, and raped you, when you were fifteen years old."

"It's none of your business. And it's over—"

"How over can it be, when just yesterday you were back in his bed?" Hansa asked, horrified. The visions of blood in his mind at that moment had nothing to do with dreams of the Abyss, and certainly weren't sexual. No, they involved Cupric, drawn and quartered, dying slowly. Hansa was pretty sure he could do it with his bare hands.

"Stay away from him," Umber whispered. "Hansa, please. I'm begging you here. *Begging.* I will get down on my knees if you need me to. Stay away from him."

Hansa might not be morally and legally aligned with the 126 anymore, but he had spent several years hunting mancers professionally. He knew what he was doing. If he prepared properly, he could—

"No!" Umber shouted, hearing the thought before Hansa had even completed it. "Hansa, stop and think for a moment."

Oh, he was thinking all right. Thinking of all the ways he could murder that man.

Umber caught both his shoulders, and pushed him back against the wall hard enough to knock his breath out. "Cupric may very well be the strongest Abyssumancer in Kavet right now," he said, voice low and cold. "Assuming he didn't kill you outright, which he might not only because it would kill me and he *does* still want Terre Verte's favor at the moment, if he finds himself in genuine jeopardy—*especially* at the hands of someone trying to protect me—what is he going to do?"

Finally, the dangerous truth sank in. Hansa could hear Cupric's voice in his head, saying, *I had two boons of Umber once. It was years ago, but the connection lingers . . .*

"Numendamned Abyssumancer," Hansa whispered.

"I got away from him once because the Quin came around and he panicked," Umber said. "I changed my name—not just the name I was using. I went through the necessary ritual to bind my power to a new name—so he wouldn't be able to summon me by blood. He doesn't want a third boon and a permanent bond any more than I do, but he's powerful enough that, whatever form the bond takes, it won't be one-sided. It might lean in his favor. If you force him to, he will risk it."

Hansa tried to swallow the lump of his heart that had wedged in his throat. "I won't do anything stupid," he said.

"I notice you're not promising to just leave him alone," Umber said. "Remember even if he doesn't have time to demand and seal a third boon, his calling me by blood would probably be enough to renew the second one. If you kill him, it might kill me. And you."

"If I see an opportunity to kill him, quickly enough and surely enough that I know he won't have a chance to call you, I'll do it," Hansa said. "I don't think I could stop myself. But I won't seek him out."

Umber nodded, slowly. He could read Hansa's mind; he knew that was all he was going to get.

"Will you agree not to tell the others?"

"We don't have to tell them everything," Hansa said, "but you have to tell them *something*. I trusted Cupric because I thought you did. They need to be on their guard. Alizarin and Cadmia especially need to know that bastard is dangerous."

"Fine, then," Umber said. "Tell them whatever you think you need to, as long as they know they can't go after him."

"You don't want to tell them yourself?" Hansa

asked. "I won't share anything you don't want me to, but if it's vague, it will sound stronger coming from you. I'll come across as the jealous lover."

Umber sighed. "Hansa . . ."

For a moment, Hansa thought Umber was objecting to the self-description Hansa had used, and then his common sense came up with the rest of the answer.

Even knowing the danger Cupric could pose, Umber hadn't told anyone. Maybe he just didn't want to share; Hansa could understand not wanting to talk about these things. But what if—

"Don't," Umber said, before Hansa could ask, *What were the first two boons?*

"Okay," he said instead. The painful compulsion caused by the magic of the boons had been enough to send Hansa down to the lowest level of the Abyss, and Hansa knew from personal experience that a boon could come with many caveats and provisions. If Cupric had included in his demands a clause about what Umber was or wasn't allowed to tell others, then Umber couldn't break that silence.

Again, Hansa thought about killing the Abyssumancer.

"Can we talk to Cadmia and Alizarin *later?*" Umber asked, voice dull with fatigue. "Right now, I want to go back to bed."

Hansa nodded. "Do you want to be alone?" Given the nature of the memories he had just dredged up,

Hansa could understand Umber needing some time *without* another man in bed with him.

In response, the spawn looked at him with tired resignation. "What? No," he said bluntly. "Stop thinking that way about me. If *you* need alone time at some point, I understand, but that's not what I want when I feel like shit. I want sex. A lot of it. With you. Now. Idiot Quin."

At least the last bit was back to its usual good-natured teasing tone. Even so, Hansa asked, "Are you sure you're up to it?" Umber looked exhausted.

"I have faith we'll find a way."

While Hansa sometimes agonized over his emotional state when he was with Umber, it was no metaphor to say the touch of the half-Abyssi's skin was magic. They started slow and leisurely, each of them aching with fatigue, but each caress was a spark set to kindling. Where their bodies came together, power flowed, and as if waking from weeks of famine to find a banquet before them, they devoured each other.

At one point, Umber hesitated, looking at Hansa with eyes that seemed to glisten wetly. Hansa opened his mouth to ask, then closed it and instead reached up his hand. Umber tensed as Hansa brushed a thumb over his cheek, acknowledging the tears without challenging them.

Then Umber ducked his head, as if the moment of honesty was too much for him.

No matter what his horny body voted, Hansa's first instinct was to stop and try to talk it out before anything else. Remembering Umber's words earlier, he instead pulled the other man's lean, trembling frame down snugly against his own, then rolled them both until Umber's head lay on the pillow and Hansa braced above him.

"This okay?" he asked.

Umber nodded sharply and pulled him closer.

Afterwards, as they collapsed against the pillows, waiting for their breathing and heartbeats to calm, Umber breathed, "Thank you."

It was Hansa's turn to feel awkward with words. "My pleasure," he managed to say.

His head tucked down against Hansa's shoulder, hiding his face, Umber murmured, "Spoiling me. What will I do when we get the bond broken and you realize your life would be simpler without a half-Abyssi pervert in it?" Umber spoke with the joking tone he used for most potentially-emotional declarations, and the words shot through Hansa, hot and cold at the same time.

At another time, Hansa might have made a joke of his own in response—something like, *Probably find a partner with fewer hang-ups and more experience.* Instead, he asked honestly, "What will *I* do, if we get the bond broken and I feel exactly the same way about you as I do now?"

Umber had used the word *when*. Hansa saw him flinch at the word *if*.

"Don't you *want* to know?" Umber asked, lifting his head. "Don't you want to know you're making your own choices because they're yours, not because there's magic in your brain telling you what to do?"

"People *change*," Hansa replied. "They change because circumstances change, or they learn something new. They change because something scares them or because they lose someone—or meet someone. One way or another, I've changed, and if losing the bond undoes all that's happened the last few months, how is that any more real? How is erasing everything I've gone through and everything I've thought about it, and perhaps digging out of my heart the people I've come to care about, any less the magic manipulating me than the original bond might have been?"

He could feel Umber withdrawing emotionally even though the spawn didn't move away physically. In fact, his fingers tightened in Hansa's hair, like an unconscious desire to hold him closer even as his words tried to do the opposite. "You don't understand," Umber said.

Hansa pushed himself up, putting a few inches of physical distance between them. Then the image came to him of a fourteen-year-old boy, scarred and trapped by an Abyssumancer. And before that, of a much younger child, who never felt he needed to question why his mother walked away from him and never returned. In Umber's earliest experiences, magical compulsion and Abyssal drives were the only reason anyone had ever claimed to love him.

Hansa knew better than to say any of that aloud, but his thinking twice about saying something never made any difference.

Umber bristled, and as if on a cue they moved away from each other, reaching for clothes like armor.

Hansa pushed to his feet—then stumbled, feeling as if the ground had shaken under him. Umber likewise seemed off-balance, and had to catch himself against the bed.

"Damn, damn, damn," Umber hissed, dropping his head as if dizzy.

"What?" Unchecked emotions hadn't taken their feet out from under them. It was magic.

"We must still have something feeding from us," Umber said. "We might not have noticed it if we had both been in good shape to begin with, but after Cupric—" He broke off, shook his head, and tried again. "I thought it was just him, that he had taken too much power from me and drained you in the process, but if that were the case we would be doing better now."

Contemplation of their relationship, future, or lack thereof could wait. Unless they literally wanted to spend the rest of their lives in bed to make up for lost power—something that only sounded pleasant as

CHAPTER 22

LYDIE

Lydie had returned from Amaranth Farms with a pounding headache, and unlike Hansa and Umber and Cadmia and Alizarin, she didn't have an easy solution. She wasn't tied to the Abyss; sex wasn't the answer to all her problems. Or *any* of her problems.

Sleep and a meal helped. Having good food available in ample amounts helped a *lot*. While the others had some private time in their rooms, Lydie ate a large meal, then walked along the cliffs behind Umber's house, brushed the snow from a bench, and imagined the ocean waves were washing over her. The spirits were quietest here, which meant she could almost hear herself think.

an idle fantasy—they needed to figure out what was going on. "If not Cupric, who? Or what?"

"My spell work is all based on raw power and instinct, not real sorcery or ritual," Umber said. "We need a mancer to help figure this out—and we don't have one."

"What about Lydie?" Umber quirked a brow at him, skeptical about how Hansa expected a necromancer to help them with Abyssal power. "The Abyss is also the realm of the dead. And Lydie was able to tie her power briefly to the Abyss. Do you think . . ." He trailed off, self-conscious about his attempt to suggest a solution involving powers he generally knew less about than anyone else.

But Umber looked contemplative. "We could ask," he said. "Good idea."

She was still there, half dozing despite the chill wind, when Hansa and Umber approached. Neither seemed as refreshed as she had expected.

Umber nodded to Hansa, as if cuing him to begin.

Hansa spoke haltingly, uncertainly, but clearly enough for her to grasp the problem. He explained about their power—oversharing a little about the bond, in her opinion, but that was fine—and how they had thought Cupric was responsible, but now believed he couldn't be.

Lydie paused him there to check one thing. "Cupric is an experienced Abyssumancer. He isn't ignorant of the dangers of the bond or power exhaustion, so he wouldn't have done something like this accidentally. So you're saying that, despite Terre Verte's injunction, you still thought he was the most likely cause of such a severe drain on your power that it might have killed both of you?"

"Yes," Hansa said, as if that was all that *needed* to be said.

Lydie started to ask more, then realized Hansa was right. That was enough to warn her that, despite all his attempts at jovial charm and startled but affable response to Umber's supposedly-unprovoked attack, he was a dangerous man.

"Umber says we need a mancer to look at what's going on, and maybe fix it," Hansa continued. He glanced at the spawn as he said it, and Umber nodded, his expression grave and drawn. "We can't go to an

Abyssumancer, but the Abyss is also the realm of the dead, so I thought maybe . . ." He trailed off, averting his gaze, as if now feeling embarrassed either by his limited knowledge of sorcery or his attempt to dabble in it.

"When a necromancer refers to the realm of the dead," Lydie said, thinking aloud as much as attempting to educate, "she generally means the one that overlaps the realm of the living." Hansa looked at her blankly, so she tried a metaphor. "Imagine you're in an open field. The wind is blowing, so the field is full of air. The sun is shining, so the same space is also full of light. Then a rancher passes by, so it's also full of the smell of horseflesh. Those things all take up the same space, yet take up no space at all. A herd of deer can fill up that field. The realm of death is like the air and light and smell, and the realm of life is the field itself and the deer. They overlap."

She was rather proud of herself for the description, and the way that Hansa nodded, his eyes widening a little with surprise at his own understanding.

Umber pressed, "Surely in that way the realm of death overlaps the Abyss and the Numen, too."

The mention of the Numen seemed to stir a cold breeze around Lydie, raising gooseflesh on her arms, though she couldn't say why. She rubbed at them and admitted, "In *theory*."

"Could you examine Hansa for any trace of this . . . death realm?" Umber asked.

"Every living creature is touched by death," Lydie explained. "When we get sick or injured, the trace grows. When someone near to us, emotionally or physically, dies, we pick up a taint from that death as well."

"Would you be able to see if there's anything that doesn't belong?"

Umber wasn't going to drop it, and an unsettling thought had just occurred to Lydie: she had almost pointed out, *And I recently linked Hansa to the realm of the dead to help him talk to his friend.* Could she be responsible for this?

"I can try."

Once more, she cast a circle of salt and earth and invited Hansa inside it so she could ensure anything she sensed came from him and not the rampant powers outside that circle. Umber, thankfully, didn't question how much of the salt he had originally purchased she had gone through; she didn't explain that she had needed to cast a true circle lately just to *sleep*. Umber's house wasn't haunted specifically, she didn't think, but the spirits in Kavet were restless and noisy lately, disturbed by all that was going on.

She focused on Hansa, and tried to sift through the power-signatures of the dead, which adhered to all the living like burrs and tree sap.

There was Hansa's own tie to the realm of the dead. All mortals owed a death, or so the saying went. Lydie's power gave her the ability to stave it off for a while in the case of illness or injury, but even she couldn't make a man immortal.

Jenkins' death clung to Hansa as a bright spot, heightened by their recent connection. As Lydie examined that bond, she noted Jenkins himself lingering outside the circle, watching anxiously. She didn't see any way the tie she had created could be enabling some Abyssi or mancer to drain away Hansa's power, thankfully.

There were other deaths on this man—so many, including too many that shone with other power. Mancers he had arrested and therefore helped kill in his previous life. She felt his fiancée's death, in the grip of the Numini and the icy water of the Kavet harbor. And there was another death—*Oh*.

"There it is," she said. It was so obvious, now that she had pushed the other distractions aside.

"Why is it?" Hansa asked.

"Hush. I think I can break it. Let me just . . ." She followed the twisting rope of power that connected Hansa to one of the dead, one who was far away, in a cavern Lydie could only barely make out . . .

The world was heat and ash, shadow and fang. He still mourned his discovery that he wasn't an Abyssi, but Modigliani had given him bones—old, powerful bones, which had belonged to the previous king of the Abyss—and working with them helped the human remember what he really was. Not Abyssi. So much more.

Black as the deepest cave on the mortal realm, those bones, which absorbed any light cast near them and deepened the darkness of his chamber.

Now they are mine.

With a discarded Abyssi claw, he cut his palm. As he worked blood and magic into the bone, it began to soften like clay under his fingertips. He could use it. Shape it. He did so once before. The blue one taught him how . . . he should know the blue one's name.

"Don't exhaust yourself," Modigliani warned, but the Abyssi seemed far away and he brushed it aside.

He couldn't hunt like an Abyssi and feeding like a human wasn't satisfying, either, which meant his center was a constant, gnawing void, filled only by scraps drawn from a tentative tie to the mortal realm. Working with the bones was the first time he felt truly good, even more than when he felt when the Abyssi's body slid along his.

"There," Lydie said again. She felt sorry for the poor, hungry soul at the base of the Abyss, but that didn't give him a right to kill Hansa and Umber by feeding on them—as he inevitably would, if the link weren't severed. She focused on the strands and began to pick at them.

The last one held, stubbornly, but—

"Hello, Arylide," Modigliani said, in a singsong, predatory tone. "Necromancer, you are gazing quite far past your own territory."

As the king of the Abyss turned his attention her way, Lydie beheld him in full. Through her link to the souls of the dead and his dominion over them, she gazed on the deepest beast in his true form—

Lydie sputtered, opening her eyes, then closing them swiftly against the immediate stinging sensation. She was cold and wet and what happened?

She smeared a hand over her eyes, wiping away the wetness that wasn't tears before cautiously opening them again, then gasped and scrambled back from the darkness that loomed over her. Living shadow, formless, but somehow possessing teeth and claws and eyes in the darkness—

"Alizarin, give her space," Cadmia's voice said, before Cadmia herself stepped between Lydie and the form that must be the Abyssi. How could Cadmia stand to be near it, have it behind her, much less touch it and make love to it?

Lydie sat up and wrapped her arms around herself. "I'm all wet," she said. Her throat was raw, and the words came out with a rasp.

"We couldn't wake you," Umber said, pushing forward. "At first I thought we should wait for you to come out of it on your own, but then you started screaming. We managed to reach Cadmia, and she remembered your saying something about ocean water disrupting your power."

She might have complained that they didn't need to pour the entire bucket over her head, but it had worked, freeing her from that infernal vision. That was what mattered.

"Thank you," she croaked. "I was—"

Her voice choked off before she could finish. She scrubbed her hands over her eyes, uselessly.

"You've said food helps, too, right?" Cadmia asked practically. "And I'll make some tea, for your throat."

They moved from her soggy circle to the table in the kitchen, where Cadmia offered bread, apples and honey as the quickest thing she could provide.

"Just bread," Lydie said. "No fruit, no honey." She had to gag the words out around a wave of revulsion, though normally she liked both.

"Abyssumancers too deep in their work often develop a revulsion for tree-fruit and honey," Hansa supplied, as Lydie stared at the bowl of apples as if it had betrayed her. She tried to imagine the crisp, white fruit she normally loved, and her gorge rose. "They're among the offerings Numenmancers often have on their altars."

Did that mean she should follow her instincts and avoid those foods until the aversion resolved on its own, or that forcing herself to eat them would help distance her from the Abyssal taint? She didn't know, but the bile in her throat as she imagined choking down an apple made the decision for her. She couldn't do it.

"Just bread," she said again, turning away from the fruit bowl.

"What happened?" Umber asked, once Lydie had taken her first bites of food.

"I—" Her breath caught. "Bones," she said aloud, struggling to remember the vision, which was fading like a nightmare. "I saw bones, black bones. Someone was . . ." She trailed off and shook her head. She had seen through someone else's eyes, but hadn't known who that someone was, or what he was doing with the bones. "He was hungry. For some reason he couldn't hunt properly, so he had to feed on a mortal. He was linked to you, Hansa, siphoning power from you. Then he turned, and I saw the Abyssi—" She caught herself before she imagined the creature too clearly, and forcibly wiped the image from her mind. "I think I severed the bond, though. How do you two feel?"

"Better," Hansa answered immediately. "I wouldn't have been able to say there was anything extra stealing power from me before, but I can feel the difference now."

"Whatever it was probably latched onto you while we were still in the Abyss," Umber speculated. "It couldn't still be Antioch, could it? Or—"

Lydie heard the distinctive *crunch* of teeth biting into an apple and turned her head to the Abyssi behind her. The apple was clear in her vision, now missing a large chunk; she saw it tumble to the ground as the dark haze seized and contorted, taking on a gray-green tinge.

"Rin? Are you all right?" Cadmia asked, eyes wide, stepping forward to wrap arms around that strange, fluid blackness.

If the Abyssi responded, Lydie couldn't hear it, but she saw the rising alarm on Cadmia's face. Umber also ran forward and put a hand on the creature.

Hansa stayed back with Lydie and said, "I know Abyssi don't eat fruit, but he wouldn't have bitten it if it were poison to him . . . would he?"

Watching sickly colors writhe through the shadowy power, Lydie wasn't so sure. Umber seemed to be pounding on the hazy smoke now, the way one might pound a man's back to dislodge something from his throat.

Exactly like that. And after a few moments, the bite of apple came back out and tumbled to the floor.

Lydie rubbed her eyes as Umber held up his arm and said, "Here."

This time the sound wasn't crisp and dry, but wet and meaty, and what disappeared was a chunk of flesh from Umber's forearm. Lydie saw the glint of bone in the wound before the blood flowed in and she turned away, gagging—and attempting to catch the stumbling Hansa, who had gone sheet pale as the pain reached him through his bond to the Abyssi-spawn.

When Umber pulled back, grabbed a dish towel, and pressed it to the fist-sized hole in his arm, Hansa fainted entirely. Lydie tried to support him as well as she could on his way down so he didn't slam his head against the wooden floor.

"Rin?" Cadmia asked again.

His one-word response, *Hunting*, reached Lydie like a whisper on the wind before the dark haze disappeared. He was gone.

What was that about?

Hansa groaned and shuddered as he pushed himself to a sitting position at the same time that Umber swayed and collapsed into a chair, still gripping the towel tightly. It was entirely crimson now, and more dripped to the ground.

"Shouldn't that heal?" Lydie asked.

Umber nodded. "It will. It's just too deep to do so immediately. Hansa?"

Hansa managed to form the words, "That. Hurt." He drew another breath, and on a moment of abashment added, "You probably noticed."

"I noticed." Umber held up his bleeding arm with a grimace. "But my pain tolerance is higher than yours."

"What was that about?" Lydie asked again.

"An Abyssi being an Abyssi?" Umber speculated, though he sounded doubtful. "We were talking about apples and he got curious?"

"With the way he usually regards our food," Hansa said, voice still breathy from pain, "that seems like me getting curious and taking a big bite out of writhing maggots."

Lydie's stomach, already unsteady from her mental trip to the Abyss and brief glimpse of Umber's flesh-bared bone, took a turn.

"I'll ask him once he's back from hunting," Cadmia said, clearly unconvinced that this bloody escapade had been the result of an idle whim. She looked at the window, outside which dawn had brightened to true morning. "In the meantime, Hansa, are you well enough to return to work? Rose helped me brush your illness off as a minor flu from your hard travels, but the longer you're away, the more gossip will start to amplify your symptoms and come up with alternative explanations. The last thing you want is for your coworkers to insist you have some sighted monk examine you for lingering magical malevolence when you walk through the door."

Hansa nodded grimly. "I can go back." He rubbed absently at the unmarked skin of his own arm, as if to assure himself it was attached. "Actually, even with this, I feel better than I have in days."

Lydie looked away quickly as Umber pulled the towel off his arm to examine his wound. There was no gush and spatter of blood, so she cautiously glanced back, and found herself immediately fascinated by what she saw. The injury was still dolefully deep, but clean now, like the wound of a corpse that had been washed of gore. Lydie could see new muscle fibers growing and reaching across the gap like the tendrils of a grasping plant.

"I'll go back to the Cobalt Hall," Cadmia said. "By now, Rose will have spread the word of what she saw among those she trusts among the Order of A'hknet.

I suspect someone will seek out either you or me, Hansa."

"To either share important information, or accuse us of sorcery," Hansa grumbled, but the words didn't sound like an argument.

Given they were both risking themselves, Lydie sighed and said, "I think someone or something powerful has been trying to reach me. *Too* powerful—I can't understand it when it speaks, and it knocks down all my shields so I end up drowning in the voices of the dead. I would like to work on a ritual so I can try to communicate with it, whatever it is. Given how this ritual went, I would feel better if someone were on hand in case I need help to snap out of it."

"I'll be here," Umber offered.

"I would like to get a second read on what happened with you and Hansa, too," Cadmia said, looking at Umber. "Could Cupric—"

"No," Hansa and Lydie said simultaneously. They exchanged a glance. Lydie was sure Hansa knew more than she did in terms of specifics, but he didn't elaborate. She added, "Cupric is good at pretending to be friendly, but he isn't on our side, and shouldn't be trusted." She held Hansa's gaze while she said it, and saw gratitude and relief there. He nodded slightly, in agreement and thanks.

A captain of the 126 was not the kind of ally she had ever expected, and she wasn't entirely sure how to feel about it.

As Hansa returned to the Quin Compound late that morning, he discovered that masking his magical aura was much less work without an Abyssal parasite pulling power from him. Comparatively speaking, it was easy. Keeping to the story he and Cadmia had crafted about a flu and a faint was even easier.

The last time he had been in the building, Hansa hadn't been thinking about much of anything beyond the immediate task of getting the manuscript for Cupric, *not* thinking about Umber being with Cupric, and not passing out or losing the veils over his power. This time, he supposed his first task should be reporting to a superior officer.

He first attempted to locate Captain Montag, who had been put in charge of Company Four's remaining men after Captain Feldgrau's death, but the captains' office and mess were both empty. He had just decided to find General Norseth, who would be Hansa's supervisor once he took captainship of Company Four, when the same too-young guard who had greeted him during his nocturnal visit shouted his name.

"Hansa! Thank Nu—Eh." He cut off the swear, which could have earned him a formal reprimand had anyone who cared overheard. His anxious posture didn't change, though. "It's good you're here," he said instead. "We have an emergency."

"What's going on?" Hansa made an effort to ask the question with a straight face, as he thought, *What's going on that you know about?*

"There are rumors of a mancer gathering in the next few days," the guard said, speaking rapidly in a low voice. "Six men from Company Three went to investigate, including Captain Grash, and never checked back in. General Norseth and Captian Montag are missing now, too, and no one has heard anything from His Eminence Indathrone. I know you were on an assignment for him recently. Do you have any idea what is going on?"

Two captains and the general missing, plus another five men from Company Three. Hansa doubted it was a coincidence. Had Verte and his cronies killed them all?

"Is anyone else missing?" Hansa asked, making no effort to conceal the simmering rage he felt as he considered those deaths. It was irrational in part; these were men who would have killed *him*, Cadmia, Umber, and Lydie without a second thought. But they were also men he had served beside, whose only thought had been to protect the people of Kavet and earn a paycheck to provide for their families. They were ignorant, but ignorance could be *fixed*. Death couldn't be.

The younger guard let out a sound that could only be called a whimper. "I . . . I don't know, sir. That's not my . . . I'm not sure who to ask." *Except you*, his expression clearly said.

Hansa nodded, mentally preparing to take control. As he had told Umber, if Verte was planning an assault on the city, the 126 were the best defense Kavet had. If Verte was planning anything less bloody, Hansa being in charge was the best defense the mancers of Kavet had.

"Where did the captains and general disappear *from*?" he asked. "Did they go to investigate? Were they on the clock, or in their homes?"

If Verte had disposed of them when they trespassed on the property he had claimed and intended to protect, Hansa would still hate him for it, but he could also understand. The mancers there couldn't be faulted for killing someone who would have killed them. On the other hand, if Verte was systematically assassinating the higher-ranked members of the guard, Hansa would need to act to protect those who were left.

"I don't know?" the kid answered.

So late, hopefully not *too* late, Hansa understood something he hadn't even stopped to think about until that moment. Verte had left a note to delay the investigation and panic about Indathrone's death not to cover their escape at that time, but to keep the 126 from realizing there was a problem and mobilizing until he had effectively removed their command structure. He had, most likely, been planning this from the moment they left the Abyss. If not before.

"Who *does* know?" Another blank look. "You do work here, don't you? What company are you in?"

The guard ducked his head, then lifted it and cleared his throat and reported with a clear voice, "Soldier Gray of Company Four, Captain, sir. I was supposed to start yesterday, but then Captain Montag went missing. I've been trying to keep busy while waiting for an official assignment."

Yesterday, Hansa thought. He couldn't blame the young man for being new and confused in that case.

"Records," Hansa sighed. "There should be records of any missions. Have you seen the captains from companies two and five?"

Soldier Gray shook his head.

"Check the sign-in logs," Hansa ordered. "If they haven't signed in today, *go to their homes*. If they're there, bring them here to report immediately. Take a half dozen more senior soldiers with you, whoever you find first." Hansa didn't have the authority to give such orders, but there seemed to be no one present with the authority to override him, either. If someone was hunting these men, Hansa didn't want an extra moment to go by before he brought them in to warn them. He also didn't want to put anyone else in charge of reading records of tips and mission logs that might include more information than Hansa wanted the 126 to have. "In the meantime, I'm going to look at records in the captains' office."

The younger guard jumped to obey, and Hansa turned toward the captains' office and the massive filing cabinets therein. He wished he had any idea how they were organized.

He started searching first for recent missions, then changed his mind and went looking for a basic duty roster instead. He needed to establish how many men were missing.

Looking at the roster for Company Four made Hansa's eyes water. There were two new names at the bottom, including Gray's, but it also still included eleven black marks, striking out good men.

Hansa's own name had been crossed out in red ink, with a note added of, *Arrested for treason, conspiracy, sorcery, aiding and abetting a mancer, and serving as an accomplice to eleven counts of murder.*

There was another note below, where his name had been returned to the list, saying simply, *Cleared of all charges.* It might as well have said, *Just kidding!* Or maybe, *Oops! If we hadn't messed that one up, maybe we wouldn't have a homicidal ex-prince hunting down our senior officers!*

Despite dealing with mancers, losses to the guard were relatively rare. Disasters like what had happened with Dioxazine and Alizarin—and, apparently, Umber's mother—were almost unheard of.

"Hansa?" He looked up as Rinnman, a career-soldier who had stepped down as a lieutenant in Company Three due to a severe knee injury that left him relying on a crutch, said his name. Rinnman's temperament was decidedly more even than Gray's. "There's someone asking to see you."

"Show him in."

"It's a her, sir," Rinnman replied. "That old A'hknet bat from the market."

"Oh . . . her," Hansa sighed, bracing himself for an encounter from the elderly lady most Order of A'hknet followers knew as Mother Avignon, and most soldiers knew as a pain in the ass. The last time he had spoken to her, she had been giving him and Jenkins a hard time about borrowing her cart so they could lug an unconscious Abyssumancer back to the cells.

If she hadn't argued with them, that Abyssumancer might have remained unconscious long enough for them to get him safely locked away.

Don't think of that just now, he told himself. They

were courting allies from the Order of A'hknet. Having Mother Avignon come here was probably a *good* sign.

The lady Avignon looked back to where Rinnman was waiting at attention in the doorway. "Can we shut the door?"

Hansa nodded. Rinnman discreetly stepped out of the room and closed the door behind himself.

Once that was done, the old woman asked, "Mind if I sit? The cold gets to my back something fierce."

"Go ahead."

She lowered herself with agonizing slowness into the chair in the far corner as Hansa took a breath in, reminding himself again that despite his instinctive irritation with her based on previous encounters, she wouldn't have bothered to come to the compound just to give him a hard time.

"I heard a disquieting rumor," she said.

She paused, long enough Hansa suspected she was hoping to find out what he already knew before she spoke. Unfortunately, there were a great many possible disquieting rumors that might be around, some more or less hazardous to Hansa's health. He schooled his face to blandness. "Oh?"

For a while she stared at him. He cleared his throat, and she jumped.

"I'm sure you know that Rose is very dear to me. Like a daughter, almost. I believe you know her as well." She said the words almost idly, but they clearly had a deeper meaning intended, one he wasn't likely to miss. Hansa hadn't forgotten the woman who had told him how to summon Umber and demand a second boon.

He wondered how much she had shared with this old woman.

"I hope she's well," he said, his voice neutral. He wasn't about to incriminate himself while sitting in the captains' office in the Quinacridone Compound.

Another tsk of disappointment. "Are you even going to *ask* me about the rumor?"

"Are you going to *tell* me?"

"I want a written declaration of immunity," she said. At his expression, she added, "I've broken no . . . major . . . laws. I've hurt no one. My crimes against the Quin are all intellectual. Not that it makes a difference these days."

"I can give you my word that I have no desire to persecute someone for 'intellectual' crimes," Hansa said honestly. *Or for most actual crimes.* "And since you surely know that any written contract could be made to disappear in this establishment as if it never existed, my word should mean more to you than such a written declaration would. Especially if you are such a close friend of Rose's, and you and she have spoken recently."

Rose knew that the second boon to Umber had been far from the end of his meddling with magic.

The old woman paused to consider those words, and finally nodded.

"Some of the small-magic users among the Order of A'hknet have been contacted recently," she said. "Just some of them, of course. I suspect those being ignored are the frauds and charlatans with magic tricks instead of real magic. But never mind that. There is word of a meeting."

Hansa nodded slowly. "Do you have any details?"

She cleared her throat. "I suspect you already know of it. What I want to know is if it's true that Terre Verte is the one holding it." Despite his efforts, Hansa's face must have revealed something. The woman's face paled. "The Terre. He's *alive*? How is that possible? The man must be a century old, for one thing, and that's ignoring the fact that half of Kavet watched him die." She paused. "Twice."

I'm an idiot.

Again. How often did this conclusion come to him?

"I'm sorry, ma'am," he said, considering again how old this hunched lady must be. "You knew Verte?"

"There aren't many of us around now who were old enough to remember and understand those days," she said. "What we went through is the kind of trial that tends to shorten the life span as well as the memory, and it's been illegal to talk about any of it in the years since. But you don't forget seeing your prince's blood splashed across the cobbles like . . .

well, like I imagine you must have seen when Jenkins was slain."

The blunt description, in addition to the implication, was enough to make Hansa tense. They had met Verte in the Abyss; they had been told he had been resurrected. Hansa had never stopped to wonder how he had died.

"Please. Tell me whatever you know."

Her eyes narrowed. "You tell me first—is it true? And if it *is* true, how is he back in this world? The dead don't just come back, and even if they drift across to where a necromancer can see them, reanimating them in mortal form is nearly impossible. One necromancer told me it might be possible to bind a spirit to a dead body, even if that body wasn't the spirit's own flesh, but he didn't have much hope for it even if the spirit wasn't three score years lost to the Abyss." The more she spoke, the more soft and rapid her speech became, until Hansa found himself leaning forward to listen.

"I want to have this conversation, but I think we should do so somewhere else," Hansa suggested, all too aware of Rinnman standing outside the door, and Gray scrambling to find as many ranked officers as he could.

"I agree," Mother Avignon agreed. "It shouldn't be anywhere at the docks, either. My children all like to eavesdrop, and will note who I meet with."

"The Drunken Horse," Hansa suggested. The casual restaurant was respectable enough for no one to

question Hansa or Cadmia going there, and specialized in private rooms with large tables, which were
popular for impromptu celebrations and gatherings.

The old woman nodded. "An hour before sunset?"
she suggested.

"We'll be there."

She noted the plural with a raised brow, but didn't
question it. Instead she stood, the process appearing
twice as painful as sitting had. Hansa walked around
the desk to offer her a hand, but she waved him off.
"The scars ache in the cold," she said. "Especially the
brand."

"It occurs to me I don't know your full name?"
Hansa admitted as he saw the woman to the door.

"Ginger Avignon," she said. "Or Ginger Cremnitz,
among some of the order who insist on using my
maiden name."

She scowled at their impertinence, which might
have amused Hansa if the name hadn't startled him.
He had seen it quite recently, on a manuscript sought
by Terre Verte. Only there, it had called her Ginger
Cremnitz of the Quinacridone.

"Yes?" she said, seeing the surprise in his face.

He shook his head. "We'll talk about it later."

"This evening," she confirmed, before adding in
an almost-absent way, "That should give you time to
talk it over with Cadmia and the spawn, and whoever
else you're associating with these days."

CHAPTER 24

CADMIA

After a frustrating day at the Cobalt Hall, aggravated by her worry over Alizarin, Cadmia was happy to get a message from Hansa telling her they were all going to meet at the Drunken Horse for supper.

When she arrived, she found Umber lounging against the outer wall chatting with a passing flower-seller. He glanced up and met her gaze briefly, nodded toward the door, then looked away without further acknowledgement.

Assuming he had his reasons, Cadmia followed his lead and stepped inside. The hostess recognized her, greeted her warmly by name, and informed her that the others for her meeting hadn't arrived yet but a private table had been reserved and she was welcome to sit.

Interesting.

The hostess was wrong. One of her dinner party had arrived—as Cadmia closed the door behind herself, she saw Alizarin on the opposite side of the room playing idly with the flame of an oil lamp, which danced cobalt whenever he blew a trickle of breath on it.

He turned to her with a grin and she tossed herself into his arms, exclaiming, "Are you all right?"

He snugged his arms and tail around her and she leaned against him, hungry for the feel of his body against hers even though it had only been a few hours. Dear Numen, sometimes she felt like she was turning into an Abyssi, while Alizarin was becoming more and more human.

"I looked for you at the house first and Umber told me to come here," Alizarin said.

His color had improved since he had first bitten the apple—Cadmia hadn't realized his fur could change color until it went a strange pale green color—but his ears and tail still drooped and the lines of his face held an expression of deep disappointment.

"You seem sad," she observed.

"I wanted an apple."

"Because we were talking about them?" Alizarin had never expressed interest in human food, disdaining it all as dirt. Cadmia had accepted that as part of his personality even before realizing that he was apparently physically incapable of swallowing fruit.

He shook his head.

"Rin, honey, you look like you're thinking a whole lot. Is there something you want to talk about?"

He paused to try to puzzle out his thoughts, but after a minute again said only, "I wanted an apple," in a small voice.

When the door opened next, Cadmia pulled back hastily, trying not to look like she was talking to and snuggling with an invisible figure. Thankfully, it was just Hansa, who dropped heavily into a chair with a sigh.

"I feel better than yesterday," he announced, "but I'm still worn-out. Thanks for coming, Cadmia. Did Umber tell you why?"

"He said we were meeting with someone from the Order of A'hknet." Umber had apparently visited Hansa at lunch and received the news then; he had passed it on to her.

Hansa nodded. "Ginger Avignon, or Ginger *Cremnitz* as she used to be called."

Cadmia knew Mother; of *course* she did. She had even known her first, last and maiden name, but had heard them used so rarely she never connected them to the names written in clean black ink until Hansa said them with such weight.

"Umber and Lydie are checking the perimeter to make sure the Order isn't planning anything unpleasant," Hansa continued. "The last time there was any hint of sorcery near Mother Avignon, you'll remember, another member of her order instantly ran to the One-Twenty-Six."

"To me, actually," Cadmia said, feeling her mouth twist at the recollection. "How are things at the Quin Compound?"

Hansa let out a half sigh, half growl. "I left two captains with orders to sleep at the compound until we figure out what happened to the *rest* of them, which raised all sorts of questions about why it was safe for me to leave on my own. Thankfully I seem to have been jumped from lieutenant to general, so no one's going to overrule me." He scrubbed a palm over his jaw. "I also left men in charge of determining what applicants were being considered to fill vacant spots, and, in the most morbid thing I had to do today, I assigned four men to start discreetly looking into President Indathrone's whereabouts." He looked up at Alizarin. "They won't find anything, right?"

The Abyssi, who had gone back to exploring the room when Cadmia had turned away, shook his head. Hansa had wanted to double-check for surety's sake, but he hadn't been overly concerned; if Alizarin said the body was gone, it was *gone*.

He did, however seem concerned as Alizarin picked up a ceramic dish shaped like a beehive from the center of the table.

"Please don't do that again," he said. The Abyss's

tail drooped. "Are you craving human food lately, or are you just bored?"

"Abyssi can't eat dirt," Alizarin replied, putting the jar back down.

"I've noticed."

Mother Avignon arrived just then, leaning heavily on her walking stick. Cadmia jumped up to help her to her chair; as she eased herself to a seat, the old woman remarked, "Rose told me I should expect you, but I wasn't sure if I should believe her. People say no one is more devout than a convert, and after you left the Order of A'hknet that saying appeared true."

Cadmia wasn't sure how to answer that. Officially, she had joined the Order of Napthol after their healers had saved her lover, Cinnabar's, life—but that had been an excuse. She had felt stifled in her life as "Scarlet Paynes' daughter," where everyone anticipated that she, too, would grow up to follow the world's oldest profession.

"Have you heard from Cinnabar?" she asked, following the train of thought. Cinnabar had ceased to be her lover when she pledged herself to the Napthol, but he had remained her friend. He had fled the city after his testimony had sent the Quin after Xaz.

"He's settled in an A'hknet meetinghouse in Tamar. He—" She broke off and her eyes locked on the door, which had just opened to admit another member of their party.

Not one they had invited. At least, not one *Cadmia*

had invited. At first, she couldn't make herself do anything but stare at the seemingly-young man who she knew was at least decades old, and whose copper eyes glowed as if molten. Out of the corner of her eye, she saw Hansa shove himself to standing and scramble back as if faced with a poisonous bug. Alizarin stepped up and wrapped his tail around Cadmia protectively.

Of all people, Ginger was the first to find her voice and say, "Na—*Naples*?"

Naples—it couldn't be Naples, he was dead, Alizarin had killed him, but somehow it was him—also appeared taken off guard by the stammered words. Still framed in the open doorway, he asked, "Do I know you?"

Hansa gasped out, "You're dead. *Why are you not dead?*"

His words, too loud and carrying, broke Cadmia from her trance. Much as she didn't want to close herself in a room with the Abyssumancer they had killed on their quest to retrieve Terre Verte, she wanted even less for their conversation to reach unsympathetic ears.

"Keep your voice down," she said to Hansa as she pulled away from Alizarin and shut the door, barely giving Naples a chance to move into the room first. "Naples, take a seat, and kindly explain to us why you're not dead."

The Abyssumancer swung himself into a chair, but his entire response was, "It seemed like the thing to do." His copper eyes rested then on Alizarin, who was watching the no-longer-dead mancer and growling lightly. "Nice to see you, too, Alizarin. Modigliani sends his regards."

Alizarin swallowed his growl and swished his tail nervously. Having Naples reference the king of the Abyss seemed a thing worth being nervous over.

Ginger's patience snapped. Her voice almost a shriek, she demanded, *What is going on?*

All three of them looked to her. Cadmia wondered if this was the kind of situation where introducing people even made sense, but she tried. "This is—"

"I know who he *is*," she said.

"And who in the Abyss are *you?*" Naples snapped.

Ginger flinched as if he had slapped her, looking momentarily not like the grizzled, powerful matriarch of the local A'hknet community and more like the girl she must once have been.

The door opened again, this time admitting Umber, who instantly began a string of profanity directed at Naples. Cadmia once more had to hastily close the door.

"We were just getting to why he isn't dead," Hansa volunteered as Umber stiffly walked past Naples to join Hansa.

"The last time I saw you," Ginger said, "you had just been devoured by an Abyssi."

Naples leaned back in his chair, and put his feet up on the one next to him. "That would be surprising,

since to my recollection that only ever happened recently." He shot a look to Alizarin. "And you weren't with us at the time."

"But . . . but . . ." Ginger couldn't seem to get the words out.

Cadmia cleared her throat. "Naples, did you and Ginger know each other *before* you ended up in the Abyss?"

Naples jumped so badly he knocked over the chair he had propped his legs on, sending it scattering loudly across the floor. *"Ginger? Ginger Cremnitz?"*

"Avignon, these days," she said coolly.

Cadmia was more than a little amused to hear how dazed Naples sounded as he said inanely, "At least you didn't marry that prat of a doctor." He leaned forward to study Ginger's face. Had they been the same age when they last met, when Naples had been the young man he still appeared?

Lydie was the last of their expected guests to arrive. Unlike everyone else in the room, she walked in, looked around, closed the door, and didn't appear remotely upset or surprised as she said, "Oh, you found the dead man!"

"Who in the Abyss is *she?*" Naples asked.

Alizarin was smiling in a way that showed too many teeth. "Necromancer," he said.

Cadmia felt a similar smile spread across her own face as she wondered aloud, "How dead *are* you, Naples?"

"I'm not dead!" Naples objected, pushing to his feet.

"*Sit*," Lydie snapped.

Naples sat, only to then shove himself back up.

"No," Lydie said as he started to step toward her. Then again, "No," when he went for the door. "Sit down, and let's talk about this like reasonable people," she suggested. Firmly. "Because you seem to be dead *enough*. And unless I'm mistaken, you're the one who nearly killed Hansa. So *sit!*"

He sat down again, though it didn't stop him from glaring.

"Way to go, Lydie," Hansa said, fighting not to laugh.

"As amusing as it would be to watch the necromancer dance our Naples about like a puppet, let's not abuse him so much he figures out how to fight back," Umber suggested. "I don't want to test a fourteen-year-old necromancer's power against a century-old Abyssumancer."

"I concur," Lydie agreed. She shrugged at Naples. "I couldn't resist."

Naples growled, an unnerving sound to hear from someone who looked human. Alizarin's hackles rose in response before Naples shook his head and grumbled, "Don't do it again."

"I'm not the only necromancer in Kavet," Lydie pointed out. "You're still wearing the taint of your own death, which is what responds so eagerly to my magic. I can see that taint sloughing off you, but un-

til it's entirely gone, it doesn't seem to matter how powerful an Abyssumancer you are—you have no protection against my kind."

The door opened one more time, this time to reveal a cheery-looking young man in the Drunken Horse's black-vest-over-green-shirt uniform. "Welcome! Should I bring a pitcher of ale for the table? Or mulled wine?" he asked.

"Fuck, *yes*," Naples replied.

The waiter started back, swiveled toward Naples' vehement response, then cleared his throat. "I'll bring both, then," he said.

"Whiskey for me," Naples added.

"And that's all," Umber said, with a glare at Naples, who didn't look remotely abashed. The moment the waiter closed the door behind himself, Umber ordered, "Explain."

Naples leaned back in his chair, languid and insolent. Honest, or a pose? Cadmia couldn't tell.

"My patron, Modigliani, was a prince of the fifth level when he made me a mancer, and has since become lord of the Abyss. You can't tell me anyone here is *shocked* to see me?"

When Naples had been killed, Umber had speculated that death might not be permanent for him. They hadn't known at the time how powerful his Abyssi was, but they had known how strong Naples himself was, and that he had been killed in a cell designed to contain power.

"*I am,*" Ginger said.

Naples' gaze settled on Ginger, and some of the lazy calm left his face as he asked, "Is anyone else still alive?"

She let out a choking gasp, as if shocked by the arrogance of the question. "How should I know? Alive and dead don't seem to be quite as *fixed* as I always thought them to be. You bastard. You're sitting there, like you haven't aged a day. Do you have any idea what we went through? Do you have *any damned idea?*"

Her voice broke, and Naples winced.

"I have some idea," he said, the last of his posturing gone, "but I hope you will tell us the rest of the tale. I'll say what I know, then I'm hoping you can help explain how we got from the last thing I remember to here. Then, we'll need Alizarin to go further back, to what the Abyssi call the time before."

They all turned toward the Abyssi—even Lydie, though she then looked quickly away, as if whatever she saw was painful to behold, and Ginger, whose brows knit with confusion before her eyes widened in alarm as she deduced who or what they were looking at.

The waiter returning with drinks, crusty bread, and plates of honeyed almond paste for dipping at that moment, provided a brief distraction. Once he was gone, Naples seemed ready to begin.

"Once upon a time," he began, with a smirk at

the fairy-tale introduction, "there was a nation called Kavet. It was ruled, as it had been for a thousand years, by a royal line known as the Terre. They were high-magic practitioners, sorcerers, but *not* mancers. The last mancer to walk the realms did so back in the days of the old wars."

"The old wars?" Cadmia asked. She couldn't remember seeing the term in her studies. "And isn't mancer another word for sorcerer?"

Naples shook his head. "We'll have Alizarin tell *that* tale, once Ginger is done with hers. For now let's just say, there were sorcerers in Kavet, some with powers that leaned toward life or death or the Numen or the Abyss. They didn't understand their powers, or why some people worked better with ice and some with blood, why some people had power and some people didn't."

He paused and took a sip of his whiskey. Ginger was nodding, following his tale. She looked poised to add to it as necessary.

"In this once-upon-a-time land, there was a prince, who was also a very powerful sorcerer. And," he added, dismissively, "there was an annoying little cult, small but rapidly growing in size, called the followers of the Quinacridone."

"Hey!" Ginger protested. "The Followers of the Quinacridone began in response to what they saw as abuses of power by the sorcerers, mostly in the city, and the over-reliance of magic to solve every-day problems, as well as the complete social isolation and aristocratic placement of the Order of the Napthol."

"Which in those days," Naples clarified, "was where those gifted with high magic went to study. It's where I grew up. It is not where Ginger grew up, as her family was devoutly and absolutely Quin." He gestured to the bracelet she was wearing, engraved with the mark of A'hknet, and added, "I notice you're wearing a different symbol these days."

She nodded, but apparently felt no need to explain her change of allegiance to Naples.

"Well," Naples said, leaning back to stare at the ceiling beams as he spoke. "Obviously, it fell apart. Terre Verte was killed protecting the country—his job, you know—and his parents lost their lives trying to save him. Sorcerers started dying from magic ripping them apart and everyone blamed the dead royal house. Oh yes, and I saw my very first Abyssi, summoned him into this world and would you believe it was an accident?"

"The king resurrected his son," Ginger said, with a questioning tone as if she weren't entirely sure of the details.

"The king . . . *half* resurrected his son," Naples corrected. "He was able to revive and sustain his body, but the prince's soul had already crossed to the next realm. It was Celadon Cremnitz, preacher-leader of the Quinacridone movement, who dragged Terre Verte's soul back from the Numen."

Around the table, there was a moment of silence.

Hansa was the one who asked, "The leader of the *Quinacridone* . . . dragged Terre Verte's soul . . . back from the *Numen*?" There were deliberate pauses between each of those highly improbable bits of information.

Naples nodded. "The leader of the Quinacridone, Celadon Cremnitz, happened to be a very powerful cold-magic user. He didn't understand what he was doing when he saved Terre Verte. He had no idea he had opened a rift to the Numen to do it, or that one of the Numini bonded to him and rode him back into the mortal realm." He took an overly-large gulp of his whiskey, then suggested, "Ginger, maybe you should take over. After all, it is difficult to imagine the way the world has changed, between the days of the Terre and today. I'll fill in the details along the way."

"All we knew," Ginger said, taking up the story, "was that magic was killing people. Celadon, my brother and the Quin's leader, somehow brought Terre Verte out of the palace, but then they . . . they . . ." She looked at Naples. "Every witness said something different. In the end, Celadon was dead. Terre Verte was dead. We thought you were dead, Naples, that you and the Terre had both been killed by that Abyssi, and several other members of the Order of the Napthol were dead. Abyssi and Numini were *killing* people, and we had no idea why."

She looked at Naples, who said, "I'll explain that later. Go on."

"So we did what we could to stop them," Ginger continued. "At first, it was just . . . suggestions, recommendations, incentives, anything we could think of that would weaken the Others' hold on the mortal realm. But the deaths continued and people got scared, and every meeting there were more people wanting to make the laws stricter. After enough time, they wrote another law. Dahlia Indathrone didn't even *like* it, but she hadn't kept a veto power for herself, and the majority voted it into power. That's when I left the Followers of the Quinacridone and joined the Order of A'hknet, the day Citizen's Initiative One-Twenty-Six passed. And that brings us to today."

Naples turned toward Alizarin.

"In all our pillow-talk," he said, a term that made Cadmia cringe as she remembered that Naples' first reason to dislike her was that Alizarin had been his lover before hers, "you mentioned your own plans, but you never mentioned the *history*. You never talked about the Gressi."

"Gressi?" Hansa asked, brow furrowed.

"Abyssumancer," Naples replied. "Numenmancer. Gressumancer."

"Gressumancers have power over all five planes: mortal, life, death, Numen, and Abyss," Lydie said. "Terre Verte seems to be one."

"Wrong. Terre Verte has power over four planes

because he inherited power from his family's years of study, and then was granted power by the Numini and the Abyssi, separately," Naples said. "A Gressumancer is something different altogether, something that begins with the Gressi, and the old war. Alizarin?"

PART TWO

Winter, Year 3988 in the Age of the Realms
Year 81 of the New Reckoning

I sing of realms and times before,
when worlds were one and life was more,
than skin and bone, but soul and pow'r
divine and ice and blood and fire.

And I sing of a love, deep and true,
forgotten by most, remembered by few
between a Numen lord, young and fleet,
and one born of Abyssal heat.
In those lakes of fire
lakes of blood
of flesh and need, and hungry lust,
crystal seeded with death
were nursery
to a slick-furred youth:
one Knet by name.

Next Aureoline from Numen ice,

full-grown and lovely like all his kind.

His wings were gold, his skin red silk,

deep sunset—or an Abyssi's milk

and from the first moment

all who knew

Aureoline loved him deep.

But none who adored him

were his desire;

none knew that he

would seduce the fire.

From "The Seduction of Knet"
Traditional Tamari Ballad

CHAPTER 25

CADMIA

"I'm young for my kind," Alizarin began. Cadmia translated for Lydie and Ginger, who could not hear him. "I was not hatched before Kavet fell to the Quinacridone. So the time before and the old war are myths to me. Even Modigliani was not alive for those days, though his sire saw the soon-after."

He continued the story, using the simple phrases and descriptions the Abyssi used to tell their history.

This is how the Abyssi note the ages: the time before, the old war, and the soon-after. Then there is this age, which is the today. We don't know what the today will be once it becomes tomorrow. Abyssi don't usually think that way.

In the time before there were no planes. The world was

full. The Abyssi delighted in the world-that-was even when it was chaos, but the Numini made order. That was fine. There was always food. The Numini tamed some of the lesser creatures and they became servants. The servants made things, and they worked in the Numini's order. They were not dirt, but the Numini were displeased when they were made meat, so the Abyssi did not hurt them unless the Numini gave them away. There was other food to be had, and the lesser creatures had other uses.

"Did you inherit memories of this?" Umber interrupted to ask. "I can't imagine a time when the Numen and the Abyss and the mortal realm were all combined."

Alizarin shook his head. "Even the oldest Abyssi are too many generations away from the time before to remember. I can only tell it the way it was told to me. Some of the Numini might remember. They live longer."

He continued.

That was the world in the time before.

There were Abyssi, and Numini, and Gressi, who were both feathers and fur. One of the Gressi, named Scheveningen, loved the lesser creatures. He wanted them to be free. The Numini did not understand the desire for freedom. He wanted them to be safe, but food cannot be safe. It can only run.

"Feathers and fur?" Lydie asked once Cadmia repeated the phrase. "What does that mean?"

Alizarin shrugged.

Cadmia conjectured, "Some combination of Numini and Abyssi?" Like the world Alizarin had described, it seemed hard to imagine. "And these lesser creatures—they're humans?"

"I always thought so," Alizarin answered.

Scheveningen and the Gressi fought against the Numini for the lesser creatures' lives. The Abyssi fought some on each side, but mostly they fed. And that was the beginning of the old war. Some of the creatures took up arms on each side. Many of them died.

At last Scheveningen set his claws into the sand and ripped the world into two. He fell into the chasm between, and he and the Gressi created the veils between the worlds. They put the Abyssi onto one side and the Numini onto the other and gave their lives to keep the third world— where they put the other beasts—protected.

"Wait—what?" Hansa asked incredulously. "These creatures created the different realms, just like that?"

"It was probably more complicated than the story makes it sound," Ginger suggested. "This is a legend passed down by creatures who barely even keep an oral history, much less a written one."

Then there was the time soon-after.

Some of the humans kept their marks of favor from their former masters. Some stayed loyal, but others used those marks to gain power over their patrons, so the Abyssi and Numini slew them.

But once those were destroyed and brought home, the last connection between the three realms was gone. The

Abyssi stayed in the Abyss. The Numini stayed in the Numen. The humans stayed in the mortal plane as long as their flesh shells survived, after which some crossed the veil one way and some the other.

"The mark of favor," Lydie asked, "is what makes someone a mancer?"

Naples nodded. "Abyssumancers or Numenmancers, anyway. Necromancers and animamancers are infected by the remains of the Gressi in this world."

"How does what is happening in Kavet fit into this narration?" Umber asked.

"Or what happened when the Terre died?" Ginger added.

"In the time-after, the Abyssi and Numini slew the mancers, only to find themselves stranded on their own planes," Naples said. "For most, that was fine, but others either wanted to regain the power their mancers gave them or—in the case of some of the Numini—they wanted to 'protect' the humans the way they had before, by imposing their own standards of order and safety." He shook his head and made a disgusted sound at the back of his throat, making it clear how he felt about that. "They started with the sorcerers, most of them nurturing lines of power for centuries just to get a foothold in the mortal realm. Then, at last . . . some succeeded."

His voice fell on the last words, as if with shame.

"The other Abyssi and Numini panicked. They saw true mancers walking the mortal realm for the first time since the old war, and they feared one of their rivals would gain control over that realm. Some feared the Numini would conquer the mortal realm and then make war against the Abyss as well. They scrambled to finish their mancers, shoving power recklessly into flesh that wasn't ready to accept it. Most of them succeeded only in tearing their chosen ones apart."

He paused, sipping his whiskey, the expression in his gaze speaking of horrors Cadmia was glad she had not been the one to see.

Ginger was obviously there with him, in a memory of the same time. "And Terre Verte was one of these?" she asked.

"No, actually. No," Naples answered, his gaze still held by memory. "I was. And Celadon Cremnitz. One of the Numini tried for generations to claim the Terre line, and might have succeeded with Terre Verte if an Abyssi named Antioch hadn't made a claim through the king's new, foreign wife, tainting the bloodline. Verte got power from both those sides, but it's too mixed for him to ever be a true Abyssumancer or Numenmancer, and none of the Others claim him directly now."

"We were told Antioch wants to distance himself from all this," Cadmia said, remembering what Alizarin had reported about the Abyssi that had once tried to claim Hansa. "If he's Verte's patron, shouldn't that weaken Verte?"

Naples shook his head. "I told you, the Terre was never a true Abyssumancer. His connection to the Other realms relies on his having *died*—twice—and crossed into that realm, only to be brought back by powerful sorcery. He doesn't have a Numini patron, either . . . which is part of the problem.

"I've spoken to Modigliani a lot in the last few weeks. He believes that, freed, Terre Verte will declare war against the Numini who had forsaken him. Should he gather enough power, he has the capacity to destroy the veils the Gressi built and break the boundary between the three realms."

Naples pushed his chair back, wobbled slightly as if dizzy, and caught himself on the table. When he turned as if to leave, Ginger exclaimed, "Where are you going? You can't just walk out after a statement like that."

"I need a walk. Or a roll in the back room. If I'm not back in five minutes you might want to ask for another waiter. Discuss amongst yourselves while I'm gone."

He walked out, ignoring their protests and leaving silence behind him.

At last Hansa said, "And here we were worried Verte might attempt a civil war here in Kavet."

"Could he do it?" Cadmia asked Alizarin. "One man couldn't possibly unmake the boundary between the realms. Could he?"

Alizarin lashed his tail and shrugged, and dipped one claw in the honeyed oil in the center of the table. He contemplated it as he spoke. "If Modigliani believes it is possible, it probably is. He is centuries older than I am, and knows many things I do not know."

"Don't—" Umber didn't finish the warning before Alizarin licked the honey off his claw. He and Hansa both flinched.

Cadmia held her breath, fearing a repeat of the apple incident—though surely even an Abyssi couldn't choke on a drop of ground almonds, oil, and honey?

Alizarin's eyes widened, and Cadmia breathed again as he let out a brief purr of approval.

Then the purr turned to a cough. Alizarin's fur rippled all over his body, crawling and rising in uneven hackles that lost their shimmer in patches and turned gray-green instead of turquoise and cobalt. He sneezed, and Cadmia jumped back from a gob of phlegm that sizzled as it struck the wood floor.

"Rin?" she asked, panicking slightly. "Do you need—?"

The world around him blackened, and he stumbled into a rift and disappeared.

"Rin!" she shouted, stupidly, belatedly, before turning toward Umber to demand, "Can you tell where he's gone?"

"Probably hunting again," Umber answered.

"In the mortal realm?" Alizarin was able to open a

rift to the Abyss, where the hunting was better, but if he crossed there in his distressed state, he wouldn't be able to get back without a mancer's help.

Umber nodded. "That rift didn't cross the planes."

Cadmia turned toward a *thunk* as Ginger dropped her head on the table and grumbled, "*This* is who I choose to ally myself with. What was I thinking?"

"I ask myself that daily," Lydie replied.

"He was all right last time," Hansa said, though he sounded only as certain as Cadmia felt.

Why was he suddenly interested in human food?

"Has he always been this way?" Lydie asked.

"I—" Cadmia broke off, realizing she had no idea. She hadn't known Alizarin before they were together in the Abyss. She looked at Hansa and Umber and they both shrugged. Then her stomach rumbled, reminding her she had skipped the official dinner at the Cobalt Hall and the hour was growing late. "I'm going to order food for the table while we wait for Naples."

"Is *everyone* at this table so tightly tied to the Abyss they can only think with their stomach and dicks?" Ginger asked waspishly.

Lydie lifted her hand. "Um, necromancer? But I still vote for food."

Ginger sighed, then waved to Cadmia as if to grant permission. She couldn't find their original waiter, but managed to track down another to order the night's special for the table. She returned just as Naples was stalking back in.

"How am I supposed to get laid if the Quinacri-done has intimidated everyone in Kavet? I mean, I could manage it, but getting that guy to roll over in timely fashion would require a little more force than anyone in this room tends to approve of."

"Since when have *you* cared?" Umber challenged.

Naples collapsed into a chair. "Since I need allies, for one. Also, I'm not desperate enough yet for him to be worth it. Though I hear Terre Verte has some power on his side I bet no one here would mind my having some fun with Incidentally, with the boons be-tween you and Cupric as old and frayed as they are, I can break them." As if the words had reminded him, Naples asked, "Where is Alizarin?"

"His food disagreed with him," Hansa said shortly. "He left to hunt. You can break the bond?"

"Not a full one like you and Umber have, but the partial one left by two boons, yes," Naples answered. "It would require my getting a little more up close and personal than you two probably trust me to be, but I can free you of him."

Trust, Cadmia suspected, was the key word. Um-ber and Hansa would need to decide that for them-selves. In the meantime, she had remembered that Naples had been Alizarin's friend long before any of the rest of them. "Do you know what is going on with Alizarin? His behavior has been odd."

Naples gave Cadmia the same long, searching look Hansa was giving him—evaluating whether or not it was worth trusting her, she suspected—before he answered, "Alizarin wants a natural connection to the Numen. He has for as long as I've known him. So far he has managed only a link to a Numenmancer, which Terre Verte could break at any moment."

"We were talking about foods that Numini and Numenmancers eat," Cadmia recalled aloud, finally making the connection. "That's what made him want the apple. And the honey. Is there some way we can help him?"

"I *did* help him, remember?" Naples snapped. "I made the knife he used to bond with Dioxazine. It worked so well and he was so grateful, he *ate me*." He stood and began to pace restlessly, swallowing a growl. "I would help him if I could. I don't know what more he can do, and I don't think he does, either."

CHAPTER 26

LYDIE

Lydie was trying to find a polite way to return the conversation to something more immediate when Ginger let out a frustrated "huff!" and asked, "Can we discuss a *plan*? Because if I've understood right, the Terre is planning a coup that might undo existence as we know it. We—"

She broke off in mid-tirade as there was a knock on the door, followed this time by the admittance of a middle-aged waitress with a bored look on her face, who brought two large loaves of bread braided around fire-roasted chicken and vegetables. They all sat in tense, irritated silence, trying to pretend that nothing

304 ALMELIA ATWATER-RHODES

was wrong and no one in the room had anything to hide.

After she left, Umber said, "All right. Let's brainstorm. We know Verte is gathering mancers and other magic users. He insists this is a 'first step' toward some unspecified goal. If he is planning to attack the Numen, then what's the point of the gathering?"

"There's nothing to say that is his only goal, or even his preeminent goal," Cadmia said. "I don't think we should assume what the Abyssi think a human will do *is* what he will do."

Even Naples nodded to that.

"We're talking about Terre Verte," Ginger said. "He won't set his sights low. If he isn't planning to attack the Numen, he will go after the Quin in an attempt to take back Kavet."

After years of keeping to the shadows, it felt unnatural to break into a conversation between such assertive figures, but there was a question no one else had acknowledged. Lydie started to raise her hand as she had once upon a time in a classroom, realized that was foolish, then asked, "I agree we don't want Terre Verte to destroy the world, but what if he *could* take back Kavet? One-Twenty-Six was written at a time when we faced different threats, ones modern mancers are able to control. What if Terre Verte could undo it?"

"Our young protégé has a point," Naples said. When he turned those eerie copper eyes her way, she wanted to sink under the table, but forced herself to hold her ground. "If Terre Verte plans to take over Kavet, do we *want* to stop him?"

"What was his Kavet like, really?" Lydie asked, looking between Naples and Ginger. "No one talks about it now. Obviously sorcery was legal. What else was different?"

"Everything," Ginger sighed.

"The Order of Napthol was made up of sorcerers?" Cadmia prompted. "That's what the manuscript Verte asked for suggested."

"The Order of Napthol was dedicated to identifying and training those born with power," Naples answered. "They also provided healing services— *real* ones, not just herbal medicine and the like—as well as exotic services and goods that were traded around the world."

Lydie tried to imagine what that would have been like, if instead of spending her childhood fighting madness and her adolescence struggling to survive and stay hidden, she could have gone to a place that would have helped her, guided her, and provided for her.

She couldn't.

"And occasionally those sorcerers and aristocrats and royals even remembered the rest of the country existed," Ginger chimed in ironically. "There's a reason the Quin rose to power even *before* the magic went mad and started killing people. I'm not saying it was all a good change," she added hastily, when Naples raised his voice to talk over her. "I've watched freedom erode for everyone, and especially for women, since the Quin took power. But I won't let you sit there and pretend everything was perfect with the Terre in control, either."

"It's irrelevant what it *used to* be like," Umber said, cutting off the argument. "It's not like Verte can step up and say 'hello everyone, I'm home, move out of the way.' His taking Kavet would mean civil war. In that case, the magic users he is gathering will be his army."

Naples looked at Ginger. "You're here. Is anyone else still alive? Henna, maybe?"

Ginger shook her head and said, "I don't know. She left Kavet when it became obvious that One-Twenty-Six was going to pass."

Lydie groped after the unfamiliar name, but it evoked nothing from her power. If the woman was dead, it was too old a death or too far away for Lydie to hear.

"What about Clay?" After a glance at the confused faces around the table, Naples explained, "Clay was . . . is . . . Terre Verte's half brother. He was less than two years old when everything happened. If he is still alive, or he has children, they have Terre blood. They might be able to appeal to Terre Verte for a peaceful solution."

"Henna took custody of Clay when Madder passed away," Ginger said. Lydie had still been searching for

Henna until that moment, which was when Naples' reaction struck her. Ginger seemed to realize the same a moment later, as she said, "He left with—Oh. Naples, I'm so—"

Naples waved a hand dismissively, but Lydie noticed he was careful not to meet anyone's eyes.

"Madder?" Lydie asked, though she probably didn't have to. The woman had died at an age that wasn't old enough to be considered golden, but wasn't young enough to be a tragedy . . . unless she was family, as she clearly had been to Naples.

Naples shook his head sharply, almost like a spasm. "One of the strongest of the cold-magic users among the Order of the Napthol," he said. "After her husband passed away, she was Terre Jaune's mistress for several years."

"And she was your mother," Ginger said, softly, but Naples had re-gathered his composure. If it hadn't been for Lydie's power, which was still humming from the sense of loss, she might have assumed he genuinely didn't care.

"You gave me up for dead," he said flatly, "and I gave all you up for dead a long, *long* time ago. I buried my mother in my mind after I took the third boon. What I *didn't* bury was Kavet. So let's focus on what's important."

Hansa cleared his throat, uncomfortably trying to do just that. He said, "Lydie, I don't know if it's the kind of thing your power could tell you, but we've had several guards disappear from the One-Twenty-Six. It would be good to know if Verte responded when they got in his way, or deliberately hunted them down. It might give us a sense of how aggressive he plans to be. Assuming they're dead . . . unfortunately, I'm assuming they're dead . . . can you tell the circumstances of their deaths?"

Lydie tried to keep her face blank, and not express so clearly how she felt about checking up on members of the 126. Hansa was right that anything they could learn about Verte's plans was for the best, but that didn't mean she was comfortable with it.

Nevertheless, she spread her power. She was about to ask the guards' names when she remembered that Naples had also mentioned another name, one she had been distracted from while searching for Henna and then responding to Madder.

Clay—

The resulting hiss of icy voices stole her breath.

Lydie coughed around the frigid air in her lungs. "Clay was a Numenmancer?" she gasped.

Naples and Ginger exchanged a look. Ginger said to Naples, "You said he couldn't be because Antioch tainted the line?"

"Antioch claimed the Terre line," Naples rephrased. Despite his obvious attempt to sound calm and businesslike, his voice had a fragile edge to it as he said, "but Clay was a bastard. My mother—his mother—used almost entirely cold magic. Is *he* alive?"

"No," Lydie answered firmly, rubbing gooseflesh from her arms.

"Well then," Naples said, a touch too loudly. "Does his being a Numenmancer change our situation, if he's dead?"

"I . . . don't know," Lydie answered. The shades had tried to tell her something else, but she hadn't caught it. Later, she could cast a circle and try again. For now, it was hard enough to make her eyes focus on the living.

"Then let's consider our options," Naples said. "Hansa, we can get back to the question of the guards in a bit. I understand you want to protect your friends in arms and all, but I don't see how it's relevant to the larger issue."

"If Terre Verte is systematically eliminating captains, then that would imply he plans to go after the Quin," Hansa explained, his voice seeming far away as Lydie still struggled to breathe. She shouldn't have tried this with a circle; the resulting hiss of voices shouting at her was too much, too overwhelming. "I can't imagine why he would bother if he weren't planning a local coup first."

"He also wanted that manuscript," Cadmia said, drumming her fingers on the table thoughtfully. "That wouldn't help him take on the Numen, but it would help him understand the modern followers of the Quinacridone. That also suggests he is preparing to move against the Quin. Lydie, are you all right?"

"Give her a minute," Naples said, his tone as almost idle as it had been when he discussed his mother's death. He was the only other mancer at the table. If anyone, he surely understood what it was to be overwhelmed by your power.

She managed to ground her power again enough that she was able to follow the conversation as it continued with increasingly obvious levels of frustration.

"If the Terre *is* planning to break into the Numen, it's a fair bet he is gathering magic users in order to boost his power. Abyssi don't guard their boundaries very well, but the Numini are very specific about who they allow to cross their territory. Or so I've heard," Naples added, with a shrug. "It's not like I'm on the guest list, or ever will be."

"If that's the plan, we should not only *not* attend the meeting, we should stop as many people—especially Numenmancers—from going as we can," Cadmia said.

"*If* that's the plan," Hansa echoed tiredly. "If he plans to attack the Quin, then we *do* want to be at the meeting. We need to gain influence among his followers, gain his trust, and know his next move."

"Flip a coin," Umber grumbled.

There is a third option.

A voice whispered in her head, one of the mortal shades who always lingered near, and suddenly an obvious solution occurred to Lydie. So obvious, she waited a few moments for someone else to bring it up. When no one did, but instead they spent several long seconds staring at each other despondently, she said, "Hansa should run for President."

Hansa gasped, *"Excuse me?"*

"Think about it," Lydie continued. "The Quin love you, and every magic user in Kavet either suspects or knows you're involved with one of the spawn, and otherwise allied with mancers. I could walk into the Quinacridone Compound tomorrow and move for an emergency election for a temporary acting President—just until Winsor Indathrone returns, of course—and Hansa Viridian, hero of Mars, would win by a landslide." She paused, biting her lower lip. "Well, *I* couldn't, since I'm not of age. But Cadmia could."

"You're mad," Hansa gasped, but as Lydie looked around the table, she saw expressions of contemplation on all the other faces.

"Maybe not," Ginger said. "I could put word in for you with the Order of A'hknet, which would earn you most of the votes in that sect. If you were in power, you could smooth the way for a Terre return, or at least a shift in the laws, in a way that wouldn't mean war."

"Or I could end up with a broken neck when Terre Verte decides I'm in the way."

Ginger let out a dismissive *"Psha.* If we make sure you're in favor with the mancer community, Terre

Verte wouldn't dare move directly against you. *Especially* if he thinks you're doing this *for* him."

Lydie picked up on Ginger's thread. "We can show up at Verte's meeting and show our support for the Terre, and turn his meeting into a campaign point."

"No, no, *no*," Hansa objected. "I'm twenty-seven, for one thing. I'm a *soldier*. I'm not leadership material."

"You wouldn't need to keep the position long," Lydie argued. *I'm twenty-seven*, he had the gall to say, talking to a *fourteen-year-old* who would have loved the choice to opt out of the oncoming war—whether civil or sorceral. Hansa had chosen to be a soldier, chosen to be a leader and supposedly a protector. He could damn well do his job. "Just long enough for us to have a chance to understand and either counter or support anything Verte tries."

Ginger and Naples exchanged a significant look, which had Hansa nearly shouting, "What *now?*"

"I was just thinking, I'm pretty sure someone said the same thing to Dahlia Indathrone," Ginger said.

"And she was probably *murdered*," Hansa retorted. "I make my case."

His objections seemed to be having absolutely no effect, as the others continued to plan around him. "I think we should have someone—not one of us, but some nice, loyal Quin—make the nomination," Naples said. "Then we can go to Terre Verte and say, 'I'm sorry, I don't know how this happened, but what do you think we should do?'"

"And if he says, 'Back off'?" Hansa asked.

"Then we know more than we did before: that he is definitely going after the Quin first, and nothing short of bloodshed will satisfy him," Ginger answered flatly. "In that case, we need to dispose of him, because the Terre Verte I knew—the one I would be willing to see rule Kavet again—would never chose the slaughter of his people over a quiet, civilized revolution. He's ruthless, but he's practical."

"Naples is right—we don't want to make the nomination ourselves," Cadmia said. "We don't want Hansa to look responsible. But if we start rumors about the President being gone, *someone* is sure to call for an interim, emergency replacement. We don't have a lot of time, so if we are even considering this plan, then we need to start immediately."

"What if I'm *not* considering this plan?" Hansa said. He looked at Umber, who had been quiet so far.

"I think . . ." Umber hesitated, giving Hansa a long look. Lydie held her breath, recognizing that Umber probably had the most power in the room to sway Hansa. "I think we *should* consider it. It's the best plan we have so far."

"Kind of like our plan to leap into the Abyss searching for a necromancer, with no supplies, no idea how to find a necromancer once we're there, and no idea how to get back?" Hansa challenged. "Or do you mean like our plan to walk into the deepest dungeon in the lowest level of the Abyss in order to resurrect someone who is now trying to destroy Kavet? As I remember it, both those plans were terrible, ended badly, and resulted from our being *manipulated*. Naples, who exactly *did* come up with those plans?"

Naples sighed. "Modigliani. And one or more of the Numini."

"Modigliani, who resurrected you and sent you up here," Hansa said, "and who is responsible for giving you all the information you've shared with us, and therefore is just as likely to be pulling our strings now as then."

"Maybe," Naples admitted.

Lydie sighed. There was no way of knowing if the Numini or the Abyssi were manipulating them at that moment. That would be true no matter what they decided.

"Based on everything you know," she asked, "who would you rather try to take the Quinacridone: Terre Verte, or you?"

"I would like a better source of information."

"Imagine you didn't know a thing about Terre Verte and his history," Lydie challenged. "You know Indathrone is dead. Sooner or later someone is going to call for a replacement. Who would you like to see take his place?"

Hansa stared at her, and she watched the last of his objections drain away. Given his previous position in the 126, he probably knew better than she did the people who would run if an election were called for.

"It looks like we're decided, then," Naples announced with a tired smile. "Nice job, Necromancer." He stood, abandoning a plate he had barely picked at. "For now, it's late, and we all have a busy day tomorrow. Hansa needs to get to the Quinacridone, Umber and I need to break a bond, and Lydie, Cadmia and Ginger need to start campaigning. If everyone is finished eating, I move we conclude this little meeting and go home to bed. And Umber . . . invite me or don't, but don't fool yourself into thinking I don't know where you live. Or for that matter that Cupric doesn't, or that Terre Verte doesn't. I'm going to the temple to catch up on rumors, and then I'm going to knock on your door. If you let me in, at least you'll know where I am."

Lydie wasn't sure if that last was supposed to sound like a threat or a flirt, but she was glad it—and the direct, copper stare and raised brow that accompanied it—weren't directed at her.

CHAPTER 27

CUPRIC

Cupric lay in bed, staring at the ceiling, wishing he were asleep but not quite daring to close his eyes again and risk it. Terre Verte had ordered him to drop by sometime this evening after the supper hour—right after he told him to stay away from Umber and Hansa. Cupric had expected that order eventually, but was disappointed by how *soon* it had come.

He stretched and frowned, realizing he couldn't remember the name of the woman sleeping next to him. She was an animamancer, which had been a new experience for him. A disappointing one, in the end; he had expected something more exciting from someone tied to life itself.

He had briefly debated trying to seduce Keppel, but one look at her while she was working reminded him that you had to be an idiot to willingly bed an Abyssumancer.

"I've got to go," he announced, shaking the woman next to him.

She opened wide doe-eyes and yawned. "Do you have to?"

I just said that I did. "I have a meeting with the Terre and Xaz."

She stretched. "That man does keep odd hours, doesn't he?" Then she adjusted her grip on the pillow, closed her eyes again, and murmured, "Sleep late tomorrow. I'll make breakfast."

Cupric stared at her for a full five seconds before deciding she was serious. "I don't think so."

"Hmm. Maybe lunch." Her eyes were still closed.

"You can't stay here," he said. Shouldn't that have been clear already? "I'm leaving. You have to leave." She was attractive, but she hadn't been nearly good enough in bed for him to want to have her waiting when he got back.

"Oh!" Her eyes opened at last and she sat up, raking hair back from her face. "Well, I'll just . . ." She blinked and frowned up at him, obviously still fighting sleep. "I'll get to my own bed. Thanks for the good time earlier, I guess, even if you are an asshole afterwards."

After the woman left, Cupric quickly washed

up and dressed, then walked toward Terre Verte's claimed home, where he found the prince in his sitting room looking over the manuscript that Umber had sent his necromancer to bring with a grave expression. Cupric had glanced at it briefly before handing it over, but hadn't understood why it was important.

"Have you learned anything interesting from that?" he asked now.

Terre Verte nodded. His words as he set the manuscript down on the table next to him, however, were not about the writing inside. "I need you to assist me in opening a rift."

Cupric was sure he must have misheard. "Excuse me?"

The Terre looked up, and for the first time, Cupric noticed the shadows under his eyes. Was scrying into the Cobalt Hall going badly? Or, just perhaps, could such a man still suffer human ailments such as anxiety?

"I need to open a rift to the Abyss," Terre Verte said, as if his first request had been unclear and that was the only reason for Cupric's surprise.

To ask, or to not ask. Cupric couldn't necessarily trust any answer he received, anyway . . .

But he asked.

"Forgive me if this is impertinent," Cupric said, "but my understanding was that you opened the rift from the Abyss to this plane with ease. You are certainly a more powerful sorcerer than I am." It galled Cupric to admit that, but he was sane enough not to deny it. "I will gladly assist you, but I am surprised that it is necessary. Is everything all right?"

"Everything's fine," Terre Verte said coldly. "My energies are directed elsewhere. Can you do it or not?"

Could he open a rift to the Abyss? Yes, certainly. Theoretically. He was an Abyssumancer and a powerful one, but so far he had been sane enough not to meddle with beings that could eat him in an instant of lost control.

"It should be within my power," he said slowly. His heart was pounding, and his hands had started to tremble. "Where are you going?"

Terre Verte shook his head. "I'm not going anywhere. I need you to assist my sister in crossing to this plane. If it is easier for you, you can cross and then return after you have rested, as long as you are back in time for the meeting."

He was speaking as if he was asking for something easy.

"It's . . . not something I've ever done before," Cupric admitted. He *should* be able to do it, but there was still the possibility of his being trapped in the Abyss if he stepped across and then his power failed. "Can she be summoned across, like one of the Abyssi?"

"In order to summon one of the Abyssi across, you need to use their power as a bridge. The spawn can't link to you like that." The air of distraction cleared from Terre Verte's gaze, and suddenly his gray eyes bored into Cupric's. "I am giving you this assignment because you have the kind of power necessary, but you should know that if you touch my sister in any way that is not with her complete and fully-informed consent, I will tear you apart. Do you believe me?"

At first, Cupric thought the sensation of ice running down his spine was a result of very rational fear, but then he realized the air had dropped in temperature. He wrapped his arms across his chest and shivered. "I believe you."

The Terre smiled, and the room warmed again. "Excellent. Let's begin."

"*Now?*"

Terre Verte nodded sharply. "Yes, *now*. If I had wanted it tomorrow, I would have asked you tomorrow."

"I'm not prepared," Cupric objected. "I need to gather tools, visit the temple, find a—"

The Terre cut him off with a wave of his hand. "I've found you an escort, and the tools you will need. Do you have any more excuses you would like to waste my time with?"

Again the temperature dropped. *Bastard.*

"Fine," Cupric said. "Who is this 'escort'?" Keppel might be able to lend power, but Cupric hoped Terre Verte didn't expect her to be *trustworthy*. Or maybe the prince would send him with some Numenmancer, to make him behave.

Terre Verte led the way into the next room. Cupric had assumed it was a bedroom, and maybe it once had been, but it wasn't anymore. It was a soft spot—not quite a temple, but somewhere the planes had been breached, repeatedly. The bed had been shoved to the side, and covered with a white silk cloth and other tools for working with the Numini. Cupric gave it a wide berth. On the other side of the room, a bookcase and low chest had been covered with leather and glass and held more familiar tools.

Cupric frowned. Where in the Abyss had the Terre been *sleeping*—with or without his Numenmancer? He looked at the bed with its silk cover, but decided no, there was no way the Numini would tolerate sex on what had obviously been transformed into an altar to them.

The white bed and the thick veil of magic had briefly distracted Cupric from one of the sources of power in the room, but at last his eyes fixed on blue. "Alizarin," he greeted the Abyssi prince. "You're my escort?"

The Abyssi nodded, his tail swishing. Cupric didn't know it well enough to translate the creature's mood, but he knew at least that a prince of the third level of the Abyss was powerful enough to make this trip not only more possible, but more pleasant.

"Alizarin will help you find your way in the Abyss,

and defend you from some of the dangers there," Terre Verte said. "He will also eat you if you cross the line with Azo."

"Does Umber know you're here?" Cupric asked. It was hard to imagine that the spawn's little crew would tolerate their Abyssi running errands for Terre Verte.

The Abyssi's tail swayed again, and this time Cupric was almost certain it was an expression of discomfort.

"Cupric," Terre Verte said warningly.

Cautious in the face of both the Abyssi's and the prince's irritation, Cupric asked instead, "How is Umber?"

The Abyssi smiled. It didn't look like a friendly expression. "He and Hansa have lots of sex. Loudly. You can taste the power all through the house. You must miss it."

The animamancer's face flashed through Cupric's mind, followed shortly after by the memory of Umber's skin, or more specifically, of his blood and the flavor of his power.

"Yes, I do," he answered.

Alizarin crossed the room in a lithe slink of beautiful blue fur, the heat in his eyes enough to make Cupric's skin tingle. "How much?" he purred, standing close.

Equally powerful instincts told Cupric to step forward, and to step backward. He ended up keeping his feet solid on the floor, doing neither. "I'm not sure I understand the question," he managed to say, his throat tight.

The Abyssi leaned forward, balancing on the balls of his feet at an angle that brought him closer to Cupric, and which would have made a human topple forward. "You're an Abyssumancer," the Abyssi said, clearly. "I've had an Abyssumancer before. They taste good."

Sweet *Numen*, the kind of power the creature was offering, if Cupric was near-suicidal enough to essentially roll over and take it. He knew what the Abyssi considered sex was brutal, but . . .

"We could work something out," he said in a voice that was so soft and breathy it didn't sound like his.

Alizarin licked his cheek, then bounced to an upright position and turned around, saying, "Good. If I get hungry, I'll eat you. Or if you ever come near Umber or Hansa. Or Caddy." The last name was practically a growl.

Cupric turned to Terre Verte, his heart now pounding not with anticipation but genuine fear. "May I have a *different* escort?"

"I'm sending you to pick up my sister," the Terre replied. "Alizarin is a perfect chaperone."

To the Abyss with all this, the Terre and his grand plans. Cupric would do this one more thing, but after that he was getting out of the way. Out of Kavet if he could. The only reason he didn't walk out of the house that instant was that, from the moment the Terre had brought up the subject, he had been able to practically *taste* the Abyss. This was exactly what his power was driven every moment to do, even if his common sense usually kept him from doing it.

But after this, he would turn tail and run like the beasts of the Abyss were after him. Mostly because it was a little too true.

CHAPTER 28

HANSA

"**Y**ou really think this is a good idea?" Hansa asked, as he and Umber fell into bed.

"I think it's the best idea we have," Umber replied. "You're over your head most of the time when it comes to Abyssal magic, but you had a good reputation when you were a guard, as a man who was fair and not just in the position for power and glory. And as much as I hate to go along with anything Naples says, he has a point. Even without Terre Verte in the equation, I would rather see you in that office than anyone else who might run for it."

"It won't take much for me to get thrown out and turned over to the Quin as a mancer, a sympathizer, or at the very least for deviant behavior," Hansa pointed out. "The majority population is fixed in its ways right now. I don't even know where I'd start."

He could see Umber smiling as he spoke. As they moved close, Umber said, "I don't know why you're asking me this. You've already moved past wondering whether you *should*, and have started wondering about how to do what you want to do next."

"Okay, I've resigned myself to it," Hansa admitted—though *resigned* wasn't quite the right word. As much as he wanted to be reasonable, to be *sane*, there was a bubbly sensation in his stomach as he considered the possibility and how he might approach it. "I'm just worried about all the ways to get killed that seem to be involved."

"There are always plenty of ways to get killed," Umber said. "This is Kavet under Quinacridone rule, after all. I'm more concerned about Naples."

"Hmm. If he does come knocking, will you let him in?"

Umber paused, drawing a deep breath. "I don't know," he said. "Probably. I'm not sure I could keep him out, and he seems to think he is on our side. For the moment, anyway."

It seemed like they had barely faded into sleep when the knock came, not on the wards or the front door but on the bedroom door.

"What?" Umber called groggily, reaching for the oil lamp on the bedside table, which obediently sparked with flame at his touch just as the door opened.

Hansa would have thought being naked in bed when Naples walked in would be awkward, but with Umber spooned against his back—and a light blanket over the both of them—it was almost fun to see the flash of envy in Naples' gaze as the Abyssumancer leaned heavily in the doorway.

"Since you're obviously capable of breaking in, couldn't you have waited until morning to announce your presence?" Umber sighed. "The guest rooms are taken, but there is a couch downstairs if you need somewhere to sleep."

Hansa, meanwhile, pushed himself up on one elbow, looking at the Abyssumancer more carefully. "Are you *bleeding*?"

"Nice of someone to notice," Naples said. He took a step farther into the room, and now Umber sat up as well, because Naples was obviously limping.

"What happened?" Umber asked.

"I went to the temple like I said I would," Naples said. "I got into a fight."

"With a Numini?" Didn't the Numini hate bloodshed? Hansa started to stand, then realized he wasn't dressed. After a brief hesitation, he decided his modesty wasn't a priority at the moment. He grabbed his pants, and managed to flash the Abyssumancer for only a second or two before he further turned up the oil lamp and went to see how badly Naples was hurt.

"With a *mancer*," Naples corrected. He dodged back as Hansa moved near. "It'll heal, Quin. I'm just here to see a spawn about a bond."

"*Now?*" Hansa wanted the bond to Cupric gone, and surely Umber wanted that even more, but it was the middle of the night and Naples was in poor shape.

"Yes, *now*," Naples snapped. "Do you think I can't hold my own against any mancer in Kavet? It's hard to win if you can't fight back. Next time I find that damned pederast I'm *not* holding back."

"Cupric?" Hansa asked. "*He* did this?"

Naples nodded sharply. "I don't think he meant to be in the temple. If I had to guess, I would say he was using it as a springboard to open a full rift into the Abyss—lazy, but effective. When I got in his way, he decided to show his teeth. You should be glad I recognized him in time."

"Why is Cupric trying to get to the Abyss?" Umber asked.

"Making friends? Getting laid? I don't care," Naples replied. "And you can care later. Because as soon as he gets *back* from the Abyss he and I are going to have a special little *chat*." Naples shook himself, in a way that Hansa had seen Alizarin do when flustered and trying to smooth down his fur. "Bastard. Maybe he *used* to be the most powerful Abyssumancer in Kavet, but he has a *lot* to learn."

Naples' hostility danced across Hansa's skin, power seeping off him. Hansa looked at Umber, who was watching Naples' rant with a strange fascination.

"Are you all right?" the spawn asked, causing Naples to jump.

"Fine. Angry," Naples replied, in short, clipped phrases. Under Umber's continued examination, he paused, drew a deep breath, and stilled himself. "Angry, impatient, hungry. Can we snap this bond before I go pick a fight?"

"Hungry?" Hansa asked. Naples had barely touched food earlier. In fact, Hansa couldn't remember seeing Naples eat a single bite of it. And now Naples was putting out waves of . . . Hunger, yes, that was the word—but it wasn't a hunger for *food*.

"Apparently there are side effects to being slaughtered and resurrected by Abyssi," Naples said, meeting Hansa's gaze with eyes that let off a faint coppery glow.

"Maybe you should rest tonight, and heal," Umber suggested. "We can work on the bond tomorrow."

"Fine," Naples said.

The Abyssumancer turned, sharply enough that Hansa felt the need to ask, "Where are you going?"

Naples glanced back with a very Abyssi smile, and answered in an equivalent tone, "Hunting."

"You're not going after Cupric, are you?"

"Not tonight."

Hansa moved closer and saw—and sensed—Naples

recoil. Hansa could see the Abyssumancer standing there, favoring one leg, with a cut down his arm that hadn't yet closed. What he could feel was a pain beyond what those wounds indicated. It was deeper and it gnawed.

"Don't *pity* me, Quin," Naples snapped, the instant the thought crossed Hansa's mind.

Hansa took a step back. "Don't do that."

"Stay out of my head and I'll stay out of yours."

"I assume the Abyssi dreams were yours, too?" Hansa asked as it occurred to him.

"Not dreams," Naples answered. "I saw through your eyes sometimes while I . . . recovered. The connection must have allowed you to see me as well sometimes."

"Explain," Umber ordered.

Naples sighed, dancing on his feet, obviously still fighting the urge to flee. "The king of the Abyss can do much, but he couldn't make me mortal on his own. He tied me to Hansa's power because he—you were the last human, living person I had touched." Halfway through the explanation he turned away from Umber to speak to Hansa directly. "It's not a permanent bond, like a mancer's to an Abyssi. I won't fall from this plane without you, and any lingering connection *should* fade, the way Lydie says my connection to the dead realm will fade, over time."

"What about the connection to the Abyss?"

Naples gave him a condescending look. "I'm an Abyssumancer."

"That's not what I mean and you know it," Hansa said. Naples just shrugged. "Does it ever *not* hurt?"

Naples leaned back against the wall with a half snarl, half laugh. "I'll let you know," he answered. "This isn't something Modigliani warned me about. Maybe it's temporary, or maybe it's a permanent consequence of coming back from the dead. If it's the latter, I wish he'd left well enough alone."

He pushed himself up again, then stumbled. Hansa caught him, surprised to realize that despite all the power Naples possessed, he was so frail. He looked twenty at most, and was lean and more than slender, as if there were nothing to him except bones, muscle, and power.

Awkwardly, Hansa drew the knife from his belt. He winced as he set the blade to his palm, drawing a fine line of blood, but not nearly as much as Naples did when Hansa pressed the new blood over the wound on the Abyssumancer's arm. It took Hansa barely a breath of power to heal that injury. How weak was Naples, that he hadn't been able to do it himself?

"Resisting temptation is not one of my strengths, Hansa," Naples growled.

Hansa knew that was true, but here Naples was *starving*, and not feeding. He could have fought Cupric and made a banquet of the other Abyssumancer, but instead he had come here to break the bond first.

"I'm gone," Naples whispered. He tried to shake Hansa's grip off his arm, going for the door.

Hansa pulled him back. In this condition, if Naples went "hunting" he would hurt someone. He might even go after Cupric, and they couldn't afford that yet. But those thoughts were secondary. Primary was the knowledge that Naples could have fed, if he had wanted to.

"*What?*" Naples demanded. The expression in his copper eyes bordered on feral, marked as it was by pain, hunger, and now fear.

Hansa stepped forward, closing the distance between them. He bent his head, meeting Naples' lips with his own, aware of how with every touch of skin to skin Naples' power fed at his. Hansa could have drawn blood again and let the Abyssumancer feed that way, but they were both most familiar with flesh as their favored coin of power.

Naples was the one who broke the kiss, turning his head to the side with a gasp and asking, "What in the Abyss was *that*?"

"Pity, probably," Hansa admitted, remembering Naples' earlier objection.

The Abyssumancer's eyes widened, copper rings almost hidden by dilated pupils. "Then I've changed my mind. Pity me. Dear *Numen*, you may pity me all you like."

Hansa glanced back at Umber, who was leaning against the wall next to the bed, watching them both. *I'm not leaving you alone with him, but if you want him to stay, he can stay,* the spawn said, silently. *I'll make sure you don't give him enough power to hurt us.*

The consent shocked Hansa momentarily beyond the echoes of desperation he could feel from Naples and back into his own mind, where his first thought was, *What am I doing?*

Naples went very still, as if he knew that anything he might say or do in that moment would tip the scales and send Hansa running the other direction.

The things Naples *wasn't* saying were enough. Hansa knew from personal experience that biting your tongue didn't help when the other person could hear your thoughts. He understood from Naples' thoughts that Naples would stay, even if they only offered to let him lie next to them. Or on the floor. The scraps of power put off by a spawn and his fleshbond when they were together were more satisfying than anything Naples could find in Kavet short of another Abyssumancer.

And Hansa knew that Naples was trying to keep those thoughts hidden, because he despised having this Quin know how weak he was.

If Hansa hesitated another few seconds, Naples would turn and bolt to keep from begging and Hansa would never have to make this decision because Naples would never come near him in this condition again.

He barely had his humanity, but Numen damn it, he had to have something he could keep and his pride was one of the few things left.

Oh, who cared? No one in this room was holding onto illusions of propriety. Hansa drew a deep breath, and as he let it out, he let himself feel the power around him—including the bond to Umber, which he tried not to focus on unless they were alone. It had been pity that had caused him to first pull Naples close, but with that power swirling around him, pity was nowhere in his mind when he decided to give up his Quin restraint and bring Naples and Umber both back to bed.

CHAPTER 29

UMBER

Umber woke, but didn't immediately move. If he moved, he might wake one of the others, and he wasn't sure yet how that would go. Hansa had seemed rational and confident about his decision the night before, despite Naples doing his best not to coerce or even *ask* the Quin for anything, but sometimes the light of day made the previous night's decisions seem poor.

Hansa always acted as if Umber's fears he might change his mind someday were paranoia, but Hansa hadn't ever been violently evicted from a man's bed when he woke up and suddenly remembered he was *living in Kavet* and *had sex with a man*. It's strange how those two facts could sneak up on a man while he was sleeping—sometimes the first time, and sometimes after months.

He opened his eyes to survey the bed. The blankets had gone Abyss-knows-where, so Umber had an excellent view of the wolf-lean, pale-skinned Abyssumancer sprawled out on his back, with Umber pinning one of his sides and the darker, broad-shouldered Quin on his other half.

Despite how clearly starved he had been, Naples had been remarkably restrained, taking what power was offered without ever grasping for more and watching Hansa for cues as to how each moment should go. Umber had glimpsed one or two of the knives Naples wore despite the spells hiding them, but he had never drawn them; he had even apologized and removed the ring he wore after the sharp blade on its back nicked Umber's arm. Umber hadn't minded, and Hansa hadn't minded in the heat of the moment, but as Naples had put it, "We didn't negotiate for blood."

Both the other men seemed asleep, but then Naples' eyes opened and immediately met Umber's. Umber saw a reflection of his own wariness in them as Naples said softly, "Thank you for letting me stay."

"It was Hansa's decision."

"If you had given any indication you wanted me gone, you know he would have kicked me out."

Naples glanced at Hansa, but he slept still, not disturbed by the soft conversation. "You two are very, very lucky."

Umber gave a half shrug, noncommittal. He had used that same word to describe Hansa once—*lucky*—but that had been before their relationship got so complicated.

The response made Naples tense. "Don't be a bastard and just admit it. You know some of the alternatives. Sweet Abyss, the link to Cupric I pulled off you would have been a soulbond if he had ever been foolish enough to demand a third boon." *Soulbond.* Dear Numen, given Cupric's power, it would have destroyed them both. "Instead you got a pretty man who, instead of blaming you for everything and hating you—which he could have—has adapted remarkably well."

If only Umber could stop questioning how much of that "adaptation" and affection were natural, versus caused by the bond. Then again, he had an expert in bed with him, didn't he?

Bracing himself, he asked, "What is a heartbond like?"

Naples shut his eyes, and his lips pressed together as if in pain as he whispered, "Dear Numen, don't ask me that."

Umber didn't repeat the question, just waited. Eventually, Naples managed to gather his courage, and speak.

"It's . . . all-consuming," he said. "If that's truly what love feels like, I don't know why any fool wants to fall in love. Azo and I, we didn't know about boons or bonds. The first boon must have been when she saved me shortly after I fell into the Abyss, but sometimes the boons don't have to be formal. The bond happened before any of us knew it was a danger.

"I started hunting, I remember. *Really* hunting. I had always drawn power from flesh and lust before, but it hurt her to see me with anyone else so I gave it up. I tried to survive on the ambient power in the Abyss and the blood of its beasts. What you saw of me last night is nothing compared to those days. You and Hansa can feed from each other, but she and I couldn't. I *wanted* to make love to her, but I've never in my life been attracted to a woman. There are ways to pleasure a woman that don't require the man's full engagement, and it brought me joy to bring her pleasure even if I received no satisfaction from it. And for a while that worked for her. But I'm a mancer, so when the bond got stronger it affected her, too, and knowing I wasn't satisfied killed the joy of it for her."

Naples trailed off, and Umber tried not to imagine those dark, awkward nights.

"And then there was the memory of everyone I had left behind," Naples continued, even softer. "A heartbond consumes you. There's nothing left of you to love anyone else. I remembered that I used to care for people—for my mother, and for Henna, and even for Ginger. I used to have crushes. I was madly, adolescently in love with a sailor named Cyan. But all those memories turned cold. It's hard enough as an Abyssumancer to not seep into the Abyss and forget your humanity, but it's even harder when you can't remember what it's like to love anyone except *her*."

Naples' words continued to come, more rapidly now, blood seeping from an old wound reopened to let infection flow out.

"I didn't even realize how far gone I was until Alizarin came to me. He needed an Abyssumancer to forge that knife. He's the one who convinced Azo that she had to tell me, force me, to feed, since I wouldn't do it unless it was for her. Only the stronger I became, the more the bond bit into both of us, so I would go days or weeks without even *tasting* power, trying to make things easier for her. Alizarin's influence allowed us to move to the court, where prey was more plentiful and survival was simpler, but . . . there was her and there was me. And either one of us would have killed ourselves to end it, except that we could never stand to harm the other that way."

He shuddered, and Hansa let out a sleepy protest and tightened his arm around Naples' waist.

"The bond itself broke when I died, but I still remember her. I remember how I felt. I remember the decades we—you're lucky," Naples said again, the words a sigh.

I am, Umber thought, but couldn't bring himself to say aloud. *But is Hansa?*

He might as well have spoken aloud. Naples answered, "That depends if you think ignorance is better than knowledge. It's easier sometimes, but I've never preferred it myself. Was Hansa happier ignorant?"

"Yes. No." It was hard to say. Hansa *had* been happy, or at least content, but he had also been hiding. How much longer would his happiness have lasted?

They would never know.

"I'd love to stay and play, and I hope I'll be invited back, but I have work to do," Naples said reluctantly. "And . . . it might be best if I'm not here when he wakes up, in case he decides this was a mistake." Umber shifted aside, and Naples slid out from under Hansa with the ease of long practice. He plucked the ring off the bedside table and put it back on the middle finger of his left hand, and only then searched the floor for his clothes.

"What's the ring made of?" Umber asked. The thing resonated power.

"Grumbacher, the previous king of the Abyss," Naples answered, pulling on his pants. "Modigliani gathered his bones from the crystal caves and gave them to me when I was trying to remember who I was."

Once dressed, he used the ring to cut across his left palm, raising power in a wave that made Hansa grumble again, this time half waking. With as little effort as most men take to open a mundane door, Naples tore a rift and stepped into it with a jaunty goodbye wave.

As the rift closed with a breath of smoke, Hansa woke with a vague, "Wha . . . ?"

"Naples has gone hunting," Umber answered.

"Oooooh," Hansa replied, flipping onto his back with a grumble. "I . . . Did I really . . ." His face turned scarlet—rather after the fact, Umber thought. "No, yes, I did."

Hansa's head was full of recriminations like, *What in the Abyss had he been doing?* But his expression was remarkably, lazily calm. One needling thought— *Umber's experiences with Abyssumancers haven't normally been this friendly*—prompted Hansa to ask, "You really don't mind?"

"I told you I didn't."

Hansa pushed himself up on his elbows. "Even though he's an Abyssumancer?"

"I'm not sure *what* he is," Umber admitted, thinking about how easily Naples had opened a rift to step across the realms, "but I don't mind having him in bed, as long as he stays this well-behaved." He glanced out the window, which showed only the barest lightening of the pre-dawn sky. "I know you need to get an early start today, but we still have a little time to spend, just the two of us. If you want to."

Hansa replied by reaching out and pulling Umber down next to him.

Hansa probably didn't realize that these were the moments Umber liked best, when the magic was sated. The bond was always there, and it responded any time they touched, but when it was sleepy and well-fed, Hansa was more playful. More timid, too, as his old shyness and inexperience spoke up when the bond wasn't demanding immediate satisfaction— but watching him conquer that self-doubt and experiment purely for enjoyment was fun, too.

Of course he doesn't realize, Umber thought. *He can't read your mind.*

With Lydie's and Naples' voices prodding him, Umber opened his mouth to say something—then suddenly, as he looked up at Hansa, he realized he was looking at a man who might very well become President of Kavet. Hansa might demur and claim he didn't want it, but once he had that power, he wouldn't give it up. He would want to use it to help his country.

Umber lived comfortably these days, but would never forget he was the same half-demon boy who had scavenged for food and been willing to give everything to the first person who had seen him as valuable. Cupric had literally drugged him and chained him down to control him, but Umber had been willing to forgive him and give him anything he wanted.

He held his words.

By the time they went downstairs, the others were already gathered in the kitchen with serious expressions on their faces—including Alizarin, who Umber hadn't seen before they all went to bed the night before.

"Welcome back," he greeted the Abyssi, whose coat had returned to its gleaming turquoise-cobalt sheen. In fact, he looked better fed than he had before the honey incident. "You found a good hunting ground?"

"In the Abyss," Cadmia answered pointedly for the Abyssi.

"I thought I heard Dioxazine calling me," Alizarin explained, his ears twitching with irritation. "I went, but only saw Terre Verte. He wanted me to help Cupric bring Azo to the meeting."

Cupric. Alizarin. Azo. There were so many awful combinations in that statement.

"And you *went*?" Hansa sounded incredulous.

Alizarin swished his tail and glared at the guard. "Azo is not fully recovered yet. I did not want to send a powerful and unfamiliar Abyssumancer to her home without an ally of hers beside him." Now Alizarin grinned, and his eyes sparkled with mischief. "Naples found me while I was hunting. He said he was look-ing for Cupric anyway, and that he could help Azo cross to the mortal plane if she wished it, so he sent me back here."

Naples and Cupric sounded like a much better combination.

"We're worried about Dioxazine," Cadmia said. "Rin says it's concerning that he thought he felt her power, but only saw Verte."

"We've also been talking about Clay," Lydie said. "Naples mentioned him. He *feels* dead to me, but there's something important about him. I've been working on a ritual to try to speak to the shade that has been trying to talk to me about him—someone very old, maybe not even in this plane, which would explain why I've had so much trouble so far. Given Clay was a Numenmancer, the Numini might know something about him, too."

All of this explanation felt like it was leading up to something Umber wasn't going to like.

"You think if you find Xaz, she might be able to help with Clay?" Hansa asked.

"No. We think the Numini might be able to help in both cases," Cadmia answered, "which is why I am going to go to the mancers' temple to try to talk to them."

Umber couldn't believe what she was saying. Be-fore she had even finished speaking, he barked out, "Absolutely not."

Cadmia squared her shoulders. "I do not need your *permission*, Umber. Alizarin will go with me. He says the power I have from the baby will protect me from the energies of the temple's rift, and Verte has done us a favor of ordering the mancers to leave us alone. The Numini spoke to me once, when we were in the depths of the Abyss, and they saved my life, so there's a chance they'll speak to me again. While we're there, Lydie is going to work on her spell to talk to the shade that has been harassing her, *you* are going to go help Ginger to spread rumors and manage nominations for President, and Hansa needs to get to the Quin Compound—unless you two have changed your plans, of course."

They hadn't. Umber opened his mouth to object, then averted his eyes from Cadmia's and caught Hansa's gaze instead.

The Quin gave a half shrug, cleared his throat, and said, "Well, I'm glad we have a plan all set up."

Hansa was right. If Umber had been able to come up with a better plan or even a rational reason why Cadmia couldn't or shouldn't go to the temple, that would have been different. But like Hansa, Cadmia was willing to risk herself to do what she saw as right and needful, and it wasn't Umber's place to protect or forbid her.

CHAPTER 30

CUPRIC

The Abyss was full of sharp things, of things that bit and stung and burned. Granted it also had its share of beautiful things—Alizarin was one example of that—but the Abyssi still fell in the category of things that would eat him if they could.

The Abyssi could have opened a rift here and spared Cupric the awkward, painful, and exhausting effort of doing it on his own, but instead Alizarin had just yawned when the Abyssumancer suggested he might be able to help. Terre Verte pointed out that if Cupric couldn't open a rift *to* the Abyss on his own, there was going to be a problem with his coming back; the clear doubt in his tone hadn't improved Cupric's mood.

Seeing Azo *had* improved his mood. She was a beautiful woman, despite Abyssal coloration, and had looked at him with appreciation in her shining blue-violet gaze when he first walked in and introduced himself.

She had spoken a single command to her servant, and within minutes food had been provided that satisfied not only his stomach but also fed his power. Of course it did; it was grown in the Abyss. The meat provided him, a little more rare than he usually took his steak, was from one of the beasts of this realm. The very *air* held power.

And stinging, burning, sharp, spiny, biting things, as he had discovered later when Alizarin had offered to take him hunting, then abandoned him about twenty minutes from Azo's home. The Abyssi claimed he had found "a friend" while hunting, which probably meant some old catamite, and had sent Cupric back on his own.

"Run afoul of fireflies, did you?" Azo asked, as she examined a burn on his upper arm.

"In Kavet, fireflies aren't actually made of *fire*," he said, somewhat defensively.

She laughed, an expression that briefly cleared the shadows of some unknown sorrow from her features. "In the Abyss, everything burns," she replies, "or bites."

"So I've come to notice."

She salved the burn, easing most of the lingering pain, and bandaged it. "And what about you?" she asked.

"Me?"

She looked askance at him as she turned away, back to the glass of wine she had been nursing when he had returned. "Yes, you," she said, with a smile. "Do you burn, or bite?"

Terre Verte's sister! his mind warned him, as Azo poured a second glass of wine and held it out to him, gaze heavy. *Back away slowly.*

He hesitated too long, and she set the wine down and walked past him. "Well, then. I suppose I'll head to bed." His heart had almost calmed from the moment of panic when she added, "You know where to find me if you change your mind."

Terre Verte's threat had been in regards to anything "that is not with her complete and fully-informed consent," right? Surely even the Terre couldn't blame him for taking a beautiful woman up on an offer that had been made so clearly.

He abandoned the wine, but followed Azo. They didn't reach the stairway, though; as she entered the front foyer, Azo stopped, frozen like stone. Only when he caught up to her did Cupric see that there was now another man in the room, standing in front of the doorway as if he had just walked in, and staring at Azo with the same stricken expression with which she was looking at him.

The man was slender, and the power he gave off was muddled; Cupric wasn't certain if he was looking at a mancer or one of the spawn. Certainly, his copper eyes glowed like something out of the Abyss. "Burn or bite" indeed. Looking at him, Cupric knew this man would burn.

Once he recovered, at least. Just then, he looked like someone had slugged him in the gut. His voice was soft as he said, "Azo . . . Alizarin told me you . . . I should have . . ."

He trailed off.

Cupric saw Azo sway and stepped forward to put an arm around her waist to steady her. "Is this man a problem?" he asked her. Spawn, mancer . . . Whatever he was, Cupric felt confident he could deal with him.

Azo shook her head, slowly.

"You're dead," Azo said, her voice a choked whisper that swiftly rose in volume. "I *felt* you die. You nearly dragged me with you. I tasted the power of your death on Alizarin when he returned here. How do you now walk back into my home?"

"I will explain everything before I leave," the other man said. "First, may I have your permission to perpetuate some violence upon your guest?"

"Excuse me?" Cupric said, the flowery phrasing not detracting from the intent of the statement.

Azo tensed. "Explain yourself, Naples."

"That Abyssumancer and I have some unfinished business," the other man—Naples, apparently—said.

Belatedly, Cupric recognized the power on him. He had seen it very briefly in the mancer temple; they had crossed paths during Cupric's first attempt to reach the Abyss, and Cupric might have been a little rough in taking power from the first place he could find it.

On the other hand, Naples hadn't put up much of a fight, so Cupric wasn't sure how he planned to avenge himself now.

"There's a lot of that in the room right now," Azo replied. "Cupric and I have our own 'business' to attend to."

Naples flinched as surely as if she had slapped him. "Please trust me, and trust that it is not jealousy speaking, when I say that this is not a man you wish to have in your bed. If you would like for me to detail the reasons why, I can."

Cupric shook his head as he stepped forward. "I can deal with this, Azo. There is no reason to concern yourself."

She looked at him, then back at Naples, and shrugged.

"You boys suit yourselves. Naples, you have my permission to do as you think necessary, but when it's done I expect you to explain."

She continued up to her room, leaving Cupric more than a little offended. He had beaten this man once, without much difficulty.

Naples watched her go, a forlorn expression on his

face as she ascended the stairs, but when he returned his gaze to Cupric the sorrow had been replaced with anger bordering on outright hatred.

Yet he smiled, an unpleasant expression that once more made him look more Abyssi than man. "If I had walked in to find you already in her bed, we wouldn't be having this little chat," Naples said. "But as it is, you haven't quite crossed that line, and Terre Verte will probably be cross with me if I kill you."

"You're allied with Terre Verte?" Well, that was interesting. Had the prince sent someone to check up on Cupric?

"More or less," Naples replied. "He doesn't know I'm back yet. Now, let's talk about Umber, shall we?" He stalked forward, and Cupric had to fight a reflex to step back, because there was something not-quite-human in the other man's gaze.

"Who *are* you?"

"My name is Naples. You're Cupric. Pleasantries over."

"You're an Abyssumancer?" Naples nodded. "You're an *Abyssumancer,* and *you're* going to give *me* a hard time about Umber?" Cupric felt more on solid ground now, knowing what he was dealing with.

"Having the Abyss in your blood will push you toward many things," Naples said. "But stalking, drugging, kidnapping, and chaining a fourteen-year-old boy? Getting him blood-drunk, so you can pass yourself off as the only one in Kavet who can possibly meet his needs? That isn't Abyssal. *Hunger* comes from the Abyss. *Impulse* comes from the Abyss. That level of premeditation is mortal or divine, and I don't think the Numini would have approved of that particular plan.

"Now, I need to pull that bond off you. Are you going to let me, or are you going to fight?"

Cupric drew himself up, tearing himself away from the copper fire that had practically hypnotized him. "I want you out of this house. You've distressed Azo enough, and if as you say you're also allied with Terre Verte, then you're getting in the way of his plans."

Naples tossed his head. "You're not the only one here capable of opening a rift to the mortal plane."

Then he did something he shouldn't have been able to do. He twisted his hand, revealing as he drew blood from his arm a sharp, barb-like backing to a black bone ring Cupric hadn't even noticed. He flicked his hand with the same showmanship some of the Abyssi would use with a claw or tail, and beside him appeared a rift.

Naples added, "And I'd say I do it better than you do. But that's all right. You're young. You'll learn, if you survive long enough and stop being a coward about your own power."

He moved close enough to touch, and Cupric drew himself up. *Young.* He easily had ten years on this boy, as well as three or four inches and several pounds of pure muscle. He also hadn't been stupid enough to do something as power-draining as opening a rift across planes in the middle of an argument.

It took only a thought for Cupric to bring his own knife to hand. It could be used to fight directly, and he appeared to have the advantage in *that* kind of fight, but being small didn't make a sorcerer any less deadly.

Cupric closed the distance and wrapped a hand around Naples' arm, over the new wound he had used to open the rift. Most Abyssumancers didn't know you could tap into another's power that way. Naples snarled as Cupric severed the link to the rift, absorbing the backlash of power into himself instead of letting it go to its natural home.

"You picked the wrong fight," Cupric said. "If you are the Terre's ally, I don't want to hurt you, but I will if you force me to it."

Instead of responding with violence, Naples wriggled forward so he could plant a kiss on Cupric's jaw. Cupric shoved him back before that razor-sharp ring got close enough to cut his throat, and Naples chuckled. "C'mon," the other Abyssumancer purred. "We could have fun together."

This was *exactly* what Cupric hated about other Abyssumancers. Everything was sex. They got angry and they wanted sex. Injure them and it was foreplay, bleed them and it was erotic. Granted, Cupric was just as guilty—he had too much Abyss in his power to not feel the same blur between the four coins of power—

but he had enough restraint to recognize when was or wasn't a good place or time.

"I don't do men," he stated.

"No, you don't, do you?" Naples replied. "With a few exceptions, of course, and that's only if there's enough power to make it worth your while. Not that I don't have more than enough power to light you up like a new star."

Cupric wasn't tempted by the offer no matter how much power this wiry little serpent had, but the other man's apparent distraction did offer an opportunity for an advantage. If Naples was distracted by the prospect of sex, it wouldn't be hard to get a strong enough loop of power around him that Cupric could then break his neck.

Naples took the invitation implied by Cupric's silence and slunk forward again. "Of course," he whispered, leaning close, "I do prefer to be face-to-face." The statement was matched by a wriggle that would have been sexy in a woman, but in this case pressed against Cupric parts he normally tried to ignore. Naples made a purring sound when he flinched. "You are *awfully* afraid of dick, for a man who keeps having sex with men. You'll let a fourteen-year-old boy go down on you but you're too Numen-cursed straight-and-narrow to so much as *touch* anything you don't want to."

"How in the three worlds do you know *any* of this?" Cupric asked. He tried to step back, but even though he knew they were in the middle of the room and there was open air behind him, it felt like he was pressing against stone.

"Abyssi watch what their mancers do, and they share the fun parts of the stories," Naples explained. Then he grinned. "I think I just figured out what I want to do to you," he said. "It seems nicely . . . poetic. The Numini might even be proud of my sense of fair play."

CHAPTER 31

CADMIA

Abyssumancers and Numenmancers, when they wanted to enter the mancers' temple, could do so one of two ways: they could go through days of elaborate and exhausting ritual to open a rift, or they could find one of the rifts that dotted Kavet. Those entrances to a place that wasn't really a place at all, a place that existed part in the mortal realm and part in the Other realms, moved around, sometimes lingering in the same spot for years and sometimes appearing and disappearing in days.

Cadmia didn't need to create or find a rift because she had an Abyssi with her. A flick of Alizarin's tail was all it took to open a portal to the temple.

It took far more than that for her to gather the courage to step *through* it.

She was not a mancer. She was not an Abyssi. She was not even spawn, herself; she only carried one in her womb. She was a scholar and proud of that fact, but she was acutely aware that she was an outsider and an intruder as she crossed the threshold into a space that pulsed and writhed with living power.

Alizarin didn't accompany her. She hoped to talk to a Numini, and the Numini were less likely to talk to Cadmia if she spoke to them with an Abyssi at her back. If she summoned him, he would come quickly, but her safety here depended mostly on Terre Verte's orders to his followers—and his control over those followers.

That was not a comforting thought, and since thoughts created reality in this place, the vague sense of walls around her constricted and shuddered.

"*Child of Napthol,*" a voice greeted her. The creature that spoke moved in a wreath of sooty power that sparkled with orange and yellow barbs, and even though Cadmia could not see the Abyssi's face here, she recognized her from their brief encounter in the Abyss. If anyone else was nearby—Abyssi, Numini or mancer—Cadmia could not sense them.

"Vanadium, of the second level court?"

The Abyssi replied in syllable tones that seemed affirmative despite the lack of words.

"I find it interesting you greet me as belonging

to Napthol," Cadmia said, "and not to Alizarin." She would have expected an Abyssi to credit her status as Alizarin's lover as more important.

"The Numini are more interesting lately than the blue prince," Vanadium replied.

"Then Napthol really is a Numini?"

Again, that hissing *yes*.

"Do you know anything about the Napthol's other chosen?" Cadmia asked. "Their mancers?"

Again, a non-verbal response. This time, Cadmia had the impression of flicking spines, a dismissive gesture.

"Your mancer is allied with Terre Verte, isn't she? Does she know anything about Dioxazine?"

"If you wish to know about the Numini's toys," Vanadium purred, "why don't you ask the Numini?"

"Do you think Napthol would speak to me?"

Vanadium retreated, her form becoming less distinct. "You have spoken that Numini's name three times now. In this place, words are power. The Numini hear. If they deign to, they will speak to you."

"Why are you helping me?" Cadmia thought to ask, belatedly. The last time she had seen this Abyssi, Vanadium had been trying to earn tribute gifts from Alizarin.

"My mancer, Keppel, is uneasy," Vanadium answered, before disappearing entirely.

The Abyssi had said Napthol had heard Cadmia's words so far, but idle questions didn't seem as respectful as speaking her request out loud, so Cadmia said into the void, "Napthol of the Numini, if you hear me and will grant me your time, please speak to me."

She waited, trying to control the space around her through sheer will. She finally managed to slow the dark pulsing of the walls, and had just started to expand the claustrophobic space when a new presence entered it, streaking the world silver and white. A Numini.

It immediately backed away, until her impression of it was distant and shadowed.

"*Careful, child,*" it said. Its voice was faint and distorted, as if heard through water. "*This place protects you somewhat, but it is not safe for mortals to behold the divine too clearly.*"

The same was true of Abyssi, Cadmia knew, but it didn't seem wise to say as much just then.

"Thank you for answering me," Cadmia said. "And for saving my life . . . that was you who saved my life in the Abyss, wasn't it?"

"It was I," the Numini said. "You are not one of our chosen . . . I do not give mortals marks of my favor, these days . . . but your sect kept my name and so I watch you still." His sigh was an icy breeze, rippling with disappointment, before he added, "It is not your fault that you have been pulled into situations you cannot control. I cannot rid you of the child you carry, but after it has been born if you need my aid you may call to me to free your body of its lingering Abyssal taint."

Cadmia had no physical body in this place, which was the only way she kept bile from rising up her throat. Only her long years of training in the Order helped her quash her revulsion so it didn't turn the temple around her to a disgusted green vortex that would attempt to wring itself free of this arrogant Numini.

Instead, she choked out, "What about now? We are looking for information about Dioxazine, or a man named Clay who we think was also a Numenmancer. Can you help me?"

The Numini's form quivered more. "I . . . I cannot aid you in this matter, not without defying the decrees of our highest Arbitrator, but I know one who can. He has been trying to reach your necromancer, but she lacks the tools she needs to speak to him. Give her this, and—"

As Cadmia felt something pressed into her hand, the Temple twisted, all that was smooth and silver and white turning puce-gray and jagged. A new form appeared, one that radiated pain and hunger.

"Flee," the Numini whispered. "He is too hungry to respect anyone's decrees. You have what you need, and all I can give you. Tell your necromancer to tell him that Napthol is loyal still."

Cadmia felt ice push her at the same time that Alizarin, perhaps sensing the same disturbance, pulled her back. Abruptly she found herself on the floor of

Umber's living room, sweat-soaked and dizzy, her hand clamped tightly around——sand?

She opened her fingers, which felt stiff, as if she had held them clenched for hours. The substance trapped within was a dull ivory, with tiny grains like fine-ground salt. It didn't look like much, but she held it carefully, trusting that it was precious.

"Do we have something I can put this in?" she asked. "A Numini gave it to me, and said to give it to Lydie to help with her spell." Recalling the kinds of tools Numenmancers used, she added, "Crystal or silver would be best, I think."

They walked together to the kitchen, where they eventually found an ornate silver teacup that hid alone in a top cabinet. Had it been part of a set once? What had happened to its companions?

She carefully poured the dusky off-white grains into the cup, and stared at them. "It doesn't look like much," she said.

"You are blind to divine power on this plane," Alizarin said. His voice was tight, and when Cadmia looked at him, she saw that his eyes had watered while he looked at the simple-looking grains. "Veronese told me all three planes have seas. The Abyss's great ocean is dry, and our smaller seas are hot and oily and poison. The mortal plane's ocean is dark and cold and salty like tears. In the Numen, there's a great ocean that is cool and fresh and perfectly clear like crystal. Souls are born there, and flow into the mortal plane to be born, and every time they do, that's when it rains here. And sometimes souls pass from the Abyss, through the mortal plane and to the Numen, and that's when the lightning comes. Or so Veronese told me."

"That's lovely," Cadmia said, sighing along with Alizarin as his gaze went distant.

"These are grains of sand from the shore of the Numen sea," Alizarin added. He reached out a hand, then drew it back as if afraid his touch would contaminate them. Knowing what she did of the Numini, Cadmia suspected he was right, though it hurt her heart to see the longing in his eyes.

She set the sand down, then wrapped her arms around her lover and pressed her cheek to his chest.

CHAPTER 32

HANSA

After spending the morning going over logs and reports, Hansa had come to the conclusion that he needed a distraction.

Of the six sighted guards who should have been in the 126, four were missing, and one had had a close call the night before.

Confining the two remaining sighted guards to the compound was not an option, not when Hansa was stuck there all day. He also wasn't willing to send them out into the city to be hunted and slaughtered by Verte's allies. Meanwhile, he needed to squelch rumors of a mancer gathering at Amaranth Farms.

He needed a distraction—something big and

splashy that would justify his sending the two remaining sighted guards and at least one of the remaining captains away from the city to investigate. And they needed to find a situation messy enough that they felt they had interrupted something.

Setting that up seemed like a good job for Umber and Alizarin. He would have them do it that night.

In the meantime, he groaned as he tried to refocus on the personnel files while waiting for someone to come in and tell him he had been nominated for President.

"Sir? Are you all right?"

Oh. Right. Rinnman had been Hansa's right-hand all day. He had been up much of the night gathering the information Hansa had requested, and then had apologized for coming in late.

He's the one who should be promoted to general and elected President, Hansa thought sourly.

"We have only one application from someone with the sight," Hansa observed, lifting his head, "and the captain who interviewed him described him as 'unstable, irrational, paranoid, and unkempt.'" Hansa didn't want to add more sighted soldiers to the guard, but ignoring the obvious need would look suspicious.

The other soldier gave a half smile before apparently deciding the expression was uncalled-for, and hiding it. "Let me know if I'm out of line, sir, but there are other applicants with the sight in the pile labeled, 'Prerequisites not met.'"

Hansa quirked a brow. "I assumed they were in that pile for a reason."

"Some of them are too young or have a history with the Order of A'hknet, but most of those were disqualified because they're women." Rinnman kept his tone even as he spoke, careful not to allow any hint of approval or disapproval enter his voice.

"Hmm." Hansa reached for the pile, which he had set aside on the floor hours ago, before remembering he *didn't* want anyone else with the sight. On the other hand . . . "If they were disqualified based on sex, I assume they never reached the interview stage?"

The other man shook his head. "I don't know how much it will help you. I worked with a few women in my earliest years in the One-Twenty-Six, and they were fine soldiers, but His Eminence doesn't approve of them in the guard these days."

Ever since Umber's mother.

No. Bonnie Holland had been an excuse, not a cause.

"His Eminence is a wise man," Hansa said. "I am sure he will see that in times like these, all possibilities must be considered." *Such bullshit.*

"It will make some of the men uncomfortable as well," Rinnman said. He didn't sound like he personally disagreed. Hansa suspected Rinnman was trying to prepare him for future arguments.

"Having men *disappear* makes me uncomfortable," Hansa replied. "Since you seem to have some familiarity with it already, I'm putting you in charge of looking through these and pulling out anyone who looks like a *likely* applicant, regardless of sex. You can conduct the first round of interviews."

Rinnman nodded. "Yes, sir."

Good. That would look productive, take time, and keep Hansa from having to directly deal with any applicants with the sight.

As the older soldier pushed himself up, leaning on his crutch, he said, "Sir, permission to speak freely?"

Hansa resisted the impulse to say, *First you can stop calling me sir when you're almost twice my age,* and instead said, "Permission granted."

Despite having been granted permission, Rinnman didn't immediately seem anxious to speak. Eventually, he managed to say, "I don't know if you recall me, but I was one of the men brought onto the panel when there were some . . . concerns . . . as to your behavior."

How could Hansa recall *anyone* from that day? He had been arrested, and would have been tried and sentenced without ever seeing those who would judge him.

It took him a moment more to realize Rinnman was referring to the *other* time.

"Yes?" he said. Years ago, he and Jenkins had been found—and had in fact *been*—innocent of sexual deviance. It was awkward having someone bring it up now that he was actually guilty of it, but he kept his face impassive.

Rinnman drew a breath, and then said, "Never mind, sir. I'll get on those interviews for you."

Well, that was curious and unsettling.

Rinnman left, and Hansa turned back to his papers, wondering what the other man had intended to say. It could have been anything, from, "I thought you were guilty" to "I still think you're guilty" to "I have a nephew who is attracted to men and would really like someone to talk to about it."

Or, "I have a nephew who was propositioned last night by a member of your dinner party."

Why the fuck did I have sex with Naples?

The thought, which had been reoccurring to him intermittently all morning, caught him off guard. Despite his calm words to Umber that morning, he couldn't quite believe he had done it, and he was glad Naples had left before he had needed to face that fact. He didn't have to deal with it again until—well, until the next time Naples knocked on that door. Which he would.

Work, Hansa!

It was a little before lunch when the first reports came, again filtered through a now-furious-seeming Rinnman: The rumors had started that President Indathrone was missing, along with several members of the 126. He promised to track down the leak. Hansa made his face appropriately grave and nodded.

Then, shortly after lunch, another knock on his door:

"Sir?" It was Soldier Gray now, dancing on his feet as he attempted to report calmly. "A group of citizens just delivered a petition for an emergency assembly. I delivered it to the city council's secretary, but thought you should be informed as well. They want to elect an interim President until President Indathrone returns."

Hansa didn't have the energy to appear shocked. He managed to say neutrally, "That sounds like a good idea."

"Cadmia Paynes has been nominated," Gray blurted out. "Isn't she the one who—um—"

Hansa was too busy blinking past his surprise to immediately understand the question. Cadmia. Why hadn't they considered that? The first President of Kavet *was* a woman, after all, and Cadmia was well-known and liked without needing Umber to clear her for maleficence and mass murder.

That thought helped him fill in the rest of Gray's stammered question. "The one who reported against me?" he suggested. Gray nodded miserably. "It was a misunderstanding. She did her job based on the information she had. I hold no grudge against her for that."

Rinnman came to the door. "The council chambers have a line stretching halfway across the plaza," he reported. "Requests for information, more nominations, and registrations for the assembly I'm sure. They just dispatched a courier to alert to the outlying towns. We . . ."

Hansa missed the rest of Rinnman's report as all his attention turned toward a rush of power that brought him mentally back to the fifth level of the Abyss, where creatures of madness and shadow reigned. His breath hissed in.

"Sir?" Rinnman asked. "Is there a problem?"

Hansa looked past Rinnman and Gray, and spotted Naples being escorted across the room by another guard. Panic choked him for an instant, thankfully cutting off his first response, before he realized that Naples hadn't been drugged or chained, but was being walked in like any other visitor.

Like a slightly drunk visitor, Hansa thought, seeing that Naples appeared just a bit unsteady on his feet.

"I need to take this meeting," Hansa said, frantically trying to remember where the two remaining sighted guards were at that moment. "It should be news I've been waiting on."

As quickly as possible, he had a closed door between himself and Naples.

"What in the three realms have you been *doing?*" Hansa asked, reeling from the heady swirls of power rising from the Abyssumancer. "And why are you doing it *here?*"

Naples crossed the room, put himself in Hansa's arms, and kissed him. The wash of power that flowed from him, seeping skin to skin, took all the strength from Hansa's knees. They both toppled back into a chair, with Naples barely catching them on the desk to keep the chair and both of them from falling over.

Hansa might not have noticed, not with the Abyssumancer seeping power and straddling him.

"I thought I should share," Naples replied. He leaned back a little, blinking slowly, and said, "I should probably ask first, shouldn't I?"

"It's polite," Hansa answered inanely, fighting the impulse to pull Naples closer again.

Above the loose collar of Naples' shirt, Hansa spotted claw marks that wrapped around the back of his neck then seemed to go down to his chest. Looking more carefully, Hansa spotted the edge of another on Naples' wrist where his cuff had hitched up. The wounds weren't bleeding anymore, but they hadn't quite healed yet, either.

"What have you been doing?" Hansa asked again, holding the clearly-intoxicated Abyssuancer at arm's length no matter how much he wanted to drag him down across the desk.

"Sennelier," Naples answered.

"Senne—*the Abyssi*?"

"He, Cupric and I had quite the threesome," Naples said.

The other Abyssumancer's name was enough to cool some of Hansa's ardor.

"Is Cupric dead?" Hansa asked.

Naples shook his head. "I didn't figure that would go over well with Terre Verte." Then he smirked.

"But it's going to be a *looooong* time before he forgets us. And I cleared any remnants of the bond from him, so he won't be able to rebuild the link from his side. And I saw Alizarin. And Azo. I brought her to Amaranth Farms, since that's where she wanted to go. She's campaigning or organizing or something for her brother I guess."

Hansa wanted to ask for details about Cupric, but when Naples spoke Azo's name, it was with a choked tone that had nothing to do with the lust and power Naples had been radiating a moment before.

"Are you all right?"

The Abyssumancer hesitated an instant, then said, "There's more than one reason I'm appreciating being really, *really* drunk right now." He squinted a little, as if to focus, and asked, "Do you mind that I came here? I could leave."

"I *wish* I could invite you to stay," Hansa groaned, "but this is probably the last place you should be right now. You're not veiling your power." Hansa doubted Naples was capable of that at the moment. "But I have a job for you, which Umber and maybe Alizarin can help you with."

"Your wish is my command, Mister President," Naples quipped.

Briefly, Hansa detailed his thoughts about how they needed a dramatic-looking distraction that would give him an excuse to send sighted solders away, and would make the other solders in the 126 feel like they were doing something about the increasing rumors about a mancer gathering. Naples' eyes sparkled in a way that made it clear he had some ideas, and was looking forward to them.

"We can do that," he said. "How about Eiderlee—is it still called Eiderlee?"

Hansa vaguely recognized the town's name, and nodded. "It's a couple days outside the city I think."

"Alizarin, Umber and I can move faster through the rifts," Naples said. "We can be home by dinner." He grinned again, but slowly the expression started to fade as he asked more seriously, "Unless you would rather I not come back with them?"

Hansa started to answer immediately, then cleared his throat. "Come for dinner," he said. "Right now I feel like saying stay afterwards, but you're glowing with enough power it's making me dizzy."

Another flash of white teeth. "I'll look forward to asking again when we're both sober. In the meantime, enjoy your day."

"Can you clean up the lobby a little without anyone noticing?" Hansa asked. "I'm not sure what the sighted guards might see when they come back, but—"

Naples gave a dramatic sigh. "You're no fun," he said, "but you can consider it done."

He sauntered out, pausing to blow a kiss over his shoulder before he opened the door. Hansa stopped to take several deep breaths and try to put the veils on his power back in place, which was what he was still doing when Rinnman stepped in.

"Good timing, Rinnman," Hansa said. "The man who was just here was a contact of mine in Eiderlee. We need to—"

"Sir," Rinnman interrupted politely, proffering a letter sealed with the symbol of the city council.

Hansa cracked the seal, feeling a bit like a figure in a dream. In the elaborate formal script of the council scribe, the letter informed him that he had been nominated by the requisite number of citizens as a candidate for interim President. There was a place at the bottom of the form for him to sign either accepting or declining the nomination.

He stared at it.

"Do you intend to accept?" Rinnman asked.

Hansa took a deep breath. He dipped his pen in the ink. And he signed his name.

CHAPTER 33

CUPRIC

Cupric had managed to crawl back to the temple, and stopped there to rest—or try to. He kept waking with a start. When he first arrived, he had thought he had sensed Alizarin, but that unreliable beast had abandoned him in the Abyss and hadn't reappeared since. Later, there had been some kind of scuffle between a pair of Numini; their crystalline voices had made his head ache.

The temple wasn't safe. It wasn't a good place to sleep. But Amaranth Farms wasn't any better, not when Cupric would need to face Terre Verte and tell him he had failed.

Damn that Abyssumancer. Who had he been? Where had he come from?

Cupric would have to return to Amaranth briefly, since that was the soft spot in the mortal plane he knew he could reach from the temple, but he wouldn't stay. If he stayed, he was going to have to kill Terre Verte in his sleep, because damn him, this was *his* fault.

Cupric could have blamed the other Abyssumancer, of course, but even *thinking* of Naples made the temple's mutable form quiver.

"*Mancer.*"

"Fuck off," he snarled to the first Abyssi who spoke to him. Then he changed his mind and said, "Wait." It growled, but Cupric could keep some control of it in this place, even in his present state. "Tell me everything you know about the Abyssumancer Naples."

The Abyssi laughed. "*Everything?*" it asked.

"You do know him, don't you?"

"*We all know him,*" the Abyssi answered. "*He is Modigliani's.*"

"Whose?" An Abyssi, probably, but the name was said as if it meant more than that.

Another voice spoke, one Cupric hadn't expected to hear. "*You do not know Modigliani?*" one of the Numini asked. It was hard to tell through the cool voice and the shift in the temple as the creature spoke, but Cupric thought it sounded surprised.

"I've made a point of not getting too personally familiar with too many Abyssi."

He cringed at the memory. He had almost thought he had the upper hand in the fight with Naples, and then the damn witch had smiled, drawn blood, and whispered, "Sennelier, I invoke you, summon you, invite you. I offer sport."

"*But you know Modigliani's Abyssumancer,*" the Numini said. "*You are a friend of Naples*?"

"*Not* a friend," Cupric responded, vehemently, before pausing to consider whether a lie could have been more profitable.

"*If you are no friend of his, and no friend of Modigliani's . . .*" It seemed puzzled, and curious. "*Are you allied with Terre Verte?*"

He had no idea what the Numini was getting at, but decided he probably didn't care. It couldn't harm him, not in the temple. The Abyssi around him would devour it if it dared violate the magical treaties here.

So he told the truth.

"Not anymore," he said.

"*If that is the case, we may have a use for you.*"

"*He isn't one of yours,*" the Abyssi said, entering into the conversation once again. "*We let you talk to Alizarin's mate because she chose you long ago, and he is odd for our kind. This one is ours.*"

"*This one,*" the Numini argued, "*is a mancer, one of the more powerful of his kind, and therefore free. He can respond to a proposal as he wishes, with or without your* consent. *Sennelier never meddles with the affairs of the mortal realm, anyway."*

"I'm listening," Cupric said, intrigued, but cautious. Numini didn't seek out Abyssumancers; they simply *didn't*. Why was this one talking to him, and what did it have to do with Naples or Terre Verte?

"Sennelier doesn't meddle," the Abyssi said, *"but he would object to your using what is his."*

"If we cannot acquire his permission, it can be done without," the Numini replied. *"We can free you of him if you wish, mancer."*

Cupric's idle curiosity shifted to alarm.

"No thank you," he said. The Numini moved closer, now seeming confused. "Look, I don't know if I can or can't help you or what you *want* me to help you with—or why—but no matter how I feel about recent events, I'm very sure I don't want to belong to the Numini. No offense, but I like a lot of things your kind doesn't approve of. And if you just mean 'free' from the Abyss, I like *power* too much to give it up."

"We cannot completely strip you of the Abyss even if we wished to," the Numini said with an impatient sigh. *"Trying to remove that power would kill you. And as you cannot help what you are, we would make no attempt to curtail your attempts to feed."*

Well, that was condescending and comforting at the same time—but what else could you expect from one of the divine realm?

He had opened his mouth to respond when the

Abyssi who had argued with the Numini moved forward again. Cupric wasn't sure if it meant to attack or not, because almost immediately there was a ringing in his ears, like the sound of someone running a damp finger around the rim of a crystal goblet. The Numini responded with the graceful beauty of frost—and an instant later, the Abyssi who had tried to interfere was simply *gone*. Cupric wasn't sure if it had been banished from the temple, or outright killed.

"*Rude,*" the Numini said, its tone utterly dismissive. "*Now, Mancer, where were we?*"

"We were at, what do you want from me, and what does my knowing and not liking Naples have to do with it?"

"*Naples belongs to the lord of the Abyss,*" the Numini replied. "*As such he is not to be trusted and not to be trifled with, directly at least. But he and I have fought before, and Modigliani is not as much of a threat as many think he is.*"

"You've fought," Cupric repeated. "Who *won*?"

The Numini laughed, and the sound was like bells and a breath of warm air amidst the chill. "*I did, naturally. I was a lord in my own right before Modigliani was ever hatched, and a simple Abyssumancer has few defenses against the divine.*"

"All at once, I'm liking you even more," Cupric said. "But let's get back to what you want from me."

"*I need a tie to the mortal plane,*" the Numini said simply. "*My Numenmancer has been taken from me and I fear I must resort to drastic measures to retrieve her.*"

"Your Numenmancer . . . Xaz?" Cupric hazarded the guess, based mostly on his earlier observation of Terre Verte's bed-turned-altar.

The Numini didn't exactly nod, not in this bubble of unreality, but the effect was the same.

"You're going after Terre Verte, then?" Cupric asked.

He must release her.

This all sounded too good to be true. Of course, there was one snag to it he already had identified. "I admit the idea of having an ally who can best Naples appeals to me, as does the idea of your interfering with Terre Verte's plans since I think he's batshit crazy. But I'm an Abyssumancer. Assuming I were willing to help you, I don't see how I *could.*"

"*The blue prince has already demonstrated the technique,*" the Numini said, "*when he formed a link to Dioxazine. Since I ask for your consent, I would have no need for his subtlety. I can mark you with my power before you leave the temple, and it will linger in you long enough for you to open a rift and for me to assist you in allowing me to cross.*"

This was madness.

Then again, so were the slices up and down Cupric's body from Sennelier's claws and teeth—not to mention Naples' knife. He could use a powerful ally. Xaz had supposedly had some trouble managing her power immediately after she bonded to Alizarin, but by the time Cupric had met her it all seemed to be under control again. If this Numini could help Cupric extract himself from what had become a painfully volatile situation, it was probably worth it.

"I want to establish a few things before I agree to anything." The Numini nodded again. "I'm *not* a Numenmancer. I won't be commanded, and I will *not* be chastised. I will sleep, or eat, or fuck, what I wish, when I wish, and I don't care if I offend your Numen sensibilities."

"I have already agreed that I would not attempt to prevent you from . . . indulging," the Numini said, distaste obvious in its voice. *"It would hardly be fair to attempt otherwise, since I will be equally free of your commands, as Alizarin has also demonstrated."*

"What would I need to do to summon you?" Cupric said, still contemplating.

"Once I have marked you, you should be able to feel our power," the Numini said. *"I have seen you open a rift once already across the planes. I am sure your attempt to reach the Numen will be awkward, but I will assist from the other side, and it will be enough."*

"I should know your name, in order to summon you."

"You may call me Doné, if you wish. It is what my intimates call me, in my realm."

It could still all go terribly, terribly wrong, but so far as Cupric was concerned, between Terre Verte and Naples, things had already gone bad.

"Okay," he said, agreeing. "You can—"

The Numini did not wait to hear more. The frost crept from Cupric's feet, up his legs, over his hips, across his torso, down to the tips of his fingers, and over his throat. At Cupric's next breath, it felt like he had walked out into the coldest of Kavet's winter days; his lungs seized as he choked on the icy air. He had long enough to think, *I wonder if it remembers an Abyssumancer can freeze to death,* and then the world went dark.

He woke, no longer in the temple, but back in his bed at Amaranth Farms. He tried to push himself to a sitting position, but the muscles in his arm trembled and it collapsed from under him. He let out a cry as he hit the bed again.

In the temple, where it was power instead of muscle that moved him, he had been able to forget how hurt he was. He needed to feed, but that was going to be difficult if he couldn't even walk.

He glanced down at his body, which was crisscrossed with cuts and darkened with bruises and the edge of curling burns. The bleeding had stopped, but that had been all he had been able to manage.

He looked closer, and realized that some of the marks he had first taken for bruises were in fact frostbite blisters. That was new, and doubtless a result of accepting the Numini's power. Well, Xaz seemed to be fine—or she had been before the Terre had done whatever he had done to her.

Time to play this game.

He rolled over onto his stomach, wincing as the movement pressed on cuts, bruises, and blisters, and shut his eyes to examine his own power. As the Numini had suggested, it was easy to reach toward the Numen; he could feel a *tug* from that direction as the Numini guided his fumbling.

I'm going to need you to help me feed, then get somewhere safe, he said as he reached the Numini he had spoken to in the Temple. *I know that's probably not what you wish to do, but if I don't feed soon, I'll lose any connection I manage to make to you.*

I will assist you.

It was like reaching into a deep lake, and having something from that darkness wrap tendrils around him and *pull*. He shuddered against the alien feel of it, but didn't fight. "Doné," he whispered, instead, knowing the name wasn't real but using it to direct his attention.

"I call you into this world." Calling one of the Abyssi didn't need to be so ritualistic, but the Numini liked ritual, their *power* liked ritual, and it was easier to use it than fight it.

"On the power of the agreement we have made I summon you and bind you to your promises.

"By my power, given to me by Sennelier, and by you, I invoke you and offer you a bond in this world.

"I call you, summon you, invoke you thrice."

As the last words were spoken, Cupric felt the air around him cool. He squinted, trying to see but needing to protect his eyes from the icy air. He wished he had had the sense to curl up in the blanket before doing this, even though he knew it wouldn't have made a difference; this cold was coming from inside.

He shut his eyes the rest of the way as light blinded him, then snapped them open as he felt a hand on his shoulder. The first thing he could make out past the glare was the shadow cast by the Numini's wings on the far wall. The glow dimmed gradually, or else his eyes adapted, and a long fall of raven-dark hair came into focus. Then skin the color of violets, and slowly, swirls of white and silver across that skin. Eyes like mercury, surrounded by black lashes. The graceful curve of a cheek, and of lips of dusky rose, then the curve of a hip, a breast, a thigh, and he realized that the Numini was not an *it* but a *she* and in fact the most beautiful creature he had ever had the honor to gaze upon.

He felt his heart skip and was certain the tears in his eyes were from neither the cold nor the glare, both of which were now tolerable.

Every fiber of his body still ached, but he found himself struggling down from the bed, conscious that his body had responded to her beauty and fearful that he would offend before he fell to his knees before her.

She reached down and caressed his cheek. His eyes closed and he sighed.

"We *will do well together, Abyssumancer*," she said, with a voice like the wind across the sea. *"Indeed we will."*

CHAPTER 34

LYDIE

Lydie groaned as Cadmia handed her the silver tea-cup and told her what was in it—both because this silver souvenir reeked of its previous owner's death, and because the last thing Lydie wanted to do was try to talk to the Numini.

"Why *me*?" she wondered aloud. Whined, perhaps. She had earned a chance to whine, hadn't she? "If a Numini wants to talk to us so badly, why doesn't it send a Numenmancer?"

She took the cup, which was bitterly cold, as if it was full of snow instead of sand.

"I got the impression the Numini have been forbidden by their own leaders from helping us," Cadmia answered—far too calmly, in Lydie's opinion.

"Forbidden," she echoed. "That doesn't trouble you, that the *divine realm* seems to oppose what we're doing?"

"The divine realm pushed us to rescue Terre Verte from the Abyss," Cadmia retorted. "I'm currently opposed to whatever they are doing, too." She shook her head. "My impression was that there is some fighting in the ranks. The one I spoke to wanted you to tell the Numini trying to reach you that Napthol is 'loyal still,' whatever that means."

Lydie had more questions, but they weren't ones Cadmia could answer. Loyal to whom, or to what? Were there factions fighting among the Numini? And most importantly: *Why was I foolish enough to get involved in all this?*

But it was too late to back out now, much as she wished she could.

"I'll see what I can do," she sighed, looking into the cup. The death attached to it was old, residue left by a shade who had died peacefully and moved on. It was only as strong as it was because someone— Umber, presumably—had kept this specifically as a memento of that loss. "Umber is rich and loves to cook. Doesn't he have some silver cookware or something like that? I can't use this." She lifted the teacup. "It's distracting."

"He's half-Abyssi," Cadmia pointed out. "I doubt

he wants to steep his food in silver. I found some linen napkins?" she suggested. "Numenmancers usually use silk, but these are new at least, as if he bought them recently but hadn't had a chance to use them."

"If this Numini is so desperate to talk to us, it will need to tolerate linen," Lydie grumbled.

As they searched Umber's linen cabinet, Cadmia asked, "Why is the teacup distracting?"

Lydie turned to stare at her, dumbfounded. "You found a single silver teacup in a cabinet somewhere—I'm guessing *not* with the rest of the dishes—and you didn't automatically assume it had come from someone dead?"

Cadmia winced, as if the thought really hadn't occurred to her, and handed Lydie one of the linen napkins. "I have a friend at the Cobalt Hall who collects silver spoons," she said. "I didn't think more about it."

Because Umber's house is littered with knickknacks and collections.

"It belonged to someone named Bonnie . . . Bonnie something," Lydie said, as she carefully poured the sand into the center of the napkin, then gratefully handed the cup to Cadmia. "She hasn't touched it in a long time, like maybe she lost it long ago, but someone—I'm guessing Umber—remembers it as hers."

"So she is dead?" Cadmia asked quietly.

It was hard for Lydie to remember sometimes that that information wasn't always widely known.

"Yes," Lydie answered. "Peacefully, if that helps, a few years ago but not too many. Should I say sorry for your loss?"

Cadmia shook her head. "I never knew her. I'll put this back where I found it."

Lydie folded the napkin carefully before letting out a relieved breath. At least she wouldn't be asked to facilitate communication with the dead again.

Just with a Numini.

She looked around the house, and frowned. She had spent the last days reinforcing walls to keep this creature out of her sleeping area, and didn't want to breach those defenses, but she also didn't want to attempt a ritual to talk to the Numini in the same spot where she had tied her power to the Abyss to help Hansa talk to Jenkins. Similarly, she wanted to avoid all the bedrooms.

It seemed there was no helping it.

Cadmia looked like she wanted to invite herself along, but Lydie had learned her lesson from having Hansa in her circle. . She returned to her room alone, and for a few minutes sat on the couch, closed her eyes, and simply breathed.

She had moved the couch to the center of the room and wrapped her protective circle around it the night before, so all she needed to do today was find the nerve to invite a massive, ethereal entity that had probably been responsible for her sleeplessness and splitting headaches to talk to her.

She also needed to decide how to use the white sand. She didn't want to mix it into her circle of salt and earth; the Numini might see that as desecration. The best she could think to do was display it in front of her in the style of an altar and gently set her fingertips to it, using it as a focus in the way she might use the personal effects of one of the dead.

As the powerful chill of the Numen crept up her left arm, she drew a breath and dropped into the realm of the dead. Here inside her circle it was peaceful and still; the shades were locked outside, awaiting her next instruction.

"I call to the entity of the Numen who has been trying to speak to me," she said, wishing she had a name with which to call it. Names were powerful.

The scraping, tapping sound came again, like branches sliding on a windowpane. This time she recognized it as a knock. There was a voice as well, but she couldn't make out the words with her walls up.

She lifted an arm to open the doorway, and said, "I invite—"

"*NO.*" The force of the negation, shoved through her walls, stole her breath. It added more softly, almost too softly for her to hear, "*Listen only. Do not look.*"

This was seeming like a worse idea by the moment. Lydie closed her eyes, then tried again. Focusing her attention on the creature beyond her walls, she said reluctantly, "I invite you in. Speak to me."

Her breath hissed in as coldness suffused her circle. This creature was touched by the dead plane, yes, which was both how she had felt it and how her wards had initially held it at bay, but it could never be mistaken for a simple shade. In some ways it reminded her of Naples, as if death was just something it had worn briefly.

"*I am sorry to disturb you, and that my attempts to communicate hurt you,*" the creature—Numini?—said. Its voice was melodious and sad. Lydie squeezed her eyes tighter shut to fight the desire to open them and see what was before her. As if sensing the impulse, the creature added, "*You must not look at me fully. I am only a shade of my previous strength, but mortals who look upon the divine are lost to its power. Our Numenmancers are immune, but no one else.*"

Lydie's skin rose in gooseflesh, but it wasn't just the warning. It was *cold*. She was starting to shiver, too. "If you have something you need to tell me, please say it fast," she urged the being.

"*I'm sorry, so sorry,*" it said again. "*You were the only one I could reach. I need to send a warning to Alizarin, and I cannot talk to him directly.*"

Lydie sighed. Once again, it seemed to be her job to pass messages. "What is the warning?"

"*Dioxazine's Numini, the one who made her a Numenmancer, is in this world. She seeks to free her Numenmancer.*

She will need to rest for some time to recover from the strain of crossing the veil, but after that I fear she will target Alizarin first. She may kill him outright, or she may just try to break the bond, but either will destroy the individual he is now."

"Alizarin is a prince of the third level of the Abyss," Lydie pointed out. "Is this Numini strong enough to win in a fight against him? And why can that Numini possibly kill Alizarin, but you can't even talk to him?"

"Alizarin is powerful, but Dioxazine's Numini is one of the three high Arbiters of the Numini, and among the oldest of our kind. As for the rest . . ." The creature's sign encompassed all the beauty of frost on the surface of a lake. *"I was banished from the Numen long ago, and then banished from the Abyss. Once I had a tie to a Numenmancer on this plane, but . . ."* Again, there was no sound, but Lydie could feel the shift in power. If the dead could weep, this is what it would feel like. *"All is ash. It is his death you feel on me, and which allows me to linger on death's plane. Allows. As if I have anywhere else to go."*

"You're a Numini . . . ghost?" Lydie clarified. "That's possible?"

"It's close enough to correct," the dead Numini replied. *"We cannot be killed by mortal means, but our own kind can destroy us. Please, you must warn Alizarin. I used him at my Numenmancer's command, but I loved him and I would not see him harmed."*

"If this Numini is so powerful, how can Alizarin protect himself?"

"Dioxazine's Numini will be more powerful when her mancer is free, which is why Terre Verte has imprisoned her, and why her Numini will first seek to free her. I do not know what horrors she may inflict on Amaranth, Terre Verte, and his mancers there, both in order to retrieve Dioxazine and once she is free."

"She's a Numini," Lydie said. "She wouldn't hurt people, would she?"

"She has tied herself to an Abyssumancer, and does not realize what that entails. She believes all things strive toward the right and the Numen given a chance, that Alizarin's recent behavior is proof of this, and that already being of the Numen she will not be tempted by Abyssal things. She does not understand the rage and hunger. It feels to her like righteous fury, which is familiar to her, not like bloodthirst, which is what it is."

"Why in the three planes would a Numini willingly bind herself to an Abyssumancer?" Lydie asked, with horror. The Quinacridone movement was proof of what happened when you mixed morality with simple human bloodlust; she didn't want to see a Numini feeling all the hungers of the Abyss for the first time.

"Because Terre Verte has imprisoned Dioxazine and in doing so made it impossible for her Numini to reach any Numenmancers. He did this to weaken the Numini, and it worked, but has created a monster."

"You didn't answer me: How can Alizarin fight this Numini? Or the rest of us, for that matter. I'm not sure slaughter is how we want to deal with the Terre Verte issue."

"*Dioxazine can fight her Numini. Numini do all but lie to hide it, but on this plane, a Numenmancer is the more powerful of the pair.*"

"You just said freeing Dioxazine will strengthen her Numini."

"*It is a double-edged sword.*"

"And you said the Numini is likely to slaughter people before she even gets to Dioxazine to free her."

The Numini-shade sighed. "*And if a Numini slays Terre Verte, his shade will instantly cross into the Numen, where he we believe he plans to make war. And if Alizarin does somehow slay this Numini, or if Terre Verte does, then the loss will kill Dioxazine and sever Alizarin's tie to the Numen and the mortal realm.*"

"Fuck," Lydie said, the word slipping out of her mouth before she anticipated it. "Let me see if I understand this. An extraordinarily powerful Numini wants to kill Alizarin, but if Alizarin kills her, it will destroy him anyway. This Numini might also kill Terre Verte, in the process expediting his war on the Numen and the destruction of the veils between the planes. Dioxazine may be able to fight this Numini—the one we can't kill even if we can fight it—but only after she is free, by which point Terre

Verte is probably dead? Do you have any *good* news to impart today, or maybe an idea? A suggestion?"

"*Wake Scheveningen.*"

Lydie struggled to place the familiar-sounding name, and at last Alizarin's story came to mind. "The Gressi?"

"*Yes, the Gressi. They are of the Numen, of the Abyss, of death and life and the mortal plane. They do not die, but only sleep. Scheveningen is the patron of the Terre line, though through the centuries of his slumber other Numini and Abyssi have fought for ownership of that bloodline as well. If Scheveningen wakes, he can strengthen the boundaries between the planes and banish those who threaten them.*"

Bringing more Others into this fiasco seemed unwise, but at least according to the story, Scheveningen was opposed to the enslavement of the human race.

"How do we wake Scheveningen?"

"*One of Terre lineage must make a sacrifice over Scheveningen's resting place.*"

Lydie almost snorted at that. "And how do you suggest we get Terre Verte to help us with that?"

"*You have spoken amongst yourselves of Clay.*"

"Spoken of, but not found," Lydie said. "I am fairly certain he is dead . . . or is that not an issue?" If she could reach and summon his shade, maybe that would be enough? After all, this Numini was supposedly dead, too.

Again that wavering, this time touched with sorrow. *"Dust and ash. He died by his own hand five years ago, after he slew his daughter Maimeri. Their spirits wail on the lowest level of the Abyss, where even I cannot reach to comfort them."*

"Died . . . slew . . . why?" Lydie stammered, then immediately regretted asking. Had she thought guilt from a mortal shade was painful? The feeling from the Numini was devastating.

"My fault," the Numini whispered. *"Clay thought his magic, the beautiful divine power I gave him, was a curse. He begged me to spare his daughter. I did. I left her only her tie to Scheveningen. She was tainted by the Numen through her father, but not enough to make her a mancer . . . just enough for her to see me, to know me, and . . ."* Mortals who look upon the divine are lost to its power. Did the Numini say that last line again, or did Lydie just hear its echo in her head? *"We had . . . mortals would call it an affair. I didn't understand the risks. It destroyed her."*

Tragic, but Lydie hadn't know the woman, and the information seemed useless, too.

It was as if the Numini needed to gather strength to speak its next words.

"Maimeri had a daughter. Pearl. She is the last of the Terre. I tried. I wanted to keep her free so when she was of age she could flee this land, but instead I must ask her to perform the sacrifice and tie herself to Kavet. With Pearl, you can wake Scheveningen. Without her, the Gressi will

not wake, and the boundaries between the planes will fall, and Alizarin will die, and Quinacridone will rule you all."

"Wait." Lydie's head was spinning with all of this information, but the last part made no sense at all. "I was following you until the end. How do the Quin end up kings of the ruins?" The one good part about destroying the world seemed to be getting rid of them.

The Numini seemed puzzled for a moment, then apparently determined the source of Lydie's confusion. *Not the Quin, the human sect of that name. Quinacridone, one of the high arbiters of the Numen. She is Dioxazine's patron. She walks this realm. When the worlds crumble, she will be left to rule."*

"She . . . what?" Lydie couldn't seem to get enough breath to form a coherent question.

"She . . . she, and I . . . thought we could make the lives of mortals better by bringing order to them." The dead Numini sighed. *"But even her attempt to teach Numen values to your kind through preachers was twisted by mortal interpretation, and eventually it all ended in disaster, and so many deaths.*

"Since then, I have come to realize we were wrong about mortals. It is the conflict and the pain that allows you to be free and to love as you do. Doné still believes you need an arbiter for your lives, but has discovered it is not easy to force her will on mortals on this plane. The Gressi protected you and your free will too well. I fear she will allow Terre Verte to destroy the veils, because she knows once

they are down, even the high justice Mir must allow her to step forward to care for the survivors."

Lydie crossed her arms, and fought to keep her eyes closed. She wanted to be done with this conversation.

"Tell me how we find your daughter," she said, "and how we summon Scheveningen. And anything else you know that might help us."

CHAPTER 35

HANSA

It had to be almost dinnertime.

Please.

Hansa looked away from the piles of papers on his desk and rolled his shoulders. The bones of his spine let out audible *pop*s as he stretched.

He had spent a half hour planning the excursion to Eiderlee, which would involve both of the remaining sighted guards and the captain of Company Five. Assisted by Rinnman and Gray, he had spent two hours after *that* filling out the paperwork that was apparently required for such a trip.

Meanwhile, the nominations had continued to come up. Hansa had been nominated thirty-seven times at last count, a number that made him worry he might need to talk to his friends about how uncomfortable he was with the idea of rigging elections. Then again, he thought at least a few of the guards had sneaked next door to place a nomination, so perhaps the number had more to do with proximity.

He hoped so.

In the middle of a meeting with Kavet's premier blacksmith, one of the only men in the country licensed to keep a forge, his door opened again, admitting a sheepish-looking Rinnman. The other soldier half closed the door behind himself before saying, "I'm sorry to interrupt, sir, but you may want to take this meeting."

From behind Rinnman, one voice momentarily separated itself from the jumble of conversation in the hall. "Let me in there, you! I'm going to strangle that boy with my bare hands!"

Hansa quirked a brow—then tried to suppress the expression, which he knew was something picked up from Umber. "You think so?" Given the babble of noise beyond the door, it took him a moment to replay the words in his mind and, only after that delay, recognize the voice. "Wait . . . is that my *mother*?"

The door pushed open, hard enough that Rinnman side-stepped barely in time to avoid being knocked over.

"Hansa!" Oh, yes. That was his mother, who strode in, glaring fiercely. "*First* you're a criminal. Then you're a hero. Oh, and you're engaged. Then that horrible event down at the docks and you're *gone*, presumed dead. Now you're alive. And you *never*—" She smacked his shoulder at that, hard enough that he winced. "You never even *bother* to tell your mother you're *alive*! Where have you been? I want to hear the truth from your own mouth." As the initial fury of the tirade wound down a bit, tears appeared in her eyes. "What have you been doing that was so important and so secret that you could let your family think the worst, for *weeks*?"

He was a grown man. He was running for President. And at that moment he was, like any man facing an irate mother, reduced to a young child once again.

"Excuse us," Rinnman said. He gestured to the blacksmith, and both men judiciously fled the room.

"I wasn't dead," was, stupidly, the first excuse that came out of Hansa's mouth. It had never occurred to him to tell his parents that he wasn't dead, because it hadn't occurred to him that he *was*. Despite his sojourn in the Abyss, he hadn't expected to be declared dead. He drew a breath, and managed more appropriate words. "I'm sorry. It was stupid of me."

"You missed Ruby's service," his mother said softly, less hostile now but with hurt more evident in her eyes. "And Jenkins'. I hadn't thought you would miss those for anything in the world."

"They gave Ruby a service?" Hansa asked, pleased but surprised. Suicides were not usually allowed such a formal farewell.

"Indathrone had sighted guards examine the

site where . . . where her body was last seen. Where you were last seen." Her voice wobbled a moment. "There was mancer magic all over it. The Quin wouldn't declare it a suicide when there was that much evidence of possible magical malfeasance—especially after someone reported that Ruby had gone to the docks and the ship seeking Cadmia Paynes for guidance."

That wasn't quite how it had all happened, but if it meant Ruby was allowed to be remembered well, Hansa wouldn't argue. "That's good," he said. She was in the Numen; whatever powers made that decision had obviously decided that she had lived rightly.

Of course, Jenkins had gone to the Abyss. Maybe the powers-that-were weren't good judges after all.

"How was Jenkins' service?" he asked, though it felt rather odd to do so, given he had talked to the man the night before.

His mother looked away as tears came to her eyes. "Beautiful," she said. "His mother . . . that poor woman. Can you believe, we're at her son's funeral, and she's trying to comfort *me*. At her own—"

She broke off, swaying. Hansa reached for her, afraid she was about to faint, and she sucked in a gasping breath. She looked up at him with unfocused eyes. "Hansa?"

"Mom?" His heart had leapt into his throat. The voice had been hers, but it was wrong, as were her movements as she looked around.

"Good," she said. "We're alone."

"What's going on?"

Now she spoke quickly, the rhythms of her speech not hers at all as she said, "Hansa, it's Lydie. You need to meet me at Umber's house. Now would be good."

She let out a quietly exhaled breath, and as she actually *did* faint, Hansa was almost too slow to catch her because he was too horrified by what had just happened. He managed to help her to a chair, where she opened her eyes and looked around in confusion.

"Hansa?" *What in the three worlds had Lydie done?* "What happened?"

"I think you fainted," he said. *Please don't remember.*

"I felt dizzy there a minute," she said. "I think maybe I should lie down."

He nodded. "Rinnman can find you an empty sitting room where you can rest awhile. I have a meeting I need to get to, but we can meet for dinner, or breakfast tomorrow? I don't know how late I'll be tonight, but I do want to tell you everything."

Wanted to tell her everything, but how much could he?

That at least was a question for another moment.

"I'll hold you to that," she answered, with a mock-glare. "I know you're a grown man, but a mother never stops worrying. Give me a hug and a kiss before you run off to do your important world-saving work."

Hansa did, and hated how frail his usually strong, vibrant mother felt. Grief and anxiety had clearly taken a toll on her the last few weeks. Hansa promised himself that, as soon as he could, he *would* tell her the truth—at least as much of it as was his story to tell.

In the meantime, he didn't think Lydie would have gone to such lengths to contact him unless it was an emergency, which meant he didn't have time to lose. He found Rinnman, saw his mother settled, gave his apologies to his next meetings and signed out for the evening.

Getting back to Umber's home unnoticed was more easily said than done, as half the population of Mars was either in the Quinacridone Compound or in the market square, and they all wanted to talk to him. He managed to evade them by ducking into his own apartment, then out a window on the back of the building.

As he hurried back to Umber's house with his head down against the bitter winter wind, he couldn't help but recall the way he and Jenkins used to tell each other ghost stories. Playground tales said that necromancers could possess people, but most of Kavet accepted that as a myth. Hansa's own mother had dismissed it as a story told to keep kids from wandering alone at night.

Other fears took hold of him as he walked. Was something wrong with Umber? Had something gone wrong while he and Naples were setting up their tableau to distract the Quinacridone in Eiderlee? Or what about Cadmia? She and Alizarin had gone to the temple. Anything could have happened there.

He moved faster.

Bursting into the house, he found Lydie and Cadmia sitting at the kitchen table, both drinking hot mulled wine, and Lydie eating anything she could fit in her mouth around her shivering.

"What's wrong?" he asked breathlessly.

"Nu-Numini," she said. "Numini . . . *ghost*." Another spasmodic shiver took her, badly enough that she had to set her mulled wine down.

Cadmia tucked the blanket over Lydie's shoulders down more tightly. "Alizarin and I met a Numini in the temple," she explained. "He gave us tools to help Lydie talk to one of them. She did some kind of ritual. By the time she called me for help, she was blue with cold. She insisted we all needed to talk together immediately."

"At least Numini ghost is a power source," Lydie said, only partly incoherently. "Wouldn't normally have . . . able to do the reaching spell."

"Reaching spell? Is that how you possessed my mother?"

Lydie's eyes widened. "*Mother*? S-sorry." She wrapped her hands tightly around her mulled wine again. Cadmia picked up a second blanket that had been warming in front of the hearth and exchanged it for the one on Lydie's shoulders. "Reached for . . . person . . . closest to you. Need t-t-t . . ." She lost the next words in a round of teeth-chattering.

"Warm up first, then talk," Hansa suggested gently. "Hopefully the others will get back soon."

As Lydie warmed, Cadmia described in more detail what she and Alizarin had heard at the temple.

Just as she finished, Naples, Umber, and Alizarin came home, all power-giddy. Their jovial moods had dissipated quickly as Lydie stopped shivering enough to form full, coherent sentences and launched into her own story about being visited by a Numini, about the tragedy of Clay and his daughter, about Pearl being the only surviving Terre, and Quinacridone—the *real* Quinacridone—walking the mortal plane, bound to an Abyssumancer, and apparently Dioxazine's patron.

"*Pearl*?" Cadmia repeated, clearly shocked. "That's—I mean, I knew she had some kind of power, but I never stopped to think what—that's why a Numenmancer kidnapped her. It seems so obvious now." Her eyes widened. Hansa couldn't help thinking about the dangers to Abyss-spawn from Abyssumancers seeking a power source. Could a Numenmancer be so cruel to a Numen-spawn child? Would the Numini tolerate it? "Or they did it at Quinacridone's command, if she's really a Terre, too," Cadmia speculated. "I feel like an idiot for not thinking of it sooner. The poor girl."

As they all exchanged overwhelmed glances, Alizarin asked, "What did the Numini you spoke with say its name was?"

Hansa didn't see why that was important, but Cadmia asked, "You think maybe it's Veronese?"

Alizarin nodded. Lydie cleared her throat, reminding them she couldn't hear Alizarin directly.

"Alizarin wants to know what the Numini was named," Cadmia said. "He knew a Numini, once."

Lydie shrugged. "It didn't give me a name."

"Who else could it be?" Cadmia asked rhetorically. "Numini can't lie, and this one said he knew and loved Alizarin."

All this was news to Hansa, but before he could say anything, Umber spoke up. "If we trust this *is* Veronese, do we trust Veronese?" he asked. "The Numini haven't been kind to us so far."

They all looked at Alizarin. He tilted his head, thoughtful. "I do," he answered at last.

"Presuming we decide we want to do it," Hansa said, "what exactly does this ritual Veronese suggests entail, other than Pearl?"

Lydie rubbed her eyes wearily. "First, you need either a necromancer or an animamancer—someone whose power naturally comes from Scheveningen. That, I suppose, would be me." She paused and drew a breath. "Next, we need to go to Scheveningen's grave, which the Numini—Veronese if that's his name—says is 'in the earth beneath the oldest structure in Kavet.' I'm hoping someone knows what that means."

Cadmia groaned. "The oldest structure in Kavet is the Cobalt Hall. Did Veronese say anything about how we were supposed to get you in there?"

"I *lived* in the Cobalt Hall," Naples pointed out. "Clay did, too. What changed between then and now?"

"The law?" Hansa suggested. "Magic responds to will and intent, right?"

"Or maybe not having a Terre heir nearby damaged the magic somehow, after Clay died," Cadmia speculated. "Pearl lives there now, but Veronese said he actively tried to keep her disconnected from that birthright."

"The Numini had Pearl kidnapped once," Umber interjected. "I think we should move quickly to protect her, even if we can't immediately figure out how to get into the Cobalt Hall. We also need to tell her what is going on."

"There shouldn't be any sighted guards in the market square right now," Hansa said, glad to have done something more useful all day than answer questions about his nomination as President, shuffle papers, and get yelled at by his mother. "We can go together."

"We need a little time to regroup first," Umber said reluctantly. "You're looking drawn from too much time spent veiling your power today. Naples, Alizarin and I enjoyed ourselves, but we also burned a lot of power out in Eiderlee. And Lydie is about to fall over."

"Veronese said Quinacridone would need to rest for a little while," Lydie reluctantly acknowledged.

"And you're right. I'll be useless until I rest and meditate to get my power under control."

"I can go ahead," Cadmia suggested. "I'll keep an eye on Pearl and make sure she stays inside. It doesn't make sense to take her out of there until we have a plan, anyway. If Alizarin can't go into the Cobalt Hall, Quinacridone probably can't, either, in which case Pearl is safer there than she would be here."

"The rest of us can stay nearby," Hansa suggested, "in case you need support."

"Do you think it's safe to use your apartment by now?" Umber asked.

The question caught Hansa off guard, and absurdly startled a laugh from him. "I'm still a little horrified by how *little* everyone at the Quin Compound suspects me. I think as long as we're careful not to draw attention to ourselves, we should be fine."

So that became the plan. Naples left his bone ring with Cadmia, since it would serve as a quick and powerful tool with which she could draw blood and summon them all without anyone noticing. As Cadmia and Alizarin said their farewells, Naples, Umber, and Hansa packed the essentials they would need, then trudged back to the center of the city and to Hansa's apartment to collapse into bed—together—and only eventually into sleep.

Hansa was in a kitchen he had never seen before, but somehow, in the way of dreams, knew was his. He was standing over the stove, making breakfast, wearing a frilly pink apron that even while dreaming he knew had to be Umber's contribution to the image.

But it wasn't Umber or even Naples that he turned, with a smile on his face, to greet. Instead, it was a woman who swept into the room, with an infant cradled in one arm and a bottle in the other hand. She was wearing a pink star sapphire ring.

Their baby in her arms, Ruby leaned close so he could kiss her.

"Aah!"

Hansa woke with a start as Naples cried out and smacked him on the shoulder.

"Ow! What in the—"

"Don't *do* that!" the Abyssumancer said, horror written across all his features.

"Do *what?*"

"Go back to sleep," Naples said. "But we do my dreams this time." He lay back down, his head resting on Hansa's chest, but his thoughts still grumbled in Hansa's head: *Damn Quin with your Numen-damned frilly dreams of women and babies.*

And yes, they did dream Naples' dreams next: dreams of power, and blood, and lust, and the viscous sea of the Abyss, and skin and fur and slick scales like silk, and the crystal caverns where Abyssi were born.

CHAPTER 36

CUPRIC

Admittedly, it wasn't how Cupric had expected things to go, but he wasn't objecting. Actually, he was buzzing. Nearly hallucinating, as he tried to figure out how to organize and control a kind of power with which he had no experience. The first time he had tried to stand up, he had fallen down, so just then he was lying on the floor, staring at the ceiling.

Doné was standing above him, looking down at him. "Get control of yourself, Mancer," she said. The tone was gentle, but the words felt like a slap.

He struggled to compose himself and stand up. "I'm sorry," he said. "It's a different kind of power than I'm used to dealing with. It's . . . disorienting."

"You said you needed to feed. You've fed. You said you needed to rest. You've rested. Now you're ungrateful."

He grabbed onto the side of the bed in order to push to his feet. "I'm grateful. I'm very grateful. But I'll admit I'm surprised."

"Who else would I feed to an Abyssumancer?" she asked. "I am the one who asked for your assistance. I wasn't about to give another to you."

The words left a knot in the pit of his stomach, and he found himself asking, "Did you . . . at least . . . enjoy it? At all?"

He had thought she had. He had tried. He had put more effort into pleasing her than he had *ever* bothered to put forth with any woman he had ever tumbled into bed with, and he had thought that he had succeeded. He hadn't known if the Numini were capable of feeling passion or physical pleasure, but no matter how power-starved he had been, he would have stopped if he hadn't been sure she was responding. Now she was standing there, still nude, and speaking as if it had been some kind of vile sacrifice.

"I'm Numini," she said.

"But—" She shut him up with a glare so cold it made his breath catch, and gooseflesh raise all up and down his arms. "Sorry," he whispered.

This was absurd. He knew it was absurd. He was an *Abyssumancer*. She had said yes—no, she had more than said yes, she had in fact initiated the encounter—

and he had done his damndest to give her pleasure. So why was he quivering at the face of her disapproval? Why did it feel like she had just stuck a knife in him?

What was *wrong* with him?

He sighed as she walked toward the window and parted the curtains to look out at Amaranth, letting misty dawn light spill through the gap. He hadn't ever looked through that window; he usually had other things to do when he was in this little box of a bedroom. Now he wondered what she was seeing.

What *was* wrong with him? He leaned back against the wall, an ache in his body he couldn't identify. It wasn't from the fight with Naples and the Abyssi. All that had healed. He was just in *pain*.

"I'm sorry," he said again. Saying it helped, a little, even as it made some part of his brain writhe in objection. "I didn't realize it would upset you. I wouldn't have . . ."

She turned. "I am fine," she said.

"I just—"

"Shh." She put a finger over his lips. "There is nothing you are capable of doing to me without my consent. I know what you are, perhaps better than you do, and it would be cruel of me to ask or expect you to be anything else. So there is no need to casti-gate yourself in my name, not over this."

"I wanted to please you," he dared say.

This time, the expression in her eyes was both gentle and sad. "I know. And it is . . . noble of you to wish it." The praise warmed him, in the same way that her next words felt like they ripped him open. "But we can all only strive with the tools we are given. You are an Abyssumancer. There is nothing I or you can do to change that. It is good of you to want to be more. That desire pleases me. But you will only find despair if you try to defy all that is your nature in order to earn the grace of the divine realm."

The statement knocked his knees out from under him; as she stepped back, he fell, sliding down the wall until he was once again sitting on the floor. He leaned his head on his knees, trying to breathe, trying not to mourn.

She touched his hair lightly. "There is something you can do for me."

He looked up, tears on his cheeks. "Anything."

She smiled, just a little, but it was enough for now. "There is a child housed at the Cobalt Hall. Her name is Pearl. Do you know her?"

He nodded. "I know who she is."

"I need her," Doné said. "I had a Numenmancer bring her to the temple recently, but his attention lapsed and she was stolen away. Bring her to me here?"

"I cannot go into the Cobalt Hall," he said. "Will she come out?"

"You can ask for her, and she will come to the door," Doné replied. She paused, then reached back and plucked a feather from her wing; it shone violet and gold, and was as long as his forearm. "Give this to her. Tell her that her father wishes to see her, and remind her that he told her the Numini could not walk in the Cobalt Hall. She will go with you."

"I can do that," Cupric said, only to then hesitate. "Will sighted guards see this? Or for that matter, will they see *me*? I'm not sure I know how to control the Numen power well enough to mask it."

"They will not be a problem," she assured him. "Hansa Viridian has kindly sent them all away. Of course, Hansa himself may be a problem; he also wants the girl, in order to spill her blood in their rites. I will keep an eye on you, and intercede if Naples or the Abyssi Alizarin is there, but the rest you should be able to handle on your own."

"Alizarin isn't a danger to you, is he?" Naples asked, his heart speeding at the fear of her being harmed.

She shook her head, and this time her smile was wider—almost hungry. "There is nothing in this world that is a danger to me. Now go. You must get the girl before they do."

"Are you coming with me?"

"I have my own errands," she replied. "You will have enough of my attention that I will be able to come to you if you need me." She touched his tear-stained cheek, kissed his forehead, and then the air swirled and the world went cold.

"Wait!" he called, leaping to his feet as she stepped backward into the new rift.

"Do this for me, and you will please me," she said. "That will get you through my absence."

Then she was gone, and he was left staring at where she had been. Gone. She had left him. He reached out as if he could touch the rift, but it had closed; he couldn't follow. He couldn't follow. But he *needed* her!

Do this for me, and you will please me.

She was right. If he just focused on the task she had given him, and on what he needed to do to accomplish it, he could survive.

Dear Abyss, what was wrong with him? All she had done was leave the room, but it felt like his heart was breaking. It was fake, all of it—it had to be; it was magic, the bond of a mancer to one of the Others. But even knowing that, he couldn't stop it.

As he left Amaranth, he passed the animamancer he had bedded before his trip to the Abyss. She smiled broadly at him, and he drew back, ashamed that he had ever touched her. That he had thought her attractive.

Horses. Terre Verte had horses. He could take one of those, to get to the city faster. Of course, Umber also had horses; Cupric had been the one to teach him to ride and, damn it, why had he done that? So the spawn could run from him faster? So he could get to Pearl faster now?

As Cupric rode, the despair twined into anger,

both at himself and at . . . Everything, anything. Except her. He wanted to be angry at Doné, but he couldn't be.

How could he ever have even *considered* risking a third boon and a bond to Umber? Would it have been like this madness? What kind of fool had he been?

As he crossed the crowded market square, accepting Doné's assurance that there wouldn't be any sighted guards and therefore not even bothering to try to hide his power, he saw more than one person step away from him—and, interestingly enough, more than one person move closer. His rapid, hostile steps could explain those who drew back, but not the others. That had to be a result of the Numini's power drawing people to him.

He hesitated before ascending the Cobalt Hall's front steps, both to push back his blatant hostility so he wouldn't scare away anyone who opened the door, and to gather his courage.

Taking the first stair was like being slapped in the face. His muscles twitched with the impulse to run back, run away as fast as possible.

Do this for me, and you will please me.

He forced himself onto the second step, which brought pressure and constriction around his lungs. His heart beat rapidly enough he feared another step would bring about a heart attack.

Yet he took it.

He leaned against the doorframe to steady himself as he knocked.

It felt like centuries but was probably only seconds before someone answered the door. Cupric wasn't sure how long he was going to be able to stand there, and didn't want to know what would happen if he passed out and they took him inside.

"Can I help you?" a young woman he didn't recognize asked.

"Can I talk to—" His breath ran out, and he had to try again.

"Are you all right?" she asked kindly.

He nodded sharply.

"Why don't you come inside and sit down?" she asked. "You don't look well."

With the invitation, the pressure pushing against him lessened a little, as if whatever magic protected the Cobalt Hall was willing to listen to its inhabitants. It remained present; he knew he wouldn't be able to step inside. But he was able to breathe, and now he did so before saying, "I need to speak to Pearl."

The woman in the doorway stiffened protectively. "Why?"

Cupric was familiar with Pearl's story, and now something occurred to him. She was blond, and one of those mismatched eyes was bright blue. It would work. He lifted his gaze, which had been focused somewhere near the ground, and said, "Would you tell her that her father would like to see her?"

The novice in the doorway would make the obvious connection, and the words wouldn't contradict what Cupric had been instructed to tell Pearl.

Her eyes widened, and she said, "Oh! Um . . . I think she's helping Cadmia make the morning meal. I'll see if she wants to see you."

The last words held that same wary mistrust, and it occurred to him that claiming to be a father who had abandoned the girl years ago could also have drawbacks.

"I'll understand if she doesn't want to," he said. "She's never had a father in her life, and I know her mother abandoned her here. I only learned about her recently."

The woman's expression softened, and she said, "I'll talk to her. Do you want to wait inside?"

"I'll wait here. I don't want to intrude if Pearl doesn't want to see me."

"I'll talk to her," she said once more, before turning away and disappearing into the Hall.

Cupric turned and sat on the lowest step to wait. He had met Cadmia once. If she came to the door with Pearl and recognized him, there might be problems. Especially since Pearl was rumored to have the sight. If she cried mancer, things could get messy.

It didn't matter; as long as he could get Pearl to leave with him, Doné could handle the rest.

CHAPTER 37

CADMIA

Pearl laughed, a sound that made Cadmia smile despite their dire situation.

Predictably, Pearl had been in her own room when Cadmia returned to the Cobalt Hall late the night before. Cadmia had wanted to talk to her right away, but even at the late hour the Hall had been buzzing with rumors of Indathrone's disappearance, the emergency election, and talk of which Sisters and Brothers had been nominated, Cadmia among them. She had been prepared to wake Pearl up to talk to her, but then in the midst of trying to calm and update Sienna she had blinked—and suddenly it was morning.

Damn, *damn* her for falling asleep. Common sense and education both told her the pregnancy was partly to blame for her fatigue, compounded with the strain and anxiety of the last few days. She had scrambled up, only to find Pearl already out on her morning cider delivery to the soldiers of the 126 ending their long, cold night shifts amid softly-falling flurries of snow. Cadmia's heart had pounded as she joined the girl and shadowed her closely, and eventually hustled her inside and convinced her to help make breakfast.

Unfortunately, the kitchen wasn't private. Cadmia couldn't tell Pearl all the things she desperately needed to know while other members of the Order drifted in and out of the room. She was still trying to think of a way she could talk to the girl alone when Sienna stepped into the kitchen and said, "Cadmia, there's a petitioner here to see you."

Cadmia blinked at the novice, as if the words had come out in a strange and unfamiliar language. "Excuse me?"

Sienna looked equally confused in response—and her confusion was more justified. She repeated slowly, "A petitioner. Are you available?" Identifying the only thing Cadmia seemed to be doing, she offered, "I can help Pearl make breakfast."

In all the chaos of trying to save the world, it was hard to remember that other people still expected Cadmia to do her official job, which was meeting with petitioners who came to her for guidance. Her specialty was working with petty criminals and abusers to help them find a path toward a healthier—and more legal—life and livelihood. It was important work that would be pointless if Quinacridone succeeded in taking over the moral realm.

"What was their name?" Maybe it was someone she had worked with before and could reasonably refer to another Sister or Brother.

"Arylide. I tried to get her to come in to the temple to wait for you, but she insisted on waiting out back in the garden," Sienna answered.

Lydie? She and the others should have been waiting at Hansa's apartment. Had something gone wrong? Had the Numini given her another message?

Cadmia wiped her hands on a towel and cast an anxious look at Pearl. "I'll be back in a few minutes," she said. "Stay here with Sienna. I need to talk to you when I get back." She tried to put all the weight of the situation into her voice and her eyes, hoping Pearl would pick up on it.

The child nodded slowly, in the thoughtful way she had when she was curious about something but wasn't sure she should ask.

As she hurried toward the back door, Cadmia heard Sienna ask Pearl, "So, what were you and Caddy making?"

Behind the Cobalt Hall had once been a scruffy alley providing a discreet way in and out of the building. It was still sometimes used that way, but over the years it had been transformed with trailing ivy, lanterns, and a pair of benches designed to give people a place to sit and meditate. The woman sitting on one of those benches now, who looked a few years older than Cadmia, was decidedly *not* Lydie.

"Who are you?" she asked, sharply enough that the woman's gaze shot up, startled.

"Excuse me?"

"You're not Arylide."

"Yes I am," the woman replied with a growing frown. "Arylide of the mender's district? I tend sails and nets and—"

"What do you want?" This *could* be a matter of a coincidental name similarity, since Arylide wasn't an entirely uncommon name, but the prickle at the back of Cadmia's neck told her otherwise.

"I came for counsel?" the woman answered, looking unsure now. "Isn't that . . . what people do here? I was told I should come to you, that you could help."

Maybe it was paranoia, but the situation was too coincidental, and the woman's tone rang false. "I'm sorry," Cadmia said, "but I am unavailable right now for a proper consult. If you come around the front of the building, you can make an appointment—"

"Wait!" the woman cried, because Cadmia was already turning away as she spoke, intending to hurry inside and check on Pearl. She caught the edge of Cadmia's sleeve and said, "Please, I need—"

That close, Cadmia caught the whiff of Abyssal

power, perhaps not *from* the woman, but *on* the woman. Maybe she was an Abyssumancer veiling her power—or maybe she had been influenced by one.

Cadmia shook the woman off and raced back inside to the kitchen. As she did, she used the sharp barb on the ring Naples had given her to nick her opposite fingertips, then sent a mental cry out: *Alizarin, get the others here, now.* If she was overreacting and it was a false alarm, so be it.

She didn't think she was overreacting.

Pearl and Sienna weren't in the kitchen anymore.

Damn. *Damn!* Near-running, Cadmia dashed from the kitchen to the front hall, where she saw an indulgent-looking Sienna smiling to herself in a dazed way. She, too, appeared tainted by Abyssal power.

"Pearl's father is here for her," Sienna said, a little too sunnily. "Isn't that—?"

Cadmia ignored her and shoved open the front door, where she found Pearl standing a few steps down, facing a pale but resolute-looking Cupric.

Cupric's gaze flickered briefly to Cadmia, but he spoke to Pearl, saying, "Obviously, I'm not actually your father. You know he can't come here, right?"

Pearl nodded.

"I also know a lot of things," Cadmia said smoothly. "One of them being how much of a bastard you are. Pearl, come inside."

She tried not to look toward the plaza, to wonder

how long it would be before the others arrived. They weren't far away.

Maybe Hansa can summon the 126, Cadmia thought dryly, though she knew the fair-minded Hansa probably wouldn't think of calling on soldiers to dispose of a mancer while he, Umber, Alizarin, and maybe even Lydie stood by hypocritically.

Pearl took a step back toward the door in response to Cadmia's words and tone, then froze as Cupric pulled something from beneath his heavy winter cloak.

At least, Cadmia *thought* he had taken something out. His hand looked empty, but as he knelt down to talk to Pearl, *she* could obviously see something, and it drew her forward again. Cadmia reached for her, but Pearl darted forward to grab whatever it was.

"Pearl!"

"It's a Numini feather," Cupric said, softly so as not to be overheard. "You would know that, if you stopped to consider why you can't see it."

"Pearl's father . . ." Cadmia hated to say it in front of Pearl, but it was better than letting her trust a man that Cadmia knew was willing to abduct and abuse one of the spawn in order to get his way. "Veronese is dead. He was slain by Modigliani. He is not the one who has been talking to you. You only want Pearl because—"

"Alizarin was mistaken," Cupric interrupted. "Numini are not easy to kill."

"I want to see him," Pearl declared.

"Pearl—"

"Cadmia, can you show *any* faith?" Cupric snapped. "You know what I am, and worse than that, *I* know what I am these days. I would claw out my own heart if it would undo what I've done, but the point of it is that it's done and the Numini asked me to talk to Pearl. I don't want to disappoint it again."

Suddenly there were tears in the Abyssumancer's eyes, and Cadmia was pretty sure they were genuine. *Too bad for him.*

"I'm sorry," Cupric said. "But Pearl, please, believe me. There are people who are going to hurt you."

"She's safe here," Cadmia said.

"She is *not* safe here," Cupric snapped.

"Mancers, spawn, and Others can't cross this threshold."

He gave what sounded like a nearly hysterical laugh. "No, we can't," he said, "but Quin guards *can*, and when they do, who's going to protect her? Alizarin? Umber?"

"Why would the Quin come for her?" Cadmia whispered. She hadn't expected this gambit, this threat.

Only a few more minutes, she thought desperately. She considered grabbing Pearl and trying to drag her inside, but if Cupric was able to overpower Umber magically, he would certainly be able to overpower Cadmia. She would rather keep him talking until reinforcements arrived instead of pushing him to use his magic.

"The Quin *will* come for her when they learn what she is," Cupric said, "and they will learn what she is because Terre Verte will tell them." He drew a deep breath. "You cannot comprehend the hatred Terre Verte holds for the Numini. He has Dioxazine locked away. He will see Pearl as another source of power in his quest to open a rift to the Numen and engage them in battle."

The words were chilling. In all their planning, they had not stopped to wonder what Verte might think of the girl.

"I will take her somewhere safe, then," Cadmia said, then thought, *Oh, thank Numen*, as she saw the others picking their way through the crowded market square. They were slowed by the people getting in Hansa's way, repeatedly stopping him. She was relieved to see that Hansa had also finally retrieved his sword from his apartment. He might have an imminent opportunity to use it.

"Where?" Cupric challenged. "Umber's house? Terre Verte has Dioxazine; that means he has his hand on Alizarin's leash. He will be able to find Alizarin any time he wishes, and through Alizarin he will be able to find you." Again he spoke to Pearl, whose eyes had gone wide. "Please, Pearl, trust me. Trust that feather you're holding. You want to see your father, don't you—" He trailed off as he noticed Cadmia's eyes darting behind him. He glanced over his shoulder, and whispered, "Oh, fu—" biting off the curse as he looked back at Pearl. "We need to go."

"Let's let Hansa and Umber decide," Cadmia declared.

"What if *I* want to decide?" Pearl asked, taking a defiant step forward.

Before Cadmia could take the two steps down to drag Pearl back again, Cupric reached forward and seized her so-close wrist. They both nearly toppled over backward as he twisted, trying to flee with the now-struggling girl, and made it almost to the bottom of the steps before Cadmia could pounce and catch Pearl's other wrist.

"Help!" Cadmia shouted. Mancer or not, Cupric would appear to any by-stander to be a stranger trying to drag Pearl out of the Hall against her will. What madness must have possessed him to think this was a good idea?

She heard Hansa yelling, "Move aside. Get out of the way!"

Naples, lean and wiry and unknown as he was, made it to them first. Over the noise, Cadmia could barely hear him growl, "Well, at least Terre Verte taught us all how to banish unwanted Numini." He drew his knife.

Cupric let go of Pearl and turned to face Naples.

Cadmia saw something ruffle the girl's hair, but that was all the warning she or any of the others had, aside from Cupric's slow-spreading smile.

Pearl took off, darting back toward the Cobalt Hall, moments before the world tightened, and seized—and lightning struck.

CHAPTER 38

HANSA

Hansa coughed, and drew a breath. The air stank of ozone and burned with cold, but that at least convinced him he was alive.

Fuck. Well, Naples was alive, too; his thought reached Hansa on their still-lingering connection.

Umber?

I agree with the Abyssumancer.

Can anyone sit up?

I can't even see yet, Naples snarled. *Or feel my hands.*

Lightning, Umber managed to say.

Hansa thought his eyes were open, but as Naples had said, he couldn't see. The world was nothing more than a wash of bright afterimages.

We're alive, he said. *I think. We are* alive, *right?*

Think so, Naples answered.

If we're alive . . . who did it hit?

The same wordless dread came from Naples and Umber in response.

If the Numini struck to kill, Naples said, his thoughts echoing with horror, *and the bolt wasn't meant for me, then it would have been for Alizarin.*

Alizarin? He tried to push himself up despite his barely-starting-to-clear vision.

"Don't move too quickly," a voice outside his mind said. It sounded tinny and far away, the result of standing inside a thunder-clap, so it took Hansa a moment to recognize it as Rinnman's. "These burns are deep. We have doctors on the way. I think you should be able to sit up, though." Gently, the other guard helped him, which was when Hansa noticed he was starting to regain feeling in his limbs.

"The others?" he asked hoarsely.

"A few others were caught in the blast. They're being tended to."

Hansa's throat seized up the next time he tried to speak, and he coughed violently before he managed to ask, "Everyone alive?"

"There's a young woman in pretty rough shape," Rinnman answered. "They don't know if she will make it. Cadmia Paynes is also unconscious, and the doctors are trying to stabilize her."

Hansa couldn't ask about Alizarin. No one else could see him.

He's not here, Naples said silently.

What does that mean?

I don't know. Nothing good. The words were heavy.

"Stop that," Rinnman whispered.

"What?"

"Whatever you're doing. It's getting in the way."

"Huh?"

"You'll be fine," Rinnman said, still speaking in low tones. "You were my priority, but I should check on your other friends now. The girl who's in the worst condition seems to be a necromancer, and they don't heal well on their own."

Hansa stared after Rinnman as he limped off.

What? Umber asked, sensing Hansa's shock. He still sounded as pained and distant as he had a few moments ago.

Rinnman knows Lydie's a necromancer, and he somehow felt me talking to you two.

Let me sleep. Thinking too loud, Naples said. His mental voice was fuzzy.

You're . . . better, Umber said to Hansa.

Hansa managed to stand, and searched for Umber, who was several feet away covered in black-purple blood-blisters. Hansa struggled to find a place on the spawn's skin he could touch without hurting him further. How was it that he was so much better, and standing already?

Rinnman limped back over, every movement slow and trembling. He looked worse off than Hansa now. "Let me see what I can do," he said. He looked from Naples to Umber, and back to Hansa again. "I don't know how much more I have left in me."

He was clearly asking, *Which one?*

Hansa nodded to Umber. It wasn't a question.

Rinnman knelt, painfully, given his injured leg, and leaned over Umber. He put a hand on the spawn's throat as if checking for a pulse, and with his eyes half-closed he leaned forward and blew a gentle stream of air at his face. It was subtle, just a man checking the injuries of another, if Hansa hadn't been watching closely.

Rinnman's eyes shot open and he looked up at Hansa with concern. "What . . . ?"

Rinnman had been able to identify Lydie as a necromancer immediately, and had sensed Hansa speaking silently to Naples. What had he sensed just then from Umber? The infernal realm itself? "Please, help him," Hansa pleaded.

Animamancer. It had to be.

Rinnman returned his attention to Umber, and a few moments later the spawn coughed and shuddered. His eyes opened, and Hansa watched as they cleared and focused.

Wow, was the whisper Hansa heard in his head.

"It's enough," Umber said.

"You're still very hurt."

"I'll heal. Don't waste your power. See if you can help Naples?"

The guard nodded and moved on.

We should be dead, Umber observed. *Most of us would be, if not for your friend-in-hiding. Once Cupric and Quinacridone realize we're alive, they'll return to finish the job. We have to get out of the city.*

Where?

*We need—*When Naples tried to reply, Rinnman hissed as if in pain and snapped, "Don't do that if you want to make sure you regain feeling in all your important extremities, understand?"

Naples didn't speak again. Hansa and Umber exchanged a glance.

By the time he pulled away from Naples, Rinnman was sweating and shivering.

"Will you be okay?" Hansa asked him, alarmed at the man's condition.

Rinnman nodded. "I'll be fine. And so should all of you. There will be some scars, but you will live. Except . . ." He hesitated.

"Except?"

"Cadmia. I can't help her. Some power in her shoves mine away." He looked up and said more softly, "The crowd is coming near again, and the doctors will be here momentarily."

"They'll want to move us to the Cobalt Hall," Hansa managed to say, thinking of Naples and Lydie.

"There's no way to pretend this was anything

other than a magical attack," Rinnman replied. "I'll have them treat you in a private wing of the Quin Compound."

"What will the doctors see?" Umber asked practically.

"Less critical injuries than they expected, but you're all still hurt, and bandages would not be a bad idea." Rinnman struggled to his feet. "They will want to put guards by your sick-room, Viridian. It could be a problem if you expect to have"—his gaze flickered, just for a moment, to Umber and Naples, before he finished with the word—"guests."

"Are any of the other guards—?"

"Like me?" Rinnman shook his head. "No. I don't know if any others might have other kinds of power."

"What happened to your leg?" Naples asked with a voice like dry parchment. "Shouldn't you be able to heal it?"

"I got in a fight," Rinnman answered. "I fought back."

He didn't wait to answer more questions, but went to greet the doctors who were finally trickling to the scene. Umber and Naples had to be carried, agonizingly, but Hansa managed to stay standing.

Lydie, it turned out, was also on her feet.

"I'm sorry," she said as she reached Hansa's side. "He would have had enough power to heal them better if he hadn't had to help me."

"Is it true that you can't heal well on your own?"

Hansa asked, as they staggered side by side toward the Quin Compound.

"I can heal," she said, "I just do it slower than most people. I wouldn't have healed from that, though. None of us would have."

They didn't have time for more before the doctors separated Hansa from Lydie and led them both into the compound.

"It's a miracle you're alive," one of the doctors said. "You must have been far enough away not to get the brunt of the blow, but you could still have internal injuries. You will need a thorough evaluation."

"It must not have been as bad as it looked," Hansa managed to mumble.

The doctor looked over his shoulder, glancing skeptically toward the plaza. Hansa turned to see what he was looking at and nearly fell over.

A few yards from the front of the Cobalt Hall, there was a slice ripped out of the ground. It was narrow enough to step across with barely an increase in stride, but as deep as a grave. Cracks and smaller craters spread out from it like a spider web, all the way to the base of the Cobalt Hall on one side, and the fountain at the center of the market on the other. The edges were coated with what looked like frost.

Looking at it made him dizzy.

He should have been dead.

He did the next best thing; he passed out.

When he woke, he was in a bed, on top of the

blankets, with much of his body wrapped in bandages. It was night; the shades were tightly drawn on the windows, but someone had left a lamp burning, turned down low.

Sitting up revealed pulled muscles and tight, blistered flesh he had felt less the last time he woke up. Maybe that was good; it meant he wasn't numb anymore. It also meant he could feel his skin, and all along that skin was a different kind of pain—a kind of burning tingling he recognized all too well. Where was Umber?

He limped to the doorway and startled the guard outside when he opened it.

"Sir! I didn't expect to see you up," Gray said. "The doctors wanted to talk to you as soon as you were awake. Do you want me to tell them—?"

"Wait," Hansa said. "I want to see my friends first. Where are they?"

Gray nodded down the hall. "They're all in the next few rooms. Rinnman said we should keep you all together, to make it easier for the doctors to treat you, and in case anything came after you. There's only one staircase that leads to this hall, and we have another dozen guards all around it. What happened? I—I'm sorry." He cleared his throat. "I'm only supposed to be here to deliver messages, not to interrogate you when you wake. Rinnman made that very clear." He straightened deliberately to attention. "I'm here if you need me."

"I need to check on my friends." Hansa walked past Gray to check the next room. The younger man didn't say anything more or try to stop him.

The first room held not Umber, but Cadmia. She was sleeping, but not peacefully. Lydie was by her side, and she looked up sleepily as Hansa walked in.

"She's dying," Lydie whispered.

"Dying?" Hansa echoed hoarsely. One side of Cadmia's face was marred by burns and blood-blisters; the other side was icy pale. That was all Hansa could see of her above the sheet. "Can you help her?" The words were a plea based on what might be nothing more than Quin hear-say and myth about a necromancer's power.

"What do you think I'm *doing* here?" Lydie snapped back. "I can't heal her, but I'm holding her from passing into the next realm. She has enough Abyssal power that it's healing her, not as fast as it would Umber or Naples, but a bit. I think it can save her, if I can keep her in her flesh long enough."

Hansa let out a breath. Lydie sounded harried and exhausted, emotional, but not despondent or desperate. She believed what she was saying, believed she could save Cadmia, given the time. Did they have time?

"Veronese managed to send Jenkins with a message, too," Lydie continued, as Hansa stared at the slow but steady rise and fall of Cadmia's chest under the light sheet that covered most of her body. "He says Veronese cannot come to help us because we may all have been tainted by the divine realm when Quinacridone attacked us, and he's worried we might be able to see him."

"Why is that a problem?" Hansa asked, frustrated. "We could use his help."

Lydie paused, expression unfocusing a little in the way it did when shades spoke to her. "Because mortals can't look on the Numini without falling in love. I didn't understand it fully when Veronese tried to tell me, but I've been listening to the shades since, and they have helped me understand. Numenmancers have natural protection because of their control over the divine realm, but others just . . . fall. That's why being exiled from the Numen drove Terre Verte to madness even before the Abyssi abused him for nearly a century. It has destroyed Cupric, not that Quinacridone cares. She sees it as an improvement." She dropped her gaze. "Veronese says it's why as soon as he tasted a Numini's tears even Alizarin fell in love, and from then onward was desperate to reach the divine realm himself. And it's why—" She choked, then continued in a whisper. "It's why Clay slew his daughter. Because she went mad with it. Pearl should be safe because she's spawn, but she is drawn to the Numini because she possesses her mother's memories of them, so she can be easily manipulated by them."

Lydie shook her head as if to clear it, then looked back at Hansa.

"We need more power than we have," Lydie wailed softly. "We need to resurrect a Gressi, or get out of Mars. We need to rescue Dioxazine and fight one of the most powerful Numini." She dropped her head in her hands. "I'm barely managing to keep Cadmia alive. I'm in over my head."

Hansa resisted the urge to sit by Cadmia's bedside; he feared he wouldn't be able to stand again. Instead, he dropped his hand onto Lydie's shoulder. "I'm worried we all are."

CHAPTER 39

DIOXAZINE

"If you don't mind a few more minutes in the snow, lovely lady, I'm sure we can find better accommodations."

Terre Verte's heavy gray gaze made her shiver, not with fear but anticipation. He was a beautiful man, and more importantly, he gave her that smoldering look knowing full well who and what she was.

She accepted his hand with a challenging grin. "I'm intrigued to see what you can come up with to try to impress me."

He charmed the necromancer who owned Amaranth Farms—if that was the word for it—with just a dash of Numen power mixed with sheer force of personality. He summoned globes of foxfire to warm the bedroom and fill it with peach-colored light, a trick a pure Numenmancer could not have managed; Xaz watched his power as he worked, wondering if her bond to Alizarin would allow her to do something similar. She would have to experiment.

In the future. At that moment, he turned toward her and all other thoughts stopped. Strangely, she didn't feel nervous. She had nothing to hide.

"Beautiful, beautiful," he whispered, and it was obvious he wasn't talking just about her body, but about her power as well.

He blew a gentle breath across her breasts, and she laughed at the sight of frost, which trailed across her skin just long enough to make her shiver before it melted away. He more than accepted what she was—he gloried in it.

She stayed with him in Amaranth, helped with his plans when she could, experimented with her own projects at other times—and enjoyed her nights in his bed. And retrospectively, she knew the exact moment that he saw . . .

Something . . .

In her power. Something disturbed him, and it was more than the taint of the Abyss.

She didn't . . .

. . . really remember anything after that.

Until now.

Dioxazine sat up with a silent scream as something ripped inside her. The violence of the severing made the magical bonds holding her shudder.

DIOXAZINE!

She looked around, trying to figure out where she was. It was like the temple, but until this moment she had been alone and powerless in a bubble of reality from which there had been no doors or windows, or even any sense of time. She wasn't sure if she had been there a moment or a month.

Now—there was a *now*, suddenly—she turned, and though she couldn't focus on the image, she knew it was one of the Numini.

"What's happening?"

We need to get you out of here before the prison adjusts to the . . . change.

With the word *change*, the bubble of power contracted with pain that made Xaz cry out.

I'm sorry, the Numini said. *Please, we have to move quickly.*

"Move . . ." She hadn't moved in . . . How long? She hadn't even been aware of moving, of anything, since that last night when Verte had come back from scrying into the Cobalt Hall, kissed her, then stepped back and looked at her like she was a stranger.

MOVE! the Numini ordered. *Do not let his sacrifice be in vain.*

"Sacrifice?"

But she didn't need the Numini to answer. She had felt it; she could feel it now.

"Alizarin," she said, and now it was her horror that caused the womblike bubble to ripple and contort. "He's—he can't be dead."

He may be destroyed or only banished, but either way the man you knew is gone from this world. The severing disrupted this prison long enough for me to reach you, but you must take over now. Please.

She wanted to ask more, particularly to demand the Numini explain what had happened to Alizarin, what it meant that he was *gone from this world*, but the Numini's urgency was infectious. Maybe if she turned her attention, like leaving the mancer's temple . . .

It was like taking a step at a right angle to everything, and it *hurt*, but she forced her way through and at last she found herself by the river in Amaranth Farms. She looked up and blinked at a hazy figure, like streaks of gold against the half-frozen river-water.

"You need to get to the city," the Numini said. "I can bring you to where Hansa and the others are. Quinacridone has worked over the years to make you afraid of your power, but you have gained much these last weeks. You may be able to help."

"The . . . what, who?" Her head was spinning.

The Numini reached for her, lifted her, and then she was falling through ice.

She found herself again, gasping, this time on a rug-warmed floor.

"The fuck?" A raspy voice spoke behind her and she turned. Naples was barely recognizable past the cuts and burns, but she would know those copper eyes anywhere. "Nearly-naked Numenmancer. Am I hallucinating?"

She shook her head—and then had the sense to look down and realize, yes, she was nearly naked. She had been in her shift when Verte had locked her away, and she wasn't wearing more now.

Naples wasn't looking though, at least not in any kind of lascivious manner. His expression spoke more of shock, which was very much what Xaz was feeling herself.

"One of the Numini released me," she said, less out of an urge to inform Naples and more because she needed to figure out what was going on. "Alizarin . . . *what happened to Alizarin?*"

Naples winced, but Xaz wasn't sure if the pain was physical or emotional. "Your Numini hit him with a bolt of lightning."

She swayed. She hadn't known the blue Abyssi long, and she had spent much of that time wanting to get rid of him, but if it hadn't been for him she would never have stood up to the Numini—she would never have stood up for *herself.* He had changed her.

"Oh, wipe that expression off your face, Numenmancer," Naples snarled. He pushed himself up to sit, but didn't stand. "You're free now, right? Does anything else matter to you?"

"My . . . Numini?" she repeated, not reacting to the jibe. "The Numini who freed me spoke as if it cared for Alizarin."

"Well, *your* Numini, the one who makes you a mancer, is Quinacridone, and he is not fond of us all. He killed Alizarin, and your being here is going to lead him right back to us."

There was too much in that brief speech for her to process it all right away. Alizarin, killed. Quinacridone. She tried to focus, but her mind was still spinning from a combination of the spell Verte had used to trap her and the shock of being pulled from it. "Then what . . . what are we doing about it?"

"*We?*" Naples leaned back against the headboard. "I can't even stand. I can't run and I definitely can't fight. I've seen what that creature can do and I doubt you have a hare's chance of winning against it, either."

"The Numini told me maybe I could help."

"Help," Naples spat. "What do you expect to *do*? Actually, you know what would weaken Quinacridone? You, dead. So why don't you go downstairs, and tell the fucking Quin you're a mancer, and let them all do us a favor for once?"

She recoiled. "I didn't—what did I—"

Despite his earlier words to the contrary, Naples managed to put his feet on the floor and struggled to rise. Unsteadily, gripping the bedpost, he stood before her as he said, "Before he was your annoying *pet*, Alizarin was my *lover*. He was the first person willing to touch me in *decades*, after I was bonded to Azo. He probably saved my life and he definitely saved my sanity. And now you dare stand there with that pained expression on your face when we both know you would have killed him to get rid of him if you could have."

His knees gave out, and he ended up kneeling on the floor.

"It's pretty obvious I'm in no condition right now to fight you," Naples said, "but I swear to you I will *find* the energy *somewhere*, if you don't get out of my sight."

She stumbled backward, barely looking out the door before she fell through it.

She was met by instant activity in the form of shouting, demanding questions from . . . *Quin guards*. They had been at the far end of the hall, but must have heard the door open and seen her, an interloper who had no reason to be in this place. She was once again inside the Quin Compound, as if Naples' words had been a curse instead of a suggestion. Why had the

Numini brought her here? For that matter, why was Naples here?

As her mind caught up to reality, it occurred to her: *Naples is dead.*

The two guards reached her, but she could only stare at them, dumbfounded. Was she dreaming? She could barely even hear what they were saying.

Another door on the hall opened, and Hansa leaned in it.

Both guards jumped to attention. "Sir! She broke in somehow. We were just about to take her downstairs."

Hansa shook his head. "Let me speak to her." He nodded back toward the room he had just left.

Xaz was surprised for a moment that they let her go with him, but then she realized that most of the guards who had witnessed her arrest had been slain that day; there was no reason either of these would recognize her not only as a mancer, but also as *that* mancer.

Also, this was probably a dream. She felt so vague and *groggy*, she had to be asleep.

She followed Hansa, only to find the room already occupied by an unconscious Cadmia and a girl Xaz didn't recognize, but who shone lightly with divine power.

Actually, Hansa seemed to be marked with that power as well; Cadmia glowed even more brightly.

"Struck by lightning?" Xaz said, remembering what Naples had said.

The girl glared. "Who are you?"

"Lydie, this is Dioxazine," Hansa said, at which point the girl's eyes widened and she paled.

"Dioxazine. The Numenmancer. The Quinacridone's Numenmancer."

Xaz winced. "Why do people keep calling me that?"

"Because apparently you *are*," Hansa said. "It's why Terre Verte locked you up. I assume you remember that—and how did you get out?" He looked at Lydie. "Did you mount a daring rescue while I was unconscious?"

"One of the Numini released me," Xaz said. "I already went over that with Naples, who likes me even less now than he used to. Why are we in the Quin Compound?"

"Long story," Hansa said.

"The short story is, there's a Numini who's planning to take over Kavet and this entire realm, and it's *your* Numini, and you're the only one who can possibly control him. Except for a Gressi, who we can only resurrect if we can somehow get into the Cobalt Hall."

"And . . . Alizarin? Where is he?" Xaz asked, hoping they would undo the ugly words the Numini and Naples had said.

They didn't. Instead they both looked away. Hansa answered, "We don't know for sure, but we haven't seen him since the lightning strike. We're hoping he was just driven back into the Abyss, and is all right there."

He may be destroyed or only banished . . . the man you knew is gone from this world. Dioxazine had interpreted the Numini's words to mean the worst, and Naples seemed convinced he was dead, but "gone from this world" didn't have to mean gone forever. Right?

Hansa looked at the girl, Lydie, who said, "I can't sense him one way or another, but I don't know what that means. I don't have any practice with Abyssi."

"Why—" Xaz's voice choked when she first tried to speak. She had to clear it before she could ask the essential question. "Why did . . . Quinacridone . . . attack you?"

Her Numini had never told her its name—deliberately. Names had power, especially among the divine, and unlike Alizarin, who had declared their bond a partnership from the start, Xaz's Numini had always clearly considered her little more than a slave. Now, as she spoke the name aloud, she could feel the Numini it belonged to. *Her* Numini.

"Shit," Hansa suddenly hissed. "Pearl. How could I have forgotten about her?"

"Lightning?" Lydie replied succinctly.

"I didn't see what happened to her. Rinnman would have said if she was hurt, right?"

"Rinnman?" Xaz echoed.

"Probably," Lydie answered half-heartedly.

"Pearl?" Xaz asked, remembering the command

that had started this entire disastrous adventure, weeks ago, when the Numini had told Xaz to get the girl and bring her to the mancers' temple.

"Quinacridone wouldn't hurt her, would he?" Hansa asked. "I mean, she's a kid, a half-Numini kid, and he's a Numini. Even if he needs to make sure we don't get to Pearl and resurrect Scheveningen, he wouldn't *hurt* her?"

Xaz pressed a hand to her temple, wincing at the pulse of anxious pain there. Who was Scheveningen?

"The Numini—*my* Numini," she said, answering the one question she could, "was furious with me when I 'allowed' Alizarin to kill Naples, even though he's an Abyssumancer and was going to kill Cadmia. He wouldn't hurt an innocent child." She started to run a hand through her hair and discovered that it was tangled as if she had walked through a windstorm. "And by the way, Naples is in the next room. I'm a little confused."

"I'm sure you are," Hansa sighed. "It's a long story. Lydie, can you tell Xaz what has been happening? I should assure the guards she's not a danger, then check on Umber."

The other girl nodded.

"I don't suppose you could find someone who could bring me some clothes?" Xaz asked as Hansa limped toward the doorway.

He nodded, then stepped into the hall.

"Okay, then," Xaz said. Naples, back from the dead.

All of them in the Quin Compound, where the guards were jumping at Hansa's orders. Quinacridone-the-Numini was in this world despite the fact that she certainly hadn't been the one to summon him because she had been bonded to an Abyssi at the time. And *dear Numen*, she had complained about Alizarin, but just thinking about him gone felt like contemplating an absent limb. She could only pray Hansa was right and Alizarin had simply been banished back to his native plane—except, of course, there was no one she dared pray to.

"Fill me in," she said to Lydie. "The highlights, at least. I have a feeling it's a long story."

CHAPTER 40

HANSA

Hansa sent Gray to get Dioxazine something to wear, after assuring the two guards that she was a friend of Cadmia's, who had raced over in such a panic after hearing that her *dear, dear friend* was injured that she had forgotten to even dress.

Strangely, it was the first lie Hansa had told that people seemed to doubt. Gray's sardonic expression suggested he had more lascivious explanations in mind; Hansa remembered Terre Verte's talk of a mistress door in Indathrone's private wing of the compound. No one questioned him, though, and he didn't think anyone would except maybe Rinnman—and that was a conversation Hansa was looking forward to.

Umber was sleeping like the dead when Hansa walked in. Though he understood why Rinnman had prioritized the way he had, Hansa wished the man had focused on healing those with *power*. Naples and Umber were the fighters of their group.

He sat by Umber's bedside, careful not to touch him, afraid to hurt him. The magic, of course, was screaming at him that if he *didn't* touch him they would both die, but Hansa doubted either of them would be up to much any time soon. How much of a problem that was going to be, how quickly, he didn't know.

So he sat there, fighting the desire to wake Umber and the knowledge that the other man needed to rest, the need to touch him and the fear of hurting him. At last he leaned down to kiss him, not the way the power wanted to, but the way *he* wanted to.

The door behind him opened and he stood quickly enough to see Rinnman avert his gaze as he hesitated on the threshold.

"I should have knocked," the other guard said. "I'm sorry."

"Come in," Hansa sighed. "And don't apologize. You saved all our lives. Shouldn't you be resting?"

"I don't sleep much," Rinnman answered.

"Is that a personal trait, or because of . . ." Hansa trailed off, afraid the question would be taken badly.

Rinnman shrugged and said, "I don't know." He crossed the room, using the crutches deftly, as extensions of himself. Hansa remembered him saying not just that he had gotten in a fight, but that he had fought back.

"Will that heal, eventually?" he asked.

Again, the man shrugged. "We'll see. Some things do, some things just don't." He put a hand to Umber's brow and his eyes widened. "Your friend here, on the other hand, is healing very quickly, even beyond what I could do." He looked up at Hansa and asked bluntly, "Indathrone's dead, isn't he?"

"Yes." It was all he could say.

Rinnman's gaze was unflinching as he asked, "Did you, or one of your friends, do it?"

"No!" Hansa hissed, shocked—only to realize that, in a way, they *had.* "It's a very long, very *complicated* story, but you need to know that I have been doing everything in my power to protect Kavet. Obviously I have some additional motives, but I am still loyal to this country."

The door opened again, and this time they both jumped up as they saw Naples there.

"You should be in bed," Rinnman gasped, as Hansa hurried over to help steady the Abyssumancer. "I'm happy to see you well enough to stand, but I can't believe you're—"

"High. Pain. Tolerance," Naples bit out. He winced as Hansa caught him around the waist, but then leaned into him, and they walked together toward the nearest chair. "Trust me when I say I'll heal better in here."

When Hansa looked up from Naples again, he found Rinnman carefully *not* looking at any of them.

"He *is* on our side, isn't he?" Naples asked.

"I think so," Hansa answered. "Rinnman?"

The other guard said, "I'm on Kavet's side, and I believe you, Hansa, when you say you are, too. I don't want to know more than I have to, and that includes . . ." A pointed glance to Hansa, Umber and Naples each in turn. "I just don't want to know. For now, I'll make sure Gray and the other guards stay a bit farther down the hall. There is only one entrance to this wing. They don't need to be right outside your door."

He walked out, pausing along the way to briefly put a hand on Naples' shoulder. Naples sighed, his body relaxing as if some of the pain were gone.

"I would like credit now for showing epic restraint," Naples said, once Rinnman had closed the door behind himself.

"For what, not getting crude with Rinnman?"

"I could have jumped him," Naples pointed out.

"You can barely *stand*," Hansa replied. "How can you *possibly* be thinking of sex?"

"I've gotten hurt worse *during* sex. You've never screwed the king of the Abyss." Naples paused, reconsidered, and said, "Hurt worse than I am *now*, at least. It would have been a close call if not for the animamancer." He winced, and shifted in his seat. "Divine wounds are more difficult to heal than infernal ones, though, so I'm not exactly at my peak at the moment. We are all going to be in trouble if Cupric or Quinacridone comes back to pick up the Numenmancer."

"Xaz said she saw you."

Naples practically snarled. "Yeah, we had a brief chat."

"She seemed dazed," Hansa said. "Is she all right?"

"Don't know. Don't care," Naples answered.

"Don't-know-don't-care if the only person among us capable of fighting the bloodthirsty Numini is up for the task?"

"Don't-know-don't-care if that bitch who doesn't have the spine to *ever* take on one of the Numini and who got my friend dead gets fed to a lesser demon," Naples spat, the vehemence as brutal as the truth in his words.

"We don't know that Alizarin is dead," Hansa said.

"Do you see him about?" Naples snapped back. "Do you see him hovering by Cadmia's side, waiting for her to wake up? Do you see him here, lending power to help us heal?" He dropped his head in his hands, and let out a cry that sounded more like an animal than a man.

Hansa struggled to swallow past the knot in his throat. "Isn't it likely he was just banished to the Abyss?" Hansa suggested, desperately. Naples knew the ways of the Abyss better than the rest of them, and every line of his expression and waver in his voice said the blue Abyssi, who Hansa had once hated and feared but had come to care for, was *gone*. "If Veronese is here when Alizarin thought Modigliani killed him, then why can't Alizarin just be in the Abyss? You could summon him back, couldn't you? He doesn't have to be *gone*."

"Well, he *is*," Naples snarled. "Maybe he's alive in the Abyss—probably he is—but I've seen Dioxazine. There isn't a hint of the Abyss on her, which means Quinacridone burned any connection to the Numen from *him*." Before Hansa could ask what that meant, Naples rose to his feet, as if despite his pain and exhaustion he couldn't stand to stay still. He explained, "Even when I first met Alizarin, he had a Numen taint, I guess from this Veronese. It's what drove him to seek a connection to the divine realm in the first place. It's what taught him to be gentle. And even it wasn't enough to ever teach him the things he learned while bonded to Dioxazine.

"I could call his name and probably summon what's left of him, but it won't be the Alizarin that you or even I know. The kind of blast that could burn him free of Xaz's divine taint wouldn't have conveniently left Veronese's in place. That means he would just be an Abyssi of the third level, a creature of hunger and lust and *nothing* else. He won't remember us as friends, or remember me or Cadmia as people he cared for, or even remember his child as something he loves. What he'll remember about us is that being around us *hurt* him, because the higher emotions do hurt, and he will do everything in his power to kill us so we don't hurt him again, because that is what an Abyssi understands."

Hansa sank down on the bed beside Umber. The movement roused the spawn, who opened his eyes with a sharp expression that instantly faded as he felt the pain in Hansa and Naples.

He reached out to pull Hansa close.

"You're still injured," Hansa said. "I don't want to hurt you."

"I'll be fine," Umber answered. "You're hurting worse."

They curled together. Naples shuffled over to them and looked down imploringly until they both reached up to pull him into the bed, too. It hurt, where bodies pressed against injuries, but it was better than being apart.

"We have to figure out what we're going to do," Hansa said.

We're going to do this first, Umber replied. He kissed him, gently, that much contact as much as either had the energy for.

I can't believe he's gone. Hansa wasn't sure whose thought that was. Maybe his own.

They lay together, sharing wordless grief and gaining comfort in nearness and touch, until the dark pool of despair changed into something harder, brighter, and more solid—but resolve.

We have to fight Quinacridone. That was Naples, the first of them to pull from a sense of numb defeat. *We can't let him get away with this. I don't care if it kills us. I've done dead before, and even if this one sticks . . . we have to fight him.*

That means we need to find Pearl, and summon Scheveningen.

And convince Dioxazine she has the power to fend off her Numini.

Their thoughts all blended together, responding to each other in what quickly became half sleep.

Dioxazine should be able to find her Numini, and Pearl might be there.

If Pearl is with Cupric, there must be a way to find him, right?

If Quinacridone isn't helping him block it, I should be able to trace my power to him. That had to be Naples. *If not, I can ask Sennelier to find him. He doesn't normally get involved in the actions of the higher planes, but he can't be pleased about Quinacridone claiming his mancer, and he won't want the Quinacridone taking over here, either.*

Somewhere in the midst of discussion, planning and commiserating, sleep claimed them—a sleep full of dreams of the Abyss and frosted by the icy rime of divine wrath.

CHAPTER 41

CADMIA

At the third level of the Abyss, there was a sea with water like black oil. The fumes that hung above it were poisonous to most creatures, as well as being volatile; one spark could send indigo fire licking across the surface, reaching out to devour any fool-ish soul who made the mistake of swimming in the viscous liquid and somehow had not yet drowned or been devoured by the red-beasts that swam beneath.

The shores of the great sea of the Abyss were the same black rock and sand that made up so much of the realm. It shone with colors unnamed by mortal words.

The first level of the Abyss was lit, during its "days," by distant fire. The second level was lit by free-floating drifts of foxfire, some of which crept along the ground and some which hung higher up. The third level was dark except for the wisps and other predatory lights. The shades who resided there knew to fear the light, because it would hunt them, for sport or pleasure even if they provided no sustenance.

Cadmia wasn't . . . *quite* . . . one of those shades. She was looking for something, and didn't want to return until she found it, and in order to walk this realm she had needed to become like the once-human ghosts who drifted there. She could still feel her tie to the mortal realm in her heart, a bit higher than the bond to the Abyss growing inside her.

She intended to convince him to come back.

When Alizarin had first returned to the court, the other Abyssi had challenged him. He had fought for hours to regain his place in the lion-like hierarchy, but had easily won those battles despite his recent sojourn. Then he hunted, then rested, and then joined the other Abyssi at play. It was all so beautiful—in its own feral way.

Then those blue eyes had lit on Cadmia as she accidentally stepped for a moment into his line of sight, and what she saw in them was not tenderness. At first it had been curiosity; he had tilted his head in a way she recognized so well. Then the expression on his face had turned to anger, and she had known he was about to pounce.

She had fled, though she had known that she would never have been able to outrun him if he wanted to give chase. Thankfully, he had been glutted with his recent kills, and hadn't cared enough to scramble after a simple shade.

Cadmia sat on the black sand, by the glutinous waters, and discovered that a shade cannot weep.

She looked up with a choked, silent scream as a shadow fell across her. She couldn't run, could only stare in horror at the creature who seemed made of shadow, blood, and claw. The other Abyssi drew away from him, even Alizarin, sinking their bodies low, and by that she recognized him.

"Modigliani."

"*Cadmia,*" he greeted her, as if greeting a friend.

"I know your Abyssumancer," she said.

"*I know,*" he replied. "*You're the one Alizarin turned on him for. You and . . .*" He ran a claw across her abdomen, lightly enough it didn't draw a single bead of blood. "*You know it is still alive back in the mortal realm?*"

She hadn't known. She had thought, since she was here, it must be, too.

"*And you are being summoned,*" the lord of the Abyss said to her.

Cadmia.

Cadmia.

There was a voice calling her, pulling at her. She had been ignoring it as she struggled to reach Alizarin.

"*I could break the necromancer's link to you and keep you here,*" Modigliani said. "*I could give you to Alizarin if you wish it.*"

"Will he recover?" she asked. She didn't intend to accept Modigliani's offer and give up her life to stay here, but she hoped the king of the Abyss knew something she did not.

"*He has recovered. The Numen taint was an unnatural infection that has weakened him for decades. It's gone now.*" He tilted his head, an expression that was heartbreakingly similar to some of Alizarin's, and said, "*Alizarin was born of crystals seeded by the previous lord of the Abyss. He would never have stayed a mere prince of the third level all this time if not for that Numen curse.*"

"If it was such a *curse,*" Cadmia spat, "why didn't you kill Veronese when you had the chance? Were you too weak, even in your own realm?"

She lashed out unwisely, in fury and hurt, but Modigliani only laughed. "*I just told you. Unhindered, our blue prince will make his way down to the fifth level someday. In a century, two at most, he will be a genuine threat to my throne.*"

"That is a long time in advance for an Abyssi to plan," Cadmia said, her gaze drawn back to the other Abyssi, who had returned to their lounging play with only occasional glances to the lord of the Abyss and the shade to whom he spoke.

"*Perhaps I, too, was touched by the divine many years ago,*" Modigliani replied sardonically. "*It was the price*

I paid when I claimed the Numini's discarded toy for the Abyss. And speaking of Terre Verte, I have a task for you to perform back in the mortal realm."

He whispered to her, and then he left her alone by the shore. The other Abyssi had noticed her, but knew he had claimed her and so they stayed far away. She could not see Alizarin anymore.

According to Modigliani, the baby was still alive. More importantly, *Cadmia* was still alive. That meant it was time to go back.

Cadmia. Cadmia. Cadmia.

The words were a chant. All she needed to do was turn her attention to them, and they pulled her closer: through the mists and marshes of the second level of the Abyss; through the bone-dry sea of the first level; through the veil of fire that separated the Abyss from the mortal plane.

Cadmia. Cadmia.

She woke weeping, not for the pain in her body but for the emptiness. Modigliani was right; the creature she had seen in the Abyss was not the man she had loved. That Alizarin, the one born when a prince of the third level tasted a Numini's tears, was gone.

She tried to put her feet on the floor and cried out at the pain, which woke Lydie, who had fallen asleep still holding onto that cord between this realm and Cadmia's spirit.

"Cadmia," the necromancer whispered, her voice small and tight. She reached out, and wiped a tear gently from Cadmia's face before saying, "I'm so sorry."

"We need to banish Quinacridone," Cadmia declared. Lydie's eyes widened as if in surprise, but how could she possibly be surprised at what was the only conclusion? Even if Modigliani hadn't explained her options, the question was not what needed to be done about Quinacridone, but only *how*.

"If we drive him from this plane, all we do is send him back to the Numen so he can try again," Lydie said.

Cadmia shook her head, then winced; moving those muscles hurt all the way down her back. "There is a prison in the Abyss," she said. "It held Terre Verte for nearly a century. It can hold a Numini."

"Just how are we supposed to get one of the most powerful Numini in existence to a prison at the lowest level of the Abyss?" Lydie asked.

Cadmia felt like she was in a trance as she spoke, and only when Lydie touched her hand did she snap out of it, gasping as if surfacing from deep water. A bottomless sea, hot as blood and thick as tar—and lit by blue eyes that looked at her without a flicker of tenderness. "As Modigliani reminded me, we are not without powerful allies. If Naples can bring Modigliani across, then when Scheveningen banishes Quinacridone, Modigliani can force him down to the lowest level of the Abyss and lock him there."

"Can Modigliani keep Quinacridone and Cupric

from killing us all, so we can get Pearl and summon Scheveningen in the first place?" Lydie asked.

Cadmia shook her head. "I don't know. I just . . ." The memory of the voice of the lord of the Abyss still echoed in her mind, and made her shudder to recall it. "We should speak with the others. Naples will know what Modigliani is capable of, and whether he's as much or more of a threat than Quinacridone. And I have a feeling we should do this all fast, before someone else makes the next move for us." Quinacridone. Cupric. Terre Verte. There were too many players on the board.

Meeting, or doing anything *fast*, turned out to be a problem. Hansa, Naples, and Umber were all in the same room, with the door locked, and while normally Cadmia would have considered protecting themselves and the world more important than sex, to those three, sex was power. They needed all the power they could get.

"You're up."

Cadmia turned slowly, leaning on Lydie's arm, as she heard a surprised male voice. The man she faced was somewhat older and leaned on a crutch; he was familiar, in that she had seen him around the Quin Compound, but she did not personally know him.

"I'm up," she agreed, glancing at Lydie.

"Cadmia, this is Rinnman," the necromancer

introduced them, obligingly. "He saved most of our lives. He's—"

"Very grateful to see you feeling better," Rinnman interrupted. "I was on my way to see Hansa, though."

"It's probably not the best time," Cadmia said, with a wince.

Rinnman nodded. "There's someone asking to see him."

"He's leading the One-Twenty-Six, has been nominated for President, and just survived a lightning strike," Lydie said. "I imagine a lot of people want to talk to him."

Rinnman frowned, looking puzzled. "That's right."

The confused expression, combined with her recent experience with the false "Arylide," was enough to make Cadmia ask tensely, "Was there something special about this visitor?"

"He's . . . I don't know." Rinnman continued to frown, thinking hard for another moment, before he said, "Well. That's . . . somewhat unsettling. He said something about asking for an audience as a 'show of good will.' I didn't think to question it. I'll go back and ask."

Cadmia was not surprised to hear a familiar voice say at that moment, "No need. I took the liberty of letting myself in."

Cadmia turned toward Verte as Rinnman moved between her and him. "Gray?" Rinnman called.

Terre Verte shook his head. "I told the two gentlemen here to take some time off," he said. "I'm sure a man such as yourself could understand why my conversation with Hansa requires privacy. In fact, why don't you leave us as well?"

Rinnman tensed, and a fine shiver seemed to pass through him, from his toes through his torso and out his fingertips, before he shook his head. "I don't think I'll do that."

"What do you want with Hansa?" Cadmia asked. She would have liked to throw Verte out of the building, but he seemed to have dispatched most of the Quin guards already, and Cadmia couldn't think of any other way to get rid of him.

Verte glanced to Rinnman briefly. "Is the animamancer in your confidence now as well?" He crossed his arms, and seemed to turn all his attention to observing the guard. "Enough in your confidence, even, that you would care to disclose the details of your conversation with Modigliani?"

Cadmia was about to say no when Rinnman shook his head. "I think I'd rather *not* be in that kind of confidence. I'm going to stand at the end of the hall. Try not to die on me."

He walked off, graceful despite the crutches and the tension lifting his shoulders.

Verte gave a half shrug, then continued with what he was saying. "I know Modigliani spoke to you. He spoke to me as well when I went to the temple trying to discover what happened to Dioxazine."

"You mean, to the woman you imprisoned?"

"I mean, the Numenmancer whose power I at tempted to dampen in order to weaken her Numini," Verte said sharply. "Now she is free, and Quinacridone is free, and that isn't good for any of us, is it? It certainly doesn't seem to be good for you, if I may be so bold as to judge by the lightning-burns that I can smell from where I'm standing." He drew a breath, calming himself, and was once again his placid, aristocratic self as he said, "We have compatible goals, and with Quinacridone in this world, we both need any allies we can get."

"Compatible . . . what *are* your goals?" Cadmia asked.

Verte gave an exasperated sign. "They are exactly what they have always been. I serve Kavet. Though I'll admit, Cupric's folly and Quinacridone's brazenness have forced me to change my *immediate* goals." He frowned. "I just hope Azo can keep the mancers at Amaranth Farms under control until I can get back. Modern magic users in Kavet have been so indoctrinated with self-hatred, I swear they must be minded like children to keep them from *eating* each other."

Fishing for a clearer understanding, Cadmia asked, "So if Hansa wins the election—"

"Let's let Hansa *live* through the election first,

shall we?" Terre Verte snapped. "After Scheveningen is raised, and Quinacridone is banished, *then* Hansa and I may discuss our relatively minor potential disagreement over the sovereignty of Kavet."

"Relatively minor?"

"Compared to Quinacridone wanting to enslave all three worlds, I would say that who rules this one island is a *minor* affair," Terre Verte said. "And it's a moot point. You need an heir to the Terre line in order to wake Scheveningen. That being so, you would be foolish to turn down the alliance I offer."

His logic would have been more persuasive if Cadmia hadn't seen him kill a man with his bare hands, and didn't know he had locked Dioxazine away without warning.

"I have never been your enemy, much as you seem to think I am," Terre Verte added. "You could try to do this without me, I suppose. Modigliani tells me that there is another heir, my father's bastard's granddaughter, but she is a child and half-addicted to the Numini. She will be unreliable, and even if she cooperates, you will be putting her through what I understand to be a *painful* ritual. Are you willing to hold that child down? Even more importantly, are you willing to risk Quinacridone killing her for fear that you may be able to use her?"

"And you can keep her safe." Cadmia said the words flatly, not sure if she believed them. *Half-addicted to the Numini*, Verte had said. According to

Veronese and Modigliani, that description could apply to Verte as well.

Terre Verte nodded. "I have a plan. If you, Hansa and the others will hear me out, we can move by dawn. Slaying the Abyssi took much of Quinacridone's energy, but she will recover swiftly."

CHAPTER 42

UMBER

Umber hadn't expected the lightning. He hadn't expected the animamancer. Most of all, he had not expected to be woken and almost physically dragged out of bed by a cranky ex-prince. But here they were, perhaps two hours before dawn, gathered in a conference room in the Quin Compound as they had once gathered in Azo's parlor in the Abyss.

Of course, Azo's parlor had been far less sterile, and Umber had felt safer near the high court of the Abyss than he did here, despite—or in some cases *because of*—his allies.

Particularly Verte, who refused to sit, but paced until everyone else had settled as comfortably as their injuries allowed. Umber had pulled his chair close to Hansa's so they could lean against each other. The burns on both their skins were fading as Abyssal power fought to expel the Numen taint and heal the damaged flesh, but the hard chair still felt sharp and painful against Umber's back. Naples had dispensed with chairs entirely and decided to sit on the floor so he could lean back against Hansa's legs and drape his left arm across Umber's.

Cadmia looked like she wanted to choose the floor, too, but had then realized the same thing that kept Umber in the chair: Verte intended to stand, which meant he would tower over anyone on the floor. Naples either didn't mind having his once-prince above him, or else there was enough Abyssi in him that the seemingly-subservient posture was meaningless to him.

Lydie had also given up formality in favor of sitting cross-legged on the floor. She didn't appear quite as uncomfortable as the rest of them, but Umber wasn't sure if that was because Rinnman had healed her more, or because she was a better liar. Her face was smooth and introspective, thoughtful but not frightened, an expression Umber didn't believe at all. Every now and then Umber caught her examining Dioxazine like some kind of fascinating bug.

Xaz pretended not to notice as she leaned against the wall next to the doorway, as if trying either to guard it or preparing to run. She seemed to have decided the best thing to do was to watch the floor and not meet anyone's gaze.

Perhaps that was for the best, since whenever Naples looked at her, he glared, and Terre Verte was doing his best to ignore her.

"Lydie has spoken to Veronese," Verte said as he paced, "and Cadmia has spoken to Modigliani. Meanwhile, I have spent most of my time speaking to the older shades that I could find in this area, and attempting to analyze the magic that protects the Cobalt Hall."

"And imprisoning your lovers," Xaz broke in frostily. "Let's not forget that."

Verte cast her an exasperated look, though Umber thought the comment well deserved.

"I *believe* we all agree that the Numini Quinacridone should not be allowed to control Kavet and the rest of the mortal realm," Verte continued, as if he had not been interrupted.

"That much, I believe we agree on," Umber conceded. "And according to Veronese, Xaz is one of the few people who might be able to control Quinacridone."

Perhaps seeing that they were not willing to let the point go, Verte sighed, and finally looked and spoke directly to the Numenmancer. "Dioxazine, you are a beautiful and fascinating woman, but like all mancers in Kavet, you have almost no formal training in sorcery. Quinacridone has deliberately kept you ignorant. Even if he had not, a mortal cannot destroy a Numini. Only another Other can. You could stand against him only so long before his power overwhelmed and broke you. So, when I realized that Quinacridone was drawing power from you—from the rituals I was trying to teach you, and therefore from all our allies at Amaranth—I needed to act swiftly. I could not sever his tie to you, so I shielded you so he could not draw power from you."

"And this 'shielding' was helpful?" Dioxazine asked ironically. "It had the effect you desired?"

Verte frowned. "No. Clearly. I did not anticipate that Quinacridone would be willing to tie himself to an Abyssumancer to cross into this realm."

"Or that he would attack Alizarin," Cadmia broke in, her voice as cutting as Xaz's. Umber was very good at compartmentalizing, and had tried repeatedly to shove his own pain over Alizarin's loss down somewhere deep in his guts. He needed to function *now*, to think clearly and plan *now*, or else they wouldn't survive the next few hours. But every time he looked at Cadmia, or every time someone mentioned the beautiful blue prince, the grief took him by surprise. He had to swallow it down like bile.

As he did so, Hansa added, "And in the process almost kill us all. So stop posturing, tell us what you know and what you *think* we should do, and then we will discuss it."

Verte's silver eyes flashed, furious. He continued,

his voice tight with irritation. "If we can kill Cupric, we can drive Quinacridone out of this realm, but that has been done before and we know it will not stop him for long. We need to destroy him. Most Abyssi would not dare cross the rulers of the Numen, but Modigliani has indicated that he is willing to assist—to a point—in order to protect his own realm from Numini invasion, and of course to protect his mancer." He glanced at Cadmia for confirmation. She nodded. "But even the king of the Abyss is weak compared to Quinacridone. The only Other who might hope to stand against a high arbiter is Scheveningen, the Gressi. That is why I believe Quinacridone will soon act to kill me, and the child you've spoken of, Pearl. For those of you doubting my motives, I hope that clarifies them."

He looked directly at Umber, as if sensing that he was the staunchest doubter in the group.

Hansa was the one who spoke up. "Why *you*?" he asked. "I've been told you're a Gressumancer, and that you're *not* a Gressumancer. I don't understand the difference, and I don't understand why your bloodline is so important. What are you?"

"I'm a sorcerer," Verte replied, with an unexpected level of patience that made Umber nervous. "I am not tied directly to one of the Others, as an Abyssumancer or a Numenmancer must be, but I have enough power from birth, bloodline, and study that I could form such a tie with a willing Abyssi or

Numini—or Gressi. That is the intention of the ritual we've been discussing, to bond me to the slumbering Scheveningen. Otherwise, Scheveningen cannot manifest physically on this plane any more than a Numini or an Abyssi can without a mancer to summon them."

Hansa nodded, taking in the words, clearly parsing it, and considering what other concerns he still had. "Those killed by Abyssi dwell in the Abyss," Hansa said, as usual happy to challenge the once-prince's assertions. "I assume those killed by Numini likewise dwell in the Numen. My understanding was that *you* wanted to return to the Numen, and were willing to go to war against them to get there. That seems to give you a conflict of interest in fighting Quinacridone, if you might get everything you want if he kills you."

"Even if I were inclined to abandon my responsibility to Kavet and rest blithely in Numen grace," Verte bit out, his patience clearly expiring, "if Quinacridone were willing to slay his enemies with divine power and embrace them in the Numen, he wouldn't have left you all alive. He already has one Abyss-tainted follower happy to do his bidding and could get more. He can find a way to murder without needing to bring the slain soul home."

Verte tried to conceal it but there at last Umber saw a flash of fear, and with it a motivation he believed: yes, Verte wanted to return to the Numen, but even more, he feared a return to the Abyss.

Hansa had done a good job addressing the same questions Umber had, so Umber jumped ahead to the next part of the conversation. "I agree with Hansa—I don't trust you—but you make a good point why we need you. So what exactly is your plan?"

"With the necromancer's help, I will tie myself to Scheveningen," Verte answered shortly. "Once that is done, I can wake him from his slumber. Together we will be able to drive Quinacridone from this realm. Unfortunately, while Arylide and I do that, we will be vulnerable. We will need protection." He looked up at Naples, who took the cue.

"Modigliani will help," Naples said, "but as you've said, even he isn't invincible. We need to control Quinacridone long enough for you to complete the ritual. Dioxazine might be able to slow Quinacridone down, but we also have Cupric to contend with. He isn't as powerful as I am, but he could still distract Modigliani, and if we kill Cupric, Quinacridone will return to the Numen and we'll lose our chance to bind him."

"Quinacridone's Abyssumancer, by definition, has an Abyssi patron who surely is not pleased with the situation. That Abyssi will be able to control Cupric, and through him steal power from Quinacridone."

"That Abyssi is Sennelier," Umber provided. "He won't want his mancer killed, either."

Hansa met his gaze briefly with a concerned query

and a thought along the lines of, *Is that a concern for you?* Umber shook his head and shrugged it off. Technically Sennelier was his sire, but he was in no way a father. Summoning him meant no more to Umber than calling any other Abyssi would.

"Even I can't summon two Abyssi at once," Naples pointed out to Verte, "and you can't summon Sennelier *and* Scheveningen at the same time."

Verte turned his eyes—now once more a deep, calm gray, as if the conversation was now going exactly the way he wanted it to—on Hansa.

Umber tensed. Hansa had some Abyssal power, but nowhere near enough to summon an Abyssi. That wasn't even something *Umber* could do.

Naples let out a surprised, "Oh. Of course."

"Of course . . . what?" Hansa asked, at the same time Umber realized what Verte was implying. No wonder Verte had been willing to explain about mancer bonds and summoning Others to the Quin.

"As plans go," Naples said, thinking aloud as if he and Verte hadn't left half the room confused, "it isn't a bad one. Hansa is—"

"Wait," Hansa interrupted, catching up as Naples spoke. "It takes a *mancer* to summon an Abyssi and tie it to this realm. I'm not a mancer. According to Alizarin, even Antioch gave up on me. *Remember?*"

"Rin also said it would be easy for another Abyssi to claim you," Cadmia said, "since all the preparation had been done already."

"An Abyssi can't have two mancers, can they?" Lydie asked. "Sennelier already has one."

"And Antioch doesn't want to be involved," Hansa said. "We don't have a lot of Abyssi friends we can just go to and ask—"

"We have Alizarin," Naples broke in softly. "We have a knife made of his bone, designed specifically to tie his power to a mortal. You do still have it, don't you, Cadmia?"

"Umber has it." He had carried it for her, since it wasn't safe to have in the Cobalt Hall.

"Won't . . . will Alizarin fight us?" Cadmia asked, her voice tight. "He doesn't know us anymore."

"That's why he won't fight us," Naples answered, his tone equally subdued. "We are asking nothing of him, and giving him a valuable power source. A mancer bonded to one of the spawn." Returning his attention to Verte, he asked bitterly, "Do you *know* what happens to one of the spawn when they're bonded to a mancer?"

"As far as I can tell," Terre Verte replied, "these two are functioning quite well together, not bonded together in impossible circumstance, the way you and Azo were. I don't see that it would make a difference, especially if they intend for it to last in the short term. Once this is done, they may still choose to break the bond anyway."

Hansa started at the reminder, as if that thought hadn't crossed his mind in a while.

"I still don't understand," Lydie objected. "What is the connection between Alizarin and Sennelier and Cupric?"

"A mancer's patron isn't the only Abyssi he can interact with," Verte explained. Given the way his gaze lingered on Hansa while he spoke, Umber suspected he was again willingly clarifying only because he assumed Hansa would be too ignorant to follow the logic. "In this case, we're setting Alizarin up as Hansa's *patron*, but only so he has the power to summon another Abyssi. Alizarin is not our ally in this, only a tool we can use to bring Sennelier over."

Umber saw Cadmia flinch and clench her jaw, her eyes narrowing at the description of her lover. He put a hand on her arm and squeezed gently, intending to be comforting, but when she put a hand over his he realized he was seeking comfort in the contact, too.

"It's a risk I'm willing to take," Umber said, "but only if it's something Hansa is willing to do." He thought by now Hansa knew enough to make an informed decision, but he wanted to make sure one particular point was clear. "Hansa, even if we break the bond between us, if you agree to this, we *won't* be able to break your connection to the Abyss afterwards. A mancer can't survive being severed permanently from his patron."

"I . . ." Hansa sighed, and scrubbed at his rough-stubble face. "I need to think."

"We don't have much time," Verte pointed out.

"Give him a minute," Xaz snapped. "Rushing to decisions hasn't been good for *anyone* here."

"No," Hansa agreed, "but he's right. I know we're short on time. I just . . ." He looked down at Naples, then at Cadmia, then Lydie. "Fuck. I'm not giving you all up. I might as well join the team."

"That's sweet," Verte drawled.

"Before we go into the technical details of making a mancer, we still haven't answered the question of how we get into the Cobalt Hall," Lydie pointed out, ever-practical. "Veronese says this needs to be done there, but mancers can't even cross the threshold."

"In my day they could," Verte replied. "It took me a great deal of effort to divine why, but at last I determined it. Scheveningen is bonded to the Terre line, but that bond was broken when I was killed, and Clay was not raised for the throne—for the *land*. The Cobalt Hall started to reject those with power when the country, led by the Quin movement, started to do the same. As such, one of two things should enable us to enter: either my blessing as a Terre, or the blessing of the chosen leader of the country."

The last was directed at Hansa, and Umber could hear the snarl of hostility in it.

"Wait—I was right?" Hansa asked, eyebrows raising. "It is responding to the laws?" Umber chuckled despite himself at the bright spark of pride in Hansa's mind. "I'm not leader yet," he added.

"No, but enough people see you as one that it might work," Xaz agreed. "I *helped* with that scrying."

"Are we ready to get started?" Verte snapped.

"One more concern," Lydie said, to which Terre Verte nodded. "Most of us can't *see* Quinacridone to fight him, which if I understand correctly is a good thing, since mortals who see the Numini go mad." She paused, regarding Verte, and probably wondering the same thing Umber had been earlier: how reliable was he going to be once Quinacridone stood before him? "The Numen taint has faded from Hansa, Umber, and Naples. That's good, except I know that because I can still see that power on Xaz, you, and Cadmia—which implies it's also on me, which makes me worry how seeing Quinacridone is going to affect Cadmia and me."

Xaz answered, her voice soft but confident. "Part of controlling Quinacridone," she said, "is suppressing her power. It isn't the form that enchants, no matter how lovely it might be, but the divinity. You two can stay behind until Modigliani and I have the Numini under control, by which point you should be safe. From that, at least."

"This might not be a big deal to anyone else," Naples broke in, "but is Quinacridone a guy or a girl? Last time I saw him, he was male, or at least possessing a man. Now you're saying *she*."

"The Others—Numini and Abyssi both—don't have a decided form or sex," Dioxazine answered, tone dismissive. "They choose their forms when they appear to mortals."

"Well." Naples sat back, patting Umber's knee idly. "That makes sense."

"Are we ready, then?" Terre Verte asked, rising.

As Hansa, Umber, and Naples seperated themselves to stand, Cadmia spoke.

"If you or Hansa can allow us into the Cobalt Hall, and in effect decide who can or cannot enter, than why can't you just refuse to let Quinacridone and Cupric in until we've woken Scheveningen?"

"Maybe we can." Terre Verte shrugged. "But the magic guarding the Hall is unconscious and reactive, not specifically controlled. Once the walls against power are down, I believe it will be all-or-nothing. If I'm wrong, we will have an unexpected advantage, but the plan we have now will work even in a worst-case scenario."

"Mm." Hansa let out a noncommittal sound, as if seeming to recall something. "Speaking of," he joked, tensely, "do you think we could possibly save the world *quickly*? I'm supposed to have breakfast with my mother."

CHAPTER 43

CADMIA

The dawn would break soon; it was still dark outside the window, but Cadmia could feel the new day pressing against her as she watched Naples, Umber, and Hansa prepare Hansa for the first step of the plan.

"How will this affect Alizarin?" Cadmia asked. She knew he wasn't the man he had been anymore, but it still felt strange using him, without his knowledge or consent.

"He will feel the connection, and the extra power it gives him," Naples answered. "It's no threat to him, so I doubt—" For a moment, his voice choked, as the words brought home again how different Alizarin was now. "He won't care. Most Abyssi are protective of their mancers since creating one takes such a commitment, but since Alizarin didn't have to *do* anything to make this bond, I doubt he'll bother. He'll accept the power it gives him. He'll use it to help him consolidate his place in the court. He won't question it." Knowing it needed to be said, he added, "It won't hurt him in any way."

Cadmia nodded. Swallowed. "Thank you."

A moment of silence passed, as Naples contemplated the arm-length black knife made of Alizarin's bone with reverence. In his gaze, Cadmia saw the same shadow of loss, pain, and rage that she could feel in herself.

"I'll return it," he promised, before turning back to Hansa.

Naples hesitated again, at which point Hansa seemed to realize he was holding his breath; he let that one out in a rush and shakily drew another.

"Umber," Naples said, "you might want to sit down. You will feel this through the bond."

"*He* should sit?" Hansa asked, sounding a little closer to hysterical now. Umber moved back to the chair he had earlier occupied, though he stretched out an arm to keep hold of Hansa's hand. "Should I ask what we need to do to make this . . . mancer . . . link?" Hansa asked, as Naples shifted his grip on the bone blade, flipping it deftly about his fingers.

Xaz asked, "Do you remember how a link to the Abyss was forced on me?"

Hansa frowned, as if unsure—and then his eyes widened, and Umber hooked an arm around his waist, holding him, as he tried to step back. Dioxazine's link to Alizarin had formed when an Abyssumancer had thrown the knife at her, burying it deep in her stomach. "Is it too late to change my—"

Before Hansa had finished speaking, Cadmia saw the nebula of power around Naples flare. When he stepped in close to Hansa, the move had the grace of a dancer on stage, including his lifted arm. Hansa let out a squeak that might have been all of a scream that could make it past his clenched jaw, and was certainly all he had time for, before Alizarin's knife slid cleanly between Hansa's ribs. Cadmia knew without a doubt that Naples had aimed for the heart, and had found it flawlessly.

Hansa swayed, not immediately falling, and Naples stepped forward so when he *did* fall, the Abyssumancer could catch him and lower him gently, one arm around Hansa's waist while the other stayed on the knife.

Naples worked quickly, his gaze distant as if he was viewing things Cadmia could not see—such as the third level of the Abyss, and the blue prince there? When he released the knife, he smoothed a hand across Hansa's chest, away from the blade and toward his shoulder. A blue-black veil of power followed, spreading from the wound.

Cadmia had to look away. Dioxazine and Verte,

she realized, were both watching with impassive expressions. Neither of them seemed surprised or worried. Lydie was staring at Hansa with curiosity, but without fear. What was the necromancer seeing? A veil of death? Or was she interested because the mortal blow hadn't resulted in . . .

Cadmia bit her lip and sat down. He *looked* dead.

No, don't look.

She raised her gaze again, and this time focused on Umber, who had slumped in his chair, unconscious but breathing steadily. Noticing, Lydie moved next to him to keep him from falling.

At last, Hansa drew a gasping, rattling breath, drawing Cadmia's gaze back to him as his entire body shuddered. His eyes opened, but never focused as Naples used a barb on the back of his ring to cut a line over his own heart. Cadmia nearly laughed when Lydie said, "Eww," as Hansa latched onto the wound.

One arm still tightly around the once-Quin's back, Naples twined the fingers of his other hand with Hansa's. He shut his eyes, drew a breath, and Cadmia saw flame flicker into life around their locked hands. Hansa flinched, trying to pull away, but Naples held tight.

When Naples finally pulled back, Hansa collapsed, coughing. The hand Naples had gripped was burned from fingertips to elbow, but as Cadmia watched, the flesh began to reform as healthy skin.

Hansa ripped the knife from his own chest without seeming to know what he was doing, and it clattered to the floor.

At last, the coughing subsided, and Hansa's breathing returned to normal. He had nearly stopped shaking before his eyes finally focused on the knife. He lifted a hand to his chest, which had healed over, leaving only the white shine of a single slender scar over his heart.

"Oh, my," he whispered. Then, "Umber." He nearly fell the first time he tried to stand, and Naples had to catch him. Umber, however, was already rousing.

"That was even more unpleasant than I imagined," Umber managed to say, as Hansa half crawled, practically into his lap.

"We need to move on," Verte said, as if knives in the heart were so commonplace that being disturbed or delayed by them was silly.

"That . . . really . . . *hurt*," Hansa managed to say.

"Blood, fire, pain, flesh," Naples replied. "Had to feed the link all four."

Hansa couldn't seem to stop checking to ensure he didn't still have a knife through his ribs. Naples meanwhile held out the knife to Cadmia, who hesitated more than a moment before taking it, at least until she confirmed that it was clean and none of Hansa's blood had stayed on it.

Verte drummed his fingers on the wall against

which he was leaning, at which point Naples looked up at him with a snarl.

"Give us a minute!" he snapped. "Scheveningen isn't going anywhere!"

"No, but we do have an angry, Abyss-marked Numini after us," Terre Verte replied bluntly, "and I would rather be further along before she arrives."

Naples drew another knife, and for a moment Cadmia thought she was about to need to break up a fight, but instead of going for Terre Verte the Abyssumancer made one quick cut on his own arm and opened a rift, into which he stepped without any hesitation or explanation.

The rift closed behind him.

"That should *not* be that easy," Umber remarked.

Terre Verte just shook his head. "The Abyss doesn't guard its borders. Only the Numen does."

"It doesn't *guard* its borders," Umber replied, "but the veils between the planes still *exist*. Could you create a rift so easily?"

Terre Verte's expression quirked for a moment in a way Cadmia couldn't recognize. He smoothed it before he pointed out, "The Numini have exiled me, and I have no desire to return to the Abyss. That leaves me with this plane."

"I agreed to this crazy plan," Hansa said, his voice still a little breathy but closer to stable, "but if I can avoid walking into the Abyss again any time soon, I would appreciate it."

Naples returned shortly, dripping glittery water with a sheen like oil, and grumbling, "Throw *me* in the lake, will you, bastard hornless . . ." He kept talking after that, but it drifted into a language Cadmia didn't recognize, but which seemed to be composed of sounds she wasn't sure the human throat could actually *make*.

"Thrown in the *lake*?" Umber asked.

Naples shook himself, sending droplets flying everywhere. Where they hit Cadmia, they were hot and oily.

"The second level of the Abyss is a little wet," he answered, "and that's where Sennelier was. He wasn't happy to see me, but I explained the situation and we managed to come to an accord. He won't fight you now, Hansa."

"Uh . . . thanks," Hansa answered.

Naples shrugged.

Verte cleared his throat, not discreetly.

Hansa glared at Verte, but then asked Naples, "So how do we do this?"

"Word of warning, you have nowhere near enough power or control over that power to be meddling with the denizens of the Abyss," Naples answered. "Do not summon anything. Do not attempt to open rifts. In fact, for now, even stay out of the temples, or you will get yourself eaten quicker than a six-day-old kitten in the crystal caves. Sennelier has agreed to assist us, and knows he will answer to me and Modigliani if he attempts to harm you, but after today you do *not* want to make the mistake of thinking you are in charge."

Hansa nodded, looking more calm rather than less, as if it were comforting to know he wasn't suddenly going to be completely different when this was all done.

Naples continued. "Normally, when you summon one of the Others, you contest your will and your power with theirs. Powerful tools help." He flipped the knife he had been holding and handed it, handle-first, to Hansa. "This was made of the bone of the previous lord of the Abyss. You may keep it."

Hansa reached for the knife tentatively. When he grasped the handle, his hand clenched spasmodically. His eyes unfocused and his lips parted slightly, as if Naples had just done something far more intimate; Naples' half smile suggested he knew exactly how Hansa felt. Cadmia fought the instinct to look away, to give Hansa some privacy—and won the fight, because her curiosity wouldn't let her miss this.

Naples waited until Hansa had shifted his grip on the knife and shook himself a little before he said, "Most of what you try to do is a matter of will and sacrifice. In this case, we're dealing with two Abyssi who are on our side and will cooperate with us, in which case the amount of power and sacrifice necessary are both significantly less. As long as I open the main rift—that's the hardest part—you should be able to call to Sennelier on your own. I'll go first." Naples drew a second blade, and with his gaze still locked with Hansa's, cut across his forearm. Blood flowed, sudden and quick, and as it dropped to the ground Naples said simply, "Modigliani."

The rift appeared with the stench of smoke, and the entire room darkened. Even Lydie stepped back, crossing her arms across her chest and looking around wildly, as if she couldn't see the rift but could *feel* it as the lord of the Abyss stepped through.

Cadmia backed up until she hit the wall, suddenly regretting her curiosity. She had seen this beast in the Abyss. Had she really wanted to see it again?

Modigliani flowed onto the mortal plane like a shadow, his form black as ink but still indistinct. He moved up behind Naples, who leaned back against the formless darkness before nodding to Hansa.

Hansa mimicked Naples' movements, but didn't appear nearly so comfortable about it. He hesitated and shut his eyes as he drew the blade across his own arm, and when he spoke Sennelier's name, it was nearly a whisper.

Either Sennelier had chosen to appear in solid form or, unlike Modigliani and Alizarin, he only had one form to begin with. Though his torso and arms were that of a man, his lower body was serpentine, with thick legs like a lizard's that helped him balance in an upright position. His face too was mostly humanoid, except the angles were all a bit too sharp, including ridges on his brow that led to a crest of spines instead of hair. From claws to face he was scaled with a pattern of burgundy and gray that gave his body a hypnotic, mosaic appearance.

"Finally," Terre Verte sighed, as the fourth-level non-royal Abyssi stepped through the rift, and paused to regard Hansa with eyes that shone with a familiar cobalt light. He had Umber's eyes . . . or, Cadmia supposed, Umber had his. "*Now* can we get a move on?"

CHAPTER 44

LYDIE

Lydie's heart pounded as she crossed the market square. She couldn't fully see the two Abyssi with them, but she could sense them as a crawling sensation down her spine and gooseflesh across her arms.

Hansa had told the guards at the Quin Compound that he was escorting Cadmia and her friends—Lydie and Umber apparently among them—back to the Cobalt Hall, where they would be tended to by the Hall's medics while safe from the mancer threat that supposedly had injured them in the first place. Lydie thought a few of the guards had started to give Hansa questioning looks, as if they were curious or concerned but not quite confident enough to speak up first.

Rinnman *did* stop them, to ask, "Where are you really going?"

"The Cobalt Hall," Hansa answered immediately.

Rinnman's gaze flickered to Lydie before he said, "Indeed?"

Lydie bristled. Having a Quin guard give her that look made her want to either fight or flee.

"We're hoping we can end this," Hansa said. "If we don't come back—" He cut off sharply, as if realizing that if they lost, Rinnman would know soon enough.

"Do you need backup?" Rinnman asked.

Hansa paused, and Lydie could see him considering it. After all, they were going after a mancer and his Other. That was the 126's job.

Lydie wasn't able to discreetly talk to Hansa directly, but she met Umber's gaze and let him see her terror there. She already had two demons at her back, and was anticipating a Numini's wrath as she worked with Terre Verte to try to summon Scheveningen. Even if Rinnman thought he could identify other Quin guards who were willing to work with them, Lydie would never be able to trust them enough to do the work that needed to be done.

Hansa jumped a little, probably as Umber spoke to him silently.

"Given what we're up against," he said, "I fear anyone else we bring in will end up being collateral damage." He looked pointedly at the gash in the ground left by Quinacridone's lightning. Lydie would have expected that someone would have at least tossed some boards across it for safety's sake, but it had been left alone. Probably no one dared go so near. "Be ready, though. If this goes wrong, I don't know what we'll face next."

"I'll organize the men we have left in the compound," Rinnman said, a bit pointedly Lydie thought. He must have known Hansa had sent many of the men on a wild-goose chase.

"Thank you."

"We need to go," Verte interrupted briskly. "Send your minion back to the barracks and then we need to get to the Hall's basement. In my day it had a dirt floor?"

Rinnman cast an assessing look at Verte, sighed, and said, "Good luck, sir," before turning back to his station.

"It's still dirt," Cadmia said, as they crossed the plaza. "It's mostly used as a wine cellar. That's where we need to do this I assume?"

She looked at Lydie. "In the earth beneath the oldest structure in Kavet," Lydie repeated, confirming.

It was easier said than done, though. As Lydie approached the Hall, she could feel the air thicken in resistance. By the time she reached the first step, her lungs burned as if she were trying to breathe molasses. She couldn't force herself up another.

Hansa could, and did, without apparent effort despite his new status. He ascended the steps without hesitation, at which point Umber and Naples exchanged a glance. Cadmia hurried to catch up to Hansa as he opened the front door.

Apparently having forgotten what he now was, and that he shouldn't be able to reach that door—never mind open it—Hansa glanced back to ask Verte, "Is there something we need to do to let people in?"

The once-prince was scowling.

Modigliani pushed forward, a faint shadow in Lydie's vision. He paused in front of Hansa, and his voice reached Lydie like a distant growl. *"May I?"*

Hansa nodded, and Lydie could see him swallow, as if his voice had flown in the face of the beast.

As the Abyssi crossed the threshold, it felt as if the building itself breathed a sigh. Lydie's ears popped with a sudden shift in pressure, and the air around her flowed freely once again, crisp and frigid with winter.

She wasn't the only one to feel it; the others took it as a sign, moving up the stairs. Hansa stepped out of the way as the rest crossed, Verte last, so the two men briefly faced each other in the doorway. Of Kavet's two leaders, one deposed and one not yet elected, the Hall had plainly chosen Hansa.

"It might have worked for you, too," Lydie heard Hansa say.

Verte shook his head and turned away, saying, "This way," as he led the way to the kitchen, and the door from it to the basement. "I think it's safe to say the barrier is fully down, that Quinacridone will have felt it, and that we'll see her shortly."

"I'm going to look for Pearl," Cadmia said, following their plan and splitting off as the rest of them went to the cellar. Cadmia hoped Pearl had run back into the building before the lightning struck. If the half-Numini child wasn't in her room at this pre-dawn hour, they had all agreed, she was probably with Quinacridone and Cupric. In that case, Verte seemed certain that Quinacridone would bring her, either to use as a hostage or as a way to help control Scheveningen when he rose.

Lydie didn't like splitting up, but Cadmia was the only one who could walk through the Cobalt Hall without attracting attention. The rest of them were hoping few people would be up at this hour, and that either Hansa could talk his way out of trouble or— more likely, in Lydie's opinion—that Umber or Verte could manipulate anyone they saw into looking the other way.

There was a lamp hanging from a hook next to the cellar door, clearly intended for anyone going downstairs, but no one bothered with it. Verte and Naples each lifted a hand, and then the winding stone stairs were lit by streaks of silver and turquoise foxfire.

"Dioxazine?" Verte prompted when they reached the bottom.

Lydie wasn't sure yet what she thought of the Numenmancer. No one had taken the time to detail

Xaz's story to their newest necromantic companion, but Lydie had picked up enough to know that Xaz's history seemed to be a series of momentary success and seeming acceptance followed by betrayal and imprisonment. She had been used, and Lydie respected the anger that now billowed around her like a cloud of divine wrath.

No, Dioxazine didn't hesitate, even to give Verte another sharp look—or acknowledge he had said her name. She spread a white sheet on the floor at the base of the stairs, settled herself onto it, and began to chant.

"Quinacridone," she chanted, "Numini of the highest level of the Numen, I summon you to me. I summon you to obey me." She continued to speak, but her voice dropped too low for Lydie to hear; she only knew that the Numenmancer was building the spell that would hopefully dampen Quinacridone's power, so when she arrived, she wouldn't instantly enchant everyone in the room.

"Terre?" Lydie prompted, as Verte looked around as if to assure himself that everyone necessary was present.

He finally looked directly at Lydie. Was that fear in his eyes? If so, was it for the ritual they were about to perform, formally tying him to the Gressi, or something else?

"Are you ready?" he asked, as if she hadn't just been asking him the same thing.

She nodded, and led the way to through the wine cellar. Amid racks and bottles, she reached out with her power, trying to sense the sleeping Scheveningen.

Nothing. She walked farther, stifling the thread of anxiety that warned her to hurry, that they had an angry Numini on its way to kill them all. Nothing. She retraced her steps. She was too young for this, hadn't had enough training. *No one* had enough training, because the stupid Quin made it illegal. No—wait. *There.*

Beneath the earth, half under a rack of wine bottles, she felt it. Like Veronese, the creature in the soil wore death like a mantle, but where the banished Numini had been tainted by death through his own destruction and exile to that realm, this one felt like a beacon.

Lydie touched the chains of power that reached from Scheveningen's resting place, and could feel that they linked to others far away, other graves where other Gressi had left their remains in the soil like nails holding the fabric of this realm together. The others were truly dead, but Scheveningen had chosen this eternal sleep; like the island of Kavet itself, he was the linchpin that held all the rest in place.

Lydie knelt and pressed her hands to the ground. It should have been impossible for her to do more than scratch the surface of the hard dirt floor, which had been packed down by countless feet over a thousand years, but her hands slid into it as if into newly-turned soil. Above her, she heard Verte's breath hitch.

"Scheveningen," Verte whispered, kneeling next to Lydie with his hands splayed flat on the ground, "please, we need you now. I am yours. Bind to me so you may walk this realm once more, mortal as this plane you created with your will."

The ground did not welcome him as it had Lydie. He was a Terre, and his bloodline had been promised to Scheveningen long ago, but Lydie was the one who had used Scheveningen's gifts all her life.

With her arm buried past the elbow, she felt a hand—skeletal and frail—grasp hers. As it did, her awareness blossomed. She could feel every grave ever dug in Kavet, from bodies sunk into shallow, marshy holes near the docks to those buried under craggy rocks on the distant shores of Quin Towers. Since Citizen's Initiative 126, bodies in Kavet had been burned instead of buried, but even those licensed pyres called to her as final resting places.

There was another side to this power, one that she knew should allow her to feel every *birth* as well, but her body wasn't capable of holding both sides of that magic.

She didn't think she wanted to.

She felt Verte next to her. *Terre.* They had all stopped using that title because they thought it meant "royal." Even Verte thought it did. But it didn't. It meant, "of the soil," or in simpler terms, "mortal."

And it meant "sacrifice."

Wielding Scheveningen's power, Lydie reached up with the hand not buried deep in the ground. She saw Verte's hand lift, as if he expected her to hold it, but that wasn't her aim. When her fingers touched his chest, they flowed through flesh and bone as easily as they had parted soil, until they coiled around his rapidly-beating heart and held it gently.

His scream was small and choked only because he couldn't draw breath to utter a louder one.

That was when the cellar door burst open, admitting Cupric in the lead and Quinacridone just behind with Pearl gripping her hand tightly.

Normally during a ritual Lydie lost awareness of the world around her, but connected to Scheveningen as she was, she saw everything in hyper-clarity.

She saw the shock on Cupric's face as he focused on the two Abyssi, which became horror as Sennelier pounced at his Abyssumancer. Quinacridone dropped Pearl's hand to respond, and suddenly Cadmia was there behind them in the doorway; she wrapped an arm around the girl's waist and took the stairs back up two at a time.

"No!" the Numen-spawn girl protested. "I need to go back! She needs my help!"

Her voice resonated through the link Lydie had made between Schenevigan and Verte, because Pearl too was a Terre. An apt sacrifice. The magic would be happy to claim her as well.

"*Get her out of here,*" Lydie breathed, sending the words to Cadmia on a breath of power.

Cadmia pleaded with the Numen-touched girl, but didn't relax her grip as she dragged her out of the ritual room. Veronese had warned them Pearl was likely to not cooperate, that her mother's memories of Veronese would include a fascination with the Numini and therefore susceptibility to Quinacridone's glamour, but it was heartbreaking to see.

That a child of my blood would wish to serve the one who once enslaved all.

That wasn't Lydie's thought. It was Scheveningen's.

Once more, Lydie's sight became expansive. She saw Amaranth Farms, where a score of mancers had gathered to argue, leaderless and restive. The Abyssumancers and Numenmancers couldn't help but sense the lord of the Abyss and a high arbiter of the Numen walking the mortal realm; they had called for the meeting, their anxiety demanding it, but now it was the animamancers and necromancers who spoke. Without understanding, they felt Scheveningen stretching in the earth.

"*Vanadium says Modigliani has promised us all a place of honor in the new world,*" the Abyssumancer Keppel reported, speaking for her Abyssi. "*She said Modigliani spoke to Verte, too. What do they mean, new world?*"

"*Where is Azo?*" another mancer asked querulously. "*Wasn't she supposed to be in charge while the Terre is gone?*"

"Maybe she didn't trust us without her brother here." Keppel grinned, but the expression was clearly forced. She cleared her throat and shook her head. "I told her the same thing I've just told you. The next thing I knew, she was gone."

Modigliani, Scheveningen thought. *What does that Abyssi youngling have planned?*

Lydie turned her attention to the closer battle.

Sennelier had Cupric pinned; Naples was helping the Abyssi keep his Abyssumancer from joining the fight, which included Numini feathers and Abyssi fur and blood spattered across the room. Modigliani and Quinacridone were locked in battle. Hansa and Umber were defending Dioxazine from—*what was that creature?* It moved like silver mist, reaching tendrils toward the Numenmancer, but it must have had a solid form somewhere underneath, since it dodged back whenever Hansa or Umber struck at it with their knives.

We called them Judgments, Scheveningen provided. *They serve the arbiters. I am ready. Pull me through.*

Lydie looked at Verte. In the wash of visions, she had almost forgotten her hand in his chest—how could she *forget* something like that? The heart in her hand was fluttering, struggling, as his lifeforce drained from him, through Lydie, and into the Gressi.

Lydie ripped her hand out of Verte's chest, and drove it too deep in the soil. The hand that gripped hers was no longer wasted, but dense and powerful flesh. She sought and found a second hand, and then started to pull the Gressi up through the soil.

The Terre collapsed, gasping, onto his hands and knees, yet he stared in wonder as Lydie pulled Scheveningen from the dirt. A gap opened in the floor, and it emitted a warm, sunny-green light utterly at odds with the battle going on.

Pearl appeared again; Cadmia must have lost hold of her upstairs. Both pounded down the stairs—then stopped, hypnotized, at the Gressi's rebirth.

The hands that broke the surface, tightly gripping Lydie's own, were scaled and clawed, but when the head emerged it wore a crest of silver-blue feathers. Dirt fell away from it like water running off an oiled tarp, leaving behind a figure that was neither male nor female, Abyssi or Numini, alive or dead.

Behind her, Lydie heard more footsteps on the wooden stairs to the cellar, but she couldn't look away from the rising Gressi even when she heard an unfamiliar woman's voice whisper, "I'm too late. Oh, you fools."

Verte stepped forward, and the Gressi wrapped its mancer in its arms. It whispered to him, *"My child, I am sorry for all you have been through."*

"I'm sorry," Verte said. "I thought—it seemed like the only—" His eyes, which had been dry through the ritual, now glistened with tears that fell down his cheeks. "When Modiglani spoke to me—" Lydie remembered her glimpse of Amaranth, and what

Keppel had said about Modigliani. And suddenly she understood, at the same time that Verte choked out, "Watch out!"

Lydie turned just in time to see Modigliani and Quinacridone pause in their battle with each other.

No, it wasn't a pause.

It was a *truce*.

The two Others, Abyssi and Numini, stepped apart as if they had been awaiting a cue. Then they pounced; Lydie felt fire and ice strike her simultaneously, throwing her away from the newly reborn Gressi as Abyssi claws and fair Numini hands rendered Scheveningen's beautiful form into blood and ozone.

CHAPTER 45

HANSA

Despite all he had gone through, Hansa was no expert on sorcery. There were, however, three critical facts he had recently learned that seemed abruptly relevant. As time seemed to freeze, his mind recounted them like a horrific laundry list:

One: An Other—an Abyssi, Numini, or apparently a Gressi—can only be truly killed by another Other.

Two: A mancer cannot survive the total severing of power from his Other.

Three: Scheveningen *was* the mortal realm.

As the newly-born form Lydie had pulled from the earth exploded in a shower of gore that settled to the ground as frost and ash, Verte staggered. The color drained from his face and he clutched at his chest.

There was no time to see more.

From the other side of the room, there was a blood-curdling growl that made every hair on Hansa's body lift. Sennelier leapt away from Cupric, took one glance at the changed situation, and said to Hansa, *"Release me, or I eat you."*

Hansa nodded. "Go," he said. He didn't know how to hold him even if he had wanted to. Of the others, he started to ask, "What do we—?"

"Do?" was lost as the ground trembled and Lydie shrieked, clenching her hands over her ears. She was bleeding from where either Modigliani or Quinacridone had struck her, but that injury didn't seem to be what had brought her down. What was she hearing?

The next sound was Azo's warlike cry as she appeared from nowhere and threw herself bodily at Modigliani in a mad attack—one that was met with a seemingly-idle bat of Modigliani's claw-encumbered paw. Azo flew backward through the air and struck the wall, where she fell, unconscious or dead. Hansa saw Naples look up, and it was as if he forgot everything else; he ran to Azo's side, leaving Cupric dazed but obviously alive.

Hansa moved to intercept the Abyssumancer, intending to leave Umber to deal with the wraith-like Numen creature they had been fighting—it was smaller now than it had been, and slower—but as he tried to circle the misty form something darker and denser scuttled out of a crack in the ground. Its shelled carapace pushed up against a shelf of wine, until with a heave it knocked the entire rack over with a *crash* of shattering bottles. The stench of cider and old wine filled the cellar.

Hansa drove his sword at the beast before his mind had even fully processed its soot-gray carapace or far-too-many vivid yellow legs. At first the blade bounced off the hard shell, but then its tip caught between two of the plates, and he bore down hard.

"*Quinacridone!*" Dioxazine shouted, her voice a dagger of ice. "*Heed me!*"

Hansa glanced up, stupidly, long enough to see that the Numini did hesitate, for a moment—but only a moment, until Cupric flung himself at Xaz.

And the ground shook again, driving them all off their feet. Hansa fell with his face inches away from the red-and-orange mandibles of the beast, and had to jerk back from its death throes.

"This whole place is going to come down," Umber shouted. "We have to get aboveground."

"We have worse things to worry about than the *building*," Cadmia pointed out, as another, smaller creature skittered across the floor. In the face of such horrors, Pearl had finally stopped struggling, and was clinging to Cadmia in terror instead.

Like a cross between a scorpion, a spider, and a snake, Hansa recognized this creature as an immature version of one of the lesser demons of the Abyss; they had seen Alizarin fight a full-grown version once. Both beasts could only be heralds of the breach in the planes caused by Scheveningen's death.

Hansa pushed himself up, pausing only to lever his sword out of the first beast, but as he looked around despair crashed on him.

Dioxazine was down, Azo was down, Modigliani and Quinacridone were working together, Lydie was holding her head and weeping as if the entire dead plane had collapsed on her at once, and Naples was kneeling by Azo's side as if the world wasn't ending—or maybe as if it were.

Because it was.

The earthquake rents in the floor were admitting more of the smaller demons. Others, cut into the walls, were starting to creep with frost.

And Hansa didn't know what to do.

He went to Umber's side. The white mist had found other prey, namely a dozen scuttling beetle-like beasts that had emerged from the Abyss, and was hovering over them as they slowly froze solid.

"I don't know," Umber said, as if Hansa had asked the question out loud: *What do we do?*

Naples stood, trembling visibly.

As Quinacridone and Modigliani stepped back from where the Gressi had been just moments before, Naples took one last look at Azo, then snarled. The sound wasn't human, and neither was the look in Naples' gaze as he drew a black-bladed sword that must have been sheathed along his spine but which—like all the Abyssumancer's tools—Hansa hadn't seen before Naples had drawn it to use. Sword in one hand and a dagger in the other, he let out a snarling cry and slashed at Modigliani.

The lord of the Abyss dodged away, then laughed, a purring, silky sound that made Hansa shudder in the same way grasping the knife had earlier. It was a *powerful* sound. He tried to block it out as he moved closer, trying to figure out if he could somehow lend strength and help without getting in the way.

Meanwhile, Quinacridone was standing in a growing halo of her own light, face set with concentration and one hand out, as if she was calling to the Numen beasts. Out of the corner of his eye Hansa saw Cadmia gripping Dioxazine's hands; the Numenmancer had woken enough that she was beginning to speak again, ever so softly but hopefully enough to staunch some of Quinacridone's power.

Hansa had no idea where Cupric was. Maybe he had fled. Hansa hoped he had been eaten by something.

"*You aren't bound to her anymore,*" Modigliani teased Naples, waving one of his nine tails dismissively at Azo's still form.

"I'll always be bound to her," Naples growled. "Even if not with magic." He lunged toward the Abyssi, who jumped away with a shocked look on his face, as if he had expected Naples to feint.

"*What is the point of this?*" Modigliani asked, as Naples' sword drew blood in a wine-violet splash. "*You are my mancer. You can't kill me without it killing yo—*"

"I can."

That soft, ringing voice echoed in Hansa's head, warning him that Xaz had lost some of her power over the Numini. For a moment his heart seemed to stop, and his body froze, and then the air became cold and fierce.

With a sound like the end of the world, everything stopped.

Then, shattering. The breath-stealing chill of the winter wind.

The lord of the Abyss screamed as his form dimmed, froze, and *fractured*, and the sound sent everyone in the room who had been standing to their knees.

Then the screaming stopped, and Hansa's first thought was, *Thank Numen*.

When he looked up, Modigliani was gone. There was no blood, not even a tuft of black fur to mark where he had been. Instead, all Hansa saw was Naples.

The Abyssumancer collapsed, the power that normally surrounded him like a nebulous halo snuffing out. Hansa struggled to reach him, but his body didn't obey his wishes fast enough. He ended up stumbling to his knees next to Quinacridone as the Numini caught Naples' still, limp form.

"*I am sorry,*" the Numini said to Naples' still form, "*that you had to make this sacrifice. The new world will be partially in thanks to you.*" Quinacridone looked up at Hansa and cradled his cheek in her hand. Her touch burned like frostbite. "*And you, Viridian . . . I can grant you your heart's desire, if you would like. You only recently accepted that bond. I can break it. The love you had pledged yourself to is in the divine realm. I can summon her now and you could be with her, as you had once planned.*"

Her. She was talking about Ruby.

Hansa opened his mouth to respond, but couldn't find his voice before another spoke.

"Do you know who *I* want to see, and have with us again?" Dioxazine asked. Before the Numini could respond, Cadmia's bone knife was in Xaz's hand—and then through Quinacridone's heart. The Numini's eyes widened in surprise as Xaz whispered, "Alizarin."

Hansa held his breath as Quinacridone's hand fell away, her arm going limp. Surely that couldn't be enough to kill it?

Yet Quinacridone was staring at the blade, which had entered just below her shoulder blade and showed its tip piercing through a breast the color of violets, with horror. Blue-black fire spread from the wound, charring the Numini's previously-flawless flesh.

The Numini looked up with wide, imploring eyes, holding a hand out to her mancer.

Xaz stumbled and coughed, then reached for Naples' still form cradled in Quinacridone's arms—or more importantly, for the long blade still gripped in his hand, the blade that, like many of Naples' tools, must have been crafted from the bones of the previous lord of the Abyss. Xaz took the sword, turned, and drove it into the Numini so it crossed Alizarin's knife.

Thunder rolled through the room and ripped Quinacridone apart, leaving only a spray of feathers. And Xaz. And Naples. Hansa's attempt to catch both of them as they fell with half-numb arms was awkward, but what else could he do?

Another tremble ran through the earth, this time accompanied by a timber disconnecting from the ceiling and crashing down. Hansa cradled the dead mancers, whose lives had been given for—for *what*? Modigliani and Quinacridone were dead, but so was Scheveningen. So was the entire *mortal realm*.

"We have to get out of here," Umber said again. He started to reach for Hansa, hesitated, then lifted Naples' body instead. Hansa followed *that*, more than anything else. Cadmia lifted Dioxazine, her mind apparently where Hansa's was: not ready to acknowledge the truth.

Certainly not ready to leave them here.

"Get Lydie and Azo," Cadmia said.

Hansa turned, prepared to face even more of the dead, but both women were still among the living. Lydie was in no condition to walk; she beat on Hansa's shoulder as he lifted her, but she was so slight, she was easy to carry. Thankfully, Azo had roused on her own and could walk on her own, though she leaned on Hansa for balance.

"Pearl?" Hansa called.

"Ran upstairs when Quinacridone turned on Modigliani," Cadmia answered. "We need to do the same."

Hansa followed the others, but as they fled the building and spilled into the market square—along with much of the population of the Cobalt Hall and other nearby buildings—he couldn't help but wonder, *What's the point?*

The sky was alight with lightning and snow, while pools of the black ichor that made up the Abyssal sea seeped from cracks in the ground. Hansa ducked as a silvery bird dived, snatching up one of the small intruders from the Abyss.

Several bystanders who had fled to the open plaza spotted him and started to run toward him. Hansa could barely hear their cries over the rumbling.

Then the shades began to rise.

Hansa blinked, thinking at first his vision had gone blurry; as the forms became more solid, he raised his sword, expecting more of the Judgements.

Instead, he found himself face-to-face with a familiar figure: Ruby.

She wasn't alone. All around Hansa, the dead had risen. Their forms were semi-solid and flickered in the wind, but they were clearly visible and recognizable.

Ruby spoke. He saw her lips move, but he couldn't hear her, could only see in her expression desperation and terrible focus.

The shade seemed to focus Lydie, though, who lifted her head as if *she* could hear something, and when Hansa put her down on her feet she turned sluggishly toward Ruby's form.

"What?" Lydie creaked out.

"Hansa!"

He turned at Pearl's shriek. The girl ran to his side, dodging beasts of the Abyss and Numen, shades, earthquake rifts, and growing pools of ice and fire. She caught his hand, and declared, "Daddy is here."

"Who?" Hansa asked.

"Veronese," Lydie reminded him. Still staring at Ruby, she said, "Veronese says we need to summon Alizarin."

"*What?*"

"Yes!" Pearl said.

"Won't he just eat us all?" Hansa objected, only to then have to scuttle back and kick at some creature that had just lunged at his ankle.

"Veronese says he can control him," Ruby said. Her voice was like the rustle of leaves on an icy ground, but still unmistakably *hers*.

"But *why?*"

"Just *do it!*" Ruby snapped. Now!"

Hansa looked back to Umber, who had Naples cradled in his arms. He shrugged, and his voice lilted through Hansa's head: *The world is ending. We might as well finish it eaten by friends.*

Sheathing his sword, Hansa drew the knife that Naples had given him. He was only vaguely aware of a chorus of cries as a significant portion of the population saw their possible future-President draw blood in the way that only a mancer ever would.

"Alizarin," he said, pausing to fight back a hysterical giggle, "get your furry blue butt up here."

He felt the pull of the Abyss, the drag at his energy . . . Was he strong enough for this? Naples had said Hansa didn't have nearly enough power to open the rift to summon Modigliani and Sennelier, but that had been before the veils had begun to disintegrate.

"Alizarin, come to me," Hansa said, and at last he felt the rift form. It grew slowly, like a flower unfurling instead of suddenly in a jagged slash, but it appeared.

"Hansa." He looked away from the rift to see Jenkins, along with a half dozen of the other guards who had died on the day Xaz first summoned Alizarin. "We're here, Lieutenant Viridian." They formed a protective ring, driving back infernal beasts that seemed drawn to the rift with spectral steel. Beyond them, living guards formed another, less-coherent ring, as if unsure whom they should be protecting from what.

Hansa stepped back, and as he felt the rift open, he put himself in Umber's arms. Umber had put Naples gently down on the rime-frosted grass, and now held Hansa tightly.

It's not the time, Umber said, *but before another crazed Numini offers you the option . . . I've decided I don't want to break the bond. If you don't.*

Hansa laughed again, and then leaned forward to catch a snowflake on his tongue.

Divine snow tasted a little like strawberries, and that, too, seemed funny.

I love you, too.

Then at last, Alizarin stood in front of him, a form of dark beauty, indigo shadows, and sharp claws. Umber's arms tightened, his body going tense, but neither of them moved to struggle or flee. Guards, living and dead, looked at Hansa and started to raise blades.

"Stay back!" Hansa ordered, as Alizarin's shape solidified, coming closer to the somewhat-feline blue form Hansa knew as Alizarin's "play" form. The Abyssi raised onto his toes and lifted his head to sniff the air, as if seeking an elusive scent.

Hansa braced himself for the attack, but it never came. Instead, Alizarin turned.

"No," Hansa whispered as the Abyssi moved not toward him and Umber, but toward Pearl, Lydie, Cadmia, and Ruby. He stalked forward, his tail swishing, then paused, rocking side to side questioningly. Something was in his way, something that, like the shades, had gradually started to come clear.

Lydie's eyes suddenly widened at the same time that Pearl shouted, *"Daddy!"*

Cadmia whipped an arm around the girl, turning her away just in time, before the Abyssi pounced.

At last and unwillingly, Hansa *could* see the Numini, who shone in all the radiant colors of the sunrise—pink and gold and white and black—for only an instant before the Abyssi tore into him as effortlessly as he had once devoured nearly a dozen guards.

Instead of blood, this time, what rained down was a mix of snow and feathers.

The world sparked, beautiful, as the first hints of true dawn shone though the carnage.

Over and over, Pearl wept, "Daddy . . . Daddy . . . Daddy!"

Alizarin shook dust from the Numini's feathers from his arm, then started to move toward Pearl again. Cadmia pushed Pearl behind her, toward the ring of living soldiers, and hissed, "Protect her," before she stood firm before Alizarin.

Alizarin looked at her. And stopped.

He turned, and his silver gaze raked the remains. *Silver?*

As Hansa watched, the Abyssi collapsed, gathering feathers with trembling hands. He lifted first one and then another before he raised his face and howled. The sound made Hansa's throat tighten and brought tears to his eyes, and at the same time pulled him forward.

"Careful," Umber warned. "You're a mancer now. You'll be drawn to your Abyssi, but that doesn't make him safe for you."

Hansa shook his head and moved out of Umber's arms until he could kneel in front of Alizarin. He put his hand on blue fur. "Alizarin?"

"*I killed him.*"

"You had to," Hansa said.

"*I killed him!*" Alizarin cried, the pain in his voice bringing Cadmia to his side.

She reached for him tentatively. "Rin?"

"*I killed him,*" Alizarin said once more. "*He was . . . I was . . .*" He dropped his head.

"Dear Numen," Umber whispered. "He's . . ."

"Veronese knew what he was doing," Ruby whispered. "He gave himself willingly." No, she wasn't whispering. She was *fading*, as were the other shades. Like a final echo in the night, Hansa heard her say to Jenkins and the others, "This way. He told me how I could bring you all . . ."

Then she was gone.

"Veronese knew," Azo said, limping up to join them, "but how did *you*, Hansa? He could have devoured you when you walked up to him."

"Couldn't you feel it?" Hansa asked. How could anyone think Alizarin would have hurt him, right then?

"We're not bound to him," Umber pointed out, still sounding dazed. "I didn't realize . . ."

Alizarin leaned forward, his body shaking with spasms, and he began to whimper.

"Step back," Hansa warned Cadmia, who was still leaning against Alizarin.

"What? Why?"

He pulled her away as feathers the color of night cut through the Abyssi's back. Inky blue with streaks of silver like stars, vast wings grew, coated with silver dust that fell to the ground when Alizarin shuddered once more, twitching them awkwardly.

"Gressi," Hansa said, as proud as a father who has just watched his first child being born.

Umber quirked a brow, started to speak, stopped, then simply said, to Hansa, "Gressumancer."

Alizarin did not stop to marvel at or even acknowledge his own divinity. Instead, he reached for Cadmia and clutched her tightly as he wept.

With an aching heart, Hansa suspected Alizarin might cry for a long time, as he learned to understand, accept, and cope with Veronese's final gift to him.

To all of us, Umber added silently. *Look around.*

The square was emptier than it had been when they had first run out here, probably due to people fleeing—that election wasn't going to be quite a landslide after all, apparently—and the abandoned streets had been ravaged by earthquake, fire, and ice, but the creatures of the Other realms had faded back into their respective planes.

"Ruby? Jenkins?"

No response. Those boundaries, too, were restored. Remembering the last words he had heard from Ruby, Hansa realized she must have led her brother and the others to the Numen after all.

Hopefully the new management is better, Hansa thought grimly. Quinacridone was dead. What were the others like? Could the Gressi still strengthen the veils to keep the Numini from breaking through again?

Gressi.

He looked at Alizarin, and finally processed Umber's words.

Gressumancer.

Those two things were required to keep the world from falling apart.

And he was one of them.

Quinacridone and Modigliani had been killed—he thought. Modigliani had been dispatched by a high arbiter of the Numen and, though technically Quinacridone had been killed by a mancer, the weapons had been formed of the bones of powerful Abyssi. They *might* really be dead.

If not, the next time they tried to break through and take over, Hansa and Alizarin would be the ones standing exactly in the way.

In the meantime, Hansa looked back, to where Cadmia and Umber had gently laid Xaz and Naples on the grass by the edge of the plaza. The realms were secure for now, but not without a bitter price.

"I'll see you in the next world," Hansa whispered to Naples. "Try not to take over before I get there."

On the other hand . . .

"Never mind. Rule the fucking place. You would be good at it." The Abyss needed a new king anyway.

He pushed himself to his feet. What next?

"Sex?" Umber suggested.

Hansa pondered the possibility, but not for very long.

"In memory of Naples," he replied, solemnly. Mentally, he prodded at the raw, tender place in his heart Naples had briefly occupied. They had been enemies first, and more recently lovers. Modigliani had resurrected Naples once, and certainly that wouldn't happen again, but it was still hard for Hansa to believe this death would be the Abyssumancer's true end any more than the previous one had been.

"Absolutely," Umber agreed.

Wait—"*Fuck!*"

"*What?*" Cadmia jumped at Hansa's vehement tone.

He hunched a little, embarrassed. "I promised my mother I would have breakfast with her."

"But . . ." Umber's eyes widened. "Earthquakes, Gressi, end of the world, and you're going to have *breakfast?*"

Hansa shrugged. "We can still have sex. Just . . . *after* you meet my mother."

Umber shook his head.

"We should've let the world end."

"It still might," Lydie murmured. "Do we stand, fight, or flee?"

"Wha—" Hansa cut off his own stupid question as he looked up and saw the company of guards that was now striding forward, led by Rinnman. There would be fast-talking necessary, some to keep himself and the others from being executed—and some to win the position of President and make it work for him.

Because now, more than ever, Hansa wanted to fix this world.

He stepped forward, to the front of the group but clearly still part of them. Umber, Lydie, Azo, and Cadmia fanned out behind him.

"We stand."

EPILOGUE

RINNMAN

It was the third time Rinnman had sat on tribunal for Hansa Viridian.

The first time, Hansa had been—at least partly—guilty. It was hard to lie to an animamancer. Hansa Viridian had not been having inappropriate sexual relations with his best friend Jenkins Upsdall, but he hadn't been entirely honest when he had denied ever having such *thoughts*.

Rinnman had voted against conviction.

The second time, Hansa had been—at least mostly—innocent. Rinnman had never believed the young, earnest lieutenant had been deceiving them all for years about Abyssal allegiances, or that he had deliberately led his men into a deathtrap. If he had meddled in black magic, he had begun to do so only after that event.

And clearly, he *had* begun to do so.

That wasn't the question at hand.

It was strange, starting with the premise that Hansa Viridian—along with Cadmia Paynes, Umber Holland, and Arylide Rackley—*had* engaged in the practice of sorcery, and then needing to debate whether or not they had committed a crime. Rinnman had been quite sure there had been another person with them, a woman with clearly unnatural traits, but she had disappeared before the arrests were made; Rinnman had deliberately encouraged the assumption that, like the otherworldly beasts and shades, she had disappeared when the veils between the realms restabilized.

He had also firmly suggested that any hint of magic on the child, Pearl, had been caused by her exposure to what had happened in the Cobalt Hall—and then had sent her back to the Hall, away from sighted guards, before anyone could question it.

Maybe, by the time she came of age, she wouldn't need to hide.

Maybe.

In the meantime, to decide what charges should be leveled against Viridian and his cohorts, they had needed to refer to the oldest archives, which still held records of the laws regarding sorcery and malfeasance from the days of the royal house. It would never have occurred to Rinnman to open those records if it hadn't been for a woman named Keppel, who had appeared at the compound with a manuscript scribed by Dahlia Indathrone in the first days after the revolution. Keppel claimed the manuscript had been stolen by the individuals truly responsible for the magical disaster that had so nearly destroyed Kavet.

Rinnman had not missed the shine of Abyssal power on the young woman, who had refused to come in to give a statement.

The most powerful statement came from another Abyssumancer, a wheat-blond man named Cupric, who had come to the compound weeping and begging for the brand. His flesh was still sizzling from the mark, which would burn away any mancer's power, when he began telling his story.

It rose Rinnman's gorge, but he listened. He invited two others in to listen. And he took notes.

Then, acting within the authority of Citizen's Initiative 126, he executed the vile creature without further discussion, debate or trial.

Then he brought the evidence before the tribunal.

"By previous vote, we have declared the four accused innocent of the crime of malfeasance. The question now at hand," he said to the group, where he was acting as secretary and judge, "is whether Viridian, Paynes, Holland, and Rackley should be pardoned entirely for their use of sorcery, as defined under the articles of Citizen's Inititive One-Twenty-Six, under the reasoning that such magic was wielded for the defense of the country of Kavet—and, as has been explained to us, of not only our entire world but the realms beyond as well."

Rinnman had considered recusing himself from the tribunal. He could have admitted to his own power and taken his place beside the others who had bravely decided to put themselves before the 126 and demand *justice*. After so many years in the 126, keeping his power carefully veiled all day every day from sighted guards, it would almost have been a relief.

Almost.

He hadn't. Partly, he had stayed because he wanted to ensure this trial happened, and was fair. None of them had fully understood what was happening when Hansa and his companions stumbled out of the Cobalt Hall with corpses and monsters among them; Rinnman had insisted that they needed to allow the accused to speak on their own behalfs, something that normally was not allowed. He had also been the one to propose that a blanket charge of sorcery was inappropriate, and the trial should be for malevolence instead—a charge he felt fairly confident this group was innocent of.

So, partly he had stayed because he wanted to ensure justice, but that wasn't the main reason. The real reason he stayed, and stayed hidden, was because he wasn't a hero. He would wield a sword to protect the innocent from evil, but he wouldn't put his neck in front of that sword's swing.

He would survive today, no matter which way the vote went.

He was a bit of a coward.

Especially since he knew, whichever way the vote went, the course of Kavet's future had been irrevocably changed by recent events.

"All in favor of granting a complete pardon for these four individuals' charges of sorcery, raise your hand now."

Some hands raised. Some stayed down. Rinnman began to count.

ACKNOWLEDGMENTS

As the Mancer trilogy comes to a close, I want to thank everyone who helped these books and this world come to life with their encouragement, advice, feedback, and support. *Mortal* had a few key beta readers, including Becky Friedman and Raeven, whose willingness to dive into this and any other story I hand them and provide fantastic and focused comments has definitely improved the quality of the book in your hands.

ABOUT THE AUTHOR

AMELIA ATWATER-RHODES is the author of the Mancer Trilogy: *Of the Abyss*, *Of the Divine*, and *Of the Mortal Realm*. She is also the author of three YA series, Den of Shadows, The Kiesha'ra, and The Maeve'ra, which have been ALA Quick Picks for Young Adults, School Library Journal Best Books of the Year, and VOYA Best Science Fiction, Fantasy, and Horror List Selections.

www.atwaterrhodes.com

Discover great authors, exclusive authors, and more at hc.com.